Dianne Blacklock lives south of Sydney with her husband and four sons. She occasionally teaches Communications at a college of TAFE when she is not busy working on her next novel.

dianneblacklock@optusnet.com.au

GW00708058

Also by Dianne Blacklock

Call Waiting

WIFE *for* HIRE

DIANNE BLACKLOCK

MACMILLAN
Pan Macmillan Australia

First published 2003 in Macmillan by Pan Macmillan Australia Pty Limited
St Martins Tower, 31 Market Street, Sydney

National Library of Australia
Cataloguing-in-Publication data:

Blacklock, Dianne.
Wife for hire.

ISBN 0 7329 1169 9.

I. Title.

A823.4

Set in 12.5/14 pt Bembo by Post Pre-press Group
Printed in Australia by McPherson's Printing Group

To the very special men in my life
Paul
Joel
Dane
Patrick
&
Zachary
With all my love

Acknowledgements

If not for the amazing Cate Paterson, this would still be a vague dream. It is impossible to thank her adequately for the care and expertise she brings to all aspects of the publishing process, or for the encouragement and support she gives to me. Thanks also to Julia Stiles for her consummate copy-editing and to Christine Mattey and Roxarne Burns for taking care of business. When I wrote my acknowledgements first time round, I had not seen the fabulous cover design by Deborah Parry, or met my publicist, the lovely Jane Novak, or the wonderful sales team at Pan Macmillan. Thank you all for your sterling efforts now and then, and while I'm at it, thanks to all the booksellers who so generously supported a first-time author.

Heartfelt thanks to Adam, Warwick, Michael, Malcolm and Glen for saving our house, and this manuscript along with it, during the Black Christmas bushfires of 2001. Worth far more than just a case of beer.

Thank you to Mum and Dad and my wonderful extended family: the Blacklocks, Naoums and Murphys, particularly to Bob, Carolyn and Ros for extraordinary support above and beyond sibling duty. Thanks to Joel for reading the first draft and putting up with my incessant yabbering about it and Dane for being a patient sounding board.

Many thanks to my gorgeous friends who give me so much including some great material, even if they don't mean to: Frances and Danny, Desley, Robyn and Lynda, Deb S., Gary and Anne, and Elizabeth; and at Loftus TAFE: Pam, Jan, Sylvia, luscious Lesley, Sally, Alison, Kay, all the Jennys and Russell the token male. Don't forget me. And I'm not forgetting Dori Stratton, my adviser on all things American, for her valuable input and encouragement. And a special thank you to Julie W. for sharing.

Welcome home Diane Stubbings. You'll always have my deepest appreciation.

When I Grow up

When I grow up I want to be a wife. My husbin will be called Tod or Brad, and he will have blond hair. He will be a doctor or a maniger.

We will have 2 kids, 1 boy and 1 girl. The boy will be called Tod or Brad (witchever I don't marry). The girl will be called Tiffiny, Sky, Kylie, Amba or Maxine. They will have blond hair to.

We will live in a 2 story house with stairs and 2 toilets and a pool. There will be daffadils and chulips in the garden all year round.

I will cook gormay for dinner and you can eat off the floor. I will go shoping on Thursdays and do the washing on Monday and do the ion-ing when days of our lives is on.

When I am a Nan, we will move to Taloombi and live in a green house with a frangipanny in the backyard.

The End

Twenty-five years later

'What did you say?'

'Didn't you hear me, or don't you understand?'

Sam's knees started to give way. She sank down into the bedroom chair. It was the one she had bought at a garage sale for eighteen dollars, but for only three hundred dollars an upholsterer had made it look like one she had seen in *Belle* for more than twice that much.

She didn't know why that came into her head right now.

'You've been accusing me for years,' Jeff was saying. 'I thought I may as well go ahead and do it.'

He was right. In every argument they had, at a certain point Sam would invariably accuse her husband of having an affair. Sometimes the accusation accompanied a sob, which always brought the fight to an end. Jeff couldn't cope with tears, so he would reassure her that he had never looked at another woman, apologise for whatever he had or hadn't done, and they would make up, more or less.

But other times the argument was vicious, and Sam would make the accusation with acrimony, not tears. Jeff would come back with 'I wish', or 'When would I find the time to have an affair?'

Sam had never, ever expected him to respond by saying 'Yes'.

'How long has it been . . . going on?' she faltered. That sounded like a line from a bad 80s pop song.

'Oh . . . six months I guess.'

Sam looked up at him. 'Six months ago? You mean March?'

He nodded. 'Yeah, maybe a little earlier.'

'You're unbelievable, honestly Jeff!'

He just frowned at her. Typical, he didn't even get it.

'March was the month we signed the contract with the builder for the pool and the pergola!' She watched his face for some sign of comprehension. 'Right after we extended the mortgage to pay for it all?'

He sighed. 'What's your point?'

'Well, didn't you even consider any of that?'

'Oh sure Sam, I took out my calendar and jotted down *Start affair*. And I made sure I picked the worst possible time, just to spite you!' Jeff exclaimed, raising his arms. 'You're acting like this is something I should have planned better. You don't plan to have an affair! At least I didn't. It just happened.'

Sam sat staring at the carpet. The word affair was echoing around in her head until it sounded odd, not like a real word at all. None of this felt real.

'Is it serious?'

He breathed out heavily. 'Well, I'm telling you.'

Jeff was sleeping in the guestroom. Sam had wanted him to leave there and then. He had somewhere else to go, after all. But he'd calmly resisted. Jeff was always calm. Dispassionate, really. That's where they were different. Sam was far more headstrong and impulsive. She often said more than she intended to, especially when she was upset or nervous. Jeff had maintained that it was important to be very careful about the way this was handled with the children. They should give it a lot of thought. He wanted to talk again tomorrow night, after it had had time to sink in.

Fuck him. Since when was he so concerned about what went on around here? He was treating this like a problem at work. Management would hold a crisis meeting, work out a strategy, then bring it to the team.

Sam turned on her side and stared at the vacant expanse of bed beside her. She had often daydreamed about this happening. Just go and have an affair, she'd thought a hundred times. It was the perfect solution. She wouldn't be in the wrong. Their friends would support her over Jeff, she was quite sure about that. There'd be no question who'd get the kids, and the house. Sam would call all the shots.

And best of all it would put an end to this catatonic marriage.

It hadn't always been like this. They were kids at school

when they started going out together. Jeff Holmes was blond and broad-shouldered, with crystal blue eyes and a killer tan. He was a spunk. And he was funny then, a bit of a clown really. He didn't like school much, he preferred surfing or skateboarding. He was just one of the boys, lacking maturity, ambition, and a girlfriend to pull him into line. He was the first guy Sam ever slept with, so she had to marry him. Not that she was a prude or anything, but back then you were a slut if you slept around.

When they left school they both went to work for the same bank, which was the standard career choice when you left school in Year 10 with no academic ambitions. That or the public service. At least working for the bank meant they were eligible for a heftily discounted interest rate on their first mortgage. Sam found a bargain-priced fixer-upper in a good street in Ryde. At first Jeff was reluctant to move so far away from the beach, but they didn't have a hope of affording anything closer. Sam assured him that if they renovated they would increase the value of the house, and they might be able to move back in a few years time. So they stripped floors, painted walls, remodelled the kitchen and bathroom, replanted the garden. When everything was just right, Sam started looking at real estate again. Jeff complained mildly at first. Couldn't they just enjoy it for a while? Take a breather? But Sam had studied the market, there was no standing still if they wanted to take advantage of the gains they had made. They had to sell up and move on.

The next house was in Epping. Brick, four bedrooms, two bathrooms and a family room. It was spacious and comfortable, situated in a leafy street with good schools around. Though no closer to the beach. Jeff didn't surf any more so it hardly mattered.

He'd climbed his way up at the bank, while Sam had quit when the children came along. When he started to work longer and longer hours, she never complained. Jeff had an executive position and she kept house. That was the way Sam liked it. Not that she was anybody's lackey, a throwback 1950s housewife. She had a job, one day a week. She hated it, but at least it gave her a cover, allowing her to join the socially acceptable ranks of women who juggled work and family, home and career.

But Sam's career was in the home. She was good at being a wife. The house ran like a finely tuned machine. There was a healthy meal on the table each night. Everyone had clean, ironed clothes before they needed them. The place was always spotless, bills paid, the chequebook balanced.

Their home was tasteful, but welcoming. They entertained regularly and Sam had developed a reputation as an accomplished hostess. She was certainly the only office wife who made a point of inviting Jeff's significant colleagues over for dinner at least once a year. She was sure this had been a factor boosting him along in his career. Sam knew she was a model wife, a prize wife, the kind of wife men secretly wished they had.

But now Jeff wanted to leave her for someone else.

Her name was Jodi, and they'd met at various corporate functions over the past year or so. The events organiser at Jeff's bank was on a fitness kick and employed Jodi because she ran a catering business that specialised in upmarket health food, whatever the hell that was. Sam really didn't want to know this much detail. Apparently Jodi was just a friend at first, someone Jeff could talk to. But there was a finality about his words, not so much in what he'd said but in the way he'd said it. He hadn't said sorry, he hadn't asked for forgiveness, he hadn't told her he would end it. He'd just told her.

Sam felt sick. Her stomach was churning, and she couldn't quite catch her breath. Her blood felt as though it had turned to lumpy jelly, rippling uncomfortably through her veins.

At least it wasn't her fault. Even her mother couldn't blame this on her.

The next day

'You've got no one to blame but yourself, Samantha.'

'Mum . . .' Sam considered hanging up right now, before she had to listen to another word.

'It's true. You've put on weight, you don't look after yourself the way you used to.'

'I haven't put on that much weight –'

'When you and Jeff were going out you always made yourself look nice. You went to that little bit of extra effort.'

'I was a teenager, Mum! I had nothing else to do but paint my nails and pluck my eyebrows. Now I've got three kids, a house, a job . . .'

'I managed to keep my figure *and* my house.'

'But not your husband.'

There was a brief, stony silence.

'Well, Samantha, maybe you'll curb some of your sarcasm now that you've found yourself in the same boat.'

Bernice Driscoll had single-handedly raised her daughters after their father deserted them. Bernice liked the term 'deserted'. She wasn't happy when the government changed the 'deserted wives' pension' to the 'sole parents' benefit'.

'How can you tell the difference between someone who is in this predicament through no fault of their own,' she'd lamented, 'and someone who, well, brought it upon *themselves*?'

According to Bernice, her husband left her because he'd always wanted a son and she hadn't been able to produce one. Pure and simple. It seemed credible, if somewhat archaic. The girls were named Alex, Sam and Max, and he left his next wife after she presented him with twin daughters, Jackie and Jaime. Well, that was the rumour Bernice had heard anyway. They'd never actually met any second wife or half-sisters. They didn't hear from their father again, but sometimes conjectured they could probably trace him by following a trail of girls with boys' names.

Bernice had carried on, like the tragic Anne Boleyn figure

she was, she often sighed to her daughters. Of course, they tried to remind her that Anne Boleyn had actually been beheaded for failing to produce a male heir to the throne and was thus perhaps at least marginally more tragic. But Bernice Driscoll didn't care to muddy the issue with facts.

'I hope this doesn't mean you won't be able to take me out to the shoe warehouse next week?' Bernice had suddenly realised that Sam's predicament could have some unfavourable repercussions on her own life. 'You know I'm desperate for new shoes, and Footrest is the only brand I can wear, but I just will not pay the prices they ask in the shops.'

Oh, no, Mum, why should my life falling apart stop me from running around at your beck and call?

'Don't worry, Mum, I'll see you next week.'

'I'm not going to talk to her about this any more,' Sam insisted later on the phone to Maxine. She knew she could count on her younger sister for support.

'I don't know what possessed you to talk about it with her in the first place,' said Max drily. 'Why did you, anyway?'

'Force of habit.'

'Would you like me to give you the "what a bastard" response?' she offered.

'Well, I wish someone would,' Sam moaned.

'What a bastard!' Max exclaimed with gusto. 'Typical bloody male with his brain in his dick. You're better off without him, Sam. And he's going to crumple into a pathetic heap without you to run around after him!' She paused. 'Do you want more?'

'No, that'll do for now. Thanks.'

'How are you really?'

'I don't know. Different to what I thought.'

'What does that mean?'

'Well,' Sam tried to explain, 'when I thought about Jeff having an affair, I didn't think it would feel like this.'

'You've actually thought about what you would feel like if he ever had an affair?'

'Yes,' she defended.

'Is that normal?'

'I don't think it's *abnormal.*'

'Mm,' Max mused. 'So, is he serious about this woman – what's her name?'

'Jodi.'

'*Jodi?* Ugh! She isn't under-age, is she?'

'I don't think he'd be that stupid.'

'When men let their penises make decisions for them, there's not a whole lot of rational thought going on.' Max sighed. 'Jodi, huh? I bet she draws those little circles over the "i". How did he meet her?'

'Through work.'

'Mm, typical, statistically speaking.'

Maxine had a statistic, an anecdote or a theory for just about everything. Often she had all three. She had been studying for a degree in psychology for the last three years, and she was almost finished first year. Not that she'd ever failed. Whenever she actually completed a subject, she usually earned a High Distinction. Max was the smartest of the three girls by far, but stuff kept getting in the way. Bad relationships, lack of money, the travel bug biting now and then. Maxine had a short attention span. She found it hard to stick at anything for long. At thirty-three years of age, she had not had one relationship that anyone could take seriously, least of all her. She avoided normal men like the plague, preferring to take her chances with an assortment of misfits and losers. Sam didn't know where Max found them, but she did, with alarming regularity.

'Do you want me to come round tonight?'

'I would, but Jeff wants to "talk".'

'Oh? Didn't you do enough talking last night?'

Sam sighed. 'We did. And I asked him to leave. But he wants to take it more slowly. He's concerned about the kids.'

'Convenient of him to think of them now.'

'That's what I said.'

'Does Alex know yet?'

'Oh I'd imagine Bernice would be broadcasting the news to her as we speak.'

Alexandra was the eldest, and she played that role to perfection. Max and Sam were both frightened of her. She lived in Melbourne now, married to Gordon who was eighteen years her senior. Max theorised it was because she needed a father figure. But Sam reckoned Alex was born old. At ten she acted like she was twenty, and at twenty she had the composure of a forty year old. She couldn't have married anyone younger than Gordon. They had one perfect specimen child, Isabella, who fitted beautifully into their precisioned life. Alex had crashed through the glass ceiling years ago, she had probably not even noticed it was there. She currently worked as a management consultant for a multinational corporation. Sam and Max had no idea what it was that she actually did.

'Well, call me and let me know what happens. Promise?' Max insisted.

'Oh, don't worry, I will. You're going to be sick of the sound of my voice before long.'

Six p.m.

'*Mummm,*' Jessica said with the tone of voice that almost-thirteen-going-on-twenty-two-year-old girls seemed to have down pat. '*Everyone* else is going, *their* parents are all letting them! What's wrong with *you*?'

'Nothing's wrong with me, thank you Jessica,' Sam replied, trying to sound firm, parental, interested. Anything but how she actually felt, which was that she didn't give a flying fig, not tonight. Things had taken a decidedly surreal turn. She had tried to keep up her normal routine throughout the day, but a vague uneasy feeling had persisted in the back of her mind that suddenly her life had become very fragile, a barely sustainable ecosystem threatened with extinction. She felt like a rainforest species in a South American jungle.

'You know the rule about school nights. I just don't understand why Brianna's party has to be midweek?'

Jessica rolled her eyes. '*Mu-umm!*' She said the word as though it had two syllables, and as though Sam had a half a brain. 'I've already explained this to you. It's the night of Tiffany and JJ's wedding!'

'Who are Tiffany and JJ?' Sam asked absently, draining the peas.

Jessica rolled her eyes again. 'They're on *Beachside*! Don't you ever listen to me?'

Sometimes Sam felt that all she did was listen to Jessica. She had a lot to say for a twelve year old. On top of that, she was glued to the phone day and night, talking loudly to her girl-friends from any room of the house, shooshing everyone if she couldn't hear. Other mothers complained that their daughters would lock themselves away in their rooms and stay on the phone. Sam wished.

'*Beachside* is a television show, right?'

'*Yes!*'

'Roll your eyes once more, girl, and it's a flat no, end of discussion.'

Jessica gave a petulant toss of her blonde mane and looked balefully at her mother, but at least her eyes did not move in their sockets.

'I'll have to talk to your father about it.'

'Why? He'll go along with whatever you say, you're just stalling.'

'That's quite enough!' Sam had all the attitude she could take for now. 'Be quiet and set the table.'

'But it's not my turn –'

'Jessica!' Sam turned back to the stove and took a couple of calming breaths. She heard rustling in the cutlery drawer. Jess had obviously decided not to push it any further for the moment. She usually figured that out, even if it took till half past the eleventh hour.

Sam looked at her watch. Josh should be home from football training by now, but he was often late these days. When she'd ask him about it, he'd just shrug, mumble something incomprehensible and shuffle off to his room. Getting any information out of him was like pulling teeth. Seemingly overnight Joshua had turned into the stereotypical teenage boy, and Sam feared she was losing him. His relationship with his father was worse. He and Jeff were like two stags butting up against one another to gain dominance. Sam supposed it was a male thing but she didn't see why Jeff couldn't just back off a bit. He was the adult after all.

She wondered how all this was going to affect Josh, and it worried her.

'Mummy? . . . Mummy?'

Sam looked down to see Ellie's wide round eyes fixed on her, unblinking. 'What's a matter, Mummy?'

She crouched down to her youngest daughter's level. 'Nothing, why?'

'You've got sadlines here and here,' she said, tracing the creases between Sam's eyebrows with her fingers. Ellie often drew attention to Sam's 'sadlines'. They were just like Nanna's, she said. That should have been enough to stop Sam frowning once and for all.

'Well, I've only got sadlines because I haven't had a hug all afternoon!'

Ellie smiled happily and wrapped her arms around her mother's neck, holding on tight. So did Sam. Ellie was her baby, the child that shouldn't have been here. They had their perfect family, a boy and a girl. Jessica had started school, and Sam was working a couple of days a week. Jeff had just been promoted again and Sam had her sights set on Cherrybrook. It was her dream suburb. If they could buy a house in Cherrybrook, she would never want to move again. She knew she would be happy there. She started driving around the streets after dropping the kids at school, picking out her ideal locations. She figured it would be another twelve to eighteen months before she could talk Jeff into moving again. He was as settled as a cat on a sunny doorstep. Sam knew not to broach it for the time being. But if a 'For Sale' sign was to go up in one of those streets . . .

After Jessica's birth, Jeff had promised to have a vasectomy. He'd agreed it was only fair, in principle. But a vasectomy in principle was not an effective method of contraception. With two young children, sex was pretty infrequent anyway and so the issue floated, unresolved. Then there was a particularly heady New Year's Eve party at Liz and Michael's. They drank a busload of champagne and neither of them could remember much the morning after.

A month later the nausea started. Ellie was born in the spring, delaying the move to Cherrybrook for the meantime, but Sam couldn't imagine their lives without their dark-haired, dark-eyed little beauty. She was the only one who had inherited her mother's physical features, but thankfully she seemed to possess her father's calmer temperament. Josh and Jess's babyhood had passed in a blur of colic, inexperience and sleepless nights, until Sam had learned the miracle of routine. And while it made things easier, their life was so regimented into nap times and bath times and mealtimes that there wasn't any time left just to enjoy the children. But Sam savoured every moment with Ellie. She let her eat when she was hungry and sleep when she was tired, and she ended up being the easiest of the three. She hated when people asked if Ellie was a mistake, noting the age gap between her and the other two. Max, in cosmic mode, said Ellie was a little soul who was always meant to be here. She had just been biding her time until the right opportunity came along. Though she didn't let on to Max, Sam liked that explanation.

They heard the front door open and close. 'That'll be your brother,' Sam said hopefully to Ellie.

'Hello gorgeous girl.' It was Jeff.

'Daddy!' Jessica exclaimed enthusiastically, throwing her arms around his neck. She knew how to manipulate her father. She would get him on side and he'd say yes to anything. She relished attention from Jeff, but sometimes out of the blue she'd snap and treat him as though he was mentally impaired. Which was the way she always treated Sam.

'You're home early,' Sam remarked as he walked into the kitchen.

'I thought it was important tonight,' he said, throwing a meaningful glance in her direction. He picked up Ellie. 'How's my other gorgeous girl?'

Jeff rarely ate with the rest of the family. He was never usually home before eight, and often it was later than that. It didn't bother Sam, she managed the afternoon routine fine without him. When Josh and Jess were babies, she'd feed them early and put them to bed before he got home, and then they would have a civilised meal together. But now she ate with the children. Occasionally she sat with Jeff while he had his dinner, maybe over a glass of wine. More often than not, though, she was halfway through a show on TV when he arrived home, so he'd eat alone. It gave him a chance to read his paper undisturbed. If he did come into the family room to join them, he invariably fell asleep on the lounge, and their only contact would be the nudge Sam would give him before she went upstairs to bed.

The sliding glass doors of the family room opened and Joshua stepped inside.

'Hi Josh,' Sam called across to him. 'You're a bit late, did training run over?'

He shrugged, not looking at them as he slid the door closed.

'Joshua,' said Jeff sternly. 'Your mother asked you a question.'

Josh glanced briefly at his father, then at Sam. 'Sorry I'm late,' he mumbled, walking away.

'Dinner's ready,' Sam called after him.

'Joshua!' Jeff persisted. But he had disappeared up the stairs. 'You shouldn't let him speak to you like that,' he said to Sam.

She shrugged. 'Let him be, Jeff. He's probably tired.'

'You're too easy on these kids. You're going to have to set a few ground rules . . .' he faltered, '. . . um, you know, to cope, in the future.'

Sam looked at him. What did he mean, cope? Without

him? She coped without him all the time! In fact it was irritating when he butted in, having an opinion, like he was doing now. They got by with very little input from Jeff. His leaving was going to make next to no difference.

'Rules are not stupid, Jess, they're in place for a reason,' Jeff was saying.

Jessica had started working on her father as soon as they sat down at the table. 'I don't have a problem with the rule, Dad,' she said sweetly, 'any other time. But this is a one-off.'

Jeff sighed, putting down his fork. 'Your mother and I have a few things to discuss tonight and this will be on the agenda, Jess. We'll let you know in the morning.'

She looked miffed, but she knew that throwing a hissy fit would sabotage any chance of getting what she wanted.

'Any more?' Josh grunted.

'Sure Josh, out on the stove,' said Sam.

'I didn't hear a "please",' said Jeff pointedly as Josh walked into the kitchen. 'Does he really need seconds?'

'Jeff, he's fourteen years old. I think he's growing a centimetre a week. Leave him be.'

Jeff sighed audibly. 'It's just an excuse to be greedy.'

What a treat it was to have him home at dinnertime, Sam thought wryly.

'Daddy, I drewed you a picture today,' said Ellie. 'For your work.'

'Did you darling?' he smiled.

Thank God for Ellie.

'Like I said to you last night, I'm well aware of the shock this will be to the children,' Jeff began. 'Let's not kid ourselves.'

Sam looked up at him dumbfounded. They were upstairs in the 'parents' retreat', which was not much more than an alcove off the master bedroom. But Sam had made it look attractive, with a pair of tub chairs, an Ikea occasional table and

a bookcase. She had stacked it with some old books that no
one wanted to read, because they hardly ever used the area.

'*Let's not kid ourselves?*' Sam repeated incredulously.

Jeff nodded.

'Why don't you just speak for yourself from here on in,
okay Jeff?' she spat. 'I'm not kidding *myself*. I haven't done anything wrong!'

Jeff sighed loudly. 'Oh, so you want to play it that way?
Someone has to bear the blame?'

'Well, what do you reckon?' she cried. 'And let's imagine for
a moment who it might be? Could it be the one who has been
responsible for the primary care of the three children, looked
after the house, taken every single worry off the other so that
he could go out and build his career?' She took a breath. 'Or
the one who's fucking a colleague?'

'Sam!' Jeff frowned. 'I don't think that's appropriate.'

'Neither do I!' she retorted.

He breathed out heavily, sitting forward in his chair and
clasping his hands together. 'It's a pretty widely acknowledged
fact that people in happy marriages don't have affairs.'

Sam rolled her eyes. 'Funny how most of the "people" who
do are men having a midlife crisis.'

'I'm not having a midlife crisis.'

'But you are having an affair. And you're married. However
you want to put it, you're breaking your vows.'

'Fine Sam, I'll be the villain, since you seem to need one so
desperately.' He paused. 'My concern now is the children.'

'That's a first,' she muttered.

'Samantha!' Jeff stood up, clearly exasperated. 'Can you cut
the attitude for just one minute? Christ! I can see where Jess
gets it from!'

Sam shifted uncomfortably in her chair. 'You expect me just
to take this all on the chin?'

'No,' he said, becoming calmer. 'I expect there'll be a lot of
anger and resentment and pain before all this is settled. But
tonight I want to talk about the kids. Can we just get over one
hurdle at a time?'

Sam felt like crying but she bit her lip, forcing back the tears. Usually they were a useful ploy during an argument. But now the rules had changed. There was no 'making up' from this.

She cleared her throat. 'Go ahead.'

Jeff sighed, sitting back down in his chair. 'I think it's going to be a shock for them. I've been doing some reading up on this and apparently in cases like ours, the kids have no idea anything was even wrong.'

'Cases like ours?'

'We don't fight all the time, there's certainly no violence, I'm not a drunk. Their lives have been normal and unaffected despite . . .' he hesitated.

What? Sam wondered.

Jeff looked as though he was searching for words. 'Well, let's just say they wouldn't be aware that you and I haven't been happy for a long time.'

She couldn't look at him. This was typical Jeff. Calmly, dispassionately doling out his opinions, handing down his assessment of the situation. She knew they weren't deliriously happy, but that didn't mean they were *unhappy*, did it? And okay, so she'd daydreamed at times about him leaving, but surely they were like most couples? She rarely heard other husbands or wives speak with any great fondness for one another after a few years, especially once children came along. .

'We don't communicate,' Jeff went on. 'We haven't really got anything in common. Except the children.'

Nothing in common? What about the house . . . and, well, their whole lives?

'Jodi and I have talked a lot about this. You'll be relieved to know that she's just as concerned about protecting the children.'

Sam wasn't going to take that. 'Well maybe she should have thought about that before she started fucking their father.'

'Sam,' he warned. 'I thought we weren't going to be like that.'

'Stop it, Jeff!' she cried, standing up and pacing across the floor. 'Just stop it!'

'What? Stop what?'

'Can't you show a little remorse? Some emotion? Something? I'm your wife, not a redundant employee you have to terminate.' She turned to face him directly. 'Actually, if I was working for you, you'd have to treat me better than this.'

His eyes flew up to meet hers.

'Don't you have to give warnings to staff, offer counselling? But when have you ever come to me before now? Ever tried to make things better? Even just come home early occasionally so we could spend some time together?' She paused. 'No, you have an affair instead and sit there and tell me you had no choice, like I drove you to it? That's just gutless, Jeff. You got somebody to escort you out of a marriage you didn't want to be in any more.'

Sam stopped, catching her breath. She could hear her own voice echoing against the walls. Jeff looked a little stunned. Eventually he cleared his throat.

'Nothing but the house and the kids has mattered to you for years,' he said in a low voice. 'If I had ever come home early from work you would have ignored me anyway.'

Sam bristled. 'So your solution was to have an affair? Come off it, Jeff. You were only thinking about yourself. Bugger the rest of us.'

Jeff looked shaken, she realised. Sam hadn't seen him appear anything but cool and composed in a long time.

'Like I said before, I didn't plan to have an affair, it just happened,' he said quietly. 'And I've struggled over what's the right thing to do, I really have. But I honestly thought it was as plain to you as it was to me that this marriage was, well, dead.'

That stung Sam. All the more because of the truth in it.

'I didn't mean to sound like this is easy or simple. It's not, I know that.' He breathed out heavily. 'But there are two ways we can do this. We can be angry and spiteful and see how much we can hurt one another. Or we can be reasonable for the sake of the kids.'

Sam swallowed down the tears that were rising in her throat. So this was what it had all come down to. Being reasonable for the sake of the kids.

They were silent for a while. Sam walked back over to her chair and sat down.

'So what do you suggest?'

Thursday morning

They decided to sit all three children down together to break the news. But as soon as they did, Sam wished they'd picked another strategy. Though she supposed it didn't matter. However they handled it, it was going to be awful.

'So, what did you say to them?' Max asked over the phone the next day.

'Jeff did most of the talking. I think he'd been rehearsing it. He gave them a little speech about how although Mum and Dad feel differently towards each other, it doesn't mean we don't love them as much as ever. Blah, blah.'

'Is that when Josh walked out?'

'I think so,' said Sam. 'Right before Jessica burst into tears.'

'What about Ellie?'

'She just looked confused.'

'Christ Sam, it sounds awful,' Max muttered. 'What happened after that?'

'Oh, Jeff stayed with Jessica and they had a long talk, which was the best way to handle her. She and I would only clash. So I took Ellie up to bed and answered her questions. I don't really think she understands what's going on. How is a four year old supposed to comprehend this?'

'What about Josh?'

'He didn't come out of his room all night.'

'Don't you think he needs to talk?'

'Yes, but he won't,' Sam explained. 'I can't get two words out of him at the best of times.'

'Maybe you're going to have to try harder.'

'He's a closed book, Max, believe me,' she insisted. 'But of course I'll try. I'll see if he wants to talk this afternoon.'

'Would he respond better to Jeff?'

'No, they just butt heads. It's better if Jeff leaves him alone.'

Max let out a loud sigh. 'This is all so depressing, Sam. I'm coming over tonight with chocolate and grog and we're going to have a serious binge.'

'We can't. Jeff asked if he can stay one more night.'

'What does he think it is, a hotel?'

'He wants another chance to talk to the kids, and then he said he'd leave for the weekend, when it might be easier on them.'

Max grunted. 'Will they even notice?'

'Funnily enough, under the circumstances they probably will,' Sam said wearily. 'I mean, I can hardly knock his intentions. I'm just pissed off that he's being so noble now, once the horse has bolted, so to speak.'

'Jeff being the horse, I take it?'

'Mm. I suppose that's the wrong metaphor for this situation.'

'Oh, it's not that. I just would have called him a different barnyard animal. Pig springs to mind.'

Sam smiled faintly.

'Alright,' said Max. 'I'll come round tomorrow night then. You should invite the crew too.'

The 'crew' was Sam's trusty band of cohorts. They'd known each other since the children were little. She sighed, realising all the phone calls she was going to have to make, all the times she was going to have to go over this.

'I don't know. I don't want the kids to think I'm throwing a party as soon as their father's gone.'

'Mm, I take your point. We could always come over a bit later. Say, nine?'

'Let me think about it. I'll see how things go tonight.'

Sam knocked lightly on Josh's bedroom door. He'd arrived home from school about twenty minutes ago. He wasn't late today. He'd dumped his bag at the foot of the stairs and walked into the kitchen, scouring the cupboards for food. Sam asked him how his day had been and got the usual grunt in reply. She let him be. She held her tongue as he took a fistful of biscuits from the pantry and she didn't even say anything when he drank milk from the carton. She pretended she hadn't seen him.

He'd been upstairs ten minutes when Sam decided to go and talk to him. He opened the door suddenly. He was changed out of his school uniform, clutching his skateboard.

'I'm goin' up the road.'

'Oh, okay,' Sam said brightly. She followed him along the hall. This was ridiculous. Something had to be said.

'Josh?'

'Mm?' he grunted, not stopping.

'Could you hang on a minute?'

He stopped at the top of the stairs. He was so tall now, but lanky, his body hadn't caught up with the growth spurt. And his face was changing too, becoming broader like a man's. He was getting more like Jeff every day. Sam had to remember not to hold that against him.

'I just want to know if you're alright?'

He shrugged. 'Yeah.'

'I meant after last night . . .'

'I know what you meant.'

Sam took a breath. 'If you want to talk . . .'

He shrugged again, but he met her eyes. 'It's okay, Mum. It's no big deal.'

She'd tried to kid herself into thinking that too. But it was a big deal. And it was only going to get bigger.

'Well, if you want to talk . . . any time.'

He nodded, and Sam watched him walk down the stairs. She heard the front door open and close again. She breathed out heavily. Well, at least she'd tried.

Jeff arrived home even earlier, determined to spend some time with the children, so after dinner Sam left them to it. She went to the bedroom and flicked through a magazine. Pages and pages of who was breaking up with whom and who was pairing up with whom. Celebrities discarding spouses like last season's wardrobe. If only it were that easy.

An hour or so later there was a tentative knock at the door. Jeff poked his head in, a sheepish expression on his face.

'I need to pack some things,' he said gingerly.

Sam nodded and he walked through the door, closing it behind him quietly. She pretended to be absorbed in her magazine as he crossed to the walk-in robe.

'I think it went alright tonight,' he said, rooting around among the shelves.

'Mm?' she murmured disinterestedly.

'Jess seems okay. She's showing a level of maturity I hadn't expected. Joshua was closed off, but that's Joshua.' He stepped back into the room, holding up an overnight bag. 'Mind if I use this? I don't need to take much at the moment.'

Sam felt like shouting at him to take everything, every last thing he owned or she would burn what was left. She felt like punching into his chest and kicking him. *Kicking him!* She'd never had an urge like that before and she had to steel herself as she got up and walked past him out of the room.

'Whatever. I'll leave you to it.'

When she came into the kitchen, everything was as she had left it. Bugger them! Didn't it occur to anyone to stack their own plate in the dishwasher? Couldn't Jeff have encouraged the kids to help out, or even, heaven forbid, have lifted a finger himself? She yanked open the fridge and poured herself a glass of wine. She would invite the girls over tomorrow night. Why should she pussyfoot around everyone else when they clearly didn't give a damn about her?

Friday

Sam parked her car at Pennant Hills Station and boarded the train to the city. Fridays were always a rush, getting the children organised for school and childcare and still making the quarter past eight train. Of course she had further to go now. There was no rail line through Cherrybrook so she had to drive the ten minutes down to Pennant Hills. A small inconvenience, she had insisted to Jeff.

They had started to look in the area in earnest when Ellie was about two. In truth, it was mostly Sam looking while Jeff got used to the idea. The day she found their house she was barely able to contain her excitement. She begged Jeff to get off early from work to come and inspect it. But he had meetings all afternoon. He insisted the weekend was soon enough. After driving him nearly mad talking at him all night, he relented and arranged to meet her there the next day.

It had five bedrooms and three bathrooms. There was a huge gourmet kitchen, a family room and casual dining area, as well as formal entertaining rooms. The master bedroom was vast, with walk-in robe, a full-size ensuite, and a parents' retreat. 'It's big,' was all Jeff could say, over and over. But it was Sam's dream house. There wasn't a pool, but there was plenty of room for one. It was even in a cul-de-sac, a 'desirable but not essential' on Sam's checklist. Max said that cul-de-sacs had bad *feng shui*. Negative energy got caught in the loop and couldn't escape. But that was just nonsense. They put a deposit on the house the next day.

Sam breathed out heavily, leaning her forehead against the window of the train. She felt tired. She hadn't slept well for the past two nights and the strain was getting to her. She couldn't face ringing the girls, she didn't feel up to going over the sorry tale over and over. So she called Max instead.

'Maxi,' she started plaintively.

'Don't call me that, it makes me sound like a feminine hygiene product.'

'Sorry, but I was wondering if you could phone the crew? I don't want to have to tell the story three times over.'

'Don't you want them to know?'

'Of course,' she insisted. 'Tell them everything, save me having to do it tonight.'

'Okay, what time do you want us?'

Sam dragged herself through the glass doors into the call centre of Metropolitan Roadside Assistance. As she signed her name on the time sheets, she realised that the last time she was here, only one week ago, she had still been somebody's wife. Now she was . . . what was she? A *deserted* wife? Despite her mother's opinion to the contrary, that just sounded pathetic.

She made her way to her workstation, trying to avoid eye contact with anyone. Today, even responding to the proverbial 'How are you?' was going to be too much effort. She sat down at the terminal and typed in her password.

'Hi Sammy, how's it going?'

Sam looked up to see Brenda's round face popping over the divider. She couldn't cope with Ms Chirpy today.

'Fine,' she said with a fixed smile. She wouldn't want the real answer to that question anyway. People didn't really want to know when they asked how you were.

'And so to work!' Sam added, putting on her headphones. She noticed out of the corner of her eye that Brenda sunk down again, out of sight. Sam looked at the screen and sighed. There was already a queue of calls.

'Location of vehicle, please.'

Sometimes Sam felt she would scream if she had to say those four words one more time. All the people she'd started with had moved on to other departments. She had been far too long in the same job, especially in a call centre. But the union delegate had argued her case when she came back from maternity leave with Ellie, and she only had to work one day a week to keep her permanent status. There weren't many jobs around for only one day a week, most people wanted more hours, not fewer. So she stayed.

But it was getting pretty bad when crank calls were the high point of her day. The poor desperates who were too cheap or too broke to call a 0055 number were Sam's favourite.

'What are you wearing?' was the inevitable opening line. Sam found it amusing, and used to go into great detail describing her navy gaberdine slacks and standard white polyester shirt with the company logo stamped all over, masquerading as a pattern.

But now they monitored calls randomly and staff had attended a one-day seminar on how to handle the 'difficult' caller. There was a company policy and procedure in place that had to be followed to the letter. So even that bit of fun had been taken away.

Eleven o'clock. Sam could hardly believe it when she checked her watch and that was the time. She knew logically it had to be right, she hadn't gone to lunch yet. But it felt like it was about four in the afternoon.

'Location of vehicle, please.'

'I don't know.'

Sam sighed. 'Could you tell me the name of the street where you are now, madam?'

'I don't know.'

'Could you give me the name of the nearest cross-street?'

'What do you mean?'

'I mean,' Sam's patience was wearing thin, 'the nearest street intersecting with the one you're in now.'

'There are no intersections.'

'Are you in a built-up area?'

'What does that mean?'

Her patience was past thin, it had become anorexic. 'Are there any street signs, distinguishing features, landmarks of any description?'

There was a pause. 'No.'

'You're standing in a nuclear wasteland, madam?' Her patience was now being booked into a clinic for eating disorders.

'Don't use that tone with me.'

Sam took a deep breath. 'Perhaps you could describe to me what you see around you?'

'There are only some nondescript houses. Not very attractive at all.'

'You realise, madam, that we can't come and help you if we don't know where you are?'

'But *I* don't know where I am! I'm lost, you stupid girl!'

'Lost where?'

'If I knew that, I wouldn't be lost!'

Sam sighed audibly. 'So, there are no street signs anywhere in the vicinity?'

'Again, no. Are you starting to understand why I'm lost?'

'What's the last place you recognised?'

'Pymble.'

'So, you're on the north shore?'

'No, not any more.'

'What do you mean?'

'I live in Pymble. I left an hour ago for Parramatta.'

That narrowed it down. Hardly.

'Well, madam, let's see if we can't figure this out. Could you describe any landmarks you passed on the way?'

'I didn't see any landmarks.'

'Even the moon has landmarks!'

'Well I'm not on the moon! I can tell you that much.'

'More's the pity.'

'What did you say?'

'I said, are you anywhere near the city?'

'Of course not, I'd know that!'

For a fleeting moment Sam considered disconnecting. When the woman called back, she was likely to get someone else. But she reached for the directory instead. 'Can you tell me where you were headed, exactly?'

That evening

'Mum, I'm sleeping over at Emma's tonight,' Jessica said breezily as she climbed into the car. She had dancing class on Friday afternoons and Sam usually picked her up after she collected Ellie from pre-school. Joshua made his own way home.

'Last time I checked, Jessica, I was still the parent,' Sam informed her. 'And the way that works is that the child asks the parent if they're allowed to stay at a friend's place. And then the parent considers it and gives the child an answer.'

She knew Jess's eyes would be spinning in her head, but Sam kept her attention on the road.

'You're not seriously going to stop me from going to Emma's? What am I, a prisoner of war?'

No, drama queen maybe. 'I'd just like a little consideration, Jess.'

She sighed. 'It's just that I knew I wouldn't be able to cope with Dad gone tonight.'

For crying out loud.

'It'll help me take my mind off it.'

'Jess, he was rarely home before nine, especially on a Friday night,' Sam reminded her, realising that a lot of that overtime was probably something else entirely. 'You seemed to cope fine before this.'

'It's different now, Mum!' Jess insisted. 'And Emma's been through it, she understands.'

Half the kids at school had 'been through it' and, as Sam recalled, Emma's parents had split when she was a baby. Still, far be it from Sam to spoil Jess's fifteen minutes in the limelight.

'I don't see why Dad can't just stay. We have an extra room.'

Sam sighed. 'It wouldn't work, Jess.'

'It's not fair that we have to do without a father just because you don't want him to live with us any more.'

'*What?*' Sam pulled up at a red light and looked squarely at her daughter. 'What did you say?'

'Dad would stay if you let him,' Jessica said airily.

Sam was gobsmacked. 'Where did you get that idea?'

'He said so, last night.'

'*What?*' Sam almost shrieked. Fuck him! What sort of a game was he playing?

'Don't have a cow, Mum!' Jessica admonished. 'He was only being honest.'

Sam glared at her, but then a car horn sounded from behind. The lights had turned green. Sam pulled off, changing gears roughly.

'Jessica,' she said through gritted teeth, 'your father is going to live with another woman. That's why he's leaving. Is that clear?'

'If you say so,' she shrugged.

Sam turned up the radio and Jessica promptly changed the channel. Sam didn't care. She couldn't speak she was so furious. How dare he say that to Jess? Where did he get off?

When they arrived home, Sam unbuckled Ellie's seatbelt and lifted her out of her booster seat. She marched determinedly inside. The girls followed her into the kitchen.

'Okay Jess, I'm presuming you want a lift over to Emma's, so go get changed and get your things together. Oh, and check that your brother's home while you're upstairs.' She turned to Ellie. 'Why don't you see if there's something on the telly, sweetheart?'

'But I'm hungry, Mummy,' she said plaintively.

'Okay, Mummy just has to make one phone call and then,' her voice dropped to a whisper, 'I'll take you to McDonald's after we drop Jessie off!'

Ellie clapped her hands and skipped out of the room. Sam picked up the phone and dialled Jeff's number at work. His assistant answered.

'Oh, hello Mrs Holmes. I'm afraid he's already left for the day.' Sam sensed the awkwardness in her voice. There was every chance she had known what was going on, long before Sam had.

'Never mind,' she said lightly. 'I'll try his mobile.'

But it was turned off. Jeff *never* turned off his mobile. He acted as though the world might spin off its orbit if he couldn't be contacted twenty-four/seven. The option came on to leave a message. Oh, she was going to leave a message alright.

'Jeff, it's me, you fucking coward! Just where do you get off telling Jess that I'm the one kicking you out? She's just given me a lecture about how I should let you stay in the spare room. This is so far below the belt it isn't funny. All your bullshit about doing the right thing by the kids – you just want to save your own arse! Call me, you spineless shithead!'

She slammed down the phone and turned around. Ellie stood wide-eyed, staring at her mother.

'There was nothing on the telly, Mummy.'

'Adults sometimes get really mad with each other and they say things that aren't very nice,' Sam was explaining to Ellie. She had brought her to McDonald's as promised. Sam wasn't eating, she just ordered a coffee. She didn't think she could stomach more than that.

She felt awful. The kids had never heard her use that kind of language. She never *used* that kind of language! Not in front of them, and only occasionally otherwise. Maybe after a few drinks with the girls. Sam was having visions of her life spiralling downwards until she became a foul-mouthed, cigarette-smoking, beer-drinking bag lady playing poker machines all day and leaving the kids locked in the car outside the casino.

'Want a chip, Mummy?' Ellie offered brightly.

'No thank you, darling.' She smiled down at her. Ellie seemed more interested in the toy that came with her Happy Meal than in listening to Sam purge. Maybe she shouldn't be so hard on herself. Ellie probably hadn't picked up on most of what she'd said on the phone anyway.

'Mummy?'

'Yes darling?'

'Why is Daddy a spiny shithead?'

Maxine arrived at seven just as Joshua was walking out the door.

'Josh! How are you going?'

'Hi Max.'

She refused to allow the kids to call her 'Aunty', claiming it made her sound old.

'That's my lift,' he said as a car horn sounded.

'Oh well, hi and bye.'

He smiled at her. He liked Max. He even let her kiss him on the cheek before he ran out to the waiting car.

'Where's Josh off to?' asked Max as she came into the kitchen.

Sam was bent over with her head in the fridge. 'Pizza with the football team,' she said, her voice muffled.

'What did you say?'

She straightened up. 'Sorry, I was just looking for olives. I'm sure I had some big green ones stuffed with anchovies.'

'Ugh!' Max pulled a face. 'Don't find them on my account! I bought chocolate!' she said, tossing two family-size blocks of Cadbury's on the bench.

Sam smiled at her sister. It was good to see her.

Max held her arms out. 'How are you, Sherlock?'

They hugged each other. Although three years younger than Sam, Max was a good six inches taller. Alex and Sam had always complained that Max got all the height. They had both stopped growing at five foot three when puberty hit. Maxine was tall, willowy, leggy. It wasn't fair. If some of her height had been distributed equally between the sisters, they all could have been average.

Though in reality, none of the three Driscoll girls could ever be described as average. With their dark hair, olive skin and coal-black eyes, they were often asked about their ancestry. Greek? Italian perhaps, from the south? Middle Eastern? Maybe even Polynesian? Sam never knew what to say. They had no idea of their father's background, and their mother was no help. Bernice refused even to have his name mentioned. The only thing he'd left behind was an Anglo-Saxon surname.

'I need a drink,' Sam announced.

'You don't want to wait for the others?'

'I could barely wait till I got home today and I'm not about to hold off a moment longer.' She took a bottle of champagne out of the fridge.

Max winced. 'Did something happen at work, or is it all just getting too much for you?'

Sam shrugged. 'I was, shall we say, less than patient with a caller. If it was monitored, I'll be summoned to Stewart's office next week and hauled over the coals.'

'Ugh, Sleazy Stew,' Max shuddered. She reached up to the top shelf for a couple of wine glasses. 'Hey, you're going to have to move these now that Jeff won't be living here. You'll never be able to reach them.'

Sam lifted an eyebrow. 'Thanks Max.'

'Just showing some empathy,' she grinned. 'Seeing how it is from your shoes, or your height. How is it from down there anyway?'

Sam popped the cork out of the bottle and poured them both a glass.

'What shall we drink to?' she said, trying not to sound pathetic.

'We will drink,' Max began, raising her glass, 'to your health, Sherlock. What doesn't kill you, only makes you stronger.'

Sam took a few gulps of her wine. She'd need strength alright, to stomach all the well-meaning platitudes she would be hearing from now on.

'Now, as for Sleazy Stew,' Max continued, 'throw yourself at his mercy. Tell him what's happened, cry, pretend you're broken-hearted.'

She was broken-hearted. 'I don't know, Max.'

'Sam, you're going to have to learn how to use this to your own advantage. Get a little savvy. You might even score a bit of compassionate leave if you play it right.'

'Mudcrab!' Ellie cried, running into the kitchen.

Max scooped her up in her arms. 'Hi Jelly Belly!'

Max had a nickname for everyone, and expected the same

in return, at least from the kids. The older two were over it, but Ellie thought it was a hoot.

'Guess what!'

'What?' said Max, settling her down on the kitchen bench.

'Daddy's gone to live with another lady.'

'Has he?' Max glanced over at Sam. She just shrugged, watching them. 'What do you think about that?'

Ellie screwed her nose up thoughtfully. 'Mmm, it's okay. Daddy said we'll still see him lots.'

'That's good.'

Ellie nodded, before leaning closer to Max. 'Mummy's mad at him but,' she whispered conspiratorially.

'Oh?'

She nodded her head seriously. 'She says he's a spiny shit –'

'Ellie!' Sam interrupted. 'Remember, you're not supposed to repeat what Mummy said when she was angry? I think it's time for bed, young lady.' There was no way she was going to let big ears hang around once the crew arrived. She'd learned enough bad language for one day.

'Oh!' Ellie looked crestfallen.

'What if I read you a story?' offered Max, turning around. 'Piggyback up the stairs.'

'So, Jeff's a spiny shit?' Max remarked when she returned to the kitchen twenty minutes later. 'Interesting metaphor.'

'I believe "spineless shithead" was the actual term I used on the phone this afternoon.'

'Never mind, she'll get it right in time for news at kindy next week.'

The doorbell sounded. Sam took a deep breath. 'That'll be the cavalry.'

Sam had met Fiona and Liz at the local baby health clinic after Joshua was born. They had all been first-time mothers and sheer terror had bonded them instantly. Rosemary had lived next door when they moved to Epping. She was not the sharpest tool in the shed, but she was very sweet, and she had the most overbearing husband Sam had ever come across. They had two boys older than Josh, who took the lead from their father. Rosemary was at the bottom rung of the family ladder and Sam had felt sorry for her. She had talked her into coming out with them one night, and though it had caused a major stir at home, Rose had gone anyway. Sam always invited Rosemary after that. She rarely came, but she appreciated being asked.

'Sammy!' Fiona cried. 'How are you?' she continued breathlessly, throwing her arms around Sam's neck and almost crushing her. Fiona was a strong woman, in every sense of the word. She had a tendency to boss the others around a little and she had an opinion about everything. She didn't realise that none of them took her as seriously as she took herself. 'He's a bastard, no other word for him.'

'Are you okay, Sam?' said Rosemary, frowning and clasping her hands. 'I can't believe he's done this to you. It's . . . he's . . .'

'An arsehole,' Liz finished for her. Max's nickname for Liz was Drizabone, for obvious reasons. She bent to kiss Sam on the cheek. 'How are you, darling?' she said in her smoky, Lauren Bacall voice.

They all crowded into the kitchen brandishing bottles of wine and greeting Max noisily. She lined up more glasses out of the cupboard.

'I brought chocolate,' Liz announced, digging in her bag.

'So did I,' said Max.

'Me too,' Fiona added.

Sam looked at Rosemary. She shrugged, opening a container to reveal a batch of chocolate spiders. Rose worked as a cook at a childcare centre and they had become accustomed to her turning up with kiddies' treats. Not that any of them complained if there was chocolate involved.

'Lucky someone had a little foresight,' said Sam, lifting a platter out of the fridge and placing it on the bench in front of them. It looked like something from a magazine. Marinated olives and char-grilled vegetables contrasted against glistening semidried tomatoes, dollops of homemade taramasalata and thick wedges of creamy cheese. Sam was good at platters. The women all murmured appreciatively.

'Does the man realise what he's giving up?' said Fiona, shaking her head and reaching for an olive.

'What? Savoury platters?' Liz frowned, slicing a hunk of cheese.

'No, I mean *everything* she does. She's so good around the house. What's his problem?'

'It's true,' Rosemary nodded. 'Who on earth could replace you, Sam? I mean, you did everything for him! And always so beautifully.'

'She's better off without him, I reckon,' said Max. 'I don't think he's ever appreciated her.'

They were all nodding knowingly. Sam felt exposed. Had they thought this all along? Why hadn't they said anything before?

'Of course, we never liked to say anything before,' said Fiona. 'I mean, while you were together. But we always thought your marriage was a little old-fashioned.'

'Not letting you work?' Liz shook her head. 'It was like something out of the Dark Ages!'

'Even Col lets me work,' added Rosemary. 'He couldn't afford to run his boat otherwise.'

'But I did work, I do work.' And it wasn't Jeff stopping her anyway.

'One day a week hardly counts,' Fiona dismissed. 'Now you'll be able to work properly, really carve out a career for yourself.'

She didn't want a career. She wanted to be a wife, that was her career. And what was wrong with that? When was the referendum that decided there was no worth in being a wife and mother?

Sam didn't expect Fiona to understand. She ruled the roost in her household, bringing in a salary twice what her husband could ever hope to make. Consequently, it was she who went back to work a few months after their first baby was born, while Gavin stayed home. Another year passed, a second daughter arrived and Fiona showed no signs of allowing parenthood to interfere with her career. Gavin was firmly entrenched as the househusband/primary caregiver/chief cook and bottle washer. The girls included him in lunch a couple of times, but they found him a bit weird. Liz said it was like his balls had been cut off. But Sam didn't think it was that. He was just weird.

Of course they always told Fiona what a wonderful man he was, staying home with the babies, supporting her career. Now Sam wondered how often they had sat around airing their opinions about her marriage when she wasn't around. Feeling sorry for her. And she thought people had envied her.

'It's always the pretty ones,' Fiona declared.

Sam frowned. 'Who? Me? Come off it.'

They all clucked, shaking their heads.

'Of course you're unselfconsciously pretty, that's your appeal,' explained Fiona.

'We'd hate you if you were up yourself,' added Liz.

'Thanks,' Sam smiled weakly. 'I know you're all trying to cheer me up, but I've been feeling so fat and frumpy lately, and the mirror isn't exactly putting up an argument.'

'Everyone puts on a few pounds after they've had kids!' said Rosemary. Rosemary had put on a few pounds with both of her children, and a few more for good measure. Her 'kids' were now young men and she never had managed to shift the weight. She had a backside she imagined was the size of Western Australia, which was a constant source of despair for her. 'It's normal, isn't it?'

'Absolutely,' Liz nodded. They all turned to stare at her, busily stuffing cheese and biscuits down her throat. After she had her baby, Liz had worn size ten jeans home from the hospital. *With a belt.*

'What?' she said, her mouth full. She swallowed. 'Okay, okay! So I have a fast metabolism! It's really hard being a thin woman in this generation, you know. Everyone hates you.'

'At least you can buy clothes that are fashionable,' Sam grumbled.

'And you don't have to panic every Spring about how you're going to look on the beach in a swimming costume,' Fiona added.

'Forget the beach,' Sam muttered. 'It's bad enough in the dressing-rooms!'

'Do we always have to talk about our weight?' Rosemary blurted suddenly.

Everyone looked at her. Rose didn't tend to put her opinions out there.

'I mean,' she continued, flustered by her own bravado, 'could you imagine men sitting around talking about how big their bums are?'

'No,' said Max. 'They'd be talking about something much more fascinating. Like football, or cars —'

'Or tits,' Liz added.

'I'm just saying that we waste so much time and energy talking about it.'

'She's right you know,' said Fiona.

'Fair enough, we should make a vow,' declared Max. 'No diet talk.'

'And no dissecting our bodies and saying how fat and ugly we are,' added Rosemary.

'And,' Liz leaned forward over the bench, 'anyone who picks up a piece of chocolate and says "I shouldn't be having this" before scoffing it anyway, has to stand in the corner for the rest of the night!'

They all drank to that. The phone started ringing.

'Take everything through into the family room. I'll just get this.' Sam picked up the handset and stepped into the hall away from the rabble.

'Hello?'

'It's me.'

Sam felt her heart sink into her stomach. She was so angry with Jeff she could hardly speak.

'Sam? Are you there?'

'Yes,' she said tightly.

She heard him release his breath. 'Sam, about your message. I didn't say those things to Jess. She must have misunderstood.'

'She seemed pretty clear this afternoon.'

'Would you mind telling me exactly what she said, if you

can remember?' His voice had an unfamiliar tone. It was almost deferential.

Sam cleared her throat. 'She said it wasn't fair that they have to lose you because I don't want you to live here any more. She said you would stay if I let you.'

'I didn't say that –'

'Well what *did* you say Jeff, to give her that idea?' Sam was becoming impatient. 'You must have said something!'

He didn't respond.

'Jeff?'

'Sorry, I was thinking.' He sighed. 'I remember she asked why I couldn't sleep in the spare room. I said it wouldn't be fair on you. That you wouldn't want me staying there under the circumstances.'

Sam could feel tears rising in her throat. She swallowed. 'Why didn't you tell her the truth?'

'I guess I didn't want Jess thinking I want to leave *her*.' He paused. 'I didn't mean it to sound the way it did. I'm sorry, Sam. Really, I can understand why you're so angry.'

She couldn't speak, she was worried she wouldn't be able to control her voice. Why was he doing this now? Being so kind in the middle of walking out on her? It was like stroking her hair as he released the guillotine.

'Let me talk to her? I'll straighten it out.'

'She's not here,' Sam said quietly.

'I'll call her tomorrow then. If that's okay with you?'

'Mm.'

'Sam, are you alright?'

Fuck. She took a breath. 'I'm fine. Look, I've got people here, I have to go.'

'Sure, I'll phone tomorrow.'

'See you.' She hung up. But she wouldn't see him tomorrow. Or the next day. Or hardly ever any more.

She walked out to the family room. The girls were scattered across the lounge chairs, all except Max, who was sprawled out on the floor. They were laughing at someone's joke.

Rosemary looked up at Sam. 'What's the matter? Who was that?'

'It was Jeff,' she said, trying to keep her voice level, keep control. But it was no use, she burst into tears. Max jumped up from the floor and put an arm around her. Liz passed her a drink.

'Come and sit down,' said Max.

Fiona sidled over to make room for them on the sofa. 'What did he say?'

'I called him earlier about something Jess said today,' Sam sniffed.

Rose passed her a tissue. 'What was that?'

'That I was kicking him out, that he would stay if I let him.'

'What?' they shrieked in unison.

'Bastard!'

'Dickhead!'

'Now, now ladies,' Liz chided. 'We don't have to lower ourselves to his level, just because the arsehole has the morals of a dog on heat.'

'What did he have to say for himself?' Max asked.

Sam wiped her eyes and nose. 'He didn't mean it the way Jess took it. He hadn't made himself clear, but she misunderstood as well.' She paused, thinking. 'He was so . . . *decent* about it. He sounded genuinely sorry.'

'So did Bill Clinton,' said Liz drily, 'after he was caught.'

Sam shook her head. 'I don't get why he's trying so hard now to do the right thing.'

'Guilty conscience,' Fiona proclaimed.

Liz nodded. 'I remember Mick acted like some kind of hero just because he gave me child support. Like he had a choice!'

Liz's first marriage had fallen apart when their son Will was barely three, on account of the fact that Mick was a 'moron' who didn't understand the meaning of fidelity, 'probably couldn't even spell it'. She married Michael five years later. He was only ever called Michael, so as not to confuse him with the first Michael, who was only ever referred to as Mick.

'I just can't help wondering if he's a better person with her,' Sam said in a small voice.

'No!' they chorused.

'It's like Fiona said,' Rosemary assured her. 'He's just feeling guilty about what he's done to you. And so he should.'

'I used to imagine him having an affair,' Sam blurted. 'Max thinks I'm odd. But you know, when it goes stale, and you're not as close as you used to be, well, I don't know,' she sighed. 'I thought it would be a good way out. That I would have all the control, send him packing. But it's nothing like that at all.'

'I'd be devastated if Gavin had an affair,' Fiona remarked. 'Not that he ever would, of course.'

'I think I know what you mean though, about having a way out,' said Rosemary wistfully.

'What about you, Liz?' asked Max. 'You've been through a marriage break-up.'

She shrugged. 'The only thing I ever daydreamed about was Mick being mauled by a Rottweiler,' she said plainly, picking up her cigarettes. 'I'm going outside for a fag.'

They were silent for a while, absorbed in their own thoughts. Sam looked at the glass in her hand and skolled down the remainder. She reached for a bottle to refill her glass.

'Hey, let's not get all morbid,' she announced. 'You're supposed to be cheering me up.'

Fiona promptly launched into the latest email joke of the day, and Sam forced herself to laugh. But she felt as though she had left her body and was watching the scene from somewhere else.

There's that sad woman whose husband left her for another woman.

After a while she walked out to join Liz, who was lighting her second cigarette.

'You don't have to stay out here, you know.'

'Yes I do, it's rude to smoke in a non-smoker's house. Especially one as pristine as yours.'

'Give me a drag then,' said Sam.

Liz passed the cigarette to her. 'You don't smoke.'

'I'm thinking of starting a few bad habits. Ooh, head spin,' she said, passing it back to Liz.

'That tends to happen when you've never smoked.'

'I used to smoke. When I was sixteen, for about a year, until I started going out with Jeff. He didn't like it so I stopped.'

'There you go, there's something worthwhile you got out of the relationship.'

They stared out at the garden. Maxine drifted out to join them.

'They're talking about the relative merits of washing powders in there. They lost me.'

'Don't be smug,' Sam corrected her. 'Of course it's boring to a single woman who doesn't have a tribe of kids to wash for.'

'No,' Liz shook her head, blowing out smoke. 'It's boring for anyone.'

'I suppose you're right.'

'The pergola looks good,' Liz remarked. 'I haven't seen it since it was finished.'

'Mm, but I wish we hadn't spent the money now,' Sam sighed. 'It's just more to pay off on the mortgage.'

'Don't worry, you'll get it back when you sell.'

'Sell?'

Liz looked at her. 'You don't intend holding on to this place, do you?'

'Why not?'

'Well, to be honest, darl, I don't think you'll be able to afford it.'

Sam felt alarmed. 'Why? Jeff's on a good wage. He wouldn't want the kids to do without.'

'They will though, Sherl, according to the statistics,' Max informed her.

'What are you talking about?'

'Children of divorces always move down a peg or two on the socio-economic ladder.'

'I think you're mixing your metaphors there,' Liz frowned.

'Maybe you don't realise,' Sam continued insistently, 'but Jeff earns *really* good money.'

'Look, you'll be better off than a lot of people. But don't forget he now has his own living expenses to cover as well.'

'The child support agency will do an assessment of what he has to give you for the kids,' Liz explained. 'It'll be fair, but you won't have any control over what he does with the rest.'

'I agree with Liz,' said Max. 'I think you'll find this house will gobble up too much of your income. And then there's maintenance, rates. I bet they're a fortune around here.'

Sam stood frozen.

There was that poor woman again, the one whose husband left her, and then she lost everything.

'Give me another drag of that cigarette.'

The following week

'Do I have to go?' Josh said for probably the tenth time since he'd found out that they were going to spend every second weekend with their father. That was as much as they had worked out at this stage.

'Yes, you do,' Sam replied brusquely, checking the back door was locked.

'Why?'

She sighed. 'Because that's the way things have to be now.' Sam had already had this argument with Jeff and she didn't feel like having it again, especially playing the other side. Sam hated that they were going to stay at the flat he shared with Jodi.

'What choice do I have?' Jeff had countered.

'Does she have to be there?'

'It's her flat, I don't think it's exactly polite to ask her to clear out for the weekend.'

'But I haven't even met the woman. I don't let the kids stay anywhere unless I've met at least one of the parents.'

Jeff sighed loudly. 'I am one of the parents, Sam, in case you've forgotten. But fine, why don't we set up a meeting?'

'Never mind,' Sam blurted. She'd rather dine on live frogs.

'Well, couldn't you take them somewhere else?'

'What are you suggesting? That I hole up in some dingy hotel room for the weekend? That'd be fun for the kids.'

'You can afford better than dingy, Jeff.'

'Maybe, as a one-off. But what difference does it make, Sam? This is where I'm living now. They're going to have to get used to it sooner or later.'

Get used to it. How carelessly that phrase was bandied about. Get used to it. Snap out of it. Get over it. Cheer up. Move on. As if it was that easy. Well, you could tell a horse to get used to being led to water, but . . .

'Now, grab your school bag, Josh, your sisters are already in the car.'

'Why?'

'Why what?'

'Why do we have to go for whole weekends?' he persisted. 'What about when football starts up again?'

'Well, your father will have to take you.' Ha. Some small consolation.

'He's never bothered before.'

'That's not quite true, Josh,' Sam admonished. 'You can't say he's *never* been to one of your games.'

'Okay, he's been like, twice,' he grumbled.

'You know it's been more than that.'

Josh followed his mother out to the garage. 'I don't see why we have to do what he wants when he's the one who pissed off.'

Sam turned around to face him. 'Because you do. Because you're fourteen years old and you don't have a choice. Your life revolves around the whims of your parents. And I'm sorry, Josh, because the last thing I want to do is hurt you, but I can't do anything about this.'

He stared down at his feet. He was much taller than Sam now and she couldn't give him a hug so easily. He wouldn't want her to anyway, with the girls peering through the car windows watching them. Instead she squeezed his arm.

'Look, if it's terrible you can sort something else out with your father. But you have to at least give it a go, Josh.'

Sam couldn't stop thinking about it all the way to work. She hated forcing anything onto Josh, but what could she do about it? Jessica was jumping out of her skin to go. Jodi's flat was in Clovelly and Jeff had promised to take them all to Bondi for breakfast on Saturday morning. Jess couldn't believe she was actually going to see where they filmed *Beachside*. She could hardly contain herself.

Ellie seemed fine. She was only worried about leaving her mother alone. Sam reassured her she would be alright, that she had lots of friends she could visit. Everyone kept telling her this was the best part about being separated. Whole weekends to yourself to do whatever you pleased. Problem was, everybody was occupied with their own families, chores, weekend sports. Even Maxine had plans. It was going to be a long weekend.

There's that sad woman whose husband left her. She does nothing all weekend but stare at old Elvis movies on the TV and drink wine out of a cask.

Sam walked wearily through the glass doors at MRA, signed on, and made her way around to her workstation.

'Morning Brenda,' she said as she passed her.

Brenda merely raised a hand, not turning around. She must have been in the middle of a call. Then Sam saw the yellow Post-it note on her monitor.

PLEASE SEE ME BEFORE YOU LOGON
STEWART

Sam sat deferentially listening to Stewart's reprimand. Not that it was harsh.

'You know this is as difficult for me as it is for you,' he said, his head bent in studied concern. 'But it's company policy.

When a breach is detected during a monitored call, the staff member in question has to be censured.'

'I understand, Stewart.'

There was a reason he was known as 'sleazy'. Stewart McEvoy considered himself a bit of a ladies' man. Sam had even overheard him telling one of the young receptionists once that he had often been mistaken for Harrison Ford. That must have been long, long ago in a galaxy far, far away. He had probably been good-looking once upon a time, but he was sadly on the decline these days. A penchant for cigarettes and alcohol hadn't helped. Still, he used his position to get away with some mildly inappropriate behaviour. No one was about to go crying harassment – he was more desperate than threatening.

'You are a valued member of the team, Samantha.' She hated the way he said her name. It was almost lascivious. 'This has never happened before so I don't imagine there will be any serious repercussions. I will have to write a report, of course. Is there anything you want me to include in your defence?'

Sam thought about what Max had said, but she hesitated. If she told Stewart it would make it more . . . real, somehow.

What was she thinking? Her kids were spending the week-end with their father and his new girlfriend. How much more real did it have to get?

She cleared her throat. 'I'm having some personal problems.'

'Well, I knew there had to be something more to it.' He came around the desk and leaned back against it, smiling down at her in a manner she could only imagine he thought was sincere.

'Is there anything in particular that would shed light? For the report,' he added.

'My husband has moved out. He's having an affair.'

'Oh Samantha!' he lamented dramatically. He got up and closed the door to his office, pulling a chair over next to her. 'What happened?'

'Like I said, he's having an affair. He left. Pretty straight-forward really.'

Stewart shook his head. 'Heartbreaking stuff, babe. I've been there.'

Yes, and he'd been the heartbreaker. He'd left wife number one for wife number two and then left her for a *very* young girl in Accounts, who at least had the good sense to dump him soon after. It was the office scandal at the time. And probably the reason he had never moved into upper management.

'Well, if you need someone to talk to, you know my door is always open.' His voice was like molasses. He sounded like that creepy guy on the radio offering an ear to the lovelorn. 'Are you going to need extra shifts? I can arrange that for you. Or maybe you'd like to take some time off?'

'I think for the meantime I'll leave things as they are.'

'Good idea,' he said, taking the opportunity to pat her on the knee. 'But you just let me know, anything I can do.'

'Thanks Stewart. I'd better get back to work.'

'Of course,' he said, clearing his throat. 'And don't worry about the incident. I'll make it go away.'

'Thank you.' She didn't like having to thank him so often. It put her in a vulnerable position.

Sam glanced at her watch. It was almost six. She had been filling in time, completing her log, dawdling. Jeff would be picking up the kids shortly. He was doing the run to preschool, dance class and then home to collect Josh. It would also give the kids a chance to get changed so that their school uniforms could be washed over the weekend. In Jeff's universe that was being considerate. She would have liked to tell him that 'considerate' would be returning their uniforms after the weekend, washed and ironed. She had no idea of Miss Jodi's laundry skills and she wouldn't trust Jeff to do it properly. It just would have been nice if he'd offered.

'What are you still doing here, Samantha?'

She jumped. 'Stewart! You startled me.'

'Sorry, I didn't mean to.' He considered her. 'You're usually out of here in such a hurry. Don't you have kids to collect?'

She breathed out heavily. 'They're spending the weekend with their father.'

'I see,' he said. 'At a bit of a loose end?'

'No,' she lied. 'This is the good part. No kids to run around after. It'll be like being a single woman again.'

'Well, if that's the case, let me take you for a drink.'

God, she'd walked right into that one, and she didn't quite know how to get herself back out.

'Come on,' he persisted. 'What are you going to do? Sit in an empty house all weekend waiting for them to get home?'

That was the plan.

'You haven't been to the Carlton since they've done it up, have you?'

She shook her head grudgingly. Maybe she should go. What harm could there be in having an innocent drink?

That was almost the last coherent thought Sam could remember having. Until about ten minutes ago, when she had emerged out of some kind of fog to find Stewart on top of her, his body heaving against hers, the smell of stale alcohol and cigarettes and sweat almost suffocating her as he rammed himself inside her. She'd wanted to scream, push him off. But instead she froze. She was frightened, terrified in fact. If she struggled she didn't know what he might do. She didn't know what he had done to get her this far. So she stayed completely still, let him think she was still passed out. It would be over soon and she could get away. He must be nearly finished. Sam bit her lip, holding back tears. She'd never slept with anyone but Jeff in her whole life. How could this have happened? Suddenly Stewart had arched, grunted, and then collapsed over onto his back on the bed beside her. He hadn't made a noise now for a while, hadn't budged. But Sam wanted to make absolutely certain he was asleep before she dared to move a muscle. She couldn't risk waking him up. So she lay there, half naked, barely breathing, trembling inside.

Finally Stewart broke into a snore and Sam mustered up the courage to move. Her heart was racing as she slithered off the bed noiselessly. She crawled around on the floor, gathering up her clothes, then crept out to the living room. She dressed quickly before tiptoeing to the front door, carrying her shoes. She opened it silently and closed it behind her with an unavoidable click.

Sam was shaking as she hurried down the stairs of the apartment block, trying to recall if she even knew where Stewart lived. She slipped on her shoes and walked out through the security door. It was a nondescript street, lined on either side with amorphous apartment blocks. She headed up the road towards an intersection. A small blue signpost under a street-light pointed to North Strathfield railway station. She breathed a sigh of relief. It was only a short walk and, as Sam had hoped, there was a taxi waiting at the entrance to the station. She hurried over and climbed into the back seat, her heart pounding almost painfully against her ribs. But it wasn't until the taxi pulled away from the kerb that Sam felt she had escaped.

'Where to, lady?'

'Um,' Sam hesitated. She didn't want to go home alone, not now. She bit her lip as tears pricked at the corners of her eyes. 'Enmore, thanks.'

Sam pulled out her mobile and dialled Max's number. Oh, please be there. Relief washed over her when she heard her sister's voice.

'Max, it's me.'

'It's the middle of the night, Sherl. Where are you?'

'I'm on my way to your place,' she said tearfully. 'Is that okay?'

'Sam, what is it, what's wrong?' Max urged. 'You sound weird, are you alright?'

'I . . .' Sam swallowed. 'I'll be there soon.'

She hung up the phone and dropped it into her handbag. She tried to remember what had happened. They'd gone to the Carlton Hotel and Stewart had bought her a glass of wine. And then another almost straight after. They'd moved to a booth, with a bottle of wine as she recalled. But Stewart only drank spirits, she was pretty sure. Had the bottle of wine been all for her?

She'd talked and talked and talked while he kept filling her glass. She told him everything, she remembered now. She found his hand on her knee comforting. She recalled getting weepy. She looked at him through an alcohol haze and remembered thinking, *'He does look a little like Harrison Ford'*.

Oh God.

A vivid image suddenly pierced through the fog in her brain. She was sitting in Stewart's car in the passenger seat. *'You can sleep it off at my place, babe.'* She remembered the smell of leather upholstery, his hand groping under her shirt, his tongue down her throat. She thought she was going to be sick. She caught sight of her reflection in the window. Who the hell are you, Samantha Holmes? What the hell have you done?

There's that woman whose husband left her. She gets drunk on Friday nights and she's anyone's.

Max had moved to Enmore to be closer to the uni, into a tiny place that was barely big enough for all her junk. But she insisted her days of house-sharing were over and she couldn't afford anything bigger on her own. Sam directed the driver to the small block of flats, paid him and got out of the cab. She was starting to feel frail as she climbed up the stairs. Max must have heard her on the landing, because she opened the door before Sam had a chance to knock. Her face was creased with worry.

'My God, what happened, Sam? You look terrible.'

That was it, Sam couldn't hold on any longer. She collapsed into her sister's arms and started to sob violently. Max held her tight, drawing her inside and closing the door.

'Sherl,' she said insistently, 'you're scaring me. Tell me you're alright.'

Sam took a deep, tremulous breath, and looked up at her. 'It's just . . . I . . . Oh God, Max, I slept with Stewart . . .'

'Sleazy Stew?' Max exclaimed.

Sam nodded, her face streaked with tears. 'I don't know how it happened. I was so drunk,' she wailed.

Max held Sam's head against her shoulder, stroking her hair. 'You're safe now, it's over.' She waited until Sam had calmed a little. 'How did it happen?'

Sam looked up at her. 'I don't know, that's the thing. We went out for a drink, and next thing I was in his bed, he was on top of me . . .' Sam started to shake, 'Oh God, what have I done, Max?'

Max held her hands to steady them. 'You're in shock. Come and lie down,' she said, walking her into the bedroom. Sam curled up on the bed and Max wrapped the covers snugly around her.

'Here,' said Max, reaching for a small bottle on the bedside table. 'Have some of my Rescue Remedy.'

'What is it?' Sam frowned.

'It's a homoeopathic mixture,' Max explained. She unscrewed the lid and drew out a glass dropper. 'Lift your tongue.'

'Why?' Sam said dubiously.

'Because you're supposed to hold it under the tongue and just let it absorb.'

'What does it do?'

'It's good for shock, it'll help you calm down.' She could see the doubt in Sam's eyes. 'Come on, it can't hurt.'

Sam opened her mouth obediently and let Max squeeze a few drops under her tongue. The taste was inoffensive enough. She sighed deeply and snuggled into the covers, closing her eyes, but all she could see was the image of Stewart bearing down on her. She opened her eyes again, startled.

'Just let go, Sam,' soothed Max. 'Get some rest. You'll feel better after you've slept.'

'But when I close my eyes I keep seeing him,' Sam said tearfully.

Max lay down behind her, on top of the covers. She wrapped her arms around her and spoke quietly, close to her ear. 'Think about the beach at Taloumbi, Sherl. Can you see it?'

Sam nodded.

'Now close your eyes. Look at the two of us running along

after Pop. It's warm, the sun is low in the sky. And Pop's taken hold of your hand, remember how big his hand was? We're heading home for dinner . . .'

Sam could see it all in her mind's eye. The beach and the ocean, the sand dunes, Nan and Pop's house. Soon the sound of the waves crashing on the shore drowned out Max's voice, and she was asleep.

Saturday morning

'Sam?'

She blinked a couple of times. The room was gloomy, but she could see daylight through a chink in the curtains. She looked up to see Max sitting on a chair beside the bed, holding a mug of tea.

'Hi,' Sam murmured sleepily.

'How are you feeling?' she asked, staring intently down at her.

Then Sam remembered what she was doing here. She felt an ache well up in her chest. 'What am I going to do, Max?'

'You're going to have a nice hot shower. And then I'm taking you to the doctor's.'

Sam frowned up at her. 'Why?'

Max sighed. 'Sam, you don't know whether Stewart used anything last night. You're going to have to take the morning-after pill.'

'What?'

'The morning-after pill. Haven't you heard of it before?'

'Sure,' Sam nodded, sitting up. Her head was throbbing. 'Do I have to, really? I've heard it makes you sick.'

'Better that than the alternative, Sherl,' said Max. 'Here, I made you a cuppa.'

Sam took it from her, the ache in her chest welling up into her throat. 'God, Max, what have I done?'

'Sherl,' Max said seriously. 'You couldn't remember much last night. Do you have any idea what happened?'

She stared into her cup. 'He asked me to come for a drink after work. I was hanging around, feeling at a bit of a loose end. I didn't want to go home to an empty house.'

'You should have told me, Sam. I could have changed my plans.'

'I didn't realise it was going to bother me that much.'

'So, what happened then?'

'It's all a bit of a blur. I remember being in his car, he was groping at me, slobbering all over me,' Sam shuddered. 'He said I could sleep it off at his place, but I don't exactly remember going inside. Next thing I knew he was on top of me . . . God, how could I do that, Max?'

'Sam! You haven't done anything. It was done *to* you. Stewart targeted you, he knew exactly what he was doing. They call it date rape.'

'I think that's overstating it. I didn't even put up a fight . . .'

'Sam, you couldn't put up a fight, you were virtually unconscious!' Max exclaimed. 'Would you ever have slept with him willingly?'

She shook her head weakly. 'I'm so stupid.'

'You're not stupid, Sherl, I won't hear you talk like that.' Max patted her arm. 'Naïve maybe, but not stupid.'

'I should have known better than to go out with Stewart in the first place. I don't even like the man.'

Max sighed. 'People do strange things under duress. Things against their character. You've had a tough few weeks. Give yourself a break.'

'I feel like I don't know who I am any more.' Her voice became a whisper as tears rose in her throat. 'Everything was one way before. I knew what to do each day, what was expected of me. Who I was.' She paused. 'Now it's all gone haywire.' Her eyes were glassy as she raised them to look squarely at Max. 'How am I going to get through this?'

Max sat on the bed next to Sam and put her arm around Sam's shoulder. 'You'll be right, Sherl. It's all part of your journey of self-discovery,' she said sagely.

Sam sniffed, brushing a tear from the corner of her eye. 'Oh don't start your new age crap.'

'It's not crap, and it's not even new age. As bad as things might get, you will find yourself through all this.'

'I didn't know I was lost.'

'Don't be trite.'

'I'm not the one being trite.'

Max turned to face her. 'Sam, this is an opportunity to spread your wings. Do what you want to do, be what you want to be.'

'You're not going to break into song are you?' Sam looked at her dubiously. 'Besides, aren't you forgetting I've still got three kids to raise? And I'll be doing it largely on my own from now on.'

'You've been doing it largely on your own all along.'

Sam was thoughtful. 'It feels different, though. I know Jeff wasn't all that involved but he was there, like a silent partner or something. It gave me a sense of security, I suppose.'

'He was your safety net,' said Max.

There *was* something terribly safe in being married, Sam realised. Your position was defined. You were *Mrs* someone. You had a husband. You could say 'my husband this', 'my husband that'. But now Sam only had an 'ex'. And what's more, she had become an 'ex' without any say in the matter. She had gone from a marriage with no life in it to a life with no marriage in it, and she wasn't sure which was worse.

'Come on,' said Max. 'We'd better get you to the doctor's.'

Sam sighed deeply. There was no competition, this was by far the worse.

'What are you doing today?' Sam asked Max, pretending for a moment she was just a woman indulging in weekend brunch with her sister. Not a woman who had just been to a clinic because she had unprotected, unwanted sex with the office lech in a drunken stupor the previous evening.

Max glanced at her uncertainly. 'Well, I have a date, but I'm going to cancel –'

'Not on my account you're not,' Sam said firmly.

'But you don't want to go home alone . . .'

'That was last night. I promise you I'm over that,' she insisted. Sam was determined to put the whole mortifying experience behind her, from the sickening images of Stewart replaying in her head, to the intrusive, embarrassing questions asked by the doctor this morning. Did she look like someone who had multiple sexual partners, for godsakes?

They were sitting at an outdoor café in the sunshine. Sam had initially baulked at the idea of food, but Max ordered her scrambled eggs anyway. She had to admit, the warm food was comforting in her stomach, and she was starting to feel normal again. Almost.

'So, who's your date?'

'You don't know him, I met him the other day at an exhibition.'

'Oh?' Sam was justifiably suspicious about Max's dates. 'What exhibition?'

'Well, he was the exhibition actually. He's a performance artist.' Max placed her cup in its saucer. 'He does this kind of postmodern interpretative dance piece tracing the fall of communism across Europe, using kitchen appliances as a percussive underscore.'

Sam winced.

Max looked blankly at her. 'What's with the face, Sam? You look like Mum.'

'Couldn't you just go out with someone normal for a change?'

'Now you sound like Mum as well.'

'I'm just saying that if you want to settle down –'

'Who says I want to settle down?'

'What, you don't want a home, a family?'

'Sure, like that really worked out for you,' Max said dubiously.

Sam stared at her cup.

'Sorry,' said Max.

She breathed out heavily. 'Don't worry, I know it's true . . .'

'But?'

'I didn't realise it was so bad. We were like most other couples. The wives complain about their husbands, the husbands complain about their wives. It's what people do. You never think it's serious. And then you hear one day that so-and-so are getting a divorce, or someone is having an affair, and you're shocked, even though you haven't heard them say a nice word to each other in years.' Sam twirled a teaspoon around in her coffee.

'Do you miss him?' Max asked, watching her.

She shrugged. 'It depends. Sometimes he's so frigging smug I can't wait to see the back of him. But then other times, he's sensitive and apologetic, like he's trying really hard to do the right thing.' Sam thought for a moment. 'That's when I want to ask him why he couldn't have put that effort in with us, instead of . . .' She sighed. 'But I already know the answer to that.'

'What?'

She looked squarely at Max. 'Whether we were happy or not, or had nothing in common any more, or whatever, is beside the point. Jeff stopped loving me. And that's what hurts the most.'

It was one o'clock by the time Sam pulled into the garage at home. She'd caught a taxi from the café to Pennant Hills Station where her car was still parked from the day before. She was feeling okay, maybe a little seedy, but that was probably just the remnants of her hangover. The doctor said she was more likely to feel nauseous after the second lot of tablets, which she was due to take twelve hours after the first. In the meantime, she was going to get on with her chores as though it was a normal Saturday. Though on a normal Saturday she would have been in and out, ferrying the kids around, Jeff would have had the weekend newspaper spread across the family room floor . . . Sam felt a sharp stab in her chest. She didn't even know what normal was any more.

As she walked into the kitchen, she was confronted by a pile of notes spread across the bench. There was a neatly written memo from Jeff with details of his new address and phone number. Just what she'd always wanted. Then a stack of notices from Josh's school. Flicking through them, Sam realised they were all asking for money: upcoming excursions, levies for extra equipment, sports fees. He could have given these to his father, she thought wryly. There was a painting Ellie must have done at pre-school. It was of all three children, with a mis-shapen heart and the letters 'MUMY' scrawled across the top. And finally an urgent note from Jess insisting she phone ASAP. Sam glanced across at the answering machine. Christ, there were eleven messages! She pressed *Play* and Jessica's voice filled the room.

'Mum, where are you? Didn't you get my message? Call me as soon as you get home . . . it's Jess.'

The other ten would be the same, only progressively more hysterical no doubt. Sam decided to ring Jeff's mobile. She didn't want to risk Jodi answering the house phone.

'Jeff Holmes.'

'Hello, it's me.'

'Hi. Jess has been trying to reach you.'

'So I gather.'

'Your mobile was turned off. You're always doing that. You should get into the habit of leaving it on, Sam.'

'Then I forget about it, the battery runs out and it doesn't work when I need it.'

'But what's the use of having a phone if you never turn it on?'

A lecture from Jeff was the last thing she needed right now.

'Anyway,' Sam said dismissively, 'can you get Jess for me, please?'

'I'll put her on.'

'*Mu-umm!* Where have you been?' Jessica whined. 'I've called you like, a *thousand* times! And I've left like, a *million* messages!'

'Jess, I have my own life too,' Sam returned. 'Now what's the big emergency?'

'You have to tape Channel 22 at six o'clock.'

'Please Mum,' Sam added.

'*Please Mum!*' Jessica repeated, exasperated.

'Why didn't you just ask your father?'

'They don't have Pay TV, they don't even have a DVD player!' Jess dropped her voice. 'It's pretty third world around here, I mean Josh has to sleep on a sofa bed in the living room. But we'll be okay. Don't worry about us.'

Sam would do her best.

'What am I taping?'

'*In Depth* with Britney Spears.'

'That's a bit of an oxymoron.'

'She's not a moron,' Jessica huffed. 'I don't make fun of your stupid, pathetic old people's music.'

'Is Ellie there?' asked Sam, ignoring Jess while she didn't make fun of stupid, pathetic old people's music. 'Could I speak to her?'

'Okay, but don't forget, will you, Mum? Channel –'

'22 at six o'clock,' Sam finished. 'I won't forget.' She never did.

'Thanks Mum. Here's Ellie.'

'Hi Mummy!'

'Hello sweetheart. Are you having a nice time?'

'Yes. But I miss you.'

'I miss you too.'

Sam could hear Jeff coaxing in the background.

'I have to go, Mummy, we're going to the beach.'

'Have fun. See you tomorrow.'

Sam waited until she heard Ellie hang up. Then she walked out to the family room, scanned the row of videotapes, neatly stacked and labelled, and found one that could be taped over. She checked the guide and programmed the VCR to start recording at six p.m. Sam and Josh were the only ones in the family who could program the VCR. Why people made such a fuss about it was beyond her. You simply read the manual and followed the steps.

She grabbed a basket from the laundry and walked upstairs. She gathered up Jess and Josh's uniforms from where they had dropped them on the floor, plus other stray bits of clothing. She came downstairs again and started up the washing machine, measured out the powder and added it to the surging water. She separated the clothes into two piles, carefully shook out each item and placed them one at a time into the machine, watching as the water eddied and tossed them around, eventually sucking them under.

There is the woman whose husband left her. She needs to get a life.

Sunday afternoon

Sam saw Jeff's car as it pulled into the driveway, because she'd been looking out since four, even though Jeff had said he would have the kids home between four-thirty and five. She'd made their favourites for dinner – potato casserole and chicken schnitzels, which was way too much fat and starch for one meal. But it wouldn't hurt this once. The house was cleaned from top to bottom. Washing and ironing was all done and put away, school lunches made, labelled and packed in the freezer. It would leave a bit of a hole in her schedule for the week, but she'd had to keep busy. She had made it through Saturday with no ill effects from the medication, but she'd slept badly last night, and all day the nausea had come in waves. Sam found if she stopped to rest, her mind wandered to why she had to take the damned pills in the first place. Or worse, the kids there at Jeff's place, the faceless figure of Jodi cooking them dinner, reading Ellie a story, listening to CDs with Jess, laughing with Josh . . .

Sam walked to the front door and opened it wide. Jeff was helping Ellie out of the car while the older two got their bags from the boot.

'Hi,' she called.

'Hi there,' Jeff returned.

Josh sauntered across the lawn towards her, carrying his backpack and skateboard.

'Hi mate, did you have a good time?' Sam asked brightly.

He grunted in what she postulated was a reasonably positive manner.

'Bye Josh,' Jeff called.

Josh made another noise as he walked into the house. Jeff didn't try to stop him or admonish him. That was progress.

Ellie ran over to her mother. 'Hi Mummy, I missed you.'

Sam picked her up, hugging her tight. 'Not as much as I missed you!'

Jeff was helping Jessica carry an assortment of bags and paraphernalia into the entry.

'My God Jess, what on earth did you take with you? You were only going for a weekend.'

'I didn't know what I'd need. I've never been there before,' she defended.

'It's okay,' said Jeff good-naturedly, ruffling her hair.

Alright for him, but Sam knew that all the clothes would be dumped in the laundry hamper whether Jess had worn them or not.

'Did you tape my show?' asked Jess breathlessly.

'Of course. How about a "Hi Mum, how are you, nice to see you"?'

'Hi Mum,' she groaned, but she was smiling, not rolling her eyes for a change. She kissed Sam on the cheek and then turned to her father. 'Bye Daddy.'

Jeff hugged her. 'I'll talk to you through the week, sweetheart.'

He kissed Ellie goodbye and both the girls skittered off inside.

'It went well,' Jeff said when they were alone. He looked quite pleased with himself. Sam felt like slapping him. 'I think they had fun. Even Josh.'

So now he thought he was Father of the Year.

'How was your weekend?'

'Oh, the usual – cleaning, cooking, washing.' That was as much as she was ever going to tell him.

'You should have had a break.'

'Sure,' Sam scoffed. 'Leave it all to the maid, eh?'

He shook his head. 'I just think you overdo it sometimes. You need to learn to relax. Everything doesn't have to be so . . . perfect.'

So, she was *too* perfect? She wished her mother could have heard that. Slapping him was too good. Patronising bastard.

'Well, real life beckons,' Sam said breezily. 'I'd best go in.'

He nodded. 'See you.'

She walked inside and closed the door, not waiting to watch him drive away.

'Mum, you should have seen it, it was amazing!' Jessica had not stopped talking about Bondi throughout dinner. 'It's like, *exactly* like it is in *Beachside*!'

'That's because it is the place in *Beachside,* you moron,' said Josh.

'What would you know?'

'More than you do, retard.'

'Now you two,' Sam interrupted. 'I hope you weren't bickering like this at your father's. What would Jodi think?' She was desperate to get information about Jodi without seeming, well, desperate. Just how young was she? Was she tall, taller than Sam? More than likely. Was she blonde, blue-eyed, reed slim and wrinkle-free? Was she everything that Sam was not? Or everything that Sam had once been? She took a deep breath, composing herself. 'I'm sure she's too young to have had much to do with kids your age.'

'She's not young, Mum. She's old.'

Sam knew that didn't mean anything. Anyone over eighteen was old to Jessica.

'Jess was saying you had to sleep out in the living room, Josh. Did that bother you?'

He shrugged. 'Nuh. There's a good skate bowl up the road. And Dad said he'll get his old boards from Grandma's and we can go surfing next time.'

Well, there you go, thought Sam as she got up to clear the table. It had all turned out alright. So why did she feel hollow? Did she want the kids to have a bad time? What kind of a mother would that make her? But she wondered if it was alright to hope that they would *prefer* to be with her?

'Mummy?'

Sam had just finished reading to Ellie and was smoothing out her quilt, tucking the sheet in tightly, just the way she liked it.

'Mm?'

'I don't like Jodi.'

'Oh?' She tried to suppress the bubble of glee that rose up in her chest, berating herself for being so childish. She sat down on the bed. 'Why not?'

Ellie thought about it for a moment. 'Well, she's doesn't smell like you, Mummy.'

'People don't all smell the same. You just have to get used to her.'

'And she didn't tuck me in. Daddy had to do it.'

Sam smiled. 'Daddy probably wanted to do it.'

'But he doesn't never tuck me in.'

'Some things are going to change, Ellie. When you visit Daddy he'll probably do a lot of things he didn't do before, because I'm not there to do them.' Was she making sense? 'He is your daddy after all, but she's not your mother.' There, that was clearer.

'Is that all that bothered you?' Sam couldn't help asking.

Ellie screwed up her face, thinking. 'Mm, she's got hair under her arms. Like mens do.'

There was a concept. 'Ladies grow hair under their arms, too.'

'You don't. You're smooth.'

'Because I shave.'

Ellie's eyes widened. 'Why do you do that?'

'So that I'll be smooth.'

'Why doesn't Jodi shave then?'

Because she's probably a sprout-eating, hippie feminazi. 'Ladies don't have to shave, Ellie, if they don't want to.'

Ellie pulled a face. 'It's yucky.'

'It's not yucky,' Sam chided gently. 'It's . . . natural.' She leaned down to kiss her. 'And it's time for sleep. See you in the morning.'

Sam walked to the door, turning back to look at her daughter before switching off the light.

'Mummy?'

'Yes sweetheart?'

'I like being with Daddy.' She paused. 'But I like it here more, with you. Is that alright?'

Sam felt a welling in her chest. 'Of course, it's perfectly alright.'

Monday

'Sam, it's Alex.'

'Hi.' Sam had been expecting this call. That didn't mean she was any the more prepared for it.

'Well, how are you?'

'Um, okay.'

There was a moment of silence. She hadn't expected her elder sister to be awkward about this.

'Yes, alright, go ahead with that.'

Sam realised then that Alex was in fact involved in another conversation.

'Sorry about that,' she said to Sam. 'You'd think I could have one phone call without being interrupted.'

'I know what you mean.'

'Pardon?'

'About trying to talk on the phone without being interrupted,' Sam explained.

'By whom?'

'Well, the kids usually.'

'Oh, yes, of course,' Alex dismissed. 'The children, how are they?'

'Fine. They seem to be coping alright, so far.'

'Good. Now the reason I'm calling is that I have business in Sydney later this week. I'd like to see you. How is 4.15 to 5.00 p.m. Thursday for you?'

'Four-fifteen to five? Couldn't she be more specific?' said Max, arching an eyebrow. She was perched on the kitchen bench with her feet on a stool, watching Sam cook dinner.

'Can you be here?' Sam pleaded.

'No, I'm sure I'm going to be busy.'

'I don't want to cope with her on my own.'

'You'll be fine. She likes you more than she likes me.'

'Why do you say that?'

Max shrugged. 'She thinks I'm a flake. Whereas you are a respectable married woman.'

'Not any more,' she sighed.

'What does Aunty Alex do, Mum?' asked Jess, coming back into the room from setting the table.

Sam and Max frowned at each other.

'She's a management consultant,' Sam explained.

'What's that?'

'Well,' she glanced at Max. 'She goes to meetings . . .'

'And she has an assistant,' Max offered.

'She has to make a lot of decisions.'

'And give orders,' added Max. 'She's good at that, she had plenty of practice on us when we were kids.'

'Do me a favour, Jess,' said Sam. 'Don't repeat that when your aunty's here, will you?'

Jess grinned. 'How much are you gonna pay me?'

'Cheek!' Sam called after her as she left the kitchen. She looked back at Max, frowning.

'What?'

'Won't you come, please?'

Max shook her head, springing down off the bench. 'Can't possibly, darling,' she said, affecting an officious tone that made her sound uncannily like Alex. 'Have an appointment with my business manager about my stock portfolio, don't you know.' She opened the fridge. 'Got anything to drink?'

4.15 p.m. Thursday

Sam took a deep breath and opened the front door.

'Hi Alex!' she said brightly.

'Samantha, good to see you.' Alex leaned forward offering her cheek for Sam to kiss, but withdrawing before they actually connected.

Everyone said Sam and Alex were most alike out of the three sisters, but Sam suspected that was only because they were both short. Alex was an upmarket version of Sam. She frequented designer boutiques while Sam shopped at department stores, she wore expensive suits, while Sam didn't even own a suit, she had her hair styled by someone who featured in the social pages of the Sunday papers, while Sam found that pulling hers back in a clip allowed her to go longer between hairdressing appointments. There was no mistaking that Alex was a high-flyer, just as there was no mistaking that Sam was a suburban mum.

'Come in,' said Sam, as Alex walked past her into the house.

Jess and Ellie were standing to attention in the living room.

'Hello Aunty Alex,' they chorused.

'Jessica, Eloise, look how you've grown,' she said perfunctorily. She stooped to offer her cheek, but they didn't quite make it to her either before she straightened up again. 'And Joshua, where is he?' she said, turning to Sam.

'Out on his skateboard,' she explained. 'He'll be along soon.'

'Okay then.' Alex stood for a moment, expectantly.

'Would you like coffee, tea?'

'Mm,' she contemplated. 'I suppose you don't have an espresso machine . . . No, don't worry. Tea will be fine.'

She followed Sam into the kitchen and put her handbag down on the bench. Sam filled the kettle and plugged it in. She reached for the loose tea canister and a pot. Alex might keel over if she used teabags. She took out some cups, the sugar, milk. When there was nothing else to do, she turned around to face her sister. Alex had perched herself on a stool, crossing her legs elegantly, her back straight as a flagpole.

'So Samantha, tell me how you are really?'

She sighed. 'As you would expect.'

'I have no expectations, dear. I hardly saw you and Jeffrey together, I wouldn't know if you were happy or not, if he'd been unfaithful before. I don't know if he beat you. I don't know anything.' She spoke like a round of bullets being fired out of a machine gun. 'Why don't you go ahead and tell me?'

Sam crossed her arms in front of her. 'He has never hit me, Alex. It's nothing like that.'

'Good.'

'I don't think he's been unfaithful before, but how would I know?'

'You would know.'

'I didn't know this time.'

Alex frowned. 'So, you'd grown apart?'

'Why do you say that?'

'Well, if you didn't know your husband was having an affair, I would think a certain distance had come between you.'

Sam poured the boiled water into the teapot and carried it across to the bench where Alex was sitting. 'I suppose,' she shrugged. She turned back for the cups.

'Sam, you were a child when you married. Of course it was bound to fail.'

Sam frowned, setting a cup down in front of Alex and pouring the tea. They'd had some good years. She didn't like to think they'd been doomed from the start.

'What I'm saying is,' Alex continued, 'you've been married since you were too young to make so important a decision. You had children straightaway. It's not surprising that things would . . . unravel, over time.'

Sam sipped her tea.

'But I don't want you thinking of yourself as a failure.'

'Like Mum does.'

'She's just bitter. Don't pay any attention to her.'

Sam was surprised. She thought Alex and Bernice were as thick as thieves.

'You're too much like her, is the problem,' Alex informed her.

She didn't particularly want to hear that.

'You were the pretty one, but smart too, though you never used your brains. You just got married and had babies.'

'But why should that bother Mum? That's what she did.'

'Exactly. She expected more of you. You deserved better than Jeffrey, you deserve better than what he's done to you.'

Sam was bewildered. All these opinions held by everyone and she never had any idea.

'Now, I want to help out,' Alex said crisply. 'I wasn't sure, I was thinking of getting you a cleaner.' She looked around her. 'But it doesn't appear you need one. You certainly keep things shipshape, don't you?'

Sam shrugged.

'So I'll find you a good solicitor.'

'Thanks Alex, but I don't think it's that serious yet.'

'Has he told you he's breaking it off with the woman?'

Sam shook her head.

'And he moved out willingly, you didn't have to force him to leave?'

She shook her head again.

'Samantha,' she said firmly, 'it's serious, whether you think it is or not. You have three children, you have property and no doubt substantial debts to go with it. You have to have someone looking out for your interests. I'll make some inquiries and get back to you next week. And I'll see to the bill.'

'I can't ask you to do that.'

'You're not asking me to do it, I'm insisting.'

'But –'

'Sam, I'm your sister. I can't have the heart-to-hearts with you. That's Maxine's job. But I can do this.' She took a sip from her cup, her first. 'Good. That's settled.' She reached into her handbag and drew out an envelope. 'Here is a voucher for a day spa. Make sure you use it.'

'A what?' Sam felt like her head was spinning.

'A day spa. Massage, facial, manicure, the works. It's all paid for.'

'Thank you,' she said, dazed.

'Not at all.' Alex stood up. 'Now I have to go.'

Sam followed her out to the front door just as Josh arrived home.

'And here's Joshua,' said Alex. 'Look at the size of you. I suppose you don't kiss aunties any more?'

He shrugged.

'Do you speak?'

'Yes Aunty Alex,' he mumbled.

'Well, you're the man of the house now, Joshua. I hope you realise how important you're going to be to your mother.'

Josh blinked as a glimmer of realisation dawned in his eyes, momentarily. Then he looked at the floor.

'Bye now, Joshua.'

'Bye Aunty Alex.' He disappeared out into the kitchen.

Sam opened the door and Alex paused on the threshold. She took hold of both of Sam's arms and pressed her cheek against hers. She still didn't actually kiss her but at least they were touching. Alex stepped back and looked at Sam for a moment before starting down the path towards her car with a cursory wave of her hand.

'I'll call you next week with the details. Oh, and remember,' she turned briefly. 'Don't pay any attention to Mum. Bye now.'

Sam wandered thoughtfully back into the kitchen. Josh was leaning against the kitchen bench nursing a biscuit tin, intent on emptying it. He looked up at his mother, swallowing down a mouthful.

'She's pretty scary.'

Friday

'I really have to get another job,' Sam moaned into the phone. She'd called Max as soon as she'd got in from work and the afternoon runaround.

'Oh no, Sam, how did it go today? Did Stewart come anywhere near you, did he talk to you? Did you spit on him?'

'No,' she sighed. 'Thank God, he avoided me like the plague all morning. I walked into the tea-room at one stage and he nearly knocked me down in his rush to get out. Then he was in meetings all afternoon.'

'That must have been a relief.'

'This is all too hard.' Sam propped the phone on her shoulder while she opened a bottle of wine. 'I want to be one of those Hollywood celebrities who book themselves into a sanatorium due to emotional exhaustion.'

'Yes, I've always found that hiding under a rock is one of the best ways to move forward,' Max sniggered. 'Okay, what we have to do first up is get you a date, someone nice this time.'

'Or I could swallow a packet of razor blades.'

'You can't let one bad experience sour you off men for good,' Max implored. 'It's like riding a bike. You have a fall, you get right back on.'

'I thought that was riding a horse?'

'Whatever.'

'The thing is, I don't want to date. I didn't even mean to go out with Stewart that night.' Sam climbed up on a stool to reach the wine glasses. Max was right, she was going to have to move them. 'Need I remind you, I haven't dated since I was a teenager. I wouldn't know the first thing –'

'*That's* like riding a bike,' Max exclaimed, relieved. 'I knew the analogy fitted somewhere.'

'What are you talking about?'

'Dating is like riding a bike. You never forget how.'

'Look,' Sam said firmly, pouring the wine. 'I need a new job, not a date, okay?'

'I'll help you with your resume.'

'You're on.'

Sam drank down one glass of wine while she decided which takeaway to have tonight. She settled on pizza because it could be delivered. She finished another glass waiting for it to arrive. Then she shared it out amongst the children and left them to eat, poured herself another glass and wandered out to the family room. She sank down onto the lounge and reached for the remote control, turning on the television. She laid there flicking channels, realising she was feeling decidedly tipsy and would probably fall asleep if she wasn't careful. She didn't have that option until she put Ellie to bed at least. Mummy passed out in front of the telly clutching a wine glass was not a good look.

Sam flicked over as *A Current Affair* came back after an ad break.

'How often have you thought,' the presenter was saying, 'I can't do all of this?'

Hardly ever, Sam thought smugly.

'In past generations women stayed at home, handling not only the housework, but all of the myriad details cluttering our day-to-day lives.'

What did she mean, *past* generations?

'Now the new breed of young power couples are finding that while they can hire a cleaner, a gardener, someone to do the ironing, wash the car, walk the dog, they need someone to co-ordinate their lives. What they really need is a wife.'

Sam sat up, pointing the remote at the TV and turning up

the volume. A plump, fortyish woman appeared on screen. She sat behind a vast desk and was wearing a red power suit, her dyed platinum hair styled to within an inch of its life.

'Meet Sheila Boland,' a male voice-over continued the story. 'She's the founder and managing director of Wife for Hire, a home help service with a difference.'

'No, this is not an escort agency,' the woman explained, her smile slightly strained. It was obviously not the first time that had been inferred. 'We don't provide that particular service, but just about anything else a wife would do. Or used to do, before women left the home to build their own careers.'

Sam listened, mesmerised. The woman spoke about their typical clients and the sorts of services they provided for them. Everything from paying the bills to organising dinner parties, shopping for gifts, making travel arrangements, dental appointments or booking the car in for a service.

'All our staff are highly disciplined women who have incredible organisational skills,' Ms Boland explained. 'They are good at juggling a dozen things at once, keeping a household running smoothly, tending to every detail. We like to call them "lifestyle managers". Our clients can get on with their careers, assured someone is in charge of their home.'

Sam felt as though she was having some kind of epiphany. She could almost hear the hallelujah chorus in the background as she wrote down the woman's name and the name of the company. *Wife for Hire*. Sam had found her calling.

Monday

'Hello, I'm ringing in response to the interview I saw on *A Current Affair* on Friday night.'

Sam had been preparing for this all weekend. She had looked up the phone number and listed questions on a sheet of

paper, as well as any details about herself she considered relevant. She had the children ready for school and out of the
house slightly earlier than usual. Then she made the call.

'Yes, that was us. How can we help you today?'

'Well,' Sam faltered. 'I was actually wondering how I might
go about applying for a position.'

'Pardon?'

'I was interested in applying for a position with your
organisation.'

'You want to work for us?'

'Yes,' she said, trying to maintain her confidence.

The woman laughed. 'We've had inquiries all morning but
you're the first person who's asked for a job!'

'Oh,' Sam's voice dropped. So much for showing initiative.

'When can you come in for an interview?'

'What? You'll see me?'

'Of course! Like I said, we've had inquiries all morning.
We're going to need more staff to cope with the demand. How
soon can you come in?'

Wednesday

'Why do you want to work for us?'

Sheila Boland was smaller than she appeared on camera, but
even more formidable. Sam was not intimidated, however. The
more she thought about this job, the more she realised it was
perfect for her. She would be able to work around the children
and she would be doing what she knew best. Now she just had
to convince Ms Boland.

'The kind of work you described on the television is what
I love doing,' Sam explained. 'And I believe I'm good at it.'

'Why do you think you're so good at it?'

'My husband has an executive position. He hasn't lifted a

finger around the house in years, he doesn't even close doors. I do everything. But I don't mind, I enjoy it.'

'That still doesn't tell me why you want a job with us.'

Sam hesitated. She had to be honest with this woman if she was going to work for her. It would come out soon enough anyhow. 'My husband and I have separated.'

'I see,' said Sheila, pursing her lips together. She sat back in her chair, considering Sam.

'I need the work, that's true,' Sam admitted. 'But I already have a job one day a week and I've been offered more shifts. I just feel that if I'm going to have to work longer hours, I would rather be doing something I love.'

Sheila was still studying her. Sam found it a little disconcerting.

'So, separated,' she said eventually, writing it down. 'How many children?'

'Three,' Sam replied. 'Two girls and a –'

'Are they all in school?' Sheila interrupted, apparently not interested in the details.

'My youngest is in pre-school two days a week.'

'And you say you do everything around the house?'

'That's correct.'

'We're not interested in housework, you understand. This isn't a cleaning service. It's how you *manage* the house that's important. Who pays the bills?'

'I do.'

'Did your husband allot you a certain amount of money for housekeeping?'

Sam had to smile. 'I'm not sure that my husband was even aware what was in his pay packet each week. I used to give him pocket money, for want of a better term.'

Sheila was busily jotting notes. 'Good, good. Who dealt with tradesmen, repairs, that kind of thing?' she continued.

'I did. We had a pool put in earlier this year and I handled everything.' She'd had trouble even getting Jeff to have input on the colour of the tiles.

'What about gift-buying?'

'I do it all.'

'For his family, his mother?'

'Yes,' she sighed. Most of the time they would actually be in the car, on the way to family birthday celebrations, when Jeff would say in a startled voice, 'Did we get something for Mum/Dad/Aunty Sal/whoever?'

'No, *we* didn't,' Sam would reply tartly. 'But *I* bought a present, wrapped it and signed the card. It's slippers, by the way.'

'What about gifts for yourself?' Sheila continued.

'Oh no, my husband handled that.' Most of the time. If she was honest she'd admit that it was probably his assistant more often than not.

'Mother's Day included?' Sheila stopped writing notes to look directly at Sam. 'I'm thinking of the school Mother's Day stall in particular. Who organises the gifts to donate to the stall?'

'I do,' said Sam in a small voice.

'And who gives the children money on the day?'

'I do,' she repeated, feeling pathetic. The kids enjoyed buying something themselves, and Jeff was always gone long before they left for school. He would have given them the money if he'd been around. But that wasn't really the issue. It didn't matter how she rationalised it, the fact was that Mother's Day largely only endured because of all the mothers who kept it going. And that was not the most comfortable realisation.

'And lastly, contraception, birth control. Who took the responsibility?'

'Pardon?' said Sam, taken aback.

'Who took responsibility for contraception?'

'Isn't that a bit personal?'

Sheila paused, considering her. 'If you're coy about getting personal, this is not the job for you. Our clients expect you to handle some highly intimate matters for them on occasion. You need to be able to take it in your stride.'

'Fine,' Sam said, drawing in her breath. 'At the time of our separation,' she faltered, 'I suppose we shared the responsibility for contraception.'

Sheila lifted an eyebrow. 'So, your husband "took responsibility" some of the time?'

Sam nodded. Once in a blue moon.

'Who purchased them?'

Now that they sold condoms in the supermarket it was hardly that big a deal. 'I did.'

Sheila hit the end of her pen on the notepad. 'Right, that's it.'

'Pardon?'

'I'll have to check your references, of course, but I'm not expecting any problems. I'll call you next week with the names of three clients to start with, and we'll take it from there.'

Sam felt a little stunned. 'Just like that? Isn't there any training involved?'

'How could I possibly train you, Mrs Holmes? You're single-handedly bringing up three children and, until recently at least, you looked after a grown adult as well. You're already a lifestyle manager. You have the skills we need. Welcome aboard.'

November

'Sounds like a glorified housekeeper to me,' Bernice sniffed.

Sam pulled a face, her back turned to her mother.

'Way to go being supportive, Mum,' said Max.

'Maxine,' Bernice frowned, 'it isn't cute to speak like an eighteen year old when you're in your thirties.'

Now Maxine pulled a face. Sam grinned. The second weekend in November was always set aside for the traditional Christmas cake and pudding baking day. Sam was disappointed this year because it was the children's weekend with Jeff, but Bernice wouldn't hear of changing it. You'd think it was written in stone somewhere – any sooner was impossibly early, and any later was unthinkable. Sam thought about swapping weekends with Jeff, but she knew that Joshua wouldn't have come anyway, and

Jess would no doubt have complained. But Ellie would have loved it. It was just the first of many traditions that would be compromised from now on, and it made Sam heartsick.

'Tell her, Sam,' said Max. 'You don't even have to do any housework, do you?'

'No, but we can arrange a cleaner if the client requests it.'

'What, these "clients" can't pick up a telephone?'

'They are very busy, pressured people.'

'"Precious" more like it,' Bernice smirked.

'Mum, it's a good job. I can work around the kids' school hours and I can do a lot of it from home.'

'But you already have a job. The MRA is a proper job, with benefits and a regular pay packet.'

'And I'm bored stupid with it.'

'Well, excuse me!' Bernice scoffed. 'These days a job has to entertain you as well as put food on the table?'

Sam wondered why she even bothered to explain anything to her mother, she was so intractable.

'How many clients do you have so far, Sam?' Max asked.

'Just three. Sheila wants me to get them started and then she'll pass along more.'

'How does it work?'

'The clients pay an upfront annual fee,' Sam explained. 'Then I'll be paid according to the time I put in. On top of that, clients are billed for any unusual or extra services, and I get to pocket all of that.'

'Have you met your clients yet?'

'I have two appointments next week – with a married couple, and an older, semiretired gentleman.'

'I thought they were all busy executives?' Bernice sniggered.

'Well, apparently his eyesight is failing and he needs a personal assistant for a couple of hours every week.'

'Who's the third?' asked Max.

'A Mr Buchanan. He's some kind of IT executive. I've emailed him, but I haven't had a response yet.'

'What's does IT stand for?' Bernice asked blankly.

'Information Technology,' said Sam.

'Computers, Mum,' Max added. 'I think it sounds interesting, Sam. How long before you'll be able to quit work?'

'You're not going to quit the MRA, are you?' said Bernice, horrified.

'Eventually, if I can build up a solid client list.'

'And what if the country goes into recession and all these rich, pampered people have to make their own phone calls? Then what happens to your house? And the children?'

'The rich are usually the last to be affected by a recession,' Max informed her drily.

'Besides, Jeff would never let the children go without,' said Sam.

Bernice stopped, wooden spoon midair. 'Are you even going to attempt to reconcile with your husband, Samantha?'

Max groaned. Sam turned to face her mother.

'Mum, my "husband" is living with another woman! He's not interested in reconciling. I have to move on, make my own life.'

That sounded so much more self-assured than she felt. If she was so ready to move on, why hadn't she contacted the solicitor Alex had recommended?

'Well, then, what arrangements have you made for Christmas?' Bernice persisted.

'What do you mean?' Sam frowned.

'When is Jeff having the children?'

'He isn't, not over Christmas,' Sam said firmly.

Both Bernice and Max stopped to look at her.

'Has he agreed to that?' asked Max.

'I don't care if he agrees or not. He chose to leave, he can't have everything his own way.' She beat the cake batter savagely with a wooden spoon. 'I can't do without the kids at Christmas. Jeff will understand.'

He wasn't going to get a choice.

Thursday

Sam checked the address again. It was correct. The house was grander than she'd expected, though she didn't know why she'd imagined it'd be otherwise. This was Woollahra after all, and Ted Dempsey had to be reasonably well off to afford the service in the first place.

She walked up to the front entrance past bowling green lawns and neatly manicured hedges. She pressed the doorbell and waited. After a few moments the door was opened by a smallish man, probably around seventy years of age, with kind eyes and an even kinder smile.

'Ms Holmes?'

'That's right.'

'You're very punctual. That's a promising start,' he smiled. He offered his hand. 'I'm Ted Dempsey, but I hope you'll call me Ted. Please come in.'

Sam stepped into the cool darkness of his house. 'Well, my name is Samantha, but everyone calls me Sam.'

'Oh, do they?' He looked mildly disconcerted. 'I hope you'll allow me to call you Samantha? It's such a beautiful name.'

She smiled. She liked him immediately, which was a good omen considering this was her first meeting with her first client. Sam followed him to the end of a broad hall, catching on either side a glimpse of rooms filled with antiques. They came to a glassed-in conservatory overlooking the back garden.

'What a beautiful home,' said Sam.

'Thank you, Samantha. I've been an antique dealer for most of my adult life.' He made a sweeping gesture around the room. 'I'm afraid a cluttered home is one of the hazards of the profession.'

There was something comforting about the furniture. Sam looked around the room, realising that every piece had a history. It had been bought and loved by someone and was special enough to be passed on, or sold again, and now to form part of a collection. Sam thought of her own formal living room – the department-store, contemporary co-ordinated settings, pale and soulless by comparison.

'Please, take a seat, Samantha,' Ted offered. 'Can I get you anything? Tea or coffee?'

Sam didn't think it was appropriate to have a client waiting on her, so she declined. They both sat down at the table and Ted patted a neat pile of papers in front of him.

'I understand Ms Boland explained to you that I require some assistance keeping up with my correspondence and other minor matters.'

Sam nodded. 'You're still in business?'

'Yes, I am, as a matter of fact. But I have a manager who runs the store, and an accountant who handles the finances. This is of a more personal nature.' He paused. 'I don't know if your employer told you that my eyesight is failing?'

'She did mention,' Sam said quietly.

'I have a condition called macula degeneration,' Ted explained. 'It has come to the point where I am unable to read normal size print even with very powerful lenses, I have to use a magnifying glass as well.'

'I'm sorry to hear that.'

'Thank you, Samantha. But please don't feel sorry for me,' he assured her. 'I have a full life, lots of dear old friends, and a driver who gets me around to see them. I love music and the opera, and I'm still involved in my business as much as I want to be.'

He paused. 'I'm just finding it hard to read. I don't want anyone else to handle my personal correspondence, I would feel that my whole life was in the hands of my accountant, or business manager, good people though they both are, you understand. I thought your organisation would be discreet, and I could keep perhaps just a small corner of my life to myself.'

Sam smiled warmly. 'That seems fair enough.'

Two weeks later

'Hello Sam?'

'Jeff, hi.' Sam felt a little wary when she heard his voice on the other end of the phone these days. There was always something new to negotiate. It was becoming a chore.

'Look, I may as well cut straight to the chase,' he began.

That's right, no need to waste pleasantries on her any more.

'I was talking to Mum and Dad last night, and they're upset they haven't seen much of the kids.'

Sam frowned. 'What's that got to do with me?'

'Well, they are their grandchildren . . .'

'I realise that. I don't have a problem with the kids seeing your parents, Jeff. Why don't you just take them for a visit next time they're with you?'

'I hardly have enough time with the kids as it is. You expect me to spend it visiting Mum and Dad?'

'What? You're not suggesting I take them?' Sam asked, confused.

'Not necessarily,' he said hesitantly. 'Maybe you could just invite them over —'

'What?' Sam could not even conceive of how excruciating that would be. 'They're your parents, Jeff. And they don't even like me!'

'That's not true. Of course they like you.'

'Oh come off it, Jeff!' Sam cried. 'I was never good enough for their precious, bloody, exalted only son. I was just a delivery chute for the grandchildren. The only good thing to come out of this separation for me is that I don't have to put up with their contempt any more.'

Jeff was silent. Maybe she had been a bit strong. But it was too late to take it back now.

'I didn't realise,' Jeff said quietly after a while. 'I don't expect you to see them if it'll make you uncomfortable. I'll handle it.'

After he hung up, Sam picked up the entire phone and held it in front of her. 'Why are you being so . . . understanding?

Why couldn't you have cared about my feelings when we were still together? Would it have been so hard?'

She stood there trembling, breathing heavily, holding the phone aloft.

'Okay, so now I'm talking to inanimate objects.'

She put the phone down on the bench.

'I must be going mad.'

December

'I actually liked Mick's parents,' Liz was saying.

Sam had arranged to meet the girls for drinks. She had to make sure she had somewhere to go after work on a Friday night when the children were at Jeff's. She told herself it was just to avoid Stewart, but it had more to do with avoiding the loneliness at home.

'Will still sees them regularly. They have a great relationship, much better than the one he has with his father. Makes you wonder what rock they found Mick under,' Liz mused.

'I have no problem at all with the kids seeing Jeff's parents,' Sam explained. 'But as for inviting them over . . .' she shuddered.

'I still remember your wedding,' Max grinned. 'Somehow his father managed to make a toast without once mentioning your name!'

'Mm, I think it was the speech he wanted to make at the twenty-first Jeff never had because we got married instead.' Sam smiled ruefully. 'And now they treat Josh exactly the same, like the heir apparent, while the girls are ignored.'

'Well, that's not your problem any more,' said Liz.

Sam looked at her.

'They'll all have their own relationships and it'll have nothing to do with you.'

'You think it's that easy?'

'Who said anything about it being easy?' Liz remarked. 'The hardest thing a woman ever has to do is give up control, especially where her kids are concerned.'

Sam became thoughtful. 'The first couple of times they went to stay at Jeff's, it was actually physically painful for me.' She breathed out heavily. 'But they came home so happy, even Josh in his own way. Jeff was spending more time with them than he had in years.'

'That's how it always is in the beginning. Everybody's on their best behaviour,' said Liz. 'Then the chinks start to appear.'

Sam nodded. 'Jess has started to complain lately. They don't get to watch much TV there, and her father won't let her stay on the phone for hours on end. She's going to miss out on a sleepover this weekend and she nearly had a conniption.'

'What is a conniption anyway?' Liz frowned. 'Is it a real thing or just something our mothers made up?'

'It's odd, though, that all the mothers made it up at the same time, isn't it?' said Max.

'Maybe it was one mother, a long time ago, and it's been passed down ever since.'

'Right,' nodded Max. 'Like Eve said to Cain, "Don't have a conniption. Your brother does not get *everything* first!"'

Sam cleared her throat. 'I believe I was talking about something serious?'

'Sorry,' they both muttered.

'How's Josh with it all?' asked Liz.

'Well, like I was saying, he was okay at first. But now he seems . . . troubled.'

'What do you mean, troubled?' Max frowned.

'I don't know. He won't talk about it.'

'Are you sure it's not a little wishful thinking?' suggested Liz.

'What do you mean?'

'Well, I can remember hating it if Will actually enjoyed himself when he was with his father. It sounds terrible, but I secretly hoped he wouldn't want to keep going.'

'I've felt that too, a little,' Sam admitted guiltily.

'You two are freaking me out!' declared Max. 'Listen to yourselves! Isn't it important that the kids have a good relationship with both parents?'

'Yes, of course it is,' Sam said in a weak voice.

'Theoretically,' added Liz. 'But just wait till you get married and have kids and then separate, and then you have to go through all this.'

Max frowned. 'And you wonder why I'm still single?'

Liz grinned. 'So, how are you going to divvy up Christmas?' she asked Sam.

'They're staying with me. I told Jeff they'd had enough changes.'

'What did he say?'

'He didn't argue. He's picking them up Boxing Day.'

'There you are!' said Fiona bursting through the crowd. 'Crikey, it's packed in here tonight.'

'Hi, we were beginning to give up on you,' said Sam.

'Oh, I couldn't get away from work, everything starts to go mad this time of the year.' She looked around the table. 'Where's Rose?'

'She couldn't get a pass out tonight,' Liz explained.

'Colonic Colin's up to his old tricks again,' said Max.

'I didn't know he'd ever stopped them. Who wants a drink?' asked Fiona.

Everyone held up their empty glasses. Fiona stared at them. 'Oh, great timing! Well, I have to go to the loo and I'm not missing any more of the conversation. Here,' she said, opening her purse and handing Max a fifty, 'you get the drinks. Make mine a margarita.'

She turned and disappeared into the crowd.

'Jeez, what did her last slave die of?'

'He didn't die, he's home minding the kids,' Liz quipped. 'And seeing as she's shouting, margaritas all round, what do you reckon?'

When they were all back at the table, Fiona suggested a toast.

'To absent friends.'

'Merry Christmas, Rosemary.'

They slurped on their drinks.

'I'm having one of these, and one only,' announced Sam. 'They are way too easy to drink and end up in one huge hangover.'

'So what have I missed?' asked Fiona. 'How's the new job, Sam?'

'Good so far.'

'Have you had any unusual requests yet?' Fiona probed, a glint in her eyes.

'What are you talking about?' Liz frowned.

'Well, I've heard that people get you to cover their bedroom floor with rose petals, or arrange a hot-air balloon flight so they can propose, that kind of thing.'

'More money than sense,' Liz muttered.

'Nothing so exciting to report as yet,' said Sam. 'I meet with a Mr Ted Dempsey once a week, to handle his correspondence.'

'Not the Ted Dempsey of Dempsey's Woollahra?' asked Fiona.

'That's him.'

'Who's that?' Liz frowned.

'Just the most respected antique dealer in Sydney, I would think. What's he like?'

'Absolutely charming.'

'Sexy?' asked Liz.

'Liz! He must be seventy years old.'

'So? He's rich, isn't he? You can overlook a slight age difference.'

Sam shook her head. 'I also had a meeting with a couple, Dominic and Vanessa Blair. Both beautiful, bright and trendy as all get out.'

'Why is it that the beautiful people always have beautiful names?' Max pondered. 'How could their parents have known what would be trendy in twenty years time? And they marry people with beautiful names too. It's always Dominic and Vanessa, or Nicholas and Madeleine, or Miles and Cassandra. I mean, you would never hear of Dominic and Ethel, or Vanessa and Wally.'

Sam looked at her. 'Doesn't your head start to hurt after a while, with all those thoughts bouncing around inside it?'

'Not at all.'

'Well, I think it's so exciting!' Fiona enthused. 'It's like being in an episode of *Lifestyles of the Rich and Famous*.'

'Dominic and Vanessa aren't famous, and they're not even that rich. Though they will be, if he gets his way.'

'Oh?'

Sam nodded. 'He has big plans for them. He wants to throw more parties and mix in the right circles. Poor Vanessa looked totally out of her depth.'

'What does she do?' asked Max.

'She's an actuary.'

'What's that?' Liz frowned.

'Something to do with statistics,' Max offered.

'It's highly specialised,' Fiona explained. 'An actuary works out risk, probability, and just about anything you need to predict from statistics. She would be phenomenally intelligent.'

'Well, you'd never know it,' said Sam. 'Dominic spoke for her most of the time, mostly about how useless she is around the house.'

'He must have a small dick,' said Liz.

'What does he do?'

'He's in advertising.'

'A very small dick,' Liz added.

'No,' Sam shrugged. 'He was very charming actually. But there's something about him, I don't know, I can't quite put my finger on it.'

'So what do you have to do for them?' Fiona asked.

'Well, he wants me to organise dinner parties, cocktails, that kind of thing. But they're going away over Christmas, so I had to make all their travel arrangements, and at the moment I'm doing their duty-free shopping.'

Fiona shook her head. 'Wow, getting paid to go shopping!'

'Yeah, not bad, is it?'

'I think we should make another toast,' Fiona announced. 'To Sam, may next year bring you everything you want, in spades.'

'And plenty of sex,' added Liz, raising her glass.

Everyone looked at her.

'What's wrong, you have a problem with that?' She raised an eyebrow. 'I think we have to get Sam a fella.'

'Don't you dare try to set me up!' Sam exclaimed, looking around the table.

'Why not?' said Liz. 'You don't want to die without sleeping with at least one other man your whole life, do you, Sam?'

Sam looked warily at Max, though she knew she could trust her not to breathe a word about Stewart.

'The last thing I need at the moment is another man to run around after.'

'But isn't that what you're doing in your new job?' asked Max.

Sam shook her head. 'I'm getting paid for it. That makes all the difference.'

January

Sam was almost finished taking the ornaments off the Christmas tree, then she would attack the tangle of lights. She usually enjoyed packing up the tree, despite a slight melancholy, because it gave a sense of closure to the season. But she wasn't enjoying it at all today. The kids weren't here to help or even get in the way, they were not due home until tomorrow. It was the sixth of January and the tree had to come down on the twelfth day of Christmas. That was tradition. Sam had to keep some things the same.

It was the only way she could cope with all the other changes. Christmas had passed uneventfully. But it hadn't felt

the same decorating the tree, it hadn't felt the same on Christmas morning. And she'd felt empty when the children had
packed up and left on Boxing Day.

The Christmas cards were the worst part. Some arrived from
friends they only heard from once a year, addressed as normal to
Jeff, Samantha and the children. There were others, uncertainly
written to the nebulous 'Holmes family', from people who had
obviously heard something on the grapevine. Then there were
the cards from those who imagined they knew everything and
couldn't miss the opportunity to gloat.

Dear Samantha,
We were so shocked to hear the news. Call me when you're up to
it. If you need a man for anything around the house, let me know
and I'll send Kevin over.

Of course, there were still others who didn't send cards at all.
They didn't want their husbands anywhere near Sam.

The house felt too big when the kids weren't here. She'd sat
alone the night after Christmas, polishing off too much of the
bottle of Baileys Aunty Gwen had given her, while watching
It's a Wonderful Life on video and sobbing freely. This wasn't supposed to be the way she was going to spend her Christmases.
You should be allowed to put a moratorium on all celebrations
after a marriage break-up. It was too hard. It only made it
painfully obvious that you weren't a family any more. Taunting
you for your failure.

It would be a relief to get back into a routine. Sam had
arranged to see Ted Dempsey this Thursday again, and the
Blairs were due back on the eighth. Sam had already sent an
email to welcome them home and set up another appointment.

She had still had no luck contacting Mr Buchanan. She'd
had to appeal to Sheila for help in the end.

'I've emailed him repeatedly to introduce myself, but he
hasn't replied,' Sam told her.

'Then call him.'

'I have, but I can't get past his assistant. I leave messages with her, but he doesn't answer those either.' Sam paused. 'The thing is, I don't understand why he would subscribe to the service and then not take advantage of it.'

'You have a point,' Sheila muttered. 'Let me just look at his file.'

Sam waited while she checked the details.

'Oh well, this may explain it. Mr Buchanan's subscription is paid by the company that contracted him. It's part of his package. He either doesn't realise, or he doesn't understand what we're all about. Have you sent him information about the kind of services we provide?'

'Yes, I used the blurb you gave me. But I couldn't tell you if he's read it. Like I said, he hasn't replied to anything.'

'You're going to have to get his attention somehow, Samantha,' said Sheila. 'Be creative. Think of it as a challenge. Once you have him on board, I have more clients for you.'

Sam knew she'd been half hoping Sheila would just fix the problem for her. But instead it had turned into some kind of test. If she didn't get Mr Buchanan on board, she would not be given any more clients. As soon as Fiona heard of her conundrum she told Sam not to worry, she'd fix it. That was Fiona's way. She had a degree in marketing and was responsible for public relations for what was, according to Fiona, the biggest accounting firm in the city. If she couldn't get Mr Buchanan's attention, it wasn't worth getting, as far as she was concerned. She was coming over tonight to help Sam compose an email message for Mr Buchanan. Something he couldn't ignore.

'What about a singing telegram?' said Liz.

Liz had tagged along with Fiona, for moral support, she claimed. The moral support had come in the shape of a bottle of nice merlot, and now they'd had too much to drink and had stopped making sense. Fiona was getting just a little impatient with the pair of them. She was taking the task quite seriously, but Sam was finding it hard to care any more.

'Sorry Fiona, it's just so frustrating,' Sam sighed. 'This guy either doesn't read his emails or he just doesn't bother answering them.'

'People get a lot of junk email,' said Fiona. 'It's easy to ignore something if you don't know what it's about. And *Wife for Hire* does sound a bit suss. Did you try calling him?'

Sam nodded. 'A few times. His secretary or assistant or whoever didn't seem that interested. Maybe she's a bit suspicious too.'

Liz reached for the bottle and refilled her glass. She handed it to Sam. 'I think you should pull out the big guns. Bombard him. Send him so many emails it clogs up his mailbox and causes a major glitch in the system, and he has to call the helpdesk.'

Fiona looked at her, frowning. 'He's an IT exec, Liz. I think he'd know how to dump the contents of his inbox.'

'Mm.' Liz took a swig from her glass. 'What about a strippergram, then?'

'Are you offering?' Sam grinned.

'No, really, you could show up at his office wearing nothing but a sandwich board with *Wife for Hire* written across it in big letters. That'd get his attention.'

Sam pulled a face. 'I want him to hire me, I don't want to make him ill.'

'I thought we took a vow not to make derogatory comments about our bodies any more,' Fiona reminded her.

'Fine, if I went into his office wearing only a sandwich board,' Sam paused, starting to giggle, 'seeing as I'm so dropdead gorgeous, he wouldn't be able to resist me, and . . .'

'What?'

'He couldn't afford me!'

Monday morning

Hal Buchanan stepped off the train at Martin Place Station and walked with the throng towards the exit. IGB had provided a car and a parking space in the basement, but he didn't imagine he'd be using either in the foreseeable future. If he had more time he could probably walk, his apartment in Ultimo was not even half an hour away on foot. But he was not a morning person and he never had been. So he woke with only enough time to shower and dress. He'd grab a coffee at the café at the base of his apartment building before taking the subway uptown.

He arrived at the foyer of the IGB tower and passed through the security screens using his magnetic identity card.

'Good morning Mr Buchanan.'

Hal smiled and nodded at the receptionist. He felt guilty that so many people seemed to know his name yet he couldn't return the courtesy. But he was only one new person for them to remember, while he had to contend with a bewildering sea of names, faces and places. So he focused on work. That was why he was here after all.

He took the lift to the twenty-second floor and walked through a series of glass corridors to his office.

'Hey Angie,' he said, passing her desk.

'Morning Hal,' she returned with a dazzling smile. The company had also provided him with an assistant. A young, ambitious, attractive assistant. He wished they could have picked someone older and a little less attractive. He had become wary of women like Angie. Perhaps he was being unfair, perhaps in fact he was cutting off his nose to spite his own face. Angie was *very* attractive, and she had that look in her eyes which stated plainly that he only had to ask. He'd seen it before often enough and he couldn't deny it was more than a little tempting. But he had a new rule – no affairs in the workplace. He hadn't come here looking for someone. Just the opposite.

He walked into his office and set his briefcase down beside the desk, turning on the computer. He sat down, keyed in his password and started checking his emails. Scrolling through the inbox, he came to an abrupt halt.

Angie appeared in the doorway to his office. 'I have your mail, Hal,' she announced. She could have handed it to him as he passed her desk, but this was her ritual every morning. Now she would ask him if he wanted coffee, even though he had told her quite clearly from the start that he didn't expect her to make him coffee.

'Can I get you a cup of coffee?' she asked.

'No, thank you,' he muttered automatically, frowning at the screen.

Angie couldn't help herself. She edged around the desk and placed one hand on the back of his chair, leaning forward. If he turned his head now he'd be eye level with her breasts, and she knew it.

'Hey, that's clever,' she remarked, pointing at the screen. She read the subject lines out loud.

From	Sent	Subject
Samantha Holmes	Friday 10:22 PM	Would you
Samantha Holmes	Friday 10:22 PM	PLEASE!!!!
Samantha Holmes	Friday 10:22 PM	Open This
Samantha Holmes	Friday 10:21 PM	Bloody Email!!
Samantha Holmes	Friday 10:21 PM	This is NOT an ad
Samantha Holmes	Friday 10:21 PM	OR junk mail
Samantha Holmes	Friday 10:21 PM	I WORK FOR YOU!

'What do you suppose that's all about?' she asked.

'Obviously someone's trying to get my attention,' said Hal, stroking his chin. 'I guess they've succeeded.'

'Fiona, you won't believe it,' said Sam breathlessly down the phone. 'Mystery Man finally made contact!'

'Fantastic! What did he say?'

'Well, I haven't spoken to him. He emailed.'

'Okay, so what did he email?'

'"You're not serious?"'

'Go on.'

'That's it.'

'That's it?'

'At least it's something,' Sam insisted. 'Until now, I wasn't even sure he existed.'

'True,' Fiona murmured thoughtfully. 'So what are you going to do now?'

'I replied of course. I said I wasn't sure if he meant was I serious that he's already a client, or serious about the service. And I asked him to call to set up an appointment.'

'Well, good luck.'

'Thanks for your help, Fiona, you know, with the email and everything.'

'So you're glad you didn't go with the sandwich board?'

Sam laughed. 'Just slightly.'

'It might have been quite effective.'

'Mm, I guess that's something we'll never know.'

Tuesday morning

From:<h.buchanan@igb.com.au   To:<holmes@webnet.com.au
Subject: Re: Answer to your Query

---

dear ms holmes
i meant are u serious about your *service*? are there really grown adults who need someone to make their appointments for them or book them into restaurants? i think i can do that for myself. thanks anyway
yours truly
hal buchanan

Tuesday afternoon

From:<holmes@webnet.com.au   To:<h.buchanan@igb.com.au
Subject: Our Services

Dear Mr Buchanan
There are many other services we could provide. I would be happy to
discuss the possibilities with you at a meeting at your earliest conven-
ience. My number is 9555 5940.
Kind regards,
Samantha Holmes

Wednesday morning

From:< h.buchanan@igb.com.au   To:<holmes@webnet.com.au
Subject: Re: Our Services

---

dear ms holmes
can u give me a hint? i really dont understand what u could do for me
hal b

'hal b' was giving Sam the shits. She had the feeling he was
taking the Mickey. She needed him as a client, but he obviously
thought he was above this. She couldn't force it on him, but
maybe she could give him a little serve in return.

Wednesday afternoon

From:<holmes@webnet.com.au   To:<h.buchanan@igb.com.au
Subject: For example

Dear Mr Buchanan
Perhaps I could teach you some basic punctuation, or at least edit your emails for you, so that you're not mistaken for a teenage boy in a chat room.
Yours sincerely
Samantha Holmes

Thursday

From:<h.buchanan@igb.com.au   To:<holmes@webnet.com.au
Subject: Re: For example

---
nobody likes a smart ass

From:<holmes@webnet.com.au   To:<h.buchanan@igb.com.au
Subject: *No subject*

Ass?

From:<h.buchanan@igb.com.au   To:<holmes@webnet.com.au
Subject: Ass?

---
not familiar with the term ms holmes? i find it hard to believe you havent been called a *smart ass* before

From:<holmes@webnet.com.au   To:<h.buchanan@igb.com.au
Subject: Re: Ass?

Smart ARSE maybe, but not smart ASS. The Yanks have taken over just about everything else in our culture, let's try to preserve a little of our own language.

Friday

From:<h.buchanan@igb.com.au   To:<holmes@webnet.com.au
Subject: Re: Ass?

---

sorry, i wasnt aware of the distinction. you see i happen to be a *yank*

Shit! said Sam out loud, staring at the computer screen. How was she supposed to know he was American?

God, what was she going to do? She had no hope of getting him as a client now. She wondered what to say to Sheila. Could she lie about it? What if he ended up making a complaint? Bugger! If only she hadn't been a smart arse he wouldn't have called her a smart ass and none of this would have happened. She had to learn to keep her comments to herself.

Sam heard the phone ring once and then stop. Jess would have pounced on it straightaway.

'Mu-um! Telephone!' she called from downstairs.

Sam picked up the receiver, hearing the clunk as Jess hung up. 'Hello?'

'Hello, Ms Holmes?'

'Speaking.'

'It's Hal Buchanan.'

Sam's heart missed a beat and she sat up straight in her chair. Goodness knows why.

'Mr Buchanan, hello, um, sorry, about the email. I didn't realise . . .'

'Don't worry about it.'

'Your accent. It's not very strong. You don't sound that American.'

There was a momentary pause. 'I take it that's your idea of a compliment?'

Shit. What was the matter with her? She swallowed. 'Sorry.'

'Look, I'm calling about this service of yours.'

'Oh?' Sam couldn't believe he was still interested.

'Maybe there is something you can do for me after all.'

'There is?' She was prepared to do anything. Well, within reason.

'I have to attend a function next Thursday evening –'

'Look, I think you might have the wrong idea,' Sam sighed, interrupting. 'This is not an escort service.'

'I realise that, Ms Holmes. I'm talking about a business function.'

'Still, it's not normally the kind of thing we do.'

'I thought you'd do anything?'

What was he, a mind reader? 'Well, within reason.'

'This is within reason.' He sighed loudly. 'Look, I'm not hitting on you. I don't even know what you look like.'

'What's that got to do with it?' Sam said indignantly.

'Plenty, if I was hitting on you!'

She didn't know what to say to that. She supposed he had a point.

'Here's the thing, I've only been in Australia a couple of months,' he explained. 'I don't know anybody, so I don't go out, and as a result I haven't met anyone I can ask when I do get an invitation.'

Sam hesitated. He sounded like a bit of a loser but she needed him as a client. 'Okay, I'll do it,' she relented. 'Let's call it a one-time-only special opening offer, and we'll never mention my earlier faux pas again. Deal?'

He laughed. 'Deal, Ms Holmes.'

'You'd better call me Samantha.'

'Oh, like the witch on TV,' he commented.

She groaned inwardly. What was it with Americans? They acted like the entire universe had its reference point in Hollywood.

'I'm going to have to ask you to meet me there,' he continued. 'I haven't really mastered the roads yet. I hope that's not too much trouble?'

Good, she'd be able to get away when she'd had enough.

'Not a problem at all, Mr Buchanan,' she said, resuming a businesslike tone.

'Please, call me Hal.'

'Okay Hal, let me take down the details. Next Thursday evening, you said?'

Wednesday

'Hi, it's me, are you home?'

'No, I'm at the movies. This is my answering service. Pretty lifelike, isn't it?' said Max in a droll tone.

'Okay,' Sam said briskly, ignoring her. 'I'm coming round to borrow your pashmina.'

'My what?'

'Your pashmina. You know, the emerald-coloured shawl,' she explained impatiently. 'With the silk fringing.'

'Oh, is that what you call it? It should be around somewhere. I haven't worn it for a while. It might need cleaning.'

'I figured that, that's why I'm coming tonight.'

'What do you want it for?'

'The thing, tomorrow night.'

'Oh, the *thing*! That's right, I nearly forgot. With the mysterious Americano.'

'I'll be there in about an hour, okay? I just have to wait for Jeff to collect the kids.'

'Oh? He's taking them in the middle of the week?'

'Well, I needed them minded and he was going to have them from tomorrow night anyway, so he offered to pick them up a day earlier.'

'He's turning into a regular Superdad,' remarked Max. 'Even taking time off work? Wonders never cease.'

'Mm,' Sam grunted. 'At least it means I can use the voucher Alex gave me for the day spa.'

'Jeez, talk about overkill.'

'Do you think? It's just that this is freaking me out. It feels like a blind date.'

'It's not a blind date. It's work, isn't it?'

'I know, but I can't help feeling self-conscious. Especially since I tried on my black dress.'

'Which one?'

'The sleeveless one.'

'That's why you want my shawl?'

Sam sighed heavily. 'I feel like a package of meat you get from the butchers, you know how they use those dark plastic bags? And they're all lumpy and misshapen? And my arms look like cocktail sausages dangling through the handles.'

Max laughed. 'How'd you come up with that?'

'I looked in the mirror,' she sighed. 'Oh Max, what if he expects me to be twenty with long blonde hair, a flat stomach and slim arms?'

'So you're not twenty and you're not blonde, you're a beautiful, thirtysomething brunette, and you're going to wear my pashma thingy so he won't see your cocktail sausages.'

Sam groaned.

'You realise he's probably middle-aged, fat and balding.'

'I should be so lucky.'

Thursday

Hal Buchanan had arranged to meet Sam at the entrance to the Inter-Continental Hotel at seven. She was ten minutes early, precisely as planned. Sam hated rushing, and she did not want to arrive red-faced and flustered because she'd been caught in traffic. Though now, standing here in the path of a fairly robust breeze, she wondered if she oughtn't go inside and wait in the foyer before her hairstyle was ruined.

The spa was fantastic, better than anything Sam had ever imagined. They started her off with a dry body brush that made her skin tingle. Then she had a lymphatic draining massage. Sam didn't care what it was supposed to be draining, she'd never had a full body massage in her life and she absolutely revelled in it. Afterwards they covered her in a seaweed concoction and wrapped her in Glad Wrap in an effort to further detoxify her lymph glands. She'd had no idea her lymphatic system was in such a terrible state. After a hydrotherapy bath that was supposed to stimulate her now apparently exhausted lymph glands, they moved on to more aesthetic considerations. She had a facial, a manicure and a pedicure, they waxed every rogue hair on her body, and they even did her make-up. That was an experience. The woman caked on so much foundation that Sam's features all but disappeared. And then she drew them all back on, only better. It was much more make-up than Sam was used to wearing, but the effect was striking. She almost believed she was, maybe, a little bit, sort of, attractive.

'Samantha?'

She spun around. She had been staring up the street but he had come from the other direction.

'Mr Buchanan?'

'Hal,' he smiled, offering her his hand. Sam took it demurely, trying not to seem obvious while she checked him out. She didn't know whether to be relieved or self-conscious again. He was fairly handsome she supposed, in a generic kind of way. Neat dark hair, tanned skin, a row of straight white teeth. She needed to get closer to determine the colour of his eyes, which she couldn't because he was quite tall.

'Well, this is a pleasant surprise,' he said with a satisfied smile.

'Sorry?'

'You, you're a pleasant surprise. Better than I expected.'

'I beg your pardon?' she said haughtily.

'Come on, you were thinking the same thing,' he said, turning towards the entrance.

'I was not.'

'Oh really?' He held the door open for Sam.

She shook her head. 'You've got tickets on yourself.'

'Pardon?' he frowned.

'You've got tickets on yourself,' she repeated.

He looked blankly at her.

'It's an expression.'

'Meaning?'

'Well,' she was embarrassed now. It was okay to make an off-hand crack, but she didn't really want to labour the point that she thought he was full of himself. 'Never mind.'

He shrugged, indicating the stairs. 'It's up this way.'

Sam was not used to her high heels and she felt a bit unsteady on the marble stairs, holding the long skirt of her dress up out of the way while trying to keep the pashmina in place.

'So,' he persisted, 'you weren't just a little relieved?'

'You're not *that* good-looking, you know.'

He raised an eyebrow. 'Okay. But I could have been sixty with a paunch and a comb-over.'

'Instead of forty with a smirk.' The moment the words came out of Sam's mouth, her shoe caught the hem of her skirt and she lurched forward. Hal reached out and grabbed her by the arm, stopping her from falling flat on her face.

'Forty with a smirk, huh?' he remarked, steadying her. 'As opposed to thirty with an attitude?'

'I'm not –'

God, what was she doing? She was about to say she wasn't

thirty. Had she gone mad? If Hal Buchanan wanted to think she was six years younger than she really was, Sam wasn't about to tell him otherwise.

'Um, I'm not, I mean, I don't have an attitude.'

He smiled down at her, releasing her arm. 'And I wasn't smirking.'

Sam felt a little shaken. She trod cautiously up the last few stairs, gripping the banister firmly. At the top, double doors opened to a large ballroom already filling with people. There was a noticeboard to one side welcoming guests to the IGB Cocktail Party.

'Perhaps you'd better fill me in,' said Sam. 'You work for IGB, don't you?'

'That's right,' he said, taking her arm and leading her into the room.

'The insurance company?'

He nodded. 'This is for the shareholders, so all the directors will be here . . . the people who hired me. That's why I thought I'd better show this time.'

'What is it that you actually do?'

'I'm a data security specialist.'

Sam looked blankly at him.

'I investigate organisations to determine their security issues,' he explained. 'Then I work with programmers to design systems to address those issues.'

'Oh.' That didn't mean a lot to Sam, and Hal realised.

'You have to key in a password to get into your PC, right?' he asked rhetorically. 'Well, that's basically data security. It just gets a little more complicated when you have to secure a system with maybe thousands of users, all with different levels of access.' He spoke in a monotone, as if the whole thing bored him a little. 'Would you like a drink?'

Sam nodded and he signalled a passing waiter. They both took a glass of champagne from the tray the young man proffered. Hal held his up briefly.

'Thanks for coming,' he said to Sam. 'I appreciate it.'

She shrugged. 'It's my job.'

He looked at her curiously for a moment before nodding. 'Good, that's good.'

'Now, here comes the guy who actually hired me,' he said in a low voice. 'I don't think he believes I do anything. Data security is largely invisible – you only notice it when it's not done properly.'

'Like housework,' Sam nodded.

He raised an eyebrow. 'I guess.'

'Hal, good to see you here for a change,' the man said as he approached.

'Evening Phillip. Samantha Holmes, this is Phillip Campbell, IGB's Director of IT.'

He shook hands with Sam. 'So you're the culprit, Ms Holmes, the reason we haven't seen Hal at any of our get-togethers?'

'Sorry, can't lay claim to that.' Sam noticed a slight uneasiness in Hal's expression. He was probably worried she was going to say why she was really here, but however she tried to explain it, it wouldn't sound right. She tucked her hand into the crook of Hal's arm, leaning coquettishly towards him.

'I can't get him away from work either, Mr Campbell,' Sam declared. 'I don't know what sort of hours you expect him to put in, but he never takes a break. It must be some contract you've got him on.'

'It's some contract alright,' Campbell nodded, cocking one eyebrow.

'Of course the worst part is that I haven't got a clue what it is that Hal actually does, I'm embarrassed to say. He tries to explain it to me, but . . .' Sam shrugged helplessly. 'You'll be thinking I'm stupid, being the Director of IT. Actually,' she mused, 'you're probably just the person I should talk to. Perhaps I could get you to explain how data security works, in language that I'd understand?'

Sam smiled sweetly at him. He looked petrified. 'Sure, maybe later,' he blustered. 'Oh, look, there's someone I really need to speak to,' he said, moving away. 'Nice to meet you.'

'You really are good at this *Wife for Hire* thing, aren't you?' Hal said later, after they had worked the room.

'I'm very good at it,' Sam said airily. It was nice to be appreciated again.

'You know, there's no need for us to hang around any longer. And I was wondering,' he hesitated. 'Well, I was wondering if you'd like to come back to my place for coffee . . .'

'I don't think so,' Sam said abruptly. She knew this was a bad idea. She had made it perfectly clear that she was not an escort, but he obviously hadn't got the message.

'Look, we can't talk here . . .' He glanced around, then took her by the elbow and led her out through the main doorway.

'What are you doing?' she frowned.

'I didn't want to discuss this with everyone around.'

She looked suspiciously at him.

'I thought you wanted me as a client?' said Hal.

'I do, but I think we may have different ideas about what that means.'

'That's why I'd like to talk about it. My apartment's not far –'

'You've got to be kidding,' Sam said, turning to start down the stairs. 'I should have known . . .'

Hal followed her. 'What? What's wrong?'

Sam stopped to look up at him. 'I'm not going back to your place –' Sam held up her fingers to mimic quotation marks, '– to *discuss business*.'

He looked askance. 'I'm not trying to get you into bed, if that's what you're thinking.'

She sighed. 'No, you just want to talk.' She turned and continued down the stairs.

'Wait up, Samantha,' he said, taking a couple of steps at a time to overtake her. He stopped in front of her, blocking her path. 'I told you on the phone I wasn't hitting on you.'

'Yeah and I came down in the last shower!'

'Excuse me?'

Didn't he understand anything? 'Never mind.'

'Look, let's get one thing straight,' he said, not hiding his frustration. 'Sleeping with you is the furthest thing from my mind!'

'You expect me to believe that?'

'I don't give a damn whether you believe it or not. I don't want to sleep with you.'

Sam stared blankly at him. 'You don't?'

'As unbelievable as it must seem to you, no, I don't.'

She swallowed.

'What? I'm so unattractive?'

Hal looked mystified. 'Damned if I do . . .'

Now she felt stupid. But did he have to be quite so adamant about it? It was not exactly flattering.

'I just thought you were getting the wrong idea about exactly what *Wife for Hire* involves,' Sam said, recovering. 'Sex is not part of the deal,' she added, lowering her voice.

He leaned forward close to her face. Now she could tell his eyes were green. 'Just like a real wife, then.'

Sam walked at a brisk pace down Macquarie Street towards the Quay.

Hal was trailing her slightly. 'Hey, wait up, Samantha. Where are you going?'

'There are plenty of places down at the Quay where we can get coffee and "talk",' she said crisply.

'Are you pissed or something?'

Sam stopped abruptly. 'No! I didn't even finish my second glass of champagne.'

'What?' he frowned. 'I was asking if you're pissed at me, you know, angry, annoyed?'

'Oh, right.' She continued walking along, slower this time. 'In Australia, if someone's pissed they're drunk. If you're angry with someone, you're pissed *off*.'

'And here I was thinking I'd come to a country where I spoke the language.'

Sam looked at him sideways. 'That was your first mistake. We speak English here.'

He shook his head. 'So, are you "pissed off" with me?'

She sighed. She didn't want to revisit the topic of how

much he didn't want to sleep with her. 'Oh, it was just that crack about wives never wanting sex. The mantra of the married man. Have you ever been married, Hal?'

'I used to be. What about you?'

'Separated.' She felt strange saying that. 'I just think that maybe you guys need to hold a great big mirror up to yourselves, lying asleep in front of the TV every night with dribble coming out of the corner of your mouths, and then ask yourselves why you're not getting any.'

Hal looked taken aback momentarily. 'So, I take it there's no bitterness over your separation?'

Sam glanced at him. 'Nobody likes a smart *ass*.'

They stopped at a place along the Opera Quays and sat at a table near the window. A waiter came to take their order.

'Do you have chamomile tea?' Sam asked.

'Certainly ma'am.'

Hal ordered a black coffee and the waiter left.

'You don't drink coffee?' he asked.

'Not at this time of night,' Sam explained. 'I was having trouble sleeping so I switched to chamomile tea. Now I can't seem to sleep unless I have a cup. I've wondered if it's some kind of conspiracy.'

'Oh, sure,' Hal grinned. 'The evil coffee barons are making it big taking over daisy fields across the world.'

'This sense of humour of yours. You've been told it's amusing?' Sam said drolly.

'I have them rolling in the aisles back home.'

'Mm, that explains it.'

Hal shook his head. 'Oh, now you're going to tell me Americans have no sense of humour?'

'I wouldn't go quite that far . . .'

'Pleased to hear it. Or else how would you explain Charlie Chaplin –'

'He was English.'

'. . . the Marx Brothers.'

'They're all dead.'

'I could go on.'

'I bet you could.'

The waiter returned and set their cups down in front of them.

'Anyway,' Sam said, stirring her tea absently, 'you wanted to talk to me about something?'

'So, when she gets cornered she changes the subject?'

'No, she just wants to get home some time before dawn, if possible.'

Hal smiled, leaning forward with his elbows on the table. 'Okay, here's the thing. I don't need you to book my car in for service, or make dental appointments for me, or pay my bills, but I could use some help . . .' He seemed to be searching for words. '*Acclimatising*, I suppose you'd call it. I just don't understand the way you guys talk, your expressions baffle me. I don't know anything about your football or cricket, which is all anybody seems to care about. Even getting around is a nightmare because you all drive on the wrong side of the road.'

'It's actually the right side of the road.'

'No, if you want to split hairs, it's the *left* side of the road.'

Sam considered him for a moment. 'Okay, here's the thing. We don't say "here's the thing".'

'Oh? What do you say?'

'We say . . .' She thought about it. 'The thing is . . .'

He frowned dubiously. 'Well that's real different.'

'And we'd say "really", not "real".'

'What?'

'I would have said, "That's really different". "Real different" is Yankee speak.'

Hal sighed. 'God, I'll be afraid to open my mouth.'

'Well, that's not such a bad thing either. Australians tend to think Americans have a little too much to say.'

He shook his head. 'You know, you guys pride yourselves on being this amazingly tolerant, multicultural society. But you openly, almost proudly despise Americans. What's the deal there?'

'We don't despise Americans,' Sam insisted. 'You're just being sensitive. Australians like everyone.'

'Oh yeah? Try being an American.'

Sam looked directly at him. 'It's not that we don't like you. God, haven't you noticed all the American shows on TV here? The movies? The kids in baseball hats? It's just . . .' She thought for a moment. 'Have you ever heard of the tall poppy syndrome?'

He shook his head.

'Well, it's a peculiarly Australian thing. I don't know if it's because we started as a penal colony or what, but we don't take to people who stand above the crowd.'

'Like a tall poppy in a field?'

'That's right. Think about it, Americans are the tallest poppies on the planet. It's in our nature to cut you down.'

Hal sat back in his chair. 'So I shouldn't take it personally?'

She shook her head. 'I don't think anyone means anything by it. We're a nation of knockers. You need to develop a bit of a thick skin if you're going to survive in Australia for any length of time. People will like you if you can laugh at yourself.'

'I'll try to keep that in mind. Any other tips?'

'I'll let you know if I think of any.' Sam sipped her tea. 'Your name's a bit of a problem.' She shook her head, cringing.

'What's wrong with my name?'

'Well, it's not a proper name, is it? Americans don't seem to have proper names. Or else they have surnames as first names, like Macauley or Parker or Forrest –'

'A character in a movie,' Hal interrupted. 'Is that where you're getting your information?'

'Come on Hal, you know I'm right. At least Hal is not a verb like "Chuck" or "Flip". You never got "Buck", from Buchanan?'

'No, I've never got "Buck".'

Sam shrugged. 'So, is Hal short for something?'

He cleared his throat. 'It is, in fact. My mother was expecting me when she was writing her doctoral thesis on *Henry IV*. That's Shakespeare, you know, perhaps you've heard of him? I believe he was British. Anyway, the young Prince Henry was better known as Hal in the play. So when I was born, my mother named me Henry, but I've always been called Hal.'

Sam just stared at him. He passed her a paper napkin.

'What's that for?' she croaked.

'That'll be for the egg you've got on your face, just there.'

The next day

'So what's he like?' Max asked Sam when she called by after work to return the pashmina. Max had suddenly decided she couldn't live without it and must have it for a date that night, even though she had previously forgotten she owned it.

Sam shrugged. 'He's a client.'

Max stopped ironing and looked suspiciously at Sam. 'What does that mean?'

'It means he's a client. What do you mean by "What's he like?"'

'Well, is he good-looking?'

'I didn't really notice.'

'Ha!' Max exclaimed. 'That means he's either drop-dead gorgeous or butt ugly.'

'Oh does it?' Sam lifted an eyebrow. 'Well, I'll tell you one thing. You're going to burn your dress if you don't move that iron.'

Max squealed, lifting it off the fabric. 'Oh shit. I should have left already. And I haven't had a shower –'

'Give me that,' said Sam, pushing her out of the way and taking the iron. 'Go and have your shower.'

Max stooped to kiss her on the cheek. 'Thanks Sherl.'

She dashed into the bathroom, dropping her robe on the way. 'Come in and talk to me.'

'I can't do that and iron your dress too.'

'Oh, okay. When you're finished then.'

'Yes sir,' Sam said under her breath. She ironed the dress in a couple of minutes and placed it carefully onto a hanger.

'Faarrghhk!' Max screeched.

'What's the matter?' asked Sam, appearing at the door to the bathroom.

'I cut my leg shaving,' she hissed, holding a face washer against her leg to stop the flow of blood. 'Bugger, bugger, bum, shit, ouch.'

'You know what they say, "Less haste, more speed",' said Sam, closing the lid of the toilet and perching herself on top.

'You're really getting that impersonation of Mum down pat,' Max remarked snidely. 'So, tell me about the American. Was he old, fat and bald like I said?'

'No,' Sam hesitated. 'He's around my age, and he's reasonably good-looking, you know, in that stereotypically American way.'

Max stuck her head around the shower curtain. 'What, is he black?'

'No, he's not black!'

'Well, statistically there are more blacks than whites in the States.'

'There are not! You're getting mixed up with South Africa.'

'Oh, am I?' Max turned off the taps and stepped out of the tub. Sam handed her a towel.

'So what's stereotypical American-looking?'

'Oh, you know, clean-cut, a little plastic, lots of teeth.'

'They do have more teeth than us, you know,' said Max.

'Don't be ridiculous.'

'I'm sure I read it somewhere,' she insisted, wrapping the towel around her hair and twisting it into a turban.

'How could they have more teeth than us? They're not a different species.'

'Just seems like it, eh?' Max grinned.

Sam followed her back to the bedroom. 'You know, that's racist.'

'It is not!'

'If you said that about someone from Asia or the Middle East, it would be considered racist.'

'Yes, but you can't be racist about Americans,' Max maintained, slipping her dress over her head. 'They rule the world. We're just the little insignificant ants having a whinge. It's like you and me with Alex.'

Sam shrugged. 'Do you want me to dry your hair?'

'Nuh, it'll be dry by the time I get there.'

She watched Max tousle her damp hair with her fingers, then flick some mascara on her lashes and dab on lip gloss. It had taken a day at an expensive beauty spa for Sam to look presentable and Max looked stunning after barely ten minutes. It had to be the three less years, the three less children, and, well, frankly a lot more than three inches in height. But things always come in threes, Sam thought ruefully.

'So what have you got to do for . . . what's his name again?' asked Max.

'Hal.'

'Hal? What is he, a Texan?' she drawled in a very bad accent.

'No, he's the son of a Shakespearian scholar,' said Sam bluntly.

'Huh?' Max frowned.

'Don't ask. Anyway, to answer your question, he wants me to help him become *acclimatised* . . .'

'How are you going to do that?'

'Well, for starters he wants to learn about football.'

Max looked shocked. 'From you?'

Sam shrugged. 'He can't join in the blokey talk at the office.'

'And he thinks you can teach him about football?' Max raised an eyebrow. 'Isn't that a bit like Osama Bin Laden teaching feminism?'

'I'm well aware of the irony,' Sam returned. 'I thought I'd ask Josh to come along.'

'Do you think he will?'

'Maybe, if I bribe him.'

Max picked up her handbag and walked out to the living room. 'Have you seen my keys?'

Sam held them up. 'They were in the door when I arrived.

You're going to get burgled, raped and murdered one day, sister of mine.'

'And then won't you miss me!' she grinned, grabbing the keys and shoving them in her bag.

'Are you going to change your handbag?'

'Why?'

'To match what you're wearing, perhaps?'

'Christ, who has the time? Swapping over all your crap whenever you change an outfit? That's too exhausting to even contemplate.'

Sam stood at the door, holding up the pashmina. Max grabbed it and flung it casually across her shoulders. It looked perfect.

'See ya. Lock up for me, will you, Sherl?' she called as she clattered down the stairs.

February

'Are you going to be home Tuesday while Ellie's at pre-school?' Jeff asked Sam when he dropped the kids off. He had hung around the doorway, waiting until they were out of earshot.

Sam frowned. 'I suppose so.'

She had plenty of work to keep her busy at home these days. Sheila had passed on three more names since Sam had confirmed she'd finally established contact with Hal Buchanan. She'd bought herself an index box and cards to keep all her client records. She knew she could set up a database on the computer, but Sam liked to have a hard copy anyway. She liked neatly printing out the details, the same format for everyone. Surname, first name. Address, telephone, mobile, fax, email. God, there were so many ways to contact a person now. She also kept job cards for each client, with the date, what she had done for them, and any notes she thought relevant.

Her work involved a lot of phone calls. Making appointments, inquiries, booking, ordering. She enjoyed the authority her position gave her, she was always calling *on behalf* of someone else and that made her bolder than she might normally be. She didn't care how many questions she asked, or how many details the person on the other end had to go and check. She was also developing index cards on the best restaurants, hotels, courier services, caterers, travel agents, anyone who had been helpful and easy to deal with.

Sam enjoyed the work, as she knew she would. She had settled into a comfortable groove. The children were back at school, and she had found a rhythm to her days again.

'Do you mind if I come over?' said Jeff tentatively. 'There are some matters I think we need to discuss.'

The rhythm suddenly jarred, like the needle scraping across a vinyl record. Sam felt sick. She'd been living on borrowed time and she knew it was about to catch up with her.

'Tuesday,' she said vaguely. 'Aren't you at work?'

'I'll take the morning off,' he explained. 'It's just that we don't get much opportunity when the kids are not around.'

'Okay,' said Sam tentatively, wishing she had an excuse. But it would only delay the inevitable.

'Good.' Jeff breathed out. He seemed relieved. 'I'll see you then, around ten?'

'Fine.'

Tuesday

Sam heard the knock at the front door right on ten o'clock. Jeff was nothing if not punctual.

'Hi,' she said as she opened the door, trying to sound bright, confident, assertive, even though she felt none of those things. Ever since he'd suggested this 'talk' she'd had the jitters. The fact was, Sam knew there was a whole lot to discuss, but she didn't really want to deal with it yet. When they were together, she had been the one who had wanted to talk about everything, while Jeff had either not been around, or hadn't been listening. So she had just turned into a nag, like most other wives she knew.

'Come in,' she said, standing back. It felt weird inviting him into his own house. He was dressed in a suit, as usual, for work. Jeff always looked impeccable, though Sam had assumed that was largely due to her.

They walked through to the kitchen and she noticed from behind that his hair was brushing his collar. He was overdue for a haircut, he usually kept it quite short. Not quite so impeccable after all.

'Would you like a coffee?'

'Thanks.'

Sam went to fill the kettle and Jeff crossed to the cupboard for the cups. They continued without speaking; she prepared the plunger, he took the milk from the fridge. It was strangely poignant.

When the coffee was ready they sat on stools at the island bench. Jeff reached into his suit pocket and drew out an envelope, placing it down between them.

'What's that?' Sam asked, not sure she wanted to know.

He cleared his throat. 'It's an assessment from child support.'

'I see.' Sam stared at the envelope. 'You applied for this?'

He nodded. 'I thought it was time we . . . settled some things.'

They sat for a while longer, not saying anything, sipping their coffees.

'Aren't you going to look at it?' Jeff asked eventually.

Sam picked up the envelope. Her heart was literally in her mouth as she drew out the folded paper, opened it and read through the contents of the letter. Most of it didn't make sense, not that it was difficult to understand, but for some reason the words didn't gel in her mind. The numbers, on the other hand, flashed at her like a neon sign.

'What do you think?'

Sam shrugged, sighing heavily. 'I'll just have to work out which of the children's activities to cut.'

'Sam,' Jeff said curtly. 'Nothing will have to be cut. That's a very generous amount.'

'How the hell would you know?' she cried, getting off the stool and pacing across the room. 'Do you even know how much the mortgage is, the electricity, the rates?'

'Yes, I do,' he said calmly.

'What?' she spun around. 'Since when?'

'Since I looked into our accounts and worked it out.'

'You're checking up on me now?' Sam shrilled. 'Who gave you the right to start snooping around?'

She noticed his jaw clench. 'You're obviously forgetting that this house is still half mine, that it's my wage paying for everything and my name along with yours on bank accounts that I have every right in the world to access!'

Sam stood there, breathing hard, tears rising in her throat.

'Oh, I see,' she said. 'Your true colours are shining through now, aren't they, Jeff? You've been all sweetness and light and understanding. But you've just been waiting to come in for the kill.'

'Don't be so melodramatic, Samantha.'

'Well, it's true, isn't it? You don't care about the kids. You just want to make sure you get to have the life you want, while we can all go to hell.'

Jeff stared at her, his eyes flinty. He went to say something, but then he stopped, dropping his head and raking his fingers through his hair. When he looked up at her again he seemed calmer.

'Come on, Sam,' he said in a level voice. 'Can't we keep this reasonable? I'm just trying to do what's fair.'

'Fair? You want to talk about fair?' The tears rose into her throat now, sticking there, making her voice sound strangled. 'Being completely faithful and loyal to you for sixteen years and then getting dumped when I got too fat or too old or God knows what. Is that fair?'

His eyes registered surprise, embarrassment, perhaps even pity. She couldn't look at him. She turned and ran out of the kitchen to the stairs, not stopping until she got to their room. But it wasn't 'their' room. It was just her room now, and it felt big and lonely and wrong.

She fell onto the bed, sobbing. She hated this. She used to be Mrs Holmes but now she was being reduced to some kind of pathetic welfare case. Jeff would dole out the money, giving her no choices, no status, no control. He must despise her.

Sam heard the bedroom door open quietly and close again, but she kept her head buried in the quilt. Bugger, she just realised this was the white damask cover – she'd be getting make-up all over it.

She felt Jeff sit down on the bed, then his hand gently touching her arm. She shook it off.

'Sam, please. This isn't the way I wanted this to happen.'

'Well you got everything else you fucking wanted. Sorry for spoiling your plans.'

'Come on, Sam,' he implored. 'The hardest part about all this is that I've hurt you so much.'

'Bullshit,' she sobbed.

He leaned over her, stroking the hair away from her face so he could see her.

'You can't think I'd want to hurt you, that I'd enjoy seeing you in pain?'

Her face crumpled and she started to sob more violently. Jeff moved close in behind her, sliding his arms under and around her. He was really hugging her, his face close to hers, gently soothing her tears.

'It isn't fair.' She twisted around to look at him. 'You have this all the time. You've got somebody to hold you, and support you and comfort you.'

Jeff stared intently down at her.

'And I've got nobody. I have to keep it together for the kids, but I've got no one to hold me, or comfort me. It's not fair,' she finished, her voice barely making it out of her throat.

He brought one hand up to cup her face, wiping the tears from her cheek with his thumb. Sam turned around fully so their bodies were pressed up against each other. Jeff started to breathe harder, and before she realised what he was going to do, his lips were on hers. They kissed voraciously, desperately, as though they were frightened to stop now they had started. Sam heard him moan faintly. Was he becoming aroused? She tugged tentatively at his shirt, pulling it up until she felt the skin of his back, grazing it with her fingertips. She felt goosebumps forming under her touch and he moaned softly again. It thrilled her that she was arousing him. That she still could. She wanted to see how much. She brought her hands around under him, fumbling with his belt buckle, clumsy in her impatience. She hadn't done this for so long, especially not like this. She pulled down the zip, feeling the tremor through his body as she took hold of him. He was hard for her. For her. He couldn't love Jodi if he was hard for her.

He reached up under her skirt and dragged her pants out of the way. Sam could think of nothing but having him inside her. She still had hold of him as they manoeuvred their bodies into position and she guided him in. He thrust hard and she gasped, wrapping her arms tight around him. She wanted to cry, this was right, this was how things should be. They could make this work, they still loved each other. He didn't need another woman when they could make love like this.

Sam felt a sudden chill. She couldn't get pregnant. That would spoil everything. 'Jeff,' she breathed, 'wait . . .'

He looked down at her, his eyes glazed.

'We have to use something.' They were lying across the bed, Sam stretched her arm up to reach for the bedside drawer. Jeff must have realised what she was doing and he lurched over, reaching the drawer easily, feeling inside until he drew out a cardboard packet. He rolled off her, wrestling with the packaging. Then Sam realised he had stopped. He was just lying there, breathing heavily. Then he sat up.

'What's the matter?' she whispered anxiously.

'I'm sorry, I can't do it. It's . . . not right.' He was slumped over, holding his head in his hands. He sounded distressed. Sam touched his back gently.

'Of course it's right. We're still married.'

Then he turned and met her eyes directly. 'Only on paper,' he said quietly. He reached across her and picked up the edge of the quilt, folding it back over her. 'I'm sorry.'

He stood up and walked slowly to the bathroom, closing the door behind him.

Sam stared after him. She must have been in shock because she couldn't move, she could hardly even breathe. What did he mean it was wrong? How could he believe it was wrong to make love to her when she was his wife and the mother of his children? He didn't mind screwing his brains out with a woman he hadn't even known a year.

It hit Sam like a punch to the stomach. She rolled over, pulling the covers tightly around her and curling herself into a ball. Jeff had left her in every sense of the word. He felt he was being unfaithful to his mistress if he slept with his wife. He was right. She was only his wife on paper.

The realisation filled her with pain. A lurching, sickly ache rose up from her stomach, wrenching through her chest and escaping out of her throat in an anguished sob. The sobs kept coming, they shook her whole body, as tears flowed from her eyes, soaking into the covers. She didn't give a fuck if they were mascara-stained any more.

The phone started to ring and for a moment she thought about ignoring it. But she hadn't turned the machine on and the kids were at school. Something may have happened. She sniffled, wiped her face on the covers and reached for the phone.

'Hello,' she said weakly.

'Samantha? Are you okay?'

Her brain wasn't working quickly enough to identify the voice.

'It's Hal Buchanan.'

'Oh, hello.'

'What's the matter? You don't sound well.'

She took a deep breath. 'It's not a good time, I'll call you back.'

'Are you alright, Samantha?' he said seriously. 'You're . . . safe?'

'I'm perfectly safe. I'll call you later.' She hung up. She lay there, gazing across the room at nothing in particular, just her life shattering into thousands of tiny pieces that, like in the nursery rhyme, could never be put back together again.

Sam heard the bathroom door open but she didn't look around. She was aware of the muffled tread of Jeff's steps on the carpet as he walked around the side of the bed and into her line of vision. He crouched down so that she had to look at his face. But she looked right through him.

'Sam, are you okay?'

'Josh's birthday last year,' she said slowly, her eyes fixed, staring. 'When you said you had to go to a conference, you were with her, weren't you?'

'I went to the conference.'

'But you were with her.'

He sighed audibly. 'Yes.'

She lay there, gazing past him, unresponsive.

'Sam, I don't want to leave you alone like this.'

'I'm not your concern any more.'

'Don't say that –'

'Oh just piss off would you, Jeff?' she cried suddenly. 'It may be half *your* house but this is my bedroom now, so get the fuck out!'

'Okay, I realise you're angry –'

'Well, aren't you the rocket fucking scientist?'

'Look, Sam, don't keep this up. Can't we talk?'

She looked at him now. 'What, so I can listen to you salve your guilty conscience? I don't think I'll give you the satisfaction, Jeff. I've had enough of your bullshit for one lifetime, thanks all the same.'

He sighed deeply and stood up. 'I'll call you later.'

'Don't bother.'

He stood there for a moment longer but she didn't move or

look at him. Then he left the room. Eventually she heard the front door close downstairs and, shortly after, his car pull away down the street. And then it was quiet again.

Sam lay there for a long time without moving. She felt warm and very safe, Hal needn't have worried. In fact, she could stay here for as long as she liked. She didn't need to get up for anything. She didn't feel like eating, she couldn't imagine eating anything again without choking on it. She would like something to drink though. There was an open bottle of wine in the fridge, but she would have to get up to go and get it. She didn't want it that much.

She would just lie here instead.

'Mum. *Mum!*'

Sam heard the voice from a long way away. She shut her eyes tighter.

'Mum?'

It sounded closer this time.

'Don't you have to pick up the girls?'

Sam roused. 'What?' she croaked.

'Are you sick?'

She blinked, squinting up at the figure above her. For a second she thought it was Jeff.

'Mum, can you hear me?'

It was Josh. She sighed, relieved. 'What's up, Josh?'

'Jess rang, freaking out 'cause you haven't picked her up.'

'Oh Christ, where is she?' Sam sat bolt upright, then had to hold her head to stop it spinning.

'She said she'd go to Emma's and wait for you there.' Josh frowned at her. 'Are you okay, Mum?'

She nodded. 'I wasn't feeling well, I must have drifted off.'

'What about Ellie?'

'What's the time?'

He glanced at the bedside clock. 'Four thirty-two.'

'That's okay, the centre doesn't close until six.' She rubbed her forehead. 'Just give me a minute, Josh,' she said. He left the room and Sam quickly changed out of her dishevelled clothes, washed her face and pulled a brush through her hair. She surveyed herself in the mirror. Ugh, she'd have to keep her sunglasses on.

Josh was hovering around the bottom of the stairs when she came down.

'Are you sure you're okay, Mum?'

'Yes, I feel a lot better now.'

'Some guy rang before, Hal somebody? He had an accent.'

Sam nodded. 'He's a client.' That was two phone calls she hadn't heard, she must have really passed out.

'He was the one who made me check your room. I didn't even realise you were home.'

She looked at Josh. Poor kid, he seemed anxious. Sam took a step closer and put her arms around him, hugging him tight.

'Mum,' he grumbled. 'Cut it out.'

She released him, smiling up at him. 'Thanks for being here, Josh. And I'm alright. I'm feeling much better, in fact.'

But driving out of the cul-de-sac, Sam still felt a little shaken. It occurred to her that a person could sink into depression in the blink of an eye. She'd lost an afternoon, that had never happened to her before. Thank God for the kids. They would keep her going. She would keep going, and move on. She could not let herself get stuck in the mire of a broken marriage.

She would contact the solicitor tomorrow and make an appointment. And then she'd ask Sheila for more clients. She was already matching her wage from the MRA and planned to resign soon. But now she'd need to build her client list further. She was going to be the star employee of *Wife for Hire* because she was a fabulous wife. The best. And Jeff could choke on that.

Eight p.m.

'Hello, is that you, Samantha?'

This time she recognised the voice.

'Hal, I'm sorry I haven't returned your call –'

'Don't worry about it. I was a little concerned, that's all.'

Sam felt uncomfortable. She hardly knew Hal Buchanan, yet somehow he had got caught up in her personal life. She had to put an end to that.

'No cause for concern, Hal. I wasn't feeling well earlier today, but it seems to have passed. Now, what can I do for you?' she said officiously.

'Um, well, I was calling about . . .' He paused. He sounded a bit vague. 'Originally, this morning, I was calling . . . Look, are you sure you're okay?'

Sam sighed heavily. 'I'm fine,' she insisted. 'What is it that you were calling about?'

'Okay. Well, actually, there's another function . . .'

'Didn't I say it was a one-off last time?'

'Yeah, but I figured that seeing you had such a good time, and you found me such unexpectedly charming company, you'd reconsider.'

Sam was smiling. He was a charmer alright.

'It's Saturday the twenty-eighth, black tie, at the Ritz Carlton.'

She glanced at the calendar. 'I have the kids that weekend.' She would also be working most of the day at the Blairs, help-ing prepare for a cocktail party.

'Didn't your husband and you ever go out, hire a sitter?'

'Occasionally, when we could afford it.' She realised that probably didn't sound very professional.

'Well, put any expenses on my account.'

'I didn't mean to imply that –'

'Look, it's fine. I don't know how all this works, but you said you were still in the red with me, so knock yourself out. The company's already paid.'

Sam thought about it. She needed to keep her clients

happy. If this is what Mr Buchanan wanted, then she would have to deliver.

'Okay, just let me take down the details.'

Thursday

Visiting Ted Dempsey each week was like respite for Sam. In the cool, tranquil quiet of his home she felt a sense of serenity that evaded her most other places these days. It almost didn't feel right being paid, especially as she barely had an hour's worth of work to do. Yet the way the billing worked, she was paid for a minimum of two hours just for showing up.

'Isn't there anything else you'd like me to do for you, Ted?' Sam asked him. 'I feel guilty taking your money for so little.'

'You are performing an invaluable service for me, Samantha,' he assured her. 'I only hope you get your fair share of my subscription fee.'

'Oh, I do,' she insisted. 'And to be honest, I think I'd do this for free.'

'Well you must be easily amused if this is any kind of a treat for you, Samantha.'

She smiled. 'It is a treat coming to your lovely home every week and sitting in the peace and quiet.'

Ted looked chuffed. 'Then I've been remiss. I haven't taken you on a tour of the house yet, have I?'

Sam had been dying to have a good look around since the first time she'd come here. But they always sat in the conservatory, looking out to the garden. As pleasant as that was, Sam was unprepared for the magnificence of the rest of the house. Every room was elegantly proportioned, with high ceilings, tall windows and grand fireplaces. Gleaming polished floors were topped with gorgeous Persian rugs, and the furniture throughout was, of course, to die for.

In the formal sitting room, Sam spotted a group of photographs in silver frames. She knew Ted was a widower and that he had a son and a grandson living in the UK. She hadn't asked Ted any personal questions, believing it was not appropriate and, frankly, not her business. Ted had said he hoped the service would be discreet, so she had made every effort to convince him it was just that, despite her curiosity.

But looking down at a large framed picture of a woman, probably taken about fifty years ago, Sam knew she was looking at Mrs Dempsey.

'Is this your wife?' she asked tentatively.

He walked over to stand next to her, nodding. 'That's Alice. She was only twenty-one in that photograph. It was just before we were married.'

'She's very beautiful.'

He smiled fondly, taking the frame in his hands and holding it closer, examining the photo lovingly. 'Yes, she was.' He looked across at Sam. 'We were married for forty-two years.'

Sam felt a sudden pang in her chest, and the back of her throat tightened. To be married all that time and still look at his wife's photo with such longing in his eyes.

'Do you miss her?'

'Every single day. But in a good way. I don't pine. Alice would not have wanted me to pine,' he said, looking back at the photo. 'I just miss the easy familiarity, sharing a thought that crosses your mind, that kind of thing.'

Sam swallowed down the lump in her throat. She hadn't spoken to Jeff since Monday. She left the answering machine on while she was home during the day and ignored his messages asking her to call. When he phoned the kids at night he asked to speak to her, but she had managed to fob him off so far, without them twigging. She wasn't going to start a cold war, she just didn't want to deal with him right now. It was too hard. She had another week's grace till it was his weekend with the kids and then she'd have to face him regardless. She might have the wherewithal by then.

'Let me show you my favourite room,' said Ted, placing the

frame carefully back into position. He directed her through an adjoining door into a large, high-ceilinged room that was lined on all four walls with books. Sam gasped.

'A library! How fantastic!'

'You like books?' he asked.

She nodded enthusiastically. 'Not that I get the time to read very often. But if I had a room like this! Just to come in here and sit would be enough.'

'It's not.'

'Sorry?'

Ted looked at her sadly. 'That's all I can do now, sit here and look. And I assure you, it's not enough.'

'Oh, I'm sorry, I wasn't thinking.' Sam paused, considering the packed shelves. 'I could read to you,' she suggested tentatively.

'No,' he shook his head, 'I told you not to feel sorry for me.'

'I'm not. I just . . .' she faltered. 'The thing is, I would *love* to read to you. I couldn't think of a more pleasant way to while away an hour or so. And we'd still have plenty of time to keep up with your correspondence.'

Ted looked at her. 'This is above and beyond the call of duty.'

'Let me be the judge of that.' Sam walked across to the shelves. 'Now, where shall we start?'

Saturday the twenty-eighth

Sam pulled the car into the visitors parking of the converted warehouse development where the Blairs had their apartment. She switched off the engine and turned to Ellie.

'Now sweetheart, remember what Mummy said . . .'

'Don't say I'm hungry all the time,' said Ellie solemnly, 'or noy Donimic and Vamessa.'

Sam smiled at her. 'Do-*min*-ic won't be here today, only *Vannn*-essa, and you won't annoy her, just try not to talk her ear off.'

Ellie nodded. 'Okay Mummy.'

'Have you got all your things?'

Sam had packed Ellie's pre-school bag with a couple of favourite toys, enough snacks for three children, as well as colouring books and pencils. She didn't dare bring textas into the Blair's all-white, minimalist designer apartment. She'd had nightmares about the very idea. Vanessa had been extraordinarily understanding, even enthusiastic, when Sam had phoned to ask if it was alright to bring Ellie along. She'd asked lots of questions about how old she was and what she liked to do. Sam kept trying to reassure Vanessa that she wouldn't even know Ellie was there, and not to be concerned, everything would be organised for the cocktail party in plenty of time. Vanessa had replied she wasn't concerned at all.

They buzzed Vanessa on the intercom before taking the lift up to the sixth floor. Sam would have to make at least a couple more trips back down to the car to bring up all the shopping. She had exchanged emails with Dominic all week, haggling over the menu. Having not had a husband who cared about this sort of thing, Sam found his obsessiveness a little irritating. She wished he would just let her get on with it. She wondered how Vanessa put up with him.

Vanessa was waiting for them at the door of the apartment. 'Hello!' she exclaimed, crouching down. 'You must be Ellie!'

Ellie nodded. 'You must be *Vannn*-essa.'

She grinned. 'Come on in.' Ellie took the hand she offered and they walked through into the living area. Sam settled the bags on the kitchen counter.

'There's more down in the car,' she said.

'Oh, do you need a hand?' Vanessa offered.

'No, that's okay. Ellie, you come with me.'

'No, I'll watch her, don't be silly.'

'Are you sure?' Sam frowned.

'Absolutely,' Vanessa insisted. 'That's if it's okay with Ellie. Do you mind keeping me company, Ellie?'

Ellie beamed. 'I'll be good, Mummy. I won't be noying.'

As it turned out, the caretaker of the building was in the foyer and, seeing Sam struggle with all the bags, he fetched a trolley and helped her get everything to the apartment in one trip.

'Look what Vanessa gave me, Mummy!' Ellie exclaimed when Sam came back. She held up a lime green box. 'It's Polly Pocket's Sparkle House!'

'Oh, Vanessa, you really shouldn't have.' It was an expensive toy and she was sure Dominic would have no idea.

'It's alright.'

'No, Vanessa, you *really* shouldn't have. I can't allow Ellie to accept this.'

Ellie's face dropped. So did Vanessa's.

'But why not, Sam?' she entreated.

'It's too expensive, and well, you're my client. It's not appropriate.'

Vanessa frowned. 'As for the cost, that's not an issue, you know that, Sam. And gosh, I had hoped we could be friends as well as clients.'

Sam looked at Ellie and Vanessa. They both had the same plaintive expression on their faces.

'Then what do you say, Ellie?'

'Thank you, Vanessa!' she exclaimed, throwing her arms around her new best friend.

'Let's go and put it together,' suggested Vanessa brightly.

The two of them skittered across the room. Vanessa dragged the coffee table out of the way and they plonked down on the rug. Sam looked through the shopping bags, sorting out what had to be refrigerated and what she should start on straightaway. Dominic had left yet another set of instructions, as if he hadn't made himself clear enough already. Sam could do this blindfolded, she really didn't need him second-guessing her.

She spent the next couple of hours chopping, slicing, stuffing and marinating. She could have organised a caterer to do this but she enjoyed it, and this way she was the one getting paid. It was very therapeutic, all this fiddly work, particularly when you didn't have the added stress of having to entertain the guests that evening. Sam thought it was probably like the feeling grandparents spoke of, relishing the time with their grandchildren all the more because they could hand them back at the end of the day.

She had not expected Vanessa and Ellie to hit it off so well. She had worried that she'd be trying to hold down a conversation with Vanessa, keep Ellie occupied and get the food prepared. But the two of them were completely absorbed. Vanessa was tireless. Sam loved her children, but there was a certain point when their games became monotonous and, frankly, boring. But Vanessa seemed nowhere near that point.

'You're very good with her,' said Sam when they took a break for lunch.

'I love kids, especially Ellie's age,' said Vanessa, her eyes shining. 'I always wanted to be a pre-school teacher.'

'Why didn't you?'

She shrugged, toying with her sandwich. 'I was good at maths and I finished the Year 12 syllabus in Year 10. So they called me and my parents in for a meeting with the principal and the maths head teacher, and someone else, I think from the uni. They asked me what I wanted to do when I left school, and I said pre-school teaching. They all laughed.' She paused. 'They didn't ask me again after that, they just told me what I'd be doing.'

'That didn't bother you?'

She put her head to one side thoughtfully. 'Mum and Dad were really proud, you know? Like I said, maths was easy for me, so I didn't mind.'

Clearly Vanessa had always done what everyone else wanted her to do. No wonder Dominic didn't faze her.

'Well, you'll have your own kids one day,' Sam offered hopefully.

Vanessa shrugged again. 'Mm. Not for a while. Dominic doesn't want to even discuss it for another five years. Hey, Ellie,' she said, changing the subject. 'Do you want to go to the park?'

Ellie glanced at her mother.

'It's quite safe, and it's not far from here,' Vanessa reassured Sam.

'That's not the problem. I really have to go over the steps for tonight, what gets put in the oven and when, the order of serving the food, that kind of thing.' Dominic had been very clear that Sam should 'train' Vanessa; he'd actually used that word.

She turned up her nose. 'Ugh. Couldn't you just write it all down? I'm fine at following instructions, really.'

Sam didn't doubt that, with Dominic for a husband. Vanessa and Ellie went off happily to the park while Sam sipped coffee and worked out a schedule for the evening. When they returned, Sam sat Vanessa down and started to take her through what she had planned. She was less than enthralled.

'Couldn't you just stay on?' she interrupted after a while.

'Vanessa!' Sam exclaimed. 'You promised me you'd be able to follow this.'

'I will, don't worry. I just thought it would be nice if you were here. It would give me someone to talk to.'

Sam looked at her. 'Why? Don't you have friends coming?'

'No. There are some people out from the UK office. That's who Dominic is with today – he's taken them out on the harbour. I don't know any of them, and they're sure to talk shop all night.' She pulled a face.

'Your evening sounds about as exciting as mine.'

'Oh really? What are you doing?'

'I have to go to a black-tie function with a client. I don't even know what I'm going to wear yet.'

'Why don't you borrow something of mine?' said Vanessa brightly.

'Oh, I couldn't do that –'

'Why not? I think we'd be similar in size, I'm just taller.'

'Everyone's taller than me,' said Sam. 'And it's very generous of you to say we're "similar" sized, but I doubt it.'

'Oh, come on,' insisted Vanessa. 'We'll find something, won't we, Ellie?'

As Sam followed them up the stairs, she realised that maybe

Vanessa was right. She was certainly taller, but she was hardly a rake. She had quite a lovely rounded figure.

In the bedroom Vanessa threw open the wardrobe doors to reveal a row of plastic-shrouded dresses. Sam surveyed them wide-eyed, spotting one designer label after another.

'I don't know, Vanessa,' she said reluctantly. 'What if I spill something?'

'Oh please!' Vanessa insisted. 'I hardly wear things more than a couple of times, Dominic always wants me to buy something new. I take them to the drycleaners and then they just hang here. It's such a waste.'

Sam sighed, reaching out gingerly to touch one. 'Have you got something in black?'

'With your colouring!' Vanessa scoffed. 'You could get away with anything. Let's try . . . purple!'

Sam looked dubiously at her, but Vanessa was off. Over the next hour Sam lost count of how many dresses she tried on. Depending on the cut, they did seem to fit the same size, but Sam was never more aware of the difference between a twenty-something and a thirtysomething body. Oh to have breasts that sat up on their own again.

She finally settled on a scarlet dress that was cut on the bias. It expanded forgivingly over those euphemisms known as child-bearing hips, and though it was low cut, she could wear a bra with it. A sheer wrap camouflaged her upper arms, and Sam begrudgingly accepted that she looked okay.

'You look beautiful, Mummy!' Ellie said rapturously. Sam eyed her daughter sceptically. She would take any compliments from her with a grain of salt, considering she was currently wearing a silver lurex top as a dress, under a fringed, beaded purple shawl, with a pair of green stilettos and an alarming amount of glittery make-up.

'You're gorgeous, Sam,' Vanessa seconded. 'Now, what about jewellery?'

Sam checked her watch. 'Oh crikey. I'm going to be late, Vanessa. I have to run.'

While Sam got back into her day clothes, Vanessa cleaned

up Ellie, all the while listening to Sam firing off instructions for the evening.

'It's all written down, isn't it?' said Vanessa calmly.

'Yes but –'

'So don't worry. Your work here is done.'

At the door she scooped up Ellie and gave her a hug. 'You'll come next time?'

'We'll see,' Sam interrupted. 'She's with her father every second weekend.'

'Then we'll have to arrange another time to get together,' Vanessa insisted happily.

Sam kept an eye on the speedo all the way home, making sure she didn't actually break the law while going as fast as she possibly could. She called Max on the mobile – she was already at the house.

'Where are you?'

'About half an hour away,' Sam explained. 'Is Josh there?'

'Yeah, but not Jess.'

'No, I have to collect her on the way home.'

'What time are you getting picked up?'

'Six-thirty.'

'Jeez Sherl, that doesn't give you much time.'

'No kidding? I'll be there as soon as I can.'

Emma's mother was never easy to get away from. Sam only hoped it didn't seem rude when she revved the engine loudly and checked her watch while the woman finished recounting something about where to get netball uniforms at a discount.

Sam flew in the door at home, running up the stairs with a shout. 'Hold the fort please, Max. He'll be here in ten minutes!'

When the doorbell rang right on six-thirty, Jessica and Ellie rushed towards the entry.

'Hold on, hold on!' said Max, as sternly as a wannabe cool aunty could manage. 'You don't want to frighten the poor man off.'

She opened the door with the girls hovering behind her. 'Hello! You must be the American.'

Hal smiled. 'And you must be the sitter.'

'Sister actually. I'm cheaper.' The girls stuck their heads around her. 'And these are the daughters, Jessica and Ellie. I'm Maxine.'

She thrust her hand towards him and he shook it. 'Nice to meet you, Maxine and Jessica and Ellie. I'm Hal.'

'Come on in, Hal.'

Max showed him into the formal sitting room because that's where Sam would have taken him. She would have preferred the kitchen herself.

'Do you realise your tie's undone?' she pointed out.

'Yeah, I can't manage these do-it-yourself bow ties. I was hoping to get some help.'

'Well, don't ask me, you'll have to wait for Sam, she's good at that kind of thing.'

'Where is Sam, by the way?'

'Sorry.' Max hit her forehead. 'Upstairs, she's running a little late. Can I get you a drink?'

'Thanks.'

'I'm not sure what she's got. I know there's bourbon.'

'Bourbon will do fine, thanks.'

Hal took a seat on the sofa and Jess sat down next to him. Ellie parked herself on the coffee table directly in front of him.

'So, how old are you, Ellie?' he asked.

'Four. How old are you?'

'I'm four as well,' said Hal. 'But with a zero added.'

'That means you're forty.'

'You're a clever little girl.'

'You're older than my dad.'

'Am I?'

'He's thirty-six, same as Mummy.'

'Put a cork in it, Jelly,' said Max, coming back into the room. She handed Hal a glass.

'Do you live in Hollywood?' asked Jessica.

'No,' said Hal.

'Have you ever been there?'

'I have, my sister lives in LA.'

Her eyes widened. 'Have you ever met anyone famous?'

'Um, let me see. I met Bill Gates once.'

Jessica screwed up her nose. 'The geek? He's like, ugly *as*!'

'But very rich.'

She shrugged. 'Have you met Britney Spears?'

'Fraid not.'

'Freddie Prinze Jnr?'

Hal shook his head.

'Heath Ledger?'

'Isn't he Australian?'

'Is he?' Jessica frowned.

'*Maxine!*' Sam called from upstairs.

'Uh oh. That sounds urgent,' said Max. 'Will you excuse me?'

'Sure.'

'And girls,' she added, 'ease off on the inquisition.'

Hal grinned. 'They're fine.'

'Have you been to Disneyland?' Ellie resumed after Max left the room.

'I have.'

'Have you been to Sesame Street?'

He laughed. 'Only on the TV.'

'Me too. Mummy lets me watch that, but not any other 'merican crap.'

'You look fab! Where'd you steal the frock?' said Max, finding Sam in the ensuite.

'Vanessa loaned it to me. Do you really think it looks alright? Does my bum look big?'

'Enormous,' Max replied, deadpan. 'Just make sure you don't walk in front of him.'

Sam frowned at her. 'What about my hair? I'm trying to get that messy, half-up, half-down look.'

'Here, I can do messy.' She took the clip out of Sam's hair and tousled it loose with her fingers. 'So, he's a bit of alright.'

'Who?'

Max rolled her eyes. 'Who do you think I'm talking about? Handsome Hal down there.'

'Oh, like I said, I hadn't really noticed.'

Max snorted. 'Sure, that's why you're all atremble, stressing about the size of your bum and your hairstyle.'

'I'm not trembling!' Sam insisted. 'And I'm stressing because I'm so late.'

'Yeah right.' Max scooped a hank of hair up and around and secured it with a clip. 'So, he's got that jaw thing happening.'

'What?'

'Hal, he's got the square jaw. It's the fourth most noticed feature on a man's face after his eyes, his smile and his hair.'

'There's not a whole lot left after eyes, smile and hair,' Sam frowned. 'I haven't heard too many women get excited over ears and noses.'

Maxine ignored her. 'Apparently weak jaw lines are the main reason men grow beards.'

'I thought it was weak chins?'

'Not on my information.' She'd finished Sam's hair. 'There, how's that?'

'Thanks Max.'

She watched Sam putting on mascara. 'So, how come he's taking you to this shindig tonight?'

Sam shrugged. 'He needed a partner.'

'Puh-lease,' Max said dubiously. 'The guy sitting downstairs in your living room does not have to go begging for a date.'

Sam frowned at her. 'This isn't a date. It's a business function and he doesn't like going alone. He's only been in Australia a few months, he doesn't know anyone.'

Max shook her head. 'He works in a big office, doesn't he? He'd only have to crook his little finger and he'd start a stampede.'

'That's a really hideous image.'

'Sam, I know you've been married forever, but you must be aware of the fact that straight, available men in Sydney are as scarce as, well, straight, available men.' Her eyes suddenly lit up. 'Hey, that's it! He's gay!'

'I doubt it. He used to be married.'

'Maybe that's why the marriage broke up?'

'Look,' Sam sighed. 'I don't think he's gay.'

'No, you're right,' Max nodded. 'I mean, he's certainly handsome enough, but he's not cut from the gay cloth. I wonder why he doesn't go out with normal women then?'

Sam stared at her sister's reflection in the mirror. 'Well, thanks for that, Max. Just what my self-esteem needed.'

'Sam,' said Max. 'I didn't mean it like that. You're the one insisting he's a client. I'm just wondering why a good-looking, eligible bloke can't get a date. Don't you think it's odd?'

Sam shrugged. 'Maybe he doesn't want to date, for some reason.' She leaned in close to the mirror to apply her lipstick.

Max rested against the vanity cabinet and folded her arms. 'The divorce was brutal,' she mused. 'And he's sworn off women for life, since he found his wife in bed with his best friend. No, his best friend *and* his best friend's wife!'

Sam rolled her eyes.

'Or,' Max continued, gathering momentum, 'his wife found *him* in bed with his best friend's wife. And maybe,' her eyes were gleaming, 'she grabbed a kitchen knife and cut off his –'

'Max!' Sam exclaimed.

'His last name's not Bobbitt, is it?'

'Shut up.'

'Maybe he has a sexually transmitted disease!' Max persisted, undaunted. 'And he doesn't want to risk going out with someone he'd be tempted to sleep with.'

Sam thought about Hal's sworn declaration that he absolutely did not want to sleep with her. She frowned.

'Oh, sorry Sam,' Max winced, seeing the expression on her face. 'That didn't come out right. It's just that guys like Hal can take their pick, and their pick is usually some stick insect with breast implants and no brain. Not a single mother of three, no matter how beautiful and clever and wonderful she is.' Max put her arms around her from behind.

'I hadn't thought of myself like that before,' Sam grimaced.

'What? Beautiful, clever and wonderful?'

'Well, that either. But I meant "single mother of three". I sound pathetic.'

'You're not pathetic, Sherl,' Max insisted. 'Actually, I'm

beginning to think you're onto something with this *Wife for Hire* gig, considering your date tonight.'

'Max!' Sam exclaimed. 'This is not a date, it's my job, he's my client, who, we have now established, is completely and absolutely out of my league!'

'Good then,' Max returned calmly. 'Takes the pressure off. You can just go and enjoy yourself. Now, do you want me to walk down first, so you can make a grand entrance?'

'Not on your life!' Sam declared. 'Walk with me, so I can hold your arm and not fall down the stairs.'

'You're expecting to fall down the stairs?'

'No, because I'm going to hang on to your arm!'

When they came into the sitting room, Ellie had planted herself on Hal's lap and was intent on tying his bow tie.

'Ellie,' Sam chided. 'Don't accost the visitors.'

'I'm not costing Hal, Mummy! I'm doing hims tie up.'

Hal turned around to look up at Sam. His face broke into a broad smile when he saw her. She felt immediately self-conscious.

'Hey Samantha. You look very –'

'Yeah, yeah,' she dismissed, scooping Ellie off his lap. 'Okay, miss, let me inspect the damage.'

Sam leaned in closer, frowning at the tangled mess that used to be a tie. 'Ellie, you've tied it in knots!'

'I just did it like my shoelaces,' she protested.

'But you can't tie your own shoelaces!'

Ellie's bottom lip started to tremble. Sam crouched down to her level. 'It's okay, honey. Where's your sister?'

'I think she got bored with me,' said Hal, 'and went to watch some American crap on the TV.'

Sam glanced at him curiously before turning back to Ellie. 'Do you remember where Daddy's ties are?'

She nodded solemnly.

'Can you go and find me one like Hal's?'

'I'll come with you,' said Max, holding her hand out to Ellie.

Hal had started to wrestle with the knot.

'Here, let me,' said Sam. She leaned over him and began working on the tortured tie.

'So, how're you doing?' he said after a while.

'Going,' Sam murmured, not looking at him.

'Sorry?'

'Australians say "How are you *going*", not "How are you *doing*".'

'You're something of a pedant, aren't you, Sam?'

'Whatever, you wanted to acclimatise,' she muttered absently. 'And stop looking down the front of my dress.'

'It's kind of unavoidable.'

She stood up straight. 'Come here then.' She led him around to the back of the sofa and he perched on the edge. They were almost level now. Sam could feel him staring at her face but she made herself focus on the tie.

'Your eyes are very brown,' he said after a while.

'Shoosh.'

'Like Ellie's. She looks just like you. Not so much Jessica.'

'No, she's like her father. So's Josh.'

'Josh?'

'My son.'

'Where's he tonight?'

'Probably in his room. Fourteen's not exactly the most sociable age.'

'How can you have a fourteen-year-old son when you're only thirty?' said Hal, feigning surprise.

Her eyes met his briefly. 'Child bride.'

'Ellie let the cat out of the bag,' he confided. 'She told me you're forty-three.'

'Forty-three!' she exclaimed. 'I beg your pardon, I'm only thirty-six.'

Hal grinned at her.

'You know, you're playing a dangerous game here. Baiting a woman who is holding as good as a rope around your neck. It wouldn't take much to tighten it.'

'You wouldn't do that, and leave those children motherless.'

'Why would my children be left motherless?'

'Well, I'm thinking strangulation might carry some kind of penalty.'

'You reckon a jury of my fellow Australians is going to put me away for knocking off an annoying American?'

'Okay, when you put it like that . . .'

Sam sighed as she discovered yet another knot. 'You shouldn't have let Ellie do this,' she reproached.

'But she's hard to resist. Like her mother,' he added.

Sam stopped abruptly and frowned at him.

'She looks like you is all I'm saying,' he protested innocently.

She had finally unravelled the last knot and she jerked roughly at the tie to release it from under his collar.

'Ow!' Hal cried.

Sam held the tie up, its gnarled, crumpled ends hanging sadly. 'Sorry!'

Ellie skipped into the room. 'Here's a new one, Mummy!'

'Just in time.' She lifted Hal's collar and, taking the tie from Ellie, she slipped it around his neck and proceeded to tie it expertly.

'I don't see why anyone wears these when you can get them ready-tied,' said Hal.

'Because they're classier.' She finished, turning his collar down and adjusting the bow tie into place. She considered him close up. She could see what Max meant by the square jaw . . . she supposed he was handsome. And definitely way out of her league. Max was right. Hal Buchanan wouldn't give someone like Sam a second glance. Which was fine with her because she was definitely not looking for anyone right now. And besides, he was a client. And he lived on the other side of the world. And –

'What is it?' said Hal.

Sam blinked. She realised she must have been staring at him and she was still holding his collar. She cleared her throat. 'There,' she said, patting the lapels of his jacket smooth. 'All done.'

'Thank you,' he replied, bemused.

'Max, I'm leaving!' called Sam, coming into the entrance. She opened the front door as the girls walked up behind her.

'A limo!' Jessica shrieked.

Sam looked around at Hal. 'I thought you were driving tonight?'

He shrugged sheepishly. 'When I checked the street map and saw how far away this was, I decided it was a bit ambitious for me just yet.'

'You should have told me,' Sam protested. 'I could have driven in myself.'

'I thought it might be fun. Have you ever had a ride in a limo before?'

Sam shook her head. She felt embarrassed, awkward, overwhelmed.

'What's your problem, Sherl?' said Max. 'Go . . . What's that expression you Americans use? Knock yourself out!'

Max and the girls stood at the door whooping and waving as they drove off out of the cul-de-sac. Sam sank back into the comfort of the soft leather seat. She was so comfortable, in fact, she was likely to doze off, given the busy day she'd had. But that would hardly be appropriate. She supposed she ought to attempt some small talk. She sat up straight and turned to Hal.

'So, where are you from?'

He looked a little confused. 'The States . . .'

'I know that. But which part?'

'Oh. All over the place.'

'Okay. Where were you born?'

Hal smiled slowly. 'Sydney.'

'Sydney? Sydney where?'

'Sydney Australia.'

Sam's eyes widened. 'You're kidding?'

'My father took a visiting professorship at Sydney University. We went back to the States when I was seven.'

'So you started school here?'

'Uh huh. Just like Mel Gibson.'

'Pardon?' Sam frowned.

'Mel Gibson lived in Australia while he was growing up too.'

'Oh, so that makes you just like him?'

He nodded, grinning. 'Only better looking.'

'So I must be just like Nicole Kidman because my husband left me for another woman?'

'Your husband left you for another woman?' Hal said seriously.

Bugger, she hadn't meant for that to slip.

'And he still has his clothes at your house?' he persisted.

Sam looked out the window. 'He takes things on a needs-only basis.' She sighed. 'I guess he hasn't needed formal wear yet.'

'So you separated recently?'

Sam thought about it. 'It'll be six months soon,' she said, almost to herself. God, sometimes it felt like six years, and other times it felt like it had only happened six days ago.

'That's not so long. What happened?'

Sam glanced at him warily. They were veering into private territory again. She had to keep the relationship professional. 'Look, no offence, but this is not really an appropriate conversation to be having with a client.'

He sighed audibly. 'Can't we be friends as well? I've been told I'm a good listener.'

Why did they all want to be friends all of a sudden? She must remember to ask Sheila if that was the norm. 'Well, be that as it may, I need clients, not friends.'

'Well good for you. I need friends. I don't have a whole bunch in this country.'

'Imagine my surprise.' As soon as the words left her mouth Sam regretted them. They lingered in the air between them, like a rotten smell. What was wrong with her? Why did she keep making nasty barbs at him?

She looked across at Hal. His jaw was clenched and he was staring straight ahead. She had always presumed that Americans were totally impervious, that nothing could put a dent in their confidence. But she'd never actually met anyone from the US until now, so how would she know?

'I'm sorry,' she said quietly. 'I don't know why I said that.'

He didn't look at her. 'You don't like me much, do you?'

'That's not it. I just . . .' she hesitated. The truth was, she was rattled. Partly because of her hectic day, partly because of running late, but it was the suggestive banter and the limousine that had really thrown her. Especially after what Max had said. Hal Buchanan wouldn't be interested in someone like her, so why all the flirting? It made her uncomfortable. Despite all his protests to the contrary the other night, Sam was not so sure he wouldn't take advantage of the situation. Did he think she was so desperate that she was easy pickings? She didn't want to be taken for a fool.

'Liking you or not liking you has nothing to do with it,' Sam said in a level voice. 'This is my job, okay? I think I should maintain a certain professional distance.'

Hal still didn't look at her. 'Absolutely. Suits me.'

March

'Imagine being able to fill one of these!' said Sam, wide-eyed, holding up a Double-D cup.

'A tube of silicone ought to do it,' Liz quipped.

Liz had dragged Sam out lingerie shopping. There was a huge sale at Grace Bros and she had insisted some new lingerie was just what Sam needed. Sam had tried to point out that in her current situation she needed new lingerie like she needed the proverbial hole in the head. But her protests had fallen on selectively deaf ears. Liz always made sure she had a flexi-day up her sleeve for important occasions like half-yearly clearances or leg waxing appointments. She was the office manager for a midsize legal practice and while she was good at her job, her motto was that one should 'work to live, not live to work'.

'What about this?' Liz suggested, holding up an almost see-through, lilac push-up bra with scalloped edges.

'It's gorgeous,' said Sam. 'But I wouldn't have anything to wear with it.'

'You don't need anything to wear with it!' Liz admonished. 'Oh, except matching undies, and I'm sure they have some here somewhere,' she said, searching the rack.

'Liz, I'm not going to spend,' Sam glanced at the price tag and frowned, 'that amount of money on something I'll never have the opportunity to wear.'

'Sam,' Liz said firmly, 'you don't keep beautiful lingerie for special occasions. You wear it any time, all the time.'

'What, under my trackies while I'm doing the housework?'

'Especially then!'

'What's the point of that?'

'It makes you feel sexy and desirable and good about yourself.'

'If I wore that while I was mopping the floor I'd feel like an idiot.'

'Okay, don't wear it while you're mopping the floor. But when you're out meeting a client and you're dressed up all businesslike, don't you think it's sensual to wear, say,' she grabbed a leopard-skin G-string off the rack, 'something like this underneath?'

'It's not sensual, it's uncomfortable,' Sam winced. 'I bought a G-string once and I ended up tossing it out. Why anyone bothers with them is beyond me.'

'To avoid a panty line,' Liz told her plainly.

'Yeah, well I need a better reason than that. Tell me that they help you avoid heart disease and I'll think about it.'

Liz sighed. 'Don't you want to keep yourself a little sexy?'

'Why?'

'So you give off different pheromones, send the message that you're out there. Guys pick that up.'

'Like dogs sniffing each other in the street?'

Liz frowned at her. 'That's disgusting.'

'My point exactly,' Sam insisted. 'Women are supposed to package themselves up and give off a scent to indicate they're available?'

'Only if you ever want to have sex again.'

'Yeah, well I'm not so sure that I do.'

Liz frowned at her. She linked her arm through Sam's, steering her away from the sensible underwear section. 'You can't be serious, Sam.'

'I'm just not that interested at the moment.'

'But how do you know until you give it a try?'

Sam hesitated. No one but Max knew about Stewart. It was like some dark, ugly secret Sam had buried at the end of the garden, and she was certainly not inclined to dig it up now.

She sighed. 'It's just something Max said. That basically anyone half decent wouldn't touch me with a forty-foot pole.'

'Did you smack her?' Liz exclaimed.

'No, she had a point. Nice eligible guys are not looking for thirtysomething single mothers with three children in tow.'

'Oh, Sam, that isn't true,' said Liz. 'I mean, you do have to be realistic. Three kids would scare off a lot of guys. But the ones who stick around are going to be pretty special. You know what they say, you have to kiss a lot of frogs before your hand-some prince comes along.'

'I don't think I'm prepared to kiss a lot of frogs, though. The whole dating thing . . . ugh,' Sam shuddered.

'That's why you need new undies,' said Liz. 'Come on, let's try on some of these.'

Sam realised then that Liz had gathered up an armful of lace and satin in almost every colour. She considered her dubiously.

'There's no harm in just trying them on,' Liz insisted, pro-pelling her towards the fitting rooms.

Inside the cubicle Sam plonked herself down on the chair provided, while Liz dropped her stash on the floor.

'Did you date much after Mick?' Sam asked, watching her sift through the pile.

'Oh, sure. You'd be surprised at the guys who come out of the woodwork. Of course a lot just thought I'd be an easy lay. You know, her husband's left, she must be desperate.'

Sam bristled. That's what she'd suspected about Hal Buchanan. But she was sure she'd seen the last of him after her

foot-in-mouth attack on the way to the black-tie dinner. The
next couple of hours had been strained, to say the least. When
the meal had barely finished, he'd informed her stiffly that she
had fulfilled her duty for the evening and the limousine driver
was waiting to take her home. She did feel bad, and she had
thought about writing a letter of apology, but she didn't really
know what to say. It was probably for the best. The dynamic
was all wrong for a client relationship, it would never have
worked.

'Then there were the ones who were desperate themselves,' Liz was saying, 'who obviously thought I couldn't be
too fussy.'

'You're not making it sound very appealing.'

'Ah, but then Michael came along, don't forget.'

'Yes, exactly,' Sam sighed. 'As if lightning's going to strike
twice. Maxine would tell you it's statistically unlikely.'

It was hard to imagine a gentler soul than Liz's Michael. He
was a physiotherapist and they'd met after Liz had sprained her
ankle in a rather embarrassing accident at a party, involving a
trampoline, a karaoke machine, and the song, 'Your Love is
Lifting me Higher'. The moment Michael laid his hands on
her, as Liz liked to tell it, she was putty. She took to having
pedicures before every appointment, wearing more and more
provocative clothing, and insisting that she still needed treatment long after her ankle had healed. She was desperate for
Michael to show some interest beyond the professional, but
week after week, nothing happened. Finally, he firmly insisted
that not only did she need no further treatment, but that he
could no longer be her therapist. Liz showed up at Sam's, dis-
traught. She couldn't bear the idea that she might never see him
again and started spouting wild ideas about injuring herself so
that she'd have an excuse. Sam had never seen Liz so unhinged,
it was not her style at all.

The following day, Michael appeared on Liz's doorstep
holding a bunch of flowers. It was unethical to date a patient,
he told her, and he had been waiting for her treatment to end
so he could ask her out. They'd been together ever since.

Sam shrugged. 'It isn't fair, you know. Jeff's separated with three kids too, but it doesn't have quite the same ring for a man.'

'He's not in the market though, is he?' Liz pulled her top over her head and tossed it on Sam's lap. She reached for a tangerine lace bra from the pile. 'He's still with what's-her-name?'

Sam nodded. 'Jodi.'

'What's she like anyway?'

Sam shrugged. 'I have no idea.'

'But what does she look like?'

'I've never laid eyes on her.'

Liz was bent over, adjusting herself into the bra. She stood up straight. 'You haven't run into each other yet?'

Sam shook her head. 'Jeff always picks the kids up and drops them off as well. She's never with him, as far as I know.'

'Oh,' Liz mused. 'She must be frightened of you. You could always pump Jess for information.'

'No, I don't want to know.'

'Really?' Liz said in a high-pitched voice.

'Really,' Sam repeated flatly. 'At first I was curious. Too curious. I started obsessing. I couldn't watch a movie without imagining Jodi as one of the characters.'

'What are you talking about?'

'Have you seen *Stepmom*?'

'God yes,' Liz rolled her eyes. 'The only bloody movie that Susan Sarandon's ever looked anything but gorgeous.'

'Well, she was supposed to be ill.'

'It was a crock, let me tell you. The first wife's a hag, and the mistress is Julia Roberts? Please. What movie executive's wet dream was that?'

'Yeah well, I watched it one weekend when the kids were with Jeff, and all I could imagine was Jodi flashing the gazillion-watt smile, driving the kids to a Pearl Jam concert, singing in the car on the way.' She sighed. 'Or else I'd see her all fragile and tragic like Nicole Kidman in *Moulin Rouge*. Or sweet and kooky like Meg Ryan in –'

'All of her movies,' Liz finished. 'Sam, you should never watch stuff like that when you're alone. Same reason they don't screen disaster films on aeroplanes. Now, what are you going to try on?'

Sam screwed up her nose.

'Listen to me, woman. It'll give you a lift. You know what Elle McPherson says.'

'Oh, this'll be good.'

'The world would be a better place if women matched their bras to their underpants.'

'She did not say that.'

'Oh yes she did. I read it in an interview with her.'

Sam shook her head. 'Heaven help us if that woman ever decides to enter politics.'

'I don't think we're in any danger of that happening,' said Liz. 'Now, the strapless in grape or the lime push-up?'

One week later

'Can I get a mobile phone for my birthday, Mum?'

'No.'

'Why not?' Jessica whined.

Sam stood the iron on its base and looked squarely at her daughter. She hated haggling with the children over things about which she had no intention of changing her mind. So she resorted to the comeback of every cornered parent.

'Because I said no.'

'That's not a very good reason,' Jess retorted.

'Well, why don't we do it the other way around and you convince me why you should be allowed to have a mobile phone.'

'Okay.' Jessica took to the task with gusto, while Sam resumed ironing Josh's school shirt. 'Firstly, remember, I am turning thirteen. I *will* be a teenager,' she announced importantly.

Why did it feel as though Jess had already been a teenager for about a decade?

'I wasn't aware it had become standard equipment for teenagers now,' Sam returned. 'I didn't get that memo from the Department of Family and Community Services.'

Jessica rolled her eyes but continued undaunted. 'Secondly, with a mobile phone I can be contacted anywhere at any time,' she stated plainly, as if that was also a perfectly self-evident notion.

'Why do you need to be contactable anywhere? Are there matters of national security that might be compromised if you can't be contacted immediately?'

'Some of my calls are important!' Jess insisted haughtily.

'Oh Jessica, give me a break. The only conversations I have ever heard between teenagers on mobiles go like this,' Sam held the iron up and mimed talking into a phone. '"Hi, where are you? Oh, okay, I'm at the station. I'm about to get on a train. Talk to you later. Bye." What's the point of that? It's like a tracking device.'

Jessica sighed noisily, pouting. 'Well, everybody else has one!'

Why did kids always use that argument? Did they ever think it was going to work? Sam wanted to know where the sucker parent was that said, 'Why yes, darling, if everyone else has one, then you absolutely must too!'

'You're going to have to come up with something better than that, Jess. In the meantime –'

'Dad said he'd buy me one,' she blurted.

Jessica took two steps backwards as she watched her mother's face turn thunderously black. Sam slammed the iron down on the board.

'That's only if you agree,' Jess continued breathlessly. 'He said I should talk to you first and then get you to call him if you want to discuss it,' she finished, talking so fast she almost tripped over her own words.

If she wanted to discuss it? Sam was past fed up with the new phase their relationship had entered since . . . well, the 'episode' was how she referred to it in her head. She certainly had not told a soul, not even Max. By the time she had seen Jeff again, neither of them had been inclined to dredge it up.

Instead he'd sent her a letter reiterating the amount he was obliged to pay under the child support scheme, and stating that he would continue with the mortgage payments on top of that, until such time as 'the property was settled'. It sounded like a pro forma business letter. She imagined Jeff sitting at his computer and the help box appearing on the screen – *It looks like you're writing a letter to screw your ex-wife over. Would you like help?*

The solicitor had told her that she would be 'ill-advised' to try to hold on to the house. The debt was too great. She had to face facts and start to consider her options. But it all felt too hard at the moment. She had put in her notice at the MRA and she was working diligently to keep her *Wife for Hire* clients happy. Why couldn't she have the luxury of concentrating on one thing at a time?

But that was never going to happen. After all, she was a woman. God had decided to make women the ones who had to think of everything, keep everyone else happy and put themselves last.

Well screw that.

If Jeff thought that Jessica should have a phone, then he could pay for the damn thing and he could put it in his name so the bills would be sent directly to him as well. Sam was going to have nothing to do with it.

'That's fine with me,' Jeff replied curtly when she gave him her conditions later, over the phone.

She had been prepared to argue with him, but he was agreeing to everything she said, if a little gruffly. 'Well, just so it's on the record, I don't approve of Jessica having a phone at her age,' Sam added.

'Apparently lots of her friends have them,' Jeff countered. So, he was the sucker parent. 'And just because you don't approve, Sam, doesn't mean it isn't right.'

She was stunned into silence.

'You'd better get used to the fact that I'm going to have a lot more input from now on.'

'So, for sixteen years you leave all the decisions to me and now you're going to tell me how to run things?'

'No,' he said firmly. 'I'm not trying to take anything away from you, Sam. I just want to be more involved. For sixteen years I worked such long hours, I hardly got to see the kids, let alone know what was going on in their lives.'

'No one was forcing you,' Sam retorted. 'Don't blame that on me.'

Jeff sighed audibly. 'Can we get away from this blame thing?' he pleaded. 'I'm just saying, I got onto this treadmill and I never questioned whether it was where I wanted to be. I just kept going. I think I was walking in my sleep for the last ten years. And now I've woken up.'

Sam swallowed hard, trying to keep down the lump that was rising in her throat. She heard beeps on the line.

'I have a call waiting,' she croaked.

'Okay then,' Jeff said. 'Bye.'

Sam hung up and took the next call. 'Hello?'

'Hi, it's me,' Max chirped.

Sam started to sob, she couldn't stop herself.

'Sam! What's the matter? What happened?'

'I was just talking to Jeff,' she sniffed.

'Oh, what's the dickhead done now?'

'Nothing,' she sighed. 'It's just, you know, he's transforming into this totally concerned father all of a sudden. Having an opinion about everything.'

'Tell him where he can shove his opinions.'

'No, it's good that he's becoming more involved. I always wanted that, I think,' she faltered.

'What do you mean, you think?'

'I'm starting to wonder if I didn't give him much of a chance. I handled everything myself. It never seemed to bother him, he just went along.'

'Well, did you take over because you had to, or did he step back because you took over?'

'That's the chicken and egg riddle, isn't it? Who knows what came first?'

Max sighed. 'Thing is, Sam, there are always two sides. Look at Mum. Sure Dad pissed off, no denying that. But whenever I spend too much time with her, I start to understand why.'

'Was I like her?' Sam asked uneasily.

'I didn't mean that –'

'But was I making Jeff live a life he didn't want, and the only way he could change it was to leave?'

'You couldn't make Jeff do anything he didn't want to,' Max insisted. 'He's a great big grown-up, for crying out loud. He made his own choices.'

Sam was all too aware of that – he'd chosen someone else.

The following week

Sam was vacuuming upstairs in Ellie's room when she thought she heard the front door slam. It gave her a fright. The kids were at Jeff's for the weekend and Maxine was coming over later. They planned to see a movie together. But that wouldn't be Max, she always sang out when she let herself in. Sam switched off the vacuum cleaner and listened. Now she could hear heavy footsteps on the stairs.

She took a deep breath, telling herself that a burglar doesn't slam doors and thud noisily up stairs. She stepped out onto the landing, sighing with relief when she saw it was Josh.

But hold on, what was Josh doing here?

'Joshua, what are you doing here?' she frowned.

He didn't look up as he passed her. 'I'm not goin' there any more.'

'What? Josh, what's this about?' She almost ran to keep up with his strides. 'How did you get home?'

'Bus and train.'

'Does your father know where you are?'

He walked into his room and turned, clutching the door-knob. 'Nuh.'

'Josh . . .' Sam stood plaintively looking up him. 'Do you want to talk about it?'

'Nuh.' He closed the door.

She breathed out. What the hell was going on? She walked downstairs to the kitchen and picked up the phone, dialling Jeff's number. He answered almost immediately.

'Jeff, it's Sam. Josh is here. What's going on?'

She heard him sigh. 'Oh, thank God. When did he get there?'

'Just a few minutes ago. What's going on, Jeff? Why did he leave?'

'I don't know.'

'What?'

'I honestly don't know, Sam. He was up before we were, he had breakfast and then he went up to the skate bowl.'

'On his own?'

'Oh, don't start, Samantha. Since when have you ever gone to watch him skating?'

'But it's a strange place –'

'He's been coming here for over six months, Sam. Besides, I went up after about half an hour to check on him and he wasn't there. We've been searching the area ever since.'

'Why didn't you call me?'

'What could you do about it? Except freak out, which is exactly what you're doing now.'

'Well, what do you reckon, Jeff? He's my son! What if something had happened to him?'

'Thank God it didn't. Did he tell you what's wrong?'

'No, of course not, he doesn't want to talk about it.' Sam paused. 'Except to say that he's not going to your place any more.'

'What?'

'What happened there, Jeff?'

'Nothing, I swear. He was quiet at breakfast and then he left.'

'Something must have happened.'

'Well, I don't know what. He's been sour for months. I don't know what's wrong with the kid.'

'His parents splitting up might have something to do with it.'

'He was sour way before that.'

'Maybe that was because his father was never around?'

'Jesus, Sam. Okay, let's fight about ancient history.'

Sam didn't say anything. He was right, it was hardly the time to be trying to score points.

Jeff sighed loudly. 'Should I come over?'

'He won't talk to me at the moment. I doubt he's going to talk to you either.'

They were both silent for a moment.

'Look,' Sam started, 'I think he wants to be left alone for now. I'll try to talk to him later. I'll let you know if I find out anything.'

'Yoohoo, it's me!'

That was Max. Damn, Sam had forgotten to phone her to call off tonight. She didn't want to go out and leave Josh on his own. Not that he had come out of his room all afternoon.

'Hi,' Sam greeted Max as she came into the kitchen. 'I should have called, I can't go out tonight.'

'Oh, what's up?'

'Josh is home.'

'What, is he sick or something?'

'No, he showed up here a few hours ago. He left Jeff's without a word to anyone. They were all out searching for him.'

'No shit,' Max murmured, plonking herself on a stool. 'What happened?'

'No one knows. Jeff swears nothing happened at his place, and Josh won't tell me anything.'

Max sat for a moment, staring at the floor. 'Do you want me to talk to him?'

Sam shrugged. 'You're welcome to try, but I'm not sure if you'll get anywhere.'

Sam realised she was pacing the kitchen floor. Max had been upstairs for more than twenty minutes. She wondered what they were talking about. Perhaps Josh hadn't told her anything, but at least he had let her stay.

She heard Max's footsteps on the stairs and she came to the doorway, watching her anxiously. Max looked pensive.

'Did he tell you anything?'

Max sighed. 'You're going to need a drink.'

'What?' Sam said fearfully, turning to follow her back into the kitchen.

Max looked at her. 'Don't worry. He's alright, I mean he's not hurt or in trouble or anything. I just think you're going to need a drink. And if you don't, then I do.'

Sam waited while Max poured them both a glass of wine. They sat on stools at the island bench.

'There's no other way to say this,' Max began. She took a mouthful of wine. 'Josh can hear Jeff and Jodi together at night.'

'Together?'

'*Together*,' she repeated meaningfully.

Sam gulped down half the contents of her glass. 'Why, how?'

'You know how he sleeps out in the living room on a sofa bed?' Max reminded her. 'Their room comes directly off the living room apparently, and he can hear them at night.'

Sam felt a little stunned. 'How is he?'

'Embarrassed, confused, angry.' Max shrugged. 'You know how hard it is for kids to cope with the idea that their parents have sex, let alone one of their parents having sex with someone else.' She paused. 'And it's been even harder on Josh because he didn't want to tell you. He didn't want to upset you.'

Sam felt tears pricking her eyes.

'The poor kid's been holding it in for months because he had no one he could talk to about it.'

'No wonder he's been sour,' Sam muttered, staring at her glass. 'Oh, shit, I'm going to have to tell Jeff.'

Max drained her glass. 'Don't envy you that one, Sherl.'

'What did you say to Josh? He didn't expect you not to tell me, did he?'

Max shook her head. 'Oh, I think he knew the escapade today was going to bring it all out in the open. So I suppose it was a kind of cry for help.'

Sam looked at Max. 'I have to do this right away, get it over with.'

She picked up the phone and dialled Jeff's number as she walked out to the family room. She heard it ring, a second time, a third. Then he picked up.

'Jeff Holmes,' he said automatically, but Sam could hear the strain in his voice.

'Hi, it's me.'

He breathed out. 'How's Josh? Have you talked to him?'

'No, but Max did.' Sam hesitated. God, she didn't know how to put this.

'So . . . ?' Jeff said impatiently.

Sam took a deep breath. 'Jeff, he can hear you and Jodi at night.'

'What? What do you mean?'

Christ. Did she have to spell it out for him? 'He can *hear* you together. At night. Think about it, Jeff!'

'Oh . . .' His voice died away.

They said nothing for a few moments. It was excruciating.

'So,' Sam resumed, 'I guess you're going to have to do some-thing about it.'

'What, you expect me not to have sex, is that it, Sam?' he said tightly.

She sighed. 'I don't expect anything, I'm just the messenger here, Jeff. Don't shoot me.'

'But you must really be enjoying this, getting to dictate to me. Ever since the issue over Jessica's phone you've been want-ing to stick it to me, haven't you?'

'Yeah, I'm loving it,' she retorted. 'I so wanted to have an argument with you about your sex life with your new lover.'

He didn't respond.

'Look,' Sam gritted her teeth. She felt pissed off that she had been put in this situation and she wasn't going to wear his anger. 'You can bonk your brains out for all I care. I'm just telling you that your son's upset because he can hear you; so, for his sake, not mine, you may have to restrain yourselves when he's there.'

She hung up the phone and tossed it on the sofa, breathing heavily. Not half a minute had passed when it rang. She picked the handset up again.

'Sam?'

'What?'

'I'm sorry,' Jeff said quietly.

She sighed. 'I'd just like to make it perfectly clear to you that I would never use the kids to get back at you in any way. You should know that. And I don't like being accused of it.'

'I know Sam, I'm sorry. And I promise I won't ever use the kids either. I shouldn't have accused you.' There was a pause. 'It's just a bit hard to deal with, okay?'

'Tell me about it.'

He sighed. 'You know, it's not as if we're at it all the time –'

'Jeff,' Sam interrupted him, 'I really don't want to know, okay?'

'Sorry.' He cleared his throat. 'Do you think he'll want to come here again?'

'I don't know, Jeff. You're going to have to work that one out with Josh.'

'He doesn't seem to want to talk to me. I thought I was making a breakthrough at first. Now he's as closed off as ever.'

'Well, there's been a reason for that.'

'I guess you're right,' he sighed. 'Do you mind if I bring the girls back a little earlier tomorrow? Give me a chance to talk to him.'

'Sure.'

'Thanks Sam. And sorry. And . . . thanks.'

April

From	Sent	Subject
Hal Buchanan	Monday 9:16 AM	What happened
Hal Buchanan	Monday 9:16 AM	you promised?
Hal Buchanan	Monday 9:16 AM	about that
Hal Buchanan	Monday 9:16 AM	Football Game
Hal Buchanan	Monday 9:15 AM	Hey

Sam found herself smiling at the screen as the emails appeared one at a time in her inbox. It had been just over a month since the black-tie dinner debacle, what was Hal Buchanan doing contacting her now? She'd avoided telling Sheila so far that he'd kind of 'dropped off' her client list, but she knew the day of reckoning was nigh and she'd have to explain herself.

But now, out of the blue, he'd given her a reprieve. All the excuses about him not being a suitable client suddenly evaporated and Sam decided he deserved a prompt and personal reply. She checked her teledex and picked up the phone, dialling the direct work number he'd given her.

'Hal Buchanan.'

'So, interested in football game, hear I you are?'

'Come again?'

'I received a very odd string of emails today.'

'Hey Samantha, nice to hear from you.'

'I'm still trying to decipher it. Do you want me to read it out to you?'

'Go ahead.'

'It says, and I quote, "What happened you promised about that football game, hey".'

'Well, that's the fault of the ISP.'

Sam laughed.

'I'm telling you, there's no way to control the order the server sends your mail.'

'So why did it work for me?'

'Beginner's luck.'

'Okay, so I won't say anything about bad workmen blaming their tools.'

'And I was so hoping I was going to get a little more of your sass.'

'Sass?' she scoffed. 'What on earth is sass?'

'It's what you're real good at. Being a smart ass.'

Sam grinned. 'Okay, I promise I'm going to bite my tongue so hard from now on, it'll bleed.'

'Well, don't do that. But, hey, what about that football game you promised?'

'Has the season started?'

There was a moment of silence. 'Do you actually know anything about football, Sam?'

She breathed out heavily. 'No,' she admitted. 'But my son knows all there is to know and he'll come with us, if that's okay with you?'

And if that was okay with Josh. She hadn't even mentioned it to him as she had not expected to hear from Hal again. Josh was lately more non-communicative than ever, if that was possible. The episode with his father had left him sullen and angry. He resented having to go there, and from what she could glean from Jessica, he made the weekends an ordeal for everyone. But Jeff hadn't complained to Sam. He wouldn't dare.

'Can I ask you something, Hal?' Sam said tentatively.

'Sure.'

'What made you decide to contact me again?'

'I'm sorry?'

'Well,' she took a breath, 'you know, after the way I acted . . .'

He didn't say anything.

Sam cleared her throat. 'I was just wondering, that's all.'

He paused. 'I contacted you because I want to go to the football, Sam. I thought that was obvious.'

Now she was embarrassed. She sounded like a schoolgirl. This was business and Hal was her client. Which was exactly how she wanted it. 'Oh, okay, sure. Right, well, I'll organise it and get back to you.'

'Great.'

'Bye then.'

'Oh, Sam?'

'Yes?'

'I also figured you deserved another chance,' he added.

Sam felt flushed. 'Oh, right. Well, I won't disappoint you.'

'I'm counting on it.'

Saturday

Sam was packing the last few things into a picnic basket when the doorbell rang.

'Get that, would you, Jess? It'll be Mr Buchanan. And be pleasant.'

Jessica sighed dramatically as though Sam had just asked her to crawl across broken glass on her bare knees. She'd been whining all morning, the football was the last place on earth she wanted to be on a Saturday afternoon, or any afternoon for that matter. But Jess was the least of Sam's problems.

Josh had surprised Sam when she'd first asked him to come to the football. He'd simply shrugged and muttered, 'Whatever'. But this morning when she reminded him, he told her flatly that he wouldn't be coming.

'But why not, Josh?'

'Cause I don't want to,' he said simply, walking away.

'Joshua, you made a commitment . . .'

He looked around. 'I didn't sign a contract, Mum, you can't make me.'

Sam felt powerless. How was she supposed to discipline him any more? He was physically bigger than her, and he seemed to be losing respect for everyone around him. She'd had a letter home from school that he'd been on detention more than three times in the past month, which required them to notify parents. Sam had called and arranged an interview with his year adviser. It was time they knew what was going on at home anyway.

'Hey Samantha,' said Hal, coming into the kitchen behind Jessica.

'Hi Hal,' Sam returned brightly.

'It's good to see you again,' he said, smiling warmly at her.

Sam hoped she wasn't blushing. She wished Max had never pointed out his square jaw. It was a bit distracting now that she was aware of it.

'Good to see you too!' she chirped. 'Come on, Ellie, we're leaving!' she called out into the family room.

Ellie ran into the kitchen, her arms laden with stuffed animals. 'Can I bring Zoey, Mum?' Zoey was a zebra, almost the size of Ellie.

'Sure –'

'And can I bring Kermie and Eeyore?'

'Yes and yes. But Ellie, where are your manners? You haven't said hello to Mr Buchanan.'

Ellie looked up at Hal, then at her mother. 'That's not Mr Blue Cannon, Mummy, that's Hal.'

He grinned. 'How are you, Ellie?'

'Good,' she smiled shyly.

'Where's your boy?' Hal asked Sam.

She sighed. 'Josh has changed his mind, unfortunately. So it looks like it's just us.'

Hal surveyed the three of them. Jessica stood scowling in the corner; Ellie had plonked herself on the floor and was busily dressing Kermit the Frog in a doll's outfit, and the manic smile on Sam's face did not mask her obvious trepidation about the whole excursion.

'Do you mind if I talk to Josh, see if I can't change his mind back again?' Hal asked.

Sam couldn't imagine that coming to any good. 'Well, if you really want to. He's not the most communicative kid.'

Hal shrugged. 'He's fourteen, isn't he? I think it's in the job description.'

Sam directed him to Josh's room and he knocked on the door. There was a grunted reply.

'Hello, Josh. It's Hal Buchanan. Do you mind if I come in?'

After a brief pause, he heard a muffled, 'It's open'.

Hal pushed the door back slowly. The boy was lying on his bed, his hands clasped behind his head, a slightly bemused expression on his face. Hal had obviously only been granted admission out of curiosity.

'Hey,' he nodded.

Josh just looked at him.

'Your mother said you've decided not to come to the football today.'

'So?'

'Well, I'd be real grateful if you'd reconsider.'

'Why?'

Hal sighed. 'You should check out the Spice Girls downstairs. Your sister looks like she'd rather chew off her own arm than come along. Ellie's bringing a zoo that she won't be able to manage by herself, so I'm gonna have to walk around carrying a stuffed zebra and a frog dressed in baby clothes. And your mother's wearing a knitted scarf that I'm pretty sure combines the colours of both teams playing today. And she's got this big picnic hamper thing happening. It's a nightmare.'

Hal thought he might just have caught a flicker of amusement in Josh's eyes. He looked around the room. The walls were lined with football posters; trophies and other paraphernalia cluttered every surface.

'You're obviously a fan, what's the problem?'

Josh breathed out. 'This is a set-up.'

'What do you mean, a set-up?'

'You're dating my mum so you want to get on the kids' good side. So how about,' he continued, affecting an American accent, 'I ask him to take me to a football game and we'll *bond*.'

Hal was amused. He leaned back against the desk. 'First of all I'm not dating your mom. I'm just one of her clients. This is for real. I know nothing about your football and I feel like a dumb Yank every time anyone talks about it.'

'Yeah, well, that's because American football *is* dumb,' Josh sniggered. 'What's with all the padding? It's so gay. And all they do is run along in a row and stop like, every five seconds. It's crap.'

Hal crossed his arms and took a deep breath. 'So, why don't you show me what's so great about your football?'

Josh eyed him suspiciously. 'You're not dating Mum?'

He shook his head. 'Truth be told, I don't even think she likes me much.'

Hal saw a smile play on the boy's lips for the first time.

Barely five minutes after Hal had gone upstairs, Sam heard what sounded like two sets of footsteps coming down. She was surprised to see Josh walking ahead of Hal into the kitchen.

'We're goin', Mum,' said Josh. 'You don't need to come. The girls either.'

'Woohoo!' cheered Jessica, skipping out of the room. 'MumcanIringEmmathanksMum,' she said, without taking a breath or waiting for a reply.

Sam looked beyond Josh to where Hal was leaning against the doorjamb. He shrugged, smiling at her.

'Maybe I should come though,' said Sam. 'I am paid to do this, after all.'

'No Mum, we'll talk about my cut when I get home,' Josh replied. 'And we'll take the food, but not in the gay basket.'

Wednesday

'Samantha Holmes?'

'Speaking.'

'Alex Driscoll calling, putting you through now.'

Alex obviously couldn't spare the time to dial her own calls. Sam wondered what that would be like. Saying to your assistant, 'Get me my sister on the line, would you? The middle one, and check her name again for me first.'

'Hello, Sam?'

'Hi, Alex. How are you?'

'I'm fine. I'm calling about the account from the solicitor –'

'Oh, I hope it wasn't too much?'

'That's not it at all. The last one was a while back and there hasn't been another since. You're not trying to cover it yourself, are you?'

'No,' said Sam. 'I've only been the once.'

'Well, what's going on?' Alex sounded surprised. 'Have you and Jeff reconciled?'

'No –'

'Then what?'

Sam sighed heavily. 'The solicitor gave me some advice and now it's up to me whether I want to take it any further.'

'What was the advice?'

'Um, well, he felt I should think about selling the house.'

'So have you?'

'What, sold the house?'

'No,' said Alex. 'Have you thought about it?'

'Well, yes, sure. It's just . . .'

'What, Sam? What?'

'It's a big step.' A no-turning-back step. Not that there was any turning back from here. But still.

'Samantha, you have bought and sold houses three times now, am I right?'

'Yes.'

'So what is the problem?'

'It's different this time. I'm scaling down, not moving up. And I'm on my own. It just feels more daunting.'

'How did you go about it before?'

Sam thought for a minute. She drove around a lot, discovered the best streets, checked every realtor in the area and calculated what would be a fair price to pay. She also read the real estate section in the newspaper religiously, even after they'd moved to Cherrybrook and she had no intention of buying or selling again. She just found it interesting.

'I suppose I did some research,' Sam offered vaguely.

'Exactly,' Alex declared. 'You're going to have to get on with it, Sam. This state of inertia is no good for anyone.'

'I just thought the children needed some time before another change was thrust upon them.'

'Fair enough,' she agreed. 'But leave it too long and you'll upset them all over again. They'll be lulled into a false sense of security, believing nothing else is going to change.'

Sam hadn't thought about it like that.

'If you don't want to go on your own, then take Maxine.'

'It's not so much going on my own, it's *being* on my own. I don't know how agents treat you when they know you're a single Mum . . .'

'I honestly think they couldn't care less, as long as they get a sale out of it.'

'I suppose you're right.'

'If it bothers you so much, don't tell them, or take a male friend, whatever. But get on and do something.'

'I will.'

'And call me.' Her voice lost its crockery-hard edge. 'Call me, okay? Let me know how you go.'

'Thanks Alex.'

May

Sam arrived at the IGB building and pushed through glass doors into a voluminous foyer. She had come into the city today on various errands for her clients and she was due to meet Vanessa and Dominic for lunch at one. Dropping in casually to see Hal Buchanan at work was a good offhand way, she felt, to broach her idea.

Which was to ask him to come house-hunting with her. She had thought this over carefully, it might even be said, obsessively. Yes, she had gone house-hunting many times on her own before. But she had a husband then. How had Max put it? Jeff was like a safety net. Sam could perform any number of complicated manoeuvres with the security of knowing he was there. She was all the more accomplished if she never actually had to fall back on him.

She supposed she could *say* she was married. But what about when she found a house? It would all come out eventually and then she'd look pathetic.

Having a man come along was the best alternative. Sam was not going to pretend Hal was her husband, and neither would she hide the fact she was separated. She wouldn't explain his presence except to say he was a friend, but the realtor was likely to surmise more. The assumption would be that Hal was her partner and that he would be involved in the purchase of the property. She had her safety net.

And why Hal? Well, first off, Sam didn't know any other single men. She supposed she could ask one of the girls if she could borrow a husband. Col was out of the question, Michael was a little shy, so that would just leave Gavin. Spending an entire day with him was an ordeal she could do without. Besides, she doubted Fiona could spare him.

Then there was the fact that Hal was American and therefore brash, confident, straight-shooting. Which was a stereotype, Sam knew, but it's how the agents would see him. That couldn't hurt. And finally, she would be killing two birds with one stone if she could convince Hal that checking out real estate was an excellent way to 'acclimatise'.

He was the obvious choice. It had nothing at all to do with his square jaw, as she'd told Maxine, who had tried to insist otherwise.

'So you're saying you're not attracted to him?'

'This is what I'm saying.'

'Have you had your eyes checked lately?'

'I can see fine, but I'm not looking, Max!' Sam had declared. 'Besides, I'm way out of his league, remember?'

'Well, as long as you're keeping that in mind.'

Sam frowned at her. 'I know, he can't be so desperate he'd be interested in me.'

'Oh, you know what I mean,' Max dismissed. 'It's just that you're seeing a lot of him lately, I've been worried about you.'

Sam sighed. 'He and Josh go to the football together. I invite him in for coffee afterwards because it's the polite thing to do.'

'Didn't he stay for dinner the other night?'

'So? Hal doesn't know anybody here. I was being hospitable.'

'I just don't want you to get your heart broken.'

'I won't get my heart broken, Max!' Sam insisted. 'I'm not even looking for a relationship, and I promise you I wouldn't consider Hal if I was.'

'You wouldn't?'

'Absolutely not. For one thing, he's a client,' she began, counting off on her fingers. 'And he's only in the country on a temporary basis. And he's a client. And he lives in the US. And have I mentioned he's a client?'

'Only like, three times,' said Max.

'I've made my point then?'

So now Sam was standing here in the foyer of the building where he worked, a chill rapidly developing in her feet. She looked across at the bank of elevators flanked by security screens, requiring an identity card to pass through. Clearly, dropping in casually was not the done thing at IGB. There was a vast reception desk to one side. Perhaps if she asked for him by name they'd let her in. She approached the desk and the receptionist smiled tersely at her.

'Can I help you?'

'I was looking for a Mr Buchanan, Hal Buchanan?'

The woman frowned slightly. 'Do you have an appointment?'

'Oh . . . no, I don't actually.' Sam faltered, wondering how best to explain herself. 'I, um, I'm just a friend.'

'Is Mr Buchanan expecting you?'

Sam shook her head lamely. The woman checked her watch. It was too early for lunch. She probably thought Sam was some desperate one-night stand stalking him the morning after.

'I can phone through, see if he's available.' She raised a questioning eyebrow. 'Would you like me to do that?'

'Yes, please . . . if it's no trouble.'

She considered Sam sceptically. 'What name shall I give him?'

'Samantha Holmes.'

The woman picked up the phone and turned just slightly away from her as she dialled. 'Mr Buchanan? It's Reception. There is a Ms Samantha Holmes here to see you.'

A moment later she replaced the receiver and cleared her throat, not making eye contact. 'Mr Buchanan will be down directly.'

'Thank you.'

Sam wandered away from the desk, gazing up into the vast atrium that stretched upwards for five or six floors. The elevator announced itself with a *ping*, and she turned around as Hal stepped through the doors. He looked over and smiled broadly at her. Sam glanced at the receptionist who was watching on the sly, eyebrows raised.

Hal walked towards her. 'Hey Sam, to what do I owe this?'

'Well, I was just passing,' she faltered. 'I thought I'd make a courtesy call, you know? I didn't realise it would be such a big deal.'

Hal glanced back at reception. 'Yeah, it's like Fort Knox around here.' He watched her fidgeting with her handbag; she looked awkward. 'What's up?'

'Nothing. Everything's fine.'

He considered her for a moment. 'Do you want to grab a cup of coffee?'

'Oh no, I didn't mean to take you away from your work . . .'

'Then that's a bonus,' he grinned.

He guided her by the elbow back out through the glass doors and into the sunshine. It was a bright autumn day. Everything seemed crisp and clean at this time of the year, even in the city. Like the place was having a loofah scrub, sloughing off the dead layers from summer.

Hal stepped up to a coffee barrow. 'How do you have it?'

'Flat white, thanks.'

'That's regular coffee with milk, isn't it?'

She nodded, and he seemed pleased with himself. A minute later he passed her a steaming cardboard cup and they walked over to a bench and sat down.

'So, just passing, eh?' Hal started.

Sam looked at him sideways. 'I was in town, I thought I'd save myself a call.'

'A call about what?'

'Well, you originally asked me to help you acclimatise, remember?'

'Turns out, your son's taking care of that quite well, as a matter of fact.'

'You're only learning about football from Josh.'

'Oh, you'd be surprised. I'm picking up quite a bit of the culture as well.'

She looked dubious. 'The only place anything Josh taught you could be of use is in the schoolyard, let me assure you.'

'You underestimate him.'

Sam considered Hal. She couldn't deny being a little curious about their relationship. Josh always seemed more animated when he came back from their outings, though as usual, he never said much.

'What do you two get up to anyway?' Sam asked.

'Wouldn't you like to know?'

'Come on,' she cajoled.

He shook his head. 'It's secret men's business.'

'Hal, he is my son −'

'Sam, we go to the football, we talk football.'

'Well, he doesn't talk to me about anything.'

'Do you talk about what interests him?'

'Like what?'

'Football.'

'I don't know anything about football.'

'There you go.'

She sighed. 'Well, does he seem alright to you?'

'He seems fine. He's a good kid,' said Hal. 'He sure loves his football, and I think he gets a kick out of showing off to an old guy like me.'

'It's very good of you −'

'He's doing me a favour,' he brushed it off.

Sam had met with Joshua's year adviser, who had struck her as an understanding person. He'd promised to keep a closer eye on Josh and inform his teachers of the situation at home. And apparently he'd settled down a little at his father's, according to Jessica. Jeff must have been showing spectacular restraint in the bedroom. Which had never been a problem while they were still together, it occurred to Sam.

'I worry about him,' she said, thinking aloud. 'I feel like I don't understand him sometimes.'

'I doubt at his age he even understands himself,' Hal returned. 'Cut the kid some slack. He's living in a house full of females, I know what that's like when you're growing up.'

'Oh, your father wasn't around either?'

'He never left us. But he was absent in a lot of ways.' Hal stared into his coffee cup. 'So what did you have in mind to acclimatise me?' he said, patently changing the subject.

Sam took a breath. 'Well, I thought I could introduce you to the wonderful world of Sydney real estate.'

'Why do I need to know about that?'

'Because you can't have a conversation at any social gathering in Sydney without having some opinion about real estate.'

'I'll just say it's overpriced.'

'They'll see right through you.'

'I'll take that chance.'

'Hal!' Sam exclaimed. 'You have to come.'

'Why?'

'Because,' she faltered, 'um, I've made appointments.'

Hal looked at her. 'What's going on, Sam?'

She sighed, she'd better just own up. 'I have to move,' she said plainly. 'I can't afford to stay in the house, or even in the area. I want to try and find something closer to the city, but it's all new territory to me.'

'So what good will I do? I don't know anything about Sydney.'

She looked at him squarely. 'I need a man.'

Hal smiled, surprised. 'Well, when you put it that way –'

'I just don't want to be written off as a single mother with no money and no prospects.'

'But you're not.'

'They don't know that.'

'They don't have to know any of your business.'

'I'd just feel better if there was a man with me.'

Hal shook his head. 'So much for the women's movement.'

'I didn't ask to be liberated,' said Sam. 'I quite like having doors opened for me, chairs pulled out . . .'

'. . . less money for the same work, not having the vote.' Hal eyed her dubiously. 'Jeez Sam, what century are you from?'

'I'm only "sassing",' she said, half-truthfully. 'So, do you want the session on real estate or not?'

Hal was quiet for a moment. 'Why didn't you just ask?'

'What do you mean?'

'Why didn't you just ask me to come house-hunting with you? Aren't we friends yet?'

'Sure,' Sam said, trying to sound offhand. 'We're friends.'

'So?'

She watched him as he stretched his arms across the back of the bench and straightened his legs out, crossing them at the ankles. 'I'm waiting,' he said, an expectant look on his face.

Sam breathed out heavily. 'Would you please come house-hunting with me on Saturday?'

'Well, I'll have to check my schedule –'

'Hal!'

He smiled broadly. 'I'd be happy to.'

Sam was meeting Vanessa and Dominic at a café along the finger wharf in Woolloomooloo. She arrived a little before one, but they were already seated. They hadn't seen her yet. Their heads were bent and Dominic was talking intently, pointing his finger a lot. Vanessa was nodding obligingly, a slight frown creasing her forehead. The picture was telling about four thousand words.

Vanessa looked up and smiled when she caught sight of Sam. She started to wave but Dominic held her hand and placed it back on the table. He stood up as Sam weaved her way towards them.

'Samantha,' he said, moving to kiss her cheek. Then he surprised her by kissing the other cheek as well. So European. Such a wanker.

Sam took a seat as Vanessa leaned over to squeeze her hand. 'Hello,' she said brightly. 'How's Ellie?'

'She's great, thanks. Though when she heard I was seeing you today she was quite miffed she wasn't allowed to miss pre-school and come along.'

'Oh really?' Vanessa cooed.

Dominic cleared his throat, regaining their attention. 'Thanks for meeting us, Samantha,' he began. 'I thought this was a pleasant way to conduct our business.'

'It is,' Sam agreed.

'Let's order first and get that out of the way.'

When the waiter appeared, Dominic took over, asking Sam what she wanted and relaying it back to the waiter. She felt like telling him that she was sure the waiter could hear her fine, but she supposed he was just playing the host. Then he ordered for Vanessa without actually asking first what she wanted. It didn't seem to bother her. Maybe they were so in tune he didn't need to ask.

'Now, Samantha,' Dominic began, passing her a manila folder. 'Here is all the information for our ski trip. The dates we're available and brochures of the lodges we prefer. I've kept these over the years, but I've highlighted the lodge where we stayed last year. And we did love it there, didn't we, Vanessa?' He didn't wait for her answer. 'That would be our first preference. So, I'll leave it with you.'

Sam took the folder. 'I'll let you know when I've booked something.'

'Fine,' he said, taking out a notepad. 'And now, onto my girl's birthday party,' he said, kissing Vanessa's hand. Sam thought it was sweet that he was so excited for her, until she noticed that Vanessa didn't look excited at all.

'When's your birthday, Vanessa?' Sam asked.

'End of the month,' Dominic answered. 'The big Three O.'

Sam tried to ignore him and focus on Vanessa. 'Have you got any ideas about what you'd like?'

'I'd like to go home for my birthday. Mum and Dad –'

'Vanessa,' Dominic chided, interrupting. 'We've already been over this, I believe. A *number* of times,' he added pointedly. 'I thought we'd settled on a party?'

No, *you've* settled on a party, Sam wanted to say. But it was not her place. She watched Vanessa smile meekly and shrug.

'Sure,' she said quietly.

'Okay,' he continued. 'I want this to be very special. I want people to walk in and say "Wow!". I want them to be talking about it for months afterwards . . .'

Sam listened to Dominic carry on in this vein for the next forty minutes. She wrote copious notes in her diary while he spat out orders and ideas and more orders. It would be a spectacular party. Dominic had superb taste, and with his advertising background, he clearly knew how to make an impression. But all the while the birthday girl sat disinterested, munching on her salad and nodding whenever Dominic said, 'You'd like that, wouldn't you?'

At least he was asking, Sam supposed, but it was lip-service at best. She wondered whether he'd bother doing anything special for Vanessa if there was no audience to look on and crow about what a wonderful husband he was.

Sam felt uneasy. She remembered Jeff's thirtieth. He'd had some foolish idea about having a beach party, but Sam had managed to talk him out of it. It may have been fun for him and some of his old mates, but what about his parents and the older relatives? And it would be a nightmare with the kids, trying to keep an eye on them. Instead Sam organised an elegant cocktail party. She hired a proper bartender, and even a string quartet, and she made all the canapes herself, from scratch. Everyone was very impressed and they all had a wonderful time. But at the end of the night she found Jeff downstairs in the rumpus room with a couple of his old schoolmates, drinking beer and listening to Bruce Springsteen records.

At the time Sam shrugged it off. He was never interested in much of the entertaining they did, even when it was his own colleagues from work. He was a bloke, it wasn't a bloke's place to fuss over dinner parties and the like. Was it?

Sam knew that was probably sexist, but in her own defence, it was more usual for a woman to take care of such things. The company was called *Wife for Hire* after all. If you replaced the word *Wife* with *Husband* or *Man*, it would carry an entirely different set of expectations.

Satisfied with what they had covered for today, Dominic announced he had to get back to work. Vanessa was in no hurry so he left her to fix up the bill, farewelling them both as he weaved his way through the tables and out onto the street. Sam saw him take out his mobile and start talking as he walked off out of sight.

'Where did you park your car?' Vanessa asked when they left the café.

'Oh, I caught the train in today,' Sam explained.

'Then I'll walk you to the station.'

'That's okay, it's not near your office.'

Vanessa smiled at her. 'So? It's a beautiful day, a walk would be lovely. Let's cut across the Domain.'

They strolled along for a while, only making small talk.

'You don't really like Dominic, do you?' Vanessa said out of the blue.

'What makes you think that?' Sam said, taken aback.

Vanessa grinned. 'I can tell you don't like him. You bristle when he does his control thing.'

Sam looked at her warily.

'Don't worry, Dominic's good at a lot of things, but reading people is not one of them. He probably thinks you adore him. Or at the very least admire him.'

'Of course I admire him.' Sam hoped Vanessa would just drop the subject.

'You're divorced, aren't you?' she asked abruptly.

Sam hadn't expected Vanessa to drop one uncomfortable subject only to replace it with another. 'No, actually, I'm not,' she replied.

'Sorry, you mentioned Ellie spending weekends with her father,' said Vanessa uncertainly. 'I just presumed –'

'Well, we are separated, but we haven't formalised it with a divorce so far.'

'Oh, are you hoping to get back together?'

Sam shook her head. That had never really been on the cards. Except for Jeff's momentary lapse months ago, there had never been the slightest suggestion they would get back together again. And ironically, that episode had been the final bell tolling.

'Was it very bad, your break-up?' said Vanessa after a while.

She sighed. 'Well, it was certainly no picnic.'

'How long ago did it happen?'

'Last September.'

'What went wrong?'

Sam looked at her. Vanessa was a sweetheart, but they probably would never have been friends in the normal course of things. They led such different lives. The trendy, child-free career woman subspecies did not usually mix with the suburban mum subspecies. But there was a neediness in Vanessa that Sam found quite poignant.

'My husband left me for another woman,' Sam said plainly.

'Oh no,' Vanessa cried. 'How could he do that? Leave *you*?

What was wrong with him? You would have been a wonder-ful wife.'

As much as Sam didn't mind hearing that, she did think Vanessa's viewpoint might be a little one-eyed. 'They say people in happy marriages don't have affairs.'

'Oh, sure!' Vanessa scoffed. 'That sounds like an excuse made up by a man having a midlife crisis.'

'That's what I told my husband when he tried it on me.'

They smiled at each other.

'How are your children coping?' Vanessa continued.

Sam shrugged. 'They have their ups and downs, and that's bound to continue. I mean, we're going to have to move house, there are still a lot of adjustments ahead of them.'

'Do you think it's harder with kids?'

Sam thought about it. 'Oh probably. But I'm glad I have them. They give me a reason to keep going.'

Vanessa smiled wistfully. 'That's what I think. No matter how much trouble children would be, you must get so much back that it makes it all worthwhile. I mean, I bet it doesn't even feel like work, looking after them. They're your flesh and blood, you'd want to do all you could for them, wouldn't you? And they must bring you so much joy.'

Sam was going to argue with her point about raising chil-dren not feeling like work, but she let it go. It was not really the issue at heart.

'Have you said all that to Dominic?' Sam asked.

'Not in so many words,' Vanessa smiled faintly. 'But it doesn't matter. He's the kind of person who sets goals and achieves them because he stays committed and never loses focus.' She was obviously parroting off something that had been said to her many times.

'You know, Vanessa . . .' Sam needed to tread carefully. This wasn't any of her business, nor was it her place to give Vanessa mar-ital advice. 'You're really supposed to compromise in a marriage.'

Vanessa looked at her. 'What are you saying?'

'If you want a baby so badly, you should tell Dominic that five years is too long, and renegotiate the "goals".'

'Oh no, I couldn't do that.'

'Why not?'

'Well, his goals are very important to him.'

Sam sighed inwardly. There was something about Vanessa's total acquiescence that she found irksome. Maybe Dominic was a little pushy, a little driven, but Vanessa certainly didn't stand in his way. In fact she barely cast a shadow.

'I'm sure Dominic wants you to be happy,' Sam said carefully. 'How is he to know if you don't tell him what's important to you?'

Vanessa was thoughtful. 'Did your husband want children?' she asked.

Sam nodded. 'I guess so. He never objected anyway. But he was happy with the two. So was I, and then Ellie came along unexpectedly.'

'What a wonderful surprise!' Vanessa gushed.

'At first I wasn't so sure, but as soon as she was born I knew she was meant to be here.'

'How did your husband handle it?'

'Oh, Jeff has a weakness for his girls. He fell in love with her at first sight.'

Vanessa smiled dreamily. 'Interesting,' she murmured.

Saturday

Hal was waiting on the street outside his apartment block, sipping coffee from a paper cup, when Sam pulled into the kerb. He approached the car with an incredulous smile.

'What's this?' he remarked, opening the door of the Landcruiser. 'Are we going off-road?'

Sam frowned. 'I don't take this off-road!'

'You don't say?' he said, climbing in. 'So what the hell are you doing with a four-wheel drive?'

'They're safer,' Sam insisted, pulling out into the stream of traffic.

'Not for anyone else on the road, especially the poor pedestrians. The wheel base is too high, and it doesn't absorb any of the impact if it hits anything, so you're three times more likely to kill somebody if you have an accident in one of these. And they're heavier on the road, they're not aerodynamic or fuel efficient, which means they use way more gas than regular cars. They're designed for off-road conditions, so when they adapt them for urban driving they're just a hulking, big, dangerous, inefficient car.' He took a breath. 'So, tell me, why did you say you have a four-wheel drive?'

Sam paused. 'Everyone else has one,' she said lamely.

He laughed out loud. 'Well, there's a good reason.'

'You know it's all your fault they got so popular.'

'My fault? How do you figure that?'

'Well, Americans started the craze.'

'How come I'm suddenly the apologist for everything bad that comes out of the US?'

'You're the only American I know.'

'There's two hundred and fifty million of us. You think there might be a little diversity? That maybe we're not all like the people you see on Ricky Lake?'

'Fair point. And maybe when you go back to the States you could make sure they understand that the vast majority of Australians have never seen a live crocodile, let alone wrestled one, that some of us don't play sport, and that kangaroos don't hop up the middle of Pitt Street.'

'Okay,' he nodded. 'Not that anyone'll know where Pitt Street is.'

She looked at him sideways.

'Go figure,' he shrugged.

Sam had done her research. Once she had accepted the inevitability of her situation, she had actually become quite focused. She'd started as she always had before, with two lists:

'Essentials' and 'Desirables'. So, three bedrooms were essential, but a fourth would be desirable. She went to the library and checked back copies of the *Herald* on CD-Rom. There was always a feature a couple of times a year on relative house prices across Sydney. They needed to move closer to the city as her clients mainly lived in the eastern suburbs, in the CBD or on the lower north shore, which were all out of her price range. The inner west was expensive too, but there were pockets that were affordable, where she had some chance of fulfilling the old adage and finding the worst house in the best street. Or at least that was the plan.

Sam had made appointments with three different realtors covering the areas she felt were worth investigating: Leichhardt, Erskineville and Summer Hill. But the morning quickly became an exercise in disappointment. The upper price limit she'd set herself turned out to be the lowest possible starting point. That's if she wanted something with hot water connected and an inside bathroom. Sam was quite amazed at the number of houses that had clearly never been touched by a renovator's hand. What had happened to the golden era of renovation? Had it died with the last millennium? These houses should have been snapped up by young, childfree, upwardly mobile couples armed with paint charts and big ideas but totally clueless as to what they were getting themselves into.

Sam didn't have the luxury of staying where she was while she renovated, and she couldn't afford it anyway. Many of the fixer-uppers she inspected were on larger blocks of land and were worth a bomb, despite the fact that bombing was about all they were good for.

The last house at the last agency was a nightmare. The carpet smelled rotten and there was rising damp in the walls, evidenced by the brown tidemark around the grotty wallpaper. Hal nearly put his hand through one wall when he leaned against it. And call her fussy, but Sam refused to live with a bathroom that had been tacked on to the back of the house as an afterthought, and had a gap between the wall and the roof where a nest of starlings had taken up residence.

When they got back to the agency, Sam followed the realtor inside and Hal said he'd wait at the car. She left her details and walked back out into the street. Hal had the newspaper spread out on the bonnet of the car and was studying it closely. He had been indefatigable. He had continued to be polite to the agents well after they had started to grate on Sam. And somehow he'd managed to put a positive spin on every house they inspected. It couldn't have been much fun for him but he'd acted as though he was enjoying himself. Sam appreciated him being there more than she'd expected.

'No more houses,' she protested, walking towards him.

'But there may be a couple −'

'No,' she said firmly. 'I'm depressed enough for one day. Come on, I'll shout you lunch instead.'

'Excuse me?'

'I'll shout you lunch,' Sam repeated. She considered Hal's blank expression. 'I'll buy you lunch,' she said slowly.

'Oh, okay,' he nodded.

'Poor Hal,' Sam grinned, walking around to the driver's side of the car. 'You must wander around in a constant state of confusion.'

'Well, if you guys would just speak English . . .'

Sam climbed into her seat. 'We speak the Queen's English in fact,' she informed him. 'Not the bastardised hybrid y'all speak over yonder in your neck of the woods.'

Hal laughed loudly, shaking his head.

'It's sass,' Sam grinned. 'I'm getting good at it, don't you think?'

'Oh, you're remarkably good,' he smiled. 'You've got it down to a fine art.'

'Why thank you,' Sam returned. 'Now, what do you feel like eating?'

Hal shrugged. 'Is there such a thing as Australian cuisine?'

'Is there such a thing!' Sam scoffed. She drummed her hands on the steering wheel, thinking. 'Ever had a real hamburger?'

'Hate to shatter your delusions, Skippy, but we have burgers in the US. In fact, you know, I think we even invented them.'

Sam started up the engine. 'I'm not talking about that plastic assembly-line pap you try to pass off as real food. I'm talking about an authentic Australian burger.'

'What's the difference?'

'You'll see.'

It took Sam longer than she expected to find the kind of outlet that would serve a true Australian hamburger. She could have picked cuisine from just about any country in the world, but she was hard-pressed to find a regular hamburger shop. There were burgers made with gourmet marinated meats, served with exotic condiments and roasted vegetables on specialty breads, or else there were the health food variety made with lentils, nutmeat or variations of tofu. She finally found a place tucked away in an industrial area, where she ordered them a burger each and chips, not fries she pointed out to Hal. They sat in a booth at a laminex table and Hal considered his hamburger warily.

'What's the red stuff?'

'Beetroot.'

'Beetroot? On a hamburger?'

'It's better than pickle. I've never met a kid who eats the slice of pickle McDonald's puts on their burgers.'

'But beets?' he said, curling his lip and eyeing his burger suspiciously.

'That, more than anything else, is what makes it Australian,' she informed him, before biting into hers.

'You're kidding me?'

She shook her head, swallowing down a mouthful. 'A few years ago, McDonald's put an Australian version on their menu and it was so popular they couldn't keep up with the demand. There wasn't enough beetroot being produced in the country. They had to withdraw it until they had a two-year surplus from farms dedicated entirely to the production of beetroot. It's a regular item on the menu now.'

'Well you're certainly a fountain of useless information.'

'And here I was thinking I was entertaining and fun to be with.'

He looked at her for a moment. 'I'm not arguing with that.'

Sam smiled shyly. 'Tell me something,' she said, changing the subject. 'Why are you here?'

'Because you wanted me to try one of your burgers.'

'No, I mean why are you in Australia?'

'Oh,' he nodded. 'It's classified. I can't tell you unless you have CIA clearance.'

'You're such a goose,' said Sam.

'And yet I just agreed that you're entertaining and fun to be with.'

Sam shrugged. 'So are you going to answer me?'

'I forgot the question.'

'What are you doing here in Australia?'

'I'm on a contract –'

'I know that,' Sam persisted. 'But why would you come all the way to the other side of the world? You must be able to get work in the US?'

'Sure. I just wanted to see where I was born.'

'That's it?'

'Pretty much.'

Sam watched him take a bite of his burger and chew it gingerly. 'Sorry,' he said, lifting the top of the bun and removing the offending crimson slice. 'I'm not taking to this beet burger idea.'

'You were married once, didn't you say?' Sam said, resuming her line of questioning.

He nodded, rearranging his burger.

'When did you break up?'

Hal looked at her. 'So, let me get this straight. Your private life is out of bounds, but mine isn't?'

'My husband left me for another woman. I told you that already and there's nothing much more to it. So what about you?'

He shrugged. 'It didn't work out.'

'That's a peculiar phrase,' said Sam. 'Very American.'

He frowned. 'Yes, only Americans have ever used the phrase "it didn't work out".'

'I mean to describe a whole marriage breaking down. "It didn't work out" sounds like you're talking about a soufflé that didn't rise.'

'Maybe it's a way of saying that you don't want to talk about it,' he said tightly, not making eye contact.

Sam's heart dropped into her stomach. She could see the pain in his expression. 'I apologise. That was completely inappropriate, it's none of my business.'

He still couldn't look at her. Now it was going to be awkward between them. Why did she keep doing this? She only seemed to open her mouth around Hal to change feet.

'It's just,' she tried to explain, 'well, you know, you told me you hadn't met anyone and that's why you asked me to partner you to those functions, and then, once I met you I knew very well you wouldn't have any trouble finding a date, and well, it was Max actually, she said "Oh come on, he'd only have to click his fingers . . ."'

Hal was frowning curiously at her.

'Oh, I'm not explaining myself very well, so what's new about that?' she said breathlessly. 'It's just that I thought there had to be some other reason why you weren't dating. You're handsome and single and straight – I mean, I presume you're straight,' she added quickly.

He nodded, considering her. 'I thought you said I wasn't *that* good looking?'

Sam could see the smile in his eyes. 'That's right, I did. It was Max who said you were handsome.'

The smile broke on his lips now, and it seemed she'd been forgiven.

'I'm going to order a coffee,' Hal said. 'Do you want one?'

Sam considered him warily. 'Haven't I taken up enough of your time . . .'

'Have a coffee with me,' he said quietly.

'Okay,' she nodded.

Hal stepped up to the counter and ordered. He returned to the booth and sat back, clearing his throat.

'Lisa and I met at the Microsoft campus in Seattle.'

'Who's Lisa?'

'My wife.'

'Hal, you don't have to tell me this –'

He held up his hand to stop her. 'I know that.' He took a breath. 'Anyway, she was my assistant. She was young, beautiful, ambitious. And she was smart. Way smarter than me, but she hadn't had the same breaks.'

'Because she was a woman?'

Hal shook his head. 'Not so much. It was her background. She'd never been to college. She didn't know who her father was, her mother was an addict. There'd been some sexual abuse, her mom's boyfriends. I don't know how she survived everything she went through. But she was tough, she pretty much brought herself up. And she was determined to have a better life. I guess I was her ticket to that better life.'

Their coffees arrived and Sam watched, trying to be patient as Hal added sugar to his cup, stirred it slowly and then took a tentative sip.

'So you're saying she used you?' she said finally, prompting him to go on.

'I allowed myself to be used,' he replied. 'I liked the whole idea that I was rescuing her, that I could make her happy. Men have knight-in-shining-armour fantasies too, you know,' he added sheepishly.

'What went wrong?'

Hal shrugged. 'Something shifted after a while. I'd been ambitious, for her sake, but I started to lose interest in the work, while Lisa was going from strength to strength. We grew apart, we didn't seem to have much in common any more . . .'

There was nothing in the marriage vows to cover bored, distant, or even 'nothing in common'. Yet that's what did it most of the time. Sam looked at Hal. He was staring into his cup, the pain had crept back into his expression. There was something else, something worse.

Eventually he spoke, his voice low. 'I was away on business, and I came back a day or two early, it was the middle of the week. Lisa was home when I got to the apartment. She said she was sick. But I'd known her to work through the flu, through anything, she never took time off.' He paused. 'She finally admitted she'd had an abortion the day before. She'd waited till I was out of town, because she didn't want to involve me.'

'Not involve you?' Sam blurted before she could help herself.

Hal looked up at her then. 'See, she wasn't sure if it was mine, so . . .' His voice faded.

Sam covered her mouth with her hand. She felt like crying, she could feel the tears stinging behind her eyes. She bit on the edge of her thumb to contain herself.

'You'll be thinking all Americans belong on Ricky Lake after all,' he said after a while.

'No, I don't think that at all,' Sam said in a small voice. 'I was just thinking, how does a person get over something like that?'

His lips formed a slight, self-conscious smile. 'They flee to the other side of the world.'

Sam looked at him. 'That's when you came here?'

'Not right away. I took a contract in New York first. Then this job in Australia came up.'

They sat quietly for a while. Sam had a dozen questions buzzing around in her head. Had they been planning to have a child? Was Lisa sleeping around, or was there someone in particular? Was she with the guy now? But none of that was any of her business and to ask Hal would be like picking away at a particularly painful sore.

'So I presume this is why you're not dating at the moment,' Sam said rhetorically.

'I'm giving my battered heart a rest.' He shook his head, smiling ruefully. 'Okay, I'm going to stop now before I start sounding like a country and western song.'

'Too late,' Sam quipped. Then she cringed. 'Sorry, I have this mouth that comes out with things before I've really thought them through.'

He smiled. 'I've noticed.'

She considered him thoughtfully. 'Why did you tell me all that?'

'So you'd know,' he said simply.

And so she wouldn't harangue him with any more questions. She took the hint.

'Well, I completely understand about the whole dating thing,' Sam said. 'My friends keep saying I should put myself out there.' She grimaced. 'But I can't face it.'

'Think of all the guys you're disappointing,' Hal said, shaking his head.

Sam grinned. 'Yes, I know, the waiting list is getting out of hand, you can imagine. I have to go through it and sort out the ones who want me for my money from the ones who just want me for my body.'

That idea really amused her, and she laughed out loud. But when she glanced across at Hal he had a curious look in his eyes. He held her gaze for a moment longer than was comfortable. Sam was sure her face had turned the colour of the discarded beetroot slice on his plate. She picked up her coffee cup and held it to her lips, sipping slowly, giving her something to hide behind.

He leaned forward after a while, claiming her attention. 'So, do you have a Plan B?'

'Hmm?'

'To find a house.'

Sam sighed heavily, setting her cup down in its saucer. 'I'll either have to borrow more money or look further out, I guess.'

'I hope your ex is doing the right thing by you,' Hal said seriously.

'He is,' she assured him. 'And we have equity in the house. I was just hoping to minimise my debt. It's a little daunting taking out a mortgage on your own with three kids.'

'I can imagine.' He paused. 'How do they feel about moving? The kids, I mean.'

Sam took a deep breath. 'That's a good question. I'll let you know.'

June

Sam decided that living close to the city had to be her priority, so she needed to stretch her budget as far as she could. And she wouldn't really know that until their house was sold. That meant telling the children.

She asked Maxine over for moral support and sat the older two down after Ellie had gone to bed. Sam didn't want her to witness any of their histrionics. She could tell her once the others had come to terms with it.

'Move!' Jessica almost shrieked. 'Why do we have to move?'

'Because we can't afford to stay here.'

'This is because of Dad, isn't it?' Josh muttered grimly.

'Well, it's because of a lot of reasons, Josh. Your father's paying more than his fair share at the moment. But he can't keep that up indefinitely.'

'Why not?' Josh persisted. 'He's the one who pissed off.'

'Josh, mind your language,' said Sam, trying to sound firm. 'This house is too big, it's too much for me to maintain on my own.'

Jessica eyed her sceptically. 'Do we have to move far? Will I be able to stay at my school?'

Here was the rub. Sam glanced at Max, whose eyes clamoured 'Don't look at me'.

'I need to be closer to my clients, and they live mostly around the city, the eastern suburbs –'

'So we could move to Bondi!' exclaimed Jessica, her eyes lighting up.

'No, we wouldn't be able to afford Bondi, Jess.'

Her face fell again.

'What about football?' said Josh.

'They play football all over Sydney, Josh.'

'Yeah, but it's midseason. I can't just leave in the middle of the comp.'

'It'll be at least a few months before we actually move. You'll be able to see the season out.'

'So where are we moving to?' Jessica whined.

Sam took a deep breath. 'I'm looking around the inner western suburbs.

'Where?' Jess frowned.

'Places like Leichhardt, or Erskineville, though they're a little out of our price range.'

'That's the other side of the bridge,' said Josh darkly. 'It's friggin' miles away.' He got up and walked towards the doorway.

'Josh . . .'

'This sucks, Mum,' he muttered, leaving the room. A minute later they heard his door slam upstairs.

Sam looked back at Jess. She was scowling. 'So I'm just supposed to leave all my friends?'

That didn't seem to bother her when she thought they were moving to Bondi.

'You'll make new friends –'

'Oh right, with tea-towel heads?'

'What?'

'Tea-towel heads. Mussos. Wogs. Whatever you want to call them.'

'I don't want to call them any such thing!' Sam exclaimed. 'Don't speak like that in my house, Jessica!'

'It's not *your* house, Mum!' she shrilled, standing up. 'If it was your house, then we wouldn't have to move!' She stormed off. They heard her silly rubber scuffs thwacking on the stairs as she ran up to her bedroom.

'Well,' Max sighed. 'That went well.'

Sam looked at her. 'I can't believe a child of mine is a racist. I didn't teach her to be racist.'

'But did you teach her anything different?'

'What do you mean?'

'All your friends and their friends are white middle class. Not that there's anything wrong with that. But they haven't known any different.'

'Well I can't stand that she thinks like that,' Sam said determinedly. 'The move will do them good.'

Sunday

'Have you got a minute?' said Jeff, wavering at the front door when he dropped the children home.

Oh, what now?

'I guess,' Sam answered vaguely.

'Let's walk?' he suggested. 'You know, out of earshot.'

Sam looked at him. What was this about? 'Okay.'

She pulled the door closed and stepped off the porch. They strolled along the grassy kerb past a couple of houses, not saying anything. He seemed to be deep in thought. Sam decided to prompt him. 'What did you want to talk about, Jeff?'

He hesitated. 'The kids told me about your plans.'

She nodded. 'I wasn't keeping them from you.'

'I know that.' He paused, rubbing the back of his neck. Something was making him uncomfortable. 'They're not very happy, I guess you realise that. They asked me to talk to you.'

Sam frowned. 'What do you want to say?'

'Is there something we can work out about the money? Maybe you could stay in the house.'

She looked at him. 'What, indefinitely? You can afford that?'

'Not indefinitely. But . . .'

'Jeff, the older two are going to be disrupted whenever I make the move, but Ellie starts school next year. I'd like to be settled before then.'

He nodded. 'Well, why can't you stay in the area, perhaps just move to a smaller house?'

Sam began to frame a response in her head and then something stopped her. 'Listen Jeff, would you like me to start dictating to you where you should live?'

By the look on his face she could tell he hadn't been expecting her to say that.

'You made a choice, all by yourself, that turned our lives upside down. You can't expect it won't have an impact and that things won't change. And you don't have a say any more.'

'Did I ever?'

'What's that supposed to mean?'

'Well, you made all the choices about where we lived, Sam, I just went along, kept the peace.'

'Bully for you! Do you want a medal for being husband of the year?'

'I'm just saying that some of those choices were the problem,' he tried to explain. 'Always the next biggest thing, never being satisfied with where we were. Playing into all that materialist crap that once we had the perfect house in the perfect street we'd be happy.'

'Keep your voice down, Jeff!' Sam hissed, conscious of the neighbours. 'What are you trying to say?' she continued in a lower voice. 'People who live in big houses can't be happy? That's a pretty simplistic argument, Jeff. Something your hippie girlfriend came up with?'

He ignored that. 'I'm just saying it might have been better for us if we'd slowed down, lived more simply maybe.'

Sam faced him squarely. 'Then you shouldn't have a problem with what I'm going to do.'

The argument had come full circle. She could see by the look on Jeff's face that he understood.

'I'll talk to the kids.' He paused. 'I'll tell them it'll be okay.'

Two weeks later

'This is a great idea, Rose,' Max declared, after the waiter had left with their orders.

'I know,' she exclaimed. 'Isn't it?'

Rosemary had organised for them to meet for brunch at the Bathers Pavilion at Balmoral Beach, and they were seated at a table with a view directly to the water. Only Fiona was unable to make it. She didn't like to leave Gavin with the kids on the weekend. She'd been working back a lot lately, she said it didn't seem fair. It was unusual for Fiona to be quite so sensitive to Gavin's needs, but the girls could hardly argue with her.

'I don't know why I never thought of this before,' Rosemary continued. 'I hardly get to come out with you guys other times, but Col's always out on his boat Sundays. He couldn't care less where I was, as long as dinner's on the table tonight.'

She grinned happily, oblivious to the shadow that passed across the faces of the other women.

'I always think going out for breakfast is so 1960s, Audrey Hepburn, don't you think?' said Liz, from behind a very large pair of dark glasses.

'Is that the reason for the Jackie O sunglasses?' asked Max.

'No, Michael and I went out with a couple of friends last night and I had a little too much of some damn fine wine. Do you know if they serve bloody marys here?'

'How was dinner, anyway?' Sam asked. 'Is Tetsuya's as good as they say?'

'Better,' Liz said plainly. 'You should have come, I told you.'

'Mm,' Sam frowned. 'Because we all know how much fun it is playing the third wheel.'

'In this case you would have been the fifth wheel,' Liz corrected her.

'The maths is the same. I'd still be the odd one out.'

'But if you'd accepted, we were thinking of asking this guy from Michael's work –'

'Well, thank God I turned you down,' said Sam. 'I've told you before, I don't want to be set up.'

'She's right Liz. Blind dates suck,' Max agreed. 'You could have asked Hal though.'

'Who's Hal?' Liz sat up, suddenly alert.

'Max!' Sam frowned. 'He's just a client,' she dismissed.

'A client who takes Josh to the football every second weekend,' Max informed them. 'Who calls in for coffee and stays for dinner –'

'Once,' Sam insisted. 'Or . . . twice maybe.'

'And,' Max continued undaunted, 'they even went house-hunting together.'

'What!' Liz and Rosemary almost shrieked at once.

'He just came along for moral support,' Sam explained. 'Max, stop giving them ideas.'

'What's he like?' Liz said eagerly.

'Too late,' Sam groaned.

'He's very good-looking,' Max started. 'Tall, with blue eyes –'

'They're green actually,' Sam interrupted.

'Right, and he's "just a client", eh Sam?' Max pulled a face. 'Oh and he's got the square jaw thing going. Very tasty.'

'Ooh, I love a strong jaw,' said Rosemary. 'Like John Travolta's.'

'No, I think his is a bit much,' Max mused. 'I'd rather Brad Pitt's. Or whatsisname, the guy from that new legal show, you know, he was in that movie with George Clooney. Now there's a jaw.'

'I heard he's gay,' said Liz.

'Who? George Clooney?' asked Rosemary, startled.

'No! The other one.'

'Oh, don't tell me that!' she protested. 'Every second guy's supposed to be gay. Who's left for a girl to fantasise about?'

'Well, I don't know about jaws. I like bums.'

They all looked at Liz.

'Nice, hard, high-set bums. What's this Hal's bum like?'

'I have no idea!' Sam declared.

'Why not?'

'Because I haven't looked,' she lied.

'Sam! It'll be a year come Spring since you broke up with Jeff!' Liz exclaimed. 'When are you going to start looking?'

'When I'm good and ready,' she returned. 'Don't you think I've got enough on my plate at the moment? Between the kids and looking for a house and coping with a new job, not to mention an ex who suddenly wants to be involved in his children's lives,' she took a breath. 'Who has time for a relationship?'

'Don't have a relationship,' Max said plainly. 'Have a fling. Hal is so flingable,' she added for the benefit of the others.

'So what happened to "he's way out of my league" and I should be careful not to get my heart broken?' Sam asked Max.

'I've revised my position,' she said.

'Since when?'

'Since he started hanging around so much. I think he might have his eye on you after all, Sam. And you could do worse. A lot worse,' she winked at the girls.

'As I keep telling you, Hal is a client.' Max mimed the words as Sam spoke them. She ignored her. 'He also lives on the other side of the world –'

'How's that?' Liz frowned.

'He's from the States,' Sam explained. 'He's only out here on a temporary contract.'

'What's the problem then?' said Liz.

'What do you mean?'

'You said you don't want a relationship, didn't you?'

'That's right, you did,' Rosemary chimed in.

'So if he's not staying in the country . . .'

'You don't have to worry about it turning into anything serious,' Max finished.

'Have some fun,' Liz urged. 'Have a fling like Max said, and then say, "So long, bud, thanks for the memories".'

'Well, um . . .' She had to put a stop to this. 'The thing is, Hal is not . . . available, as such.'

'I knew there had to be something,' said Max triumphantly.

'Is he married?' Liz asked.

'No.'

'Don't tell me he's gay!' Rosemary said, defeated.

'No, he's not gay.'

'Come on then, out with it,' Max urged.

'I'm not at liberty to say, you'll just have to take my word for it, Hal is not available,' said Sam. 'Oh, here comes breakfast.'

'Don't change the subject.'

'No really, here's our food.'

Two waiters fluttered around them for the next few minutes, until they all had juice, coffee and platter-sized dishes jostling for space on the table.

'This is delicious,' said Sam, tucking into her eggs.

'Mind you, anything cooked by someone else always tastes better,' said Rosemary.

'I reckon,' Sam agreed.

'Oh no you don't,' said Max.

'Don't I?'

'You're not leaving us hanging with "he's not available", thanks very much.'

'I'm not saying another word,' Sam said, pointing her fork in the air for emphasis. 'It's none of your business and, besides, it's extremely personal.'

The girls all put their glasses down simultaneously and scraped their chairs, bringing them in closer to the table.

'No,' Sam insisted. 'I'm not telling.'

'Why not?'

'Because my clients have to be able to trust that I'll protect their confidentiality.'

'Come on, Sam,' Liz retorted. 'It's us. You're not giving the story to the papers. We'll never tell, we don't even know him.'

'Max does.'

'What?' she blinked. 'I won't say anything. Do you think I'm going to blurt "Oh, I heard your wife cut off your penis" next time I see him?'

'Is that what happened?' Rosemary exclaimed, wide-eyed.

'Of course not!' Sam groaned. Their imaginations were even worse than the truth. She put down her fork and dabbed her mouth with a napkin. 'You promise me you won't breathe a word to another living soul?'

'Of course not!'

'Never.'

'Promise.'

They all craned in closer to hear.

Sam took a deep breath, and paused, looking around the table at their eager faces. 'Oh, I don't think this is right –'

'*SAM!*'

'Okay! Hal broke up with his wife because she had an

abortion without telling him.' Sam said it quickly so it almost didn't count.

'No shit,' Liz murmured.

Max sat back in her chair. 'Well, hold on, we don't know the whole story. It's her body, her right.'

Liz tilted her head, thinking. 'I don't know about that. I mean, I fully support a woman's right to choose and all. But it was his baby too. Doesn't he have some rights?'

'At least to be told,' Rosemary nodded.

'Maybe she didn't want a baby and he did, and she had no other way out,' Max suggested.

'That's not what happened at all.'

They all looked back at Sam.

'What else do you know?' Max narrowed her eyes.

At this point it was hardly worth keeping the rest of the story from them. 'The thing is, she didn't know whose baby it was.'

No one said anything for a while, they just stared at the food on their plates.

'Poor bugger,' Liz said, breaking the silence.

'Why does shit always happen to nice people?' Max pondered. 'It doesn't seem fair.'

Rosemary looked a little bewildered. 'I'm not sure if I've missed something. Why isn't he available?'

'D'oh,' Max groaned. 'He's nursing a broken heart, of course.'

'Oh, poor man,' Rosemary said wistfully.

'Let's not take up a collection just yet,' said Liz. 'I bet he's still getting his end in.'

Sam shot a look at her. 'That is such a disgusting expression. Why would you say that?'

'He's a guy. You know how it is, they can't survive without sex.'

'That's a myth perpetrated by men,' Max drawled. '"Oh, you don't understand, if I don't have sex at least every three days, I'll explode from the build up of sperm in my system." What a crock.'

'Well,' said Liz, 'if he's spreading his sorry tale around, he'd have women falling over themselves –'

'Seduction by sympathy,' Max nodded. 'Works like a charm.'

'I don't think he'd do that,' Sam bristled. 'It was very painful for him to even speak about it.'

'So how come he told you?' asked Liz.

Sam shrugged. 'To shut me up, I suspect. I was being nosy, asking too many questions.'

'There's a reason I nicknamed you Sherlock,' Max nodded.

'God, Sam,' said Liz. 'I just realised, you mustn't have had sex for like, a year.'

'Thereabouts.'

Max sat up straight. 'Why don't you and Hal –'

'Max!'

'What?' She looked squarely at Sam. 'You're both consenting adults. And it sounds like you have a very honest, open thing going. Why not be upfront about this?'

'What are you suggesting? That I say, Hal, I haven't had sex for a while. Would you mind?'

'I bet you fifty bucks you wouldn't get a knockback,' Liz grinned.

'Would you actually say that to a guy?' Sam demanded.

'I would say, and I have said,' Max returned calmly, '"I think there's something going on between us, would you be interested in taking it further?"'

'My sister the tart.'

'I'd rather be a tart than a nun.'

Sam decided not to respond to that, in fact to leave the whole conversation behind. 'These eggs Florentine are to die for.'

'You're changing the subject again.'

'I'll have to start calling you Einstein.'

Thursday

Sam was currently reading *Great Expectations* to Ted after he discovered she had never read the Dickens classic before. She could only vaguely recall the old black and white film with the graveyard scene at the very beginning, which quite frankly had given her the creeps. She didn't remember the Miss Haversham character, she probably hadn't made it that far. But now Sam was fascinated by the pathetic old woman still dressed in the wedding finery she had been wearing when she was jilted at the altar, sitting forlornly at the wedding breakfast, the table covered in cobwebs and run over by mice.

'It's a little incredible, don't you think, Ted?' Sam commented.

'What do you mean, Samantha?'

'I'm just wondering what's going on in her mind. I mean, she's independently wealthy. So what if the jerk left her at the altar, life goes on.'

'Ah, but Samantha, you must remember that in her time women had no status unless they were married. She could have been the richest woman in England, but until she became somebody's wife she was a nobody. It's not like it is today.'

Sam wondered if it was all that different.

'Look at yourself,' he continued. 'You're bringing up those children all on your own and no one thinks any the less of you.'

'Oh, there are still a few outdated attitudes hanging around, let me assure you, Ted.'

'Are there, Samantha?' Ted seemed concerned. 'Have you experienced anything like that?'

'A little.'

'Such as?'

'Well, recently I had to bring a male friend along when I was looking for houses so I would be taken seriously.' Sam smiled lamely. 'I'm not so sure it worked though. It seems I can only afford the worst house in the worst street in the worst suburb.'

Ted looked crestfallen. 'Oh dear, Samantha. Is there anything I can do to help?'

Sam realised he was taking her possibly a little too literally. He was such a kind man, she didn't want to alarm him.

'I'm sorry, Ted, I'm exaggerating. I just have to do my homework. I'm sure I'll find something.'

'I know some people in real estate around here,' Ted offered.

'Oh, thanks Ted. But this area is way beyond me.'

'But they would have colleagues all over Sydney,' he insisted. 'Will you allow me to make some calls on your behalf?'

Sam hesitated. 'It's very kind of you, Ted, but you shouldn't be doing favours for me.'

He looked genuinely surprised. 'But why not? You do nothing but favours for me.'

'But that's my job. You pay me.'

Ted considered her. 'Well Samantha, what if we make a deal? I'll make a few calls for you, and you could do a favour for me in return.'

'Once again, Ted, "favours" are what I'm paid to do.'

'This is extra.'

Sam was curious. 'Go ahead.'

Ted sat back in his armchair. 'You know I have a son who lives in the UK?'

Sam nodded. Although she dealt with all of his private correspondence, she had never seen so much as a postcard from his son, and she worried that there had been some kind of rift. She couldn't imagine Ted in conflict with anyone, but who knew the things that went on inside families? It was certainly not unheard of for children to bite the hand that had once fed them.

'My son and I talk on the telephone every few weeks, which is an absolute delight,' Ted explained.

Sam was relieved.

'But he is obsessed with email, he's constantly sending me snippets of conversation. It's quite extraordinary.'

'He's not alone, Ted,' Sam smiled. 'It seems to be the preferred mode of communication these days, along with SMS messaging.'

'Well, I'm not even going to ask what that is,' said Ted. 'The thing is, Samantha, until recently I was able to enlarge the font so that I could still read it, but it's becoming tiresome. I'm scrolling one or two words across the screen at a time and, well, it spoils the flow, you can imagine. And replying has become a nightmare.' He paused. 'I've tried to manage myself because, I'm sure you understand, he's my son, I wanted to keep it between the two of us.'

Sam knew what he was getting at. 'Ted, nothing would make me happier than scribing for you to your son. But why don't you just tell him you can't read it and talk more often on the phone instead?'

Ted looked sheepish. 'He doesn't know about my condition, Samantha. And I don't want him to know. He'll only worry. I'm managing very well, as you know, but he would imagine it was far worse than it is.'

Pride would be a factor too, but Sam didn't begrudge him that.

'Well then, we have some emails needing a reply,' she said briskly. 'We'd better get on with it, if you feel we're quite finished with Mr Dickens for today?'

Ted smiled at her warmly, and Sam wished she was doing so much more to deserve the depth of appreciation she could see in his eyes.

July

Sam raced inside from hanging clothes on the line and just made it to the phone before the machine kicked in.

'Samantha? Sheila.' Her boss was always a little abrupt. Sam wondered how she had ever got into this line of work. She couldn't imagine Sheila showing the kind of congeniality her clients seemed to appreciate.

'I've been checking your time sheets,' Sheila continued. 'Do you realise you haven't claimed anything for Mr Buchanan since April?'

'Uh huh,' Sam confirmed, catching her breath.

'Well, what's going on?'

'Nothing,' she said defensively. 'Nothing's going on.'

'Then why haven't you recorded time spent?'

'Well,' Sam hesitated. 'I just, I haven't done much for him for a while.'

'This doesn't make any sense, Sam. I've just been reading a feedback questionnaire from Mr Buchanan, full of praise for you.'

'What feedback questionnaire?'

'Oh, we send them out from time to time. Client feedback is vital to us. I mean, this business is all about keeping clients happy. They're the only ones who can tell us if we're succeeding.'

'Oh, sure,' Sam murmured. 'I just wasn't aware you did that.'

'Well, you don't have anything to worry about, Samantha. I've received some excellent feedback from your clients.'

'You have?'

'Absolutely,' she declared. 'I didn't expect it from you when you first came into the office, I thought you might be a little precious. But it seems that everyone adores you. Mr Dempsey even wants to increase his subscription, you'll be getting a pay rise.'

'Oh no.' Sam was going to have to take this up with him. 'Ted's an absolute pleasure to work for. I couldn't accept more money from him.'

'Customer's always right, Samantha,' Sheila dismissed. 'Now, what about Mr Buchanan?'

'Well, um,' Sam was taken aback. 'What did he tell you?'

'He's ticked excellent in every box on the questionnaire. And in the space for comment at the end he wrote . . .' she paused. Sam could hear the shuffling of papers. 'Oh, yes, here it is. "Ms Holmes is professional, thorough and tireless. She has been an enormous help as I've acclimatised to a new country, I couldn't have got by these past few months without her invaluable assistance."'

Sam was blushing. There was no one around to hear what Sheila had just said, but she was blushing nonetheless.

'He's American,' she said in a small voice. 'You know how they exaggerate.'

'Well, whatever, you must have done something to earn such high praise.'

'It hasn't been that much —'

'Samantha, this is not only for your sake. IGB is a huge client, and they generally review the service every year. If I don't show that the hours they have already paid for are being used by the client, they may decide their money could be spent in better ways.'

'Sorry. What do you want me to do?'

'Look over your records for the last few months, work out the hours you've spent on Mr Buchanan. Anything and every-thing, and don't forget phone calls. It's obviously meant a lot to him, whatever you've been doing. You should be getting paid for it.'

Sam sat staring at her index card for Hal. She hadn't touched it since the emails had arrived in April. She'd simply recorded the date and next to it the words '*Contact restored!!!*', in what now looked like a rather over-excited hand. She sighed. How could she bill Hal for coming house-hunting? Or for taking Josh to the football? Or for the phone calls he'd made to see how things were going for her? It didn't seem right. She had to do some-thing for him for a change. She picked up the phone and dialled his direct number at work.

'Hal Buchanan.'

'Hi, Hal, it's me, Samantha Holmes.'

'Hey Sam.' His tone softened instantly. 'How're you doing?'

She smiled. He still hadn't picked up 'How are you going', but Sam decided she liked the way he said it. 'I'm fine, thanks. But listen, I've just been talking to my boss, and she told me all the lies you've been spreading about me.'

'What lies?'

'About everything I've supposedly been doing for you. You didn't have to say all that, Hal.'

'But it's true. I asked to be acclimatised and you've been doing a fine job.'

'Oh sure,' Sam said dubiously. 'Letting you take my son to the football, dragging you around house-hunting . . .'

'Ah now, but that had a purpose, didn't it? You should hear me these days when the conversation turns to real estate.'

'Oh yeah? What do you say?'

'That it's overpriced.'

Sam grinned. 'I believe you had that figured out before.'

'Mm, but now I can say it with authority.'

'Well, my boss is expecting me to put in revised time sheets claiming the time spent with you.'

'So?'

'It doesn't feel right.'

'Sam, it's not coming out of my pocket. Who keeps the money if you don't claim it?'

'The business, I guess.'

'So knock yourself out.'

'I just wanted you to know.' She hesitated. 'And to say thanks.'

'You're very welcome.'

'And now you have to let me do something for you.'

'Oh? What do you have in mind?'

'I don't know, Hal. You have to help me out here. There must be something you want?'

'But you told me sex wasn't part of the deal?'

'Hal!' Sam exclaimed. She knew she was blushing now.

'Gotcha,' he laughed. 'Okay, okay, let me think. What's a quintessential Australian day out?'

'What do you mean?'

'Quintessential means . . .'

'I know what *quintessential* means. But what do you mean by a quintessential Australian day out?'

'That's what I was asking you. What did you do on a day out when you were a kid, for example?'

Sam thought about it. They didn't have those kinds of days out when she was a child. Her mother usually worked on weekends and she palmed the three girls off to their grandparents in the school holidays. Picnics and outings were for kids with fathers.

'I'll have a think about it,' said Sam eventually, flipping through her diary. 'The kids are with their father this weekend, are you free Saturday?'

'Let me just check,' he said slowly. 'You wouldn't believe the women I have begging to take me out. You know, being handsome and single and straight in this city is such a burden.'

Sam smiled. 'I've created a monster.'

'Turns out you're in luck. Saturday's fine.'

'Then I'll pick you up, say around ten?'

'I'll look forward to it.'

Saturday

Sam pulled up in front of Hal's apartment block a few minutes after ten, but at least he was waiting for her now. She'd already driven around the block twice after arriving early and having no chance of finding a park. She didn't know how people lived in the middle of the city. She hoped it wasn't going to be an issue when she moved. 'Garage' was on her list of desirables but she had better add 'Parking' at least to her essentials.

'Hey Sam,' he smiled, climbing into the car. 'So, where are we headed?'

Sam pulled off up the street. 'Well, you were after a typical Australian day out, am I correct?'

'That's right.'

'Okay, the first thing you have to understand is that it's not a proper day out unless you drive a long way.'

'Oh?'

'Australians are happy to drive the distance on a weekend that most Europeans would only travel on their holidays. The maxim seems to be the further you go, the better time you'll have.'

'So, where are you taking me?' he asked suspiciously. 'Mom will worry if I'm not home before nightfall.'

Sam grinned. 'Just up the coast a little way. There's a place I used to visit when I was little.'

'You're still little.'

She looked sideways at him. 'Younger then.'

'So what did you do at this place up the coast when you were younger?'

'We spent a lot of time at the beach, naturally. Any authentic Australian experience has to include the beach.'

'The beach?'

Sam nodded. 'The myth is that we all live outback in the bush, but hardly any of us do. Twenty million people, fewer than in New York I think, and we're all loitering around the shore, dipping our toes in the water. You want a classic Australian day out, then you need to get sunburnt, dumped in the surf till your cossies are full of sand, dragged out by a rip and dragged back in by a lifesaver. Oh, and stung by a bluebottle.'

'I didn't understand half of what you just said. What's a bluebottle?'

'I think it's some kind of jellyfish, I'm not really sure exactly. But it's only small, and it looks like a transparent blue plastic bag with tentacles hanging off it. And it stings like buggery.'

'What?'

'They entangle themselves around your limbs, and when you try to pull them off, they grip tighter, and get tangled up in your fingers, and they keep on stinging.'

'Is it bad?'

Sam looked at Hal's pained expression. 'They can't kill you or anything. They just hurt like hell. It feels like an electric shock. When I was a girl they used to sponge you down with vinegar, or paint you all over with this blue stuff if you were stung. Now the treatment may be a little more sophisticated.'

She sighed. 'But summer's not really summer without one decent bluebottle infestation.'

Hal was shaking his head. 'Honestly, you Australians are crazy. You've got poisonous snakes and spiders and deadly things in the water, and yet you blithely carry on as though they're not there.'

'No we don't. We take the proper precautions.'

He glanced at her dubiously. 'I was at the beach one day when I first arrived in the country. Not swimming, just looking. Anyway, a siren sounded and everyone got out of the water. I asked someone nearby what was going on –'

'It would have been a shark alarm.'

'That's what they told me,' Hal nodded. 'Then after a little bit, the alarm sounded again and everyone went straight back into the water. I'm saying you're all crazy.'

Sam laughed. 'There are hardly ever any sharks.'

'Sorry, "hardly ever" is too often for me.'

'So I take it you don't go to the beach much?'

He shook his head. 'You don't swim in the ocean in the States. Not where I come from.'

'Why not?'

'It's too cold.'

'So do you swim at all?'

'Sure. I spent all my summers as a boy at the lake.'

'But you grew up here?'

'Just till I was seven. For the rest of my childhood we went to the lake.'

'I don't like swimming in lakes and rivers,' said Sam, turning up her nose.

'Why not?'

'Well, you don't know what's under there. There could be all kinds of creepy-crawlies.'

Hal shook his head. 'At least there are no man-eating sharks or blue-tentacled creatures that give you an electric shock.'

'Or box jellyfish,' Sam added. 'Step on one of them and you're dead in a few minutes. Then there's the blue-ringed octopus, the crown-of-thorns starfish . . . oh, and I was reading about this new one they've discovered. I can't remember its name, but it's only the size of a peanut, and if its tentacles so much as brush against your skin, you end up in hospital.'

Hal was looking at her in horror.

'You don't have to worry,' she grinned. 'They're only found up the top end, and only at certain times of the year.'

'Are we going to the beach today?' he asked dubiously.

'Just for a walk,' she assured him. 'I wouldn't take you swimming in the middle of winter.'

He shook his head. 'Winter in Sydney. It's a bit of a joke, isn't it?'

'Why? It gets cold.'

'You people don't know the meaning of the word cold.' He looked out the window into the bright blue sky. They were just crossing the Harbour Bridge. The water was flecked fluorescent from the sunshine. 'Just look at this beautiful day. It has no business calling itself winter.'

Sam glanced out across the harbour. The sky was clear to the horizon, there wasn't a cloud in sight. She should have hung out a few loads of washing before she left.

What was that? When had a clear, cloudless day only come to mean a good drying day? Or a good day for airing the doonas, or washing the floor? When had she become such a boring, joyless person?

'What is it?' asked Hal.

She looked at him.

'You're frowning.'

'Oh, I didn't mean to,' she said, breaking into a smile. 'I was just thinking, it really is a beautiful day.'

They talked easily as they drove out of the city, eventually joining the expressway north. Hal had never really told Sam much about his home, and she was intrigued. There was a perception that Americans were ignorant about Australia, which was probably true, but Sam was embarrassed to admit that her own perceptions of America were shaped largely by what she saw in the movies or on TV. New York was full of wisecracking thirty-somethings who spent a lot of time in each other's apartments or in coffee shops. And the mob lived over, was it the Brooklyn Bridge? Chicago had Oprah, and apparently a lot of hospitals, given that so many medical dramas seemed to be set there. Boston was full of lawyers and LA was Movieworld. She didn't know where Vermont was, which was where Hal's family had settled on their return from Australia. He explained it was between New York state and New Hampshire in the New England region. At least Sam knew that meant the east coast. It snowed in the wintertime and it was nowhere near the ocean, Hal added, which was why he was not accustomed to swimming in one.

The conversation flowed without effort. It was actually a pleasant experience to be driving along, chatting amiably with another adult. Usually when they had travelled anywhere as a family it had been an ordeal, shouting above the kids to stop them fighting, or bickering over directions or bad driving habits. Sam didn't like the way Jeff drove right up the back of other cars, or his obsession with overtaking, or that he was a bit elastic with the speed limit. And he didn't like her pointing out any of those things.

Sam turned off the freeway at the Gosford exit and followed the winding road that would take them to the coast. She had done this trip at the start of almost every school holiday when she was growing up. Her mother didn't like the road and refused to drive on it, so Pop would come down to pick them up. Nan never came, and Pop never stayed over at their house. He'd stop for lunch, stretch his legs, but he wouldn't linger more than an hour or so. It became clear to the girls as they grew older that their mother and her parents didn't really get along, but they didn't delve into it. Sam and Max thought they were the luckiest children alive to be able to spend their holidays in the little green cottage in Taloumbi, so they asked no questions.

They only spent Easter and part of the Christmas holidays together at home. And that was more than enough. Bernice Driscoll thought holidays were best spent on projects around the house. They cleaned windows, washed curtains and blinds, stripped and polished floors, cleared out cupboards. Maxine hated it with a passion and put more energy into avoiding than doing. Alex usually had school assignments and, later on, part-time work at the local supermarket. Sam was her mother's mainstay, and she had to admit she found the whole exercise strangely satisfying, which was probably a bit odd for such a young girl.

Alex stopped coming to Taloumbi after a few years when she decided she was old enough to look after herself during the school break, thank you very much. Bernice didn't argue with her eldest daughter. Even then no one argued with Alex. Certainly not Sam and Max. Alex bossed them around even more at Nan's, overseeing how many scones they ate and what time they went to bed. It was much more fun without her.

They lost Pop the year Sam turned fifteen, and Nan the year she turned sixteen. The first holiday she spent at home she started going out with Jeff.

As they approached the town centre of Taloumbi, Sam started to feel the same sense of anticipation she had as a girl. She hadn't been here since before she was married, so she shouldn't have been surprised that the quiet little village had turned into a busy shopping centre. But it made her a little sad. She had always meant to bring the children to show them the place but she had never got around to it. It probably wouldn't mean that much to them anyway, it was just a little green-painted fibro house on a big, wide, flat block of land, a stone's throw from the beach.

'It's not far now,' she told Hal. 'I used to spend all my holidays up here when I was a girl.'

'Oh? Did your family have a place here?'

Sam shook her head. 'My grandparents lived here. My mother had to work full-time after my father left, so they looked after my sisters and me in the school holidays.' She glanced across at Hal who looked as though he wasn't sure what he should say. 'Don't worry, they were the happiest times of my childhood.'

Sam had checked a map at home to make sure she would remember where to go, which was just as well because the area had changed considerably. There were many more blocks of flats and flashy houses, but Dolphin Parade was still where it had always been. It was a long street stretching from the main thoroughfare all the way to the beach. Sam drove slowly – she hardly had a choice considering the obstacle course of speed humps and roundabouts she had to negotiate. After a while she began to feel uneasy. There was one block of flats after another; she couldn't imagine the dear little green house sitting there all alone, overshadowed by its neighbours.

Sam steered around the final roundabout. This was the last stretch of road before the beach. She scanned ahead, looking for a gap between the buildings. She pulled up where number seven should have been. But there wasn't even a number '7' any more. There were only the words *Bella Vista* in black iron curlicues on the front of a blonde-brick three-storey block of flats. Sam stared at it, uncomprehending. She blinked, hoping that when she opened her eyes the green house would be sitting there again. She was unaware that Hal had said her name a couple of times. She only remembered he was there at all when she felt his hand on hers, still clutching the steering wheel. It gave her a start, and she looked at him for a moment without really seeing him. She turned away and got out of the car, leaving the door open as she hurried down the road towards the beach.

'Sam!'

She stopped at the street sign at the corner and stared at it, the letters burning into her eyes. Dolphin Parade. She hadn't made a mistake. So where was the house?

Hal caught up to her as she started back up the street again. He grabbed her by the arm. She looked at him, startled.

'Sam, you left the car running,' he said, holding the keys. 'What's wrong, what's the matter?'

'I can't find Nan's house,' she said tearfully, pulling away and running back up to where it should have been. She stopped for a moment, breathless, out the front of *Bella Vista*. Then she started down the driveway.

'Sam!' Hal had followed her. He caught her arm again and swung her around. 'You're sure this is the right street?'

She nodded, blinking back tears, the ache in the back of her throat making it hard to speak.

Hal held both her arms gently. She looked like a bewildered little girl. He barely had the heart to say anything. 'Then the house is gone, Sam,' he said quietly. 'It must have been pulled down a long time ago.'

She looked at him for a while as the truth dawned on her. 'I have to call my mother,' she said, breaking away from him and heading back to the car. She opened the door and reached across to her bag for her mobile. She dialled the number and leaned on the car, waiting for it to connect. Hal stayed back, propped against the brick fence of *Bella Vista*.

She heard her mother's voice. 'Hello?'

'Mum, it's Sam.'

'Oh, Samantha. I can't hear you very well, it's a bad connection. Where are you calling from? Are you on the mobile?'

'I'm in Taloumbi.'

'You're calling from Taloumbi on your mobile? It'll cost you a fortune.'

'Mum,' Sam interrupted brusquely. 'What happened to Nan and Pop's place?'

'Why, I sold it. Years ago.'

Sam breathed out heavily. 'Why didn't you tell me?'

'I'm sure I did –'

'No, you didn't,' Sam said firmly. 'You never told me anything about it.'

'Well, it was right around the time you were getting married, you probably don't remember.'

'You never told me!' she insisted sharply. 'I would remember.'

'Fair enough, if you say so. Why did you want to know anyway?'

Sam paused, catching her breath. 'I drove up to see it today, for old times' sake.'

She heard her mother chuckle. 'Honestly Samantha, you

always were sentimental. If it had still been standing it would have been such a dump by now.'

'So you knew they were going to pull it down?'

'Of course! What else would they do with a little fibro shack, especially on such a prime block of land. We sold it to a developer for quite a tidy sum. Some of it paid for your wedding.'

Well, wasn't that a bitter fucking irony.

'Sam, are you there? I think I must be losing you.'

For some reason, Sam didn't say anything.

'She must have dropped out,' her mother muttered to herself. Then she hung up. Sam sighed heavily and turned off the phone in case she tried to ring back. Not that her mother would ever do that, it would be too expensive.

Sam glanced over towards Hal. God, he must think she was cracked. She should never have brought him here. And now she was going to have to do the right thing and see this day out when all she felt like doing was crawling under a rock.

She dropped the phone back into her bag and reached for a tissue. When she turned around again Hal was wandering slowly over to her, his hands thrust in his pockets.

'Are you okay?'

She nodded, mustering a smile. 'Let me assure you, the quintessential day out does not usually involve a woman having a loony attack. That's an optional extra.'

'You had a bit of a shock,' he said. 'It's understandable.'

Oh, don't be nice. If he was nice, she was going to burst into tears, she just knew it.

'Did you find out what happened?' he asked.

Sam nodded. 'My mother sold it to a developer to help pay for my wedding. Talk about throwing good money after bad!' she scoffed. She was trying to lift the mood but Hal just looked sadly at her. Shit.

'I just don't understand why everything has to change,' Sam sighed. 'Why some things can't stay the same.'

'They call it progress,' he said ruefully.

'Who says?'

'I'm sorry?'

'When we're little we don't want to throw out the old, we cling to it,' Sam said testily. 'Old teddies, raggedy blankets, we cherish what's familiar. We love it despite it being old and tatty, perhaps even because of it. And then somewhere along the way we're taught to believe that new is better, younger is more attractive. We discard people as though they had a use-by date.'

Sam realised she'd been tearing her tissue up savagely as she spoke. What the hell was she going on about? She glanced up at Hal. He still had that sympathetic expression on his face. God, he must think she was loopy.

'This isn't much of a day out for you,' she said.

'Don't worry about me.' He leaned back against the car next to her and folded his arms. 'Would you rather go home?'

Sam shook her head. It was hardly fair on Hal to drag him all the way up here only to turn around and go home again. And he was being so decent about it all. She looked down the street to the beach. At least it hadn't changed. 'Do you want to go for a walk?'

'Sure.'

They strolled slowly down to the end of the road.

'You must have been very close to your grandparents,' said Hal after a while.

Sam nodded. 'Coming here was the most normal family experience we had. I have such fond memories of the house. It was just a simple little cottage, but . . .' she sighed. 'My mother thought it was nothing but an old shack. She didn't really see eye to eye with her parents. But we loved them. I named Ellie after Nan.'

They came to the track through the sandhills that would take them to the beach.

'And your grandfather?' Hal prompted Sam to continue.

'Oh, we adored Pop. I used to follow him around the entire time, but he didn't seem to mind. I think he may have enjoyed it.'

'I'm sure he did.'

They came to an octagonal viewing platform set on the crest of the sandhills. There were signs with information about the dune regeneration project being undertaken along the beach, the reason the track was cordoned off.

'Max and I used to play hide and seek in these dunes. And then when we got a little older, we'd hide and watch the guys when they came out of the surf. They'd do these really complicated manoeuvres with their towels wrapped around them, getting their boardshorts or wetsuits off and dry clothes on. We used to watch, hoping we'd see something, but if we ever had, I'm sure we would have died.'

Hal smiled.

'Coming from an all-female household made us overly curious and incredibly naïve. Boys were a mystery, like another species. It was quite an education having one of my own, let me tell you.'

'When did your father leave?'

'Just after Maxine was born. I was only three, I don't really remember him.'

'You never saw him again?'

Sam shook her head. She didn't like talking about her father. Most of the time she forgot she even had one.

They continued down the track towards the sand.

'I love the beach,' said Sam. 'It takes me back to being a kid. You know, carefree, no responsibilities. I've always said if I ever won the lottery, I'd go lie on a beach somewhere for a month.'

'I can't imagine you doing that,' said Hal.

She looked at him. 'Why not?'

'I don't know,' he shrugged. 'I can't see you staying put for that long. You're always so busy.'

Sam smiled. 'I'd like to give it a go. See what it'd be like to have nothing to do for a while.'

They had reached the shore and Sam stooped to untie her sneakers. Hal did the same. She stepped forward to test the water.

'Oh my God! It's freezing,' she gasped.

Hal followed her. 'It's not cold,' he scoffed. 'It's . . .'

Sam looked at him expectantly.

'Bracing,' he finished.

They continued along the shoreline, their feet sinking in the damp sand, leaving a trail of footprints. Sam remembered walking along with Max in single file behind Pop, stepping in his footprints. When they were little they used to have to leap from one to the next to match his strides.

'So you had a pretty idyllic childhood?' Sam asked Hal after a while.

'What makes you say that?'

She shrugged. 'Oh, I don't know. Summers by the lake, skiing in the winter. Sounds not bad to me.'

Hal chuckled.

'What?'

'Australians have some funny ways of expressing themselves. You say "not bad" when you mean something's good, and "not too good" when something's bad.'

'It's so we can never be accused of overstating anything. So, how was your childhood?' she asked pointedly.

'Not bad,' he quipped.

'Any brothers or sisters?'

'One sister, ten years older than me.'

'So you were spoilt rotten?'

Hal smiled. 'No, I was nurtured and cherished and ended up growing into a very well-balanced adult. Haven't you noticed?'

Sam eyed him. 'And your parents were both academics?'

'How did you know that?'

'I listen Hal, I'm a woman.'

He shook his head. 'Okay. My father was a professor of literature. My mother was originally one of his students.'

'Sounds a bit scandalous.'

'No, nothing happened until she came back as a graduate. She was studying for her masters degree and he was her adviser. She was very bright, probably more intelligent than my father. I think it threatened him a little.'

'Oh?'

He nodded. 'Anyway, they married, and pretty soon she was pregnant with my sister. She gave up academia and devoted herself to Portia –'

'Portia?'

'Mm,' Hal smiled. 'From *The Merchant of Venice*. My mother had a thing for Shakespeare.'

'I remember "Prince Hal",' said Sam. 'She had a PhD, didn't you say?'

'Not quite,' he explained. 'She was invited to take up a research position and complete her PhD at Dartmouth College, which was very prestigious, it's an Ivy League school. But out of the blue, my father accepted the post in Australia. She worked on her thesis out here, and then I came along. She never finished it. Portia thinks that's just how my father wanted it.'

'What do you think?'

Hal shrugged. 'I don't know why Mom made the choices she did, I don't know what went on behind closed doors. I was just a kid, she was a very loving mother. She seemed happy to me.'

'Maybe she was.'

'Portia will always believe she was trapped in the marriage and wasn't able to express herself. I suggested once that maybe Mom found expression in her role as our mother. Portia nearly bit my head off. She said that was just the kind of typical, misogynist, male egotism that fuelled our patriarchal society and kept women as the underlings,' he recited.

'What did you say to that?'

'I took it right back. Portia can be pretty scary. Especially when you're ten years old and she's twenty and she's at college, and she comes home and all she does is fight with everybody.' He paused, staring down at the sand as he walked. 'She was always yelling at Mom, telling her to break out, live her own life. It used to worry me as a little kid. I didn't understand, I thought she'd go and I'd be left alone with my father.'

'I'm assuming that never happened?'

Hal sighed heavily. 'She died the year I went to college. Cancer.'

'Oh Hal, I'm sorry.'

They didn't say anything for a while. They had come to

the headland and they started to pick their way over the rocks
until the encroaching waves forced them back. The swell was
huge today. They sat on a flat rock staring out towards the
horizon.

'What about your father?' Sam asked eventually.

'He's still alive. He spends most of his time on his own,
writing and researching. He has the occasional paper published.
I don't think he ever got over losing Mom, despite the fact that
he never really appreciated her while she was there.'

'Oh?'

'According to Portia,' he smiled faintly.

'Do you see him much?'

'It's a little difficult at the moment.'

'I realise that,' said Sam. 'But when you were back home?'

'Well, we lived on opposite sides of the country . . .' Hal
glanced at her briefly before looking back out at the sea. 'He's
not an easy person to get close to. We don't really have a lot in
common.'

Sam sensed he didn't want to say too much more about that.
'What about Portia?'

'She lives in LA, somewhere she knew my father would
never come to visit. There's no love lost between those two.'
Hal leaned forward, resting his elbows on his knees. 'Portia's
the activist of the family. I think she believes she's giving Mom
the voice she never had. She never married but she had a
daughter, who's all grown up now, married with children of
her own. All very respectable. Portia thinks she failed with her,'
Hal grinned.

'Do you keep in touch?'

'Sure,' he nodded. 'We haven't lived nearby each other since
I was a kid, but we have a very fiery email relationship. She
blames me for all the sins of men because I am one, for multinational corporations because I work for one, and for
technology because of what I do.'

'How did you end up working in IT anyway?' Sam asked as
the thought occurred to her. 'You know, coming from a liter-
ary family. Were you being a rebel?'

Hal smiled. 'Maybe a little, but it was mostly by accident. I floundered a bit after Mom died, dropped out of college and took a job in an electronics workshop. I didn't really imagine it would become my career.'

'A career you don't even like any more?' Sam suggested.

He looked at her. 'You really do listen, don't you?'

She smiled.

'It's probably just typical middle-class, middle-aged, ego-centric male angst,' said Hal. 'At least that's what Portia would call it.'

'Did you ever have a dream to do anything else?'

'Sure.'

'Like what?' Sam urged.

He turned around to face her. 'Well, there was cowboy, fire-man and then astronaut, or maybe it was the other way around. Astronaut and then fireman.'

'Okay, anything after the age of ten?' Sam persisted.

'Well, that was the year my parents bought me my first sailboat –'

'You really were spoilt.'

Hal ignored that. 'I spent my teenage years dreaming up ways to make a living sailing around the world.'

'But you never did?'

'After I quit college I crewed a boat around the Caribbean for a few months. But that was about it.'

'Do you still sail?'

'Sure, all the time.'

'Really?' Sam exclaimed. 'Here in Australia?'

He nodded. 'I was out on the harbour last weekend.' He looked at her. 'Why are you so surprised?'

Sam realised that ever since the girls had planted the seed, she'd had images of Hal trawling the bars in his spare time, picking up women to take home for sympathy sex.

'It probably just doesn't fit with my mental picture of you.'

He raised an eyebrow. 'You have a mental picture of me? What am I wearing?'

'Shut up.'

'I told Josh I'd take him sailing. He didn't mention it?'

She looked at Hal. 'That would involve opening his mouth and forming words into some sort of meaningful communication.'

Hal smiled, shaking his head. 'I'll have to take you sailing sometime.'

'No thanks,' she baulked.

'Why not? You can't be afraid of the water, not after braving bluebottles and octopus and God knows what else.'

'As long as my feet are on the bottom and my head is above water, I'm fine,' Sam returned. 'But I don't like the idea of being in a boat with a flimsy sail flapping about, going this way and that, being tossed around by the wind and the waves.'

Hal laughed. 'That's not how it is. You have to learn to control the boat, use the conditions to your advantage.'

'I'm sure you never have *complete* control,' Sam said.

'You don't need to have complete control. Giving up a little and letting the boat take you is part of the attraction. The freedom.'

'It doesn't sound like freedom, it sounds scary.' Sam twirled her toe around in a tiny pool that had formed in the rock. She was aware that Hal was watching her. 'Well,' she said briskly, standing up. 'You must be getting hungry.'

'What are you going to subject me to this time?'

'Mm,' she said, starting along the rocks back to the sand. 'Ever had a Chiko roll?' She turned to look at him. He shook his head. 'What about a battered sav?'

'A what?'

'No, I couldn't do it to you,' Sam grinned, skipping across the rocks ahead of him. She didn't want to waste the day being sad. It might be the last day she'd have to herself for a while.

Her mother had said she was overly sentimental, like it was a bad thing. But perhaps she was right. Sam had too much baggage, she had to learn what to leave behind, what was not worth dragging around any more. It just made her feel heavy and heartsore. Clearly she wasn't the only person in the universe with sadness in her past. Maybe her grandparents' house was gone, but the memory of her childhood years spent with them was still intact. And she could keep that with her forever.

Friday

Sam stepped into the lift and pressed the button for the eighteenth floor. Although she knew where Vanessa worked, she had never actually been to her office. She just wanted to drop off the itinerary for their ski trip while she was in the city.

The eighteenth floor was quiet when Sam stepped out of the lift. She walked through a pair of glass doors to a dimly lit reception area and asked the woman behind the desk for Vanessa Blair, her voice not much above a whisper. She would have felt like she was shouting even if she spoke in a normal tone, the atmosphere was so muted.

Vanessa appeared a minute later, smiling brightly as she always did, but she also spoke softly. 'Hello Samantha. It was really good of you to come in just for this.'

'Oh, don't worry about it, I always have a few errands to run while I'm in the city.'

Sam followed Vanessa down a grey-carpeted corridor between rows of office cubicles. They walked into one that was barely distinguishable from the others, except for the few touches Vanessa had obviously added to make it her own. Cutesy figurines and stuffed animals peeked out from behind an in-tray and the computer monitor, another lot were grouped on top of a filing cabinet. A polka-dotted cylinder was filled with novelty pens and pencils and her screensaver was a picture of Tweety Pie.

Sam looked across the maze of partitioned walls to the grey vertical blinds that enshrouded the entire office area. Surely there was a reasonable outlook from this building, considering its proximity to the harbour, so why would they keep all the blinds closed? Too distracting for the workers? Sam felt sad for Vanessa. She lived and worked in environments that seemed so at odds with her sunny disposition.

'Take a seat,' Vanessa offered.

Sam sat down and drew out a packet from her handbag. 'This is all the information about your trip, your book-in times –'

'That's fine,' said Vanessa, clearly disinterested. 'Dominic will go through it all and call you if he has any questions.'

'Don't you want to know?'

Vanessa shrugged. 'Skiing is Dominic's thing. I just go along and try to keep warm!' she smiled.

'I think a holiday at the snow would be wonderful. We used to talk about taking the kids,' Sam mused. 'I don't know when I'll ever be able to afford to take a holiday again.'

Vanessa looked abashed. 'I didn't mean to appear ungrateful. It's a lovely place we stay in . . .'

Sam knew that was the truth, she'd authorised payment of the tariff.

'How are your children anyway? How's Ellie?' Vanessa asked.

'She's fine, they're all fine.'

'And the house-hunting? Have you found anything yet?'

'I'm closing in.'

It turned out that the houses she'd been shown on her first sojourn out with Hal were really scraping the bottom of the barrel. Just the agents pouncing on an unsuspecting punter in the vague hope of shifting properties that had lain fallow in their books for months.

Sam was not quite that stupid. And she had spent a lot more time and legwork getting to know the areas better and coming up with a realistic price range. She had actually been pleasantly surprised by Marrickville. It was still in the general vicinity she was targeting, but it was a little more affordable. And she had discovered more than a few wide, leafy streets off the main roads and away from the industrial area. Of course, demand was higher there too. The canny buyer had to be ready to run out and inspect something the minute an agent called, and be prepared to bid on it the same day. Ted had made inquiries, and Sam now had a couple of trustworthy realtors looking out for her interests.

'I'll be putting my house on the market shortly.'

Vanessa winced. 'How are the children coping with that? Leaving the family home and all?'

Sam sighed. If Jeff had talked to Josh and Jess it was hard to tell. They were both stubbornly sullen and disconsolate.

'Oh, they'll be alright. Children are very adaptable,' she said, trying to convince herself as well. 'They don't have much of a choice, I guess. It's going to happen anyway.'

Vanessa was thoughtful. 'Do you think it's easier to accept something that's inevitable?'

'Sure, I suppose. What else can you do?' Sam wondered what she was getting at.

'Did you ever do something and tell your husband about it later?'

Sam let out an involuntary peal of laughter, before remembering where she was. The place was as solemn as a church. She cleared her throat and resumed in a low tone. 'I don't think it's unusual for a wife to tell her husband something after the event. You know, haven't you ever pretended a new dress was something you've had for ages, that kind of thing?'

Vanessa looked at her blankly. 'No, Dominic likes me to buy new clothes.'

Lucky her. 'Mm, well, it was just an example,' Sam dismissed. 'What I'm trying to say is that people who live together probably blur the edges of the truth from time to time.' She sighed. 'That sounds so . . . underhanded. But in practice it's really about avoiding conflict. You get to know someone after living with them for a long time. What needs to be said, what's better left unsaid.'

Vanessa seemed to be very intent on Sam's words.

'I'm not sure I'm the person you should be asking about this,' said Sam.

'Why not?'

'Well, I don't exactly have a successful record.'

'How long were you married?'

'Sixteen years.'

'That's not bad. You survived two seven-year itches,' Vanessa smiled.

'I suppose that's one way of looking at it.'

'And besides, he left you. Don't you believe those stories that an affair doesn't end a marriage. That's the guilty party's excuse, remember.'

Sam had begun to wonder, though. More and more lately. When she thought about their marriage, the image that came to mind was a kind of wasteland. There was nothing there. Jeff had said once that the house and kids were all that mattered to her, and perhaps he was right. The last few years played in her mind like a home video. The kids' birthday parties, Josh's football games, Jess in her dancing costumes, the pool going in . . . and Jeff was never in the frame.

'I'd better let you get back to work,' said Sam all of a sudden. She picked up her handbag and got to her feet. She had no time for regrets, for moping about the past. And she was not going to start taking the blame for what had gone wrong between them. Jeff had put himself out of the frame, she hadn't pushed him. And Sam hadn't gone anywhere. If he had wanted to reach out she would have been there. But he hadn't. He'd reached for someone else.

August

'Are you very busy for the next few weeks?' barked Sheila when Sam picked up the phone.

Sam hated being asked questions out of the blue like that. She would rather hear what it was about before she committed herself.

'Why? What are you offering?'

'I've got a big job for you, a huge job in fact. But it will take up a lot of your time this month. Interested?'

She felt torn. Life was frenetic at the moment, to say the least. The house had sold at a little above the asking price, the first weekend it was listed. This was a highly desirable location, Sam had been right about that much. And she was finally closing in on a couple of properties in Marrickville that were about as good as she was going to get. She had put in an offer for her first choice and was waiting to hear if it had been accepted.

Then of course she had the prospect of packing up the contents of a house three times the size of the one she was moving to, finding schools for the children, selling the Landcruiser – too cumbersome with parking at a premium. And yes, she had begrudgingly admitted, to Hal's smug amusement, too expensive to run. And then the endless paperwork. So what was Sheila's question? Was she very busy?

'The client is prepared to pay a higher rate. And he's offering a bonus if he's satisfied with the job.'

Sam took a breath. She could use the extra money. 'Well, what's it about? What does he want me to do?'

'I'll go through it if you accept the job upfront. Haven't got time otherwise, I'll have to find someone else.' Sheila paused. 'I came to you first, Sam, because I know you can do it. So what do you say, are you in?'

For a penny and a pound by the sounds of it. 'Sure.'

'Okay. The client's name is Alan Mitchell . . .'

Wednesday

Sam decided it was best to start as soon as possible, and she was curious to see what she had got herself in for. Ellie was not in pre-school today, but Sam didn't think it would be a problem bringing her along.

Sheila had explained that the fourth Mrs Mitchell had left a few months ago. She'd handled everything in the house apparently. Nothing unusual in that, but since then Mr Mitchell had allowed things to slide to the point where he claimed the place was virtually unliveable. Sheila thought that was probably a gross exaggeration, but Sam was required to bring the house back to normal, whatever the cost. He would continue to pay at a particularly attractive rate if someone could oversee the running of the household from then on.

Sam knew Alan Mitchell could afford it. He had made his fortune in the metropolitan freeway boom of the last twenty years. Wherever you drove around Sydney you were more than likely to be driving on Mitchell concrete.

She pulled up in front of an imposing concrete mausoleum on the waterfront at Drummoyne. The house was an eyesore, one of those places that would have had the neighbours shaking their heads and wondering how council had allowed it. It was designed to bellow, 'I'm bigger than all of you, and I've got more money, too'.

She helped Ellie from the car and walked up to the security gate. Sam had visited Mitchell's offices yesterday to meet him and get her instructions. He was a big man, well into his fifties, with a ruddy complexion and the bulbous nose of a drinker. He was not ageing gracefully. His hair had formed a thin web that sat precariously on top of his head, and the skin on his face was as coarse as the outside of a rockmelon.

'Here's the key, security code, everything you'll need to get in,' he'd said, sliding an envelope across the desk towards Sam. 'You'll find a pile of old mail to go through, should find who you have to contact to get everything goin' again. Sheila's got the authority to pay for it all. I'm goin' away this arvo for a few weeks, so come and go as you please.'

Sam keyed in the numbers that would disengage the alarm and then unlocked the gate. They crossed a concrete courtyard to the front door. The shrivelled remains of what was once some kind of flowering shrub filled an enormous concrete planter by the door.

'Bloody wife, just pisses off one day.' Mitchell had gone on to explain. 'Dya believe it? Fucking disappears! Oh, sorry love, 'scuse the French. But Chrissakes, just to up and leave? Without a trace? The others hung around, even if it was just to give me hell.'

Sam and Ellie walked into the entry and down a few stairs into the living area. Peach was the first thing that struck Sam. Peach walls, peach vertical drapes, peach leather lounge and peach carpet. The next thing that struck her was the mess.

'Anyways, first thing, friggin' Foxtel gets cut, missed the bloody heavyweight title bout. I thought she done it outta spite. Then the phone's dead. Then one day I come home, and the friggin' lights aren't workin'. Power's out! Jeez, I had to empty out the fridge by torchlight. Beer was still cold, thank Christ.'

There was hardly a flat surface not covered with empties, overflowing ashtrays, Chinese takeaway containers and pizza boxes. As she and Ellie gingerly made their way across the room, Sam automatically stooped to pick up discarded clothing, shoes, bottles. But she didn't know what to do with what she'd collected, so she just tossed it all onto the lounge. She opened the vertical blinds to let in some light, and was confronted by the sight of the swamp that was once a swimming pool.

'Yucky, Mummy!' Ellie exclaimed. 'It's all green.'

'Worse thing,' Mitchell had croaked, leaning forward across the desk, 'the rumour is, it was with the pool man.' He shook his head ruefully. 'I mean, what a fuckin' cliché, fuckin' pool man! Oh, sorry about the French, love.'

'I think we'll skip the kitchen,' said Sam now, grimacing. 'Are you ready to check out upstairs?'

Ellie nodded her head warily. They crossed back to the entry and clattered up the curved, tiled staircase to a railed landing. There were three archways, the central one being the largest. They walked through into a huge bedroom, again all in peach. Walls, vertical drapes, carpet, what was not covered in discarded clothes and shoes. Sam supposed the bedcover was peach too, but it was lost in a jumble of sheets and blankets twisted up on the bed. Ellie walked over and looked up.

'Mummy, why is there a mirror on the roof?'

Good grief. 'I suppose so they can see how they look before they get up in the mornings.'

There were smaller archways either side of the bedhead and Sam walked through one into what she realised was Alan Mitchell's dressing room. Again, clothes were strewn every-where, drawers hung open, shoes littered the floor. The man was worse than a child, couldn't he pick up *anything* after him-self? The dressing room led through into a bathroom, another vision in peach and as filthy as the rest of the place. Sam took the round trip, out through the door of what she presumed was the estranged Mrs Mitchell's dressing room. But here it was tidy, pristine in fact. The only thing out of place was a card-board box that looked as though it had been tossed in here, landing on its side. Sam knelt on the floor and turned the box over. It was filled with photograph frames. She lifted one out and looked at the face of a woman around her own age, sitting at a table at some sort of formal function. Alan Mitchell was beside her, his mouth gaped open, mid-guffaw. But the woman wasn't smiling. She was clutching a wine glass and she looked . . . empty, Sam supposed. Her eyes had this hollow, vacant cast that Sam found chilling.

Ellie walked up behind her. 'She looks sad, Mummy.'

'Yes, she does.'

Sam realised then that the hanging rails were full, the shoe racks too. There was a neat line-up of handbags across one shelf. She opened the drawers, one at a time. Even the under-wear drawer appeared to be full. A couple of slim drawers were divided into trays to store jewellery. They were filled with gold chains and bracelets, even a wristwatch. The woman had taken nothing from this slob. She must have left with barely the clothes on her back. Though Sam suspected she had at least held on to her dignity.

They came back down the stairs. Now she just had to decide where to start.

'What are we going to do now, Mummy?'

'I was wondering the same thing, sweetheart.'

Before she'd left the office yesterday, Mitchell had stopped her. 'No questions, nothing else you want to know?'

Sam shook her head. 'I'll work it out, Mr Mitchell. That's my job.'

'Christ, you don't have much to say for a woman. You get the place fixed up by the time I get back and I might have to propose!'

'A bonus will do,' she'd said plainly.

Sam took a notepad and a couple of pens out of her bag. She cleared a spot on the dining-room table, noticing the beer bottles had left a spirograph of white rings on the surface. If she was going to do this properly, she might have to see about getting a French polisher in. But first things first.

'Here, Ellie,' she said, tearing a page out of her pad, 'why don't you draw me a picture?'

Ellie screwed up her nose. 'I haven't got any colouring-in pencils but, Mummy.' Then her eyes lit up. 'I could write Daddy a letter!'

'Good idea.'

Sam started a list. She wrote 'cleaner' first, she had no intention of lifting a finger around here. It would be enough to organise the army of people that would be needed to attack this mess. Her mobile phone started to ring and she picked it up out of her bag.

'Samantha Holmes.'

'I can only ever seem to catch you on the mobile these days, Samantha.'

She sighed. 'Hang up then, Mum. I'll call you back.'

'It's not that. I just don't know how you can afford to keep that phone going when you've got to sell your house and your car and heaven only knows what else.'

'I need the mobile for my work, Mum.'

'Well, if you'd stayed at the MRA —'

'Mum!' Sam stopped her. She took a breath. 'What is it that you were ringing about?'

'No need to get snappy, dear. It's just that I noticed Lincraft was having a sale, and you know I was telling you that I wanted new curtains for the living room . . .'

Her voice trailed away, waiting for Sam to jump in any time and say, 'I'll take you, Mum, what day suits you?'

But something made her resist. 'I don't know if I can do it this time, Mum. I'm terribly busy. I've started packing and I've got a huge job at the moment, that's where I am right now.'

'So, you have the time to help out total strangers, but not your own mother?'

'Mum, they're clients. They pay me.'

'I see, it's like that now, is it, Samantha? If I need your help, I'm going to have to pay for it? You were never so money-grubbing.'

Sam steeled herself. 'You know you have three daughters, Mum.'

'Maxine is irresponsible, she can't be relied upon. Besides, she doesn't even have a car,' she pointed out. 'And Alex is interstate.'

'But you never asked Alex to do anything for you even while she was still living here.'

'She has an extremely important position, I can't expect her to run around after me.'

'Isn't my work important?'

'Honestly, Samantha, aren't you a bit old to be playing tit-for-tat?'

Sam stopped arguing so that she could get her mother off the phone. She didn't have the time. She had a lot of calls to make this afternoon to get things moving at the Mitchell house. And she needed to stop at the mall to exchange something for Josh on the way home. Sam had bought the wrong CD for his birthday, and didn't he rub it in. It seemed she couldn't do anything right by the children these days, the older two at least.

She wasn't looking forward to breaking the news about the house. The agent had rung this morning to tell her that someone had beaten her offer. She told him to go ahead with Ermine Street, her second choice.

Of course she was getting second best. It was becoming the story of her life. The other house had three bedrooms and a small enclosed sunroom as well. It would have made an ideal bedroom for Ellie, meaning Jess could still have had a room to herself. The house in Ermine Street had no such options. There was a tiny bedroom for Josh, and two larger rooms, the biggest of which Sam was prepared to give to the two girls. But Jessica was going to hit the roof when she found out she would be sharing with Ellie. When she'd got wind there was even a chance of this she'd been ropable.

'Why do I have to share my room?'

'Why can't she share with Josh?'

'Why do we have to move?'

'Why have you ruined my life?'

Sam parked in the mall car park and rushed along the seesaw of ramps to the entrance.

'Hurry up, sweetie,' she said over her shoulder to Ellie, trying not to sound impatient.

'Why are we in a hurry for, Mummy?'

'Because Mummy has a lot to do.'

'Why?'

'Because . . . I just do.'

'Cause you have to clean up that man's filfy house?'

'That's right.'

'Why do you have to clean his house, Mummy?'

'Well, you saw it, Ellie, it's very messy, isn't it?'

'But why do *you* have to do it?'

'Because it's my job.'

'But you're not that mans's wife, Mummy.'

Sam swung around to look at her daughter. 'It's not only a wife's job to clean the house, Ellie. Mr Mitchell is quite capable of cleaning up after himself, but he chooses not to.'

'Why?'

'He has a lot of money and so he'd rather pay someone else to do it.' Sam took hold of Ellie's hand and walked on briskly into the entrance to the mall.

'Doesn't Daddy have a lot of money any more?' said Ellie after a while.

'What?'

'He has to do the cleaning now, but he didn't used to.'

'Oh?' said Sam, raising an eyebrow.

Ellie nodded emphatically. 'He has to wash up the dishes, and clean up the kitchen, and sometimes he cooks the dinner.'

'Well, what do you know.'

'Doesn't Daddy have enough money to pay Jodi to do it?'

Sam was trying to think about how to answer that. But she gave up. 'No more questions, Ellie. Mummy's got a lot of things on her mind.'

They walked into the CD shop and Sam headed straight for the sales desk. Last time she'd handled it herself. She thought she had done the right thing. Josh had wanted a CD with a particular song on it and she had found it amongst the racks without any assistance. She'd left the shop quite smug with her savvy ability to negotiate the modern music scene.

How was she to know there was a live version and a studio version? She wasn't Molly Meldrum, for godsakes. Josh had been glum and ungrateful, chalking it up as just another example of how his parents were failing him.

Sam was going to get it right this time. She approached the desk. A young man with lots of studs and rings punctuating his face, smiled brightly at her.

'Hiya, how can I help you today?'

Sam placed the CD in its original bag, with the docket, on the desk in front of the pierced man. She always kept the docket and the original bag.

'I bought this Nevada album for my son, but apparently I got the wrong one.'

He slid the CD out of the bag while she spoke. 'Oh, you mean Nirvana?'

'Isn't that what I said?'

He smiled. 'He wants the studio album, I s'pose? Never mind.'

That was kind. Despite his piercings, he seemed like a decent young fellow. She'd bet he wouldn't grumble at his mother the way Josh did.

'Thank you for understanding. I mean, it's not that big a deal to change it, is it? I told him that. I was only trying to get him what he wanted. It'd be nice to get a little appreciation for all the things I do right that no one seems to notice. But they certainly notice when I get it wrong.'

Sam took a breath. The pierced man's expression had turned from kindness to bemusement.

'*Nevermind* is the name of the album you're after. I'll just get it.'

Friday evening

'What's wrong with me, Max?' Sam moaned. 'Now I'm pouring out my problems to complete strangers.'

'It's called overload,' said Max plainly. 'You're bound to have a bit of spill-over now and then.'

'Too right. And now in the middle of the busiest month of my life, I have to go to Mum's and measure up her windows for curtains and then take her off to Lincraft, where of course she won't like anything they have on sale, and then it'll turn into this huge project while we traipse the city looking for fabric for curtains, that she only decided to change because of the sale, and I'll be still making them for her come Christmas time.' Sam took a breath.

'Well, that was your choice.'

'No it wasn't!'

'All you had to do was say no.'

'To Mum? I tried to, but she makes me feel so guilty.'

'No she doesn't.'

'Oh yes she does!'

'She can't *make* you feel anything, Sam. You have to take responsibility for your own emotions.'

'Don't start with the psychobabble, Max.'

Max ignored her. 'You know I'm right. Why do you give her so much power over you?'

Sam paused. 'It's okay for you, she doesn't even ask you.'

'That's right, because I've carefully cultivated a solid reputation for unreliability over the years. You're about the only person who has any expectations of me at all. And look where that's got me! Packing coffee cups on a Friday night! Where did I go wrong with you?' she grinned.

Each night Sam had aimed to sort through one cupboard in the house in an attempt to whittle away at the overwhelming task that lay ahead of her. But everything she unearthed seemed to have some memory attached to it, happy, sad or unexpected. There were long-forgotten wedding presents still in their boxes, souvenir tea-towels bought on holiday, tiny baby clothes, favourite toys and puzzles she'd kept just to remember.

But now remembering hurt. Sam decided that happy memories were yet another casualty of a broken marriage. She wondered if she would ever be able to think about her old life without feeling sad or bitter.

'Then, to add insult to injury,' Sam continued, waving a piece of paper around, 'this arrived in the mail today.'

Liz walked in from outside where she had been having a smoke. She'd shown up to help because pretty much anything was preferable to Friday-night football. 'What is it?' she asked.

'An invitation to my school reunion.'

'What's wrong with that? Sounds like fun.'

Sam pulled a face. 'That's what I thought, till I noticed that partners are also invited.'

'So?'

'Of course, I know why that was decided. Bloody Robyn Johnson is one of the organisers and we all know who she married.'

'We do?' Liz frowned at Max, who shrugged.

'Yes. One of the cricketers, played for Australia, I think he has a brother who plays too.'

'Don't they all have a brother who plays?' Max asked Liz.

'Steve, or Mark,' Sam said vaguely. 'No, it's definitely Steve, Steve something. Or maybe Mark.'

'I thought they were all called Steve or Mark,' Liz muttered aside to Max.

'Steve Bremer! That's it. Oh, she's probably just dying to come and show off her celebrity husband.' Sam paused. 'And I don't even have a regular one to take any more.'

'So Sherl, you're not going to go out ever again because you haven't got a husband?'

'No, I'm just not going to this,' she said, screwing up the paper.

'Here, give it to me,' said Max. 'Don't waste a good bit of packing paper.' Sam tossed it to her, and she wrapped it around a coffee mug and placed it in the cardboard box at her feet. 'There, that one's about full. What's next?'

Liz smiled. 'A drink, I reckon.'

Two weeks later

Sam stood staring at the bottom of Alan Mitchell's pool. She could actually see it now. The same water that had been pond-scum green was now glistening turquoise. When the pool man had first come to take a look he had scratched his head in disbelief when Sam asked if he could get it cleaned up inside a fortnight.

'I mean, maybe, but it'll take so many chemicals, you wouldn't be able to swim in it for at least that long again.'

'That's okay,' Sam told him. 'The owner obviously hasn't swum in it for a long time anyway.'

'Yeah, I think only his wife ever used the pool.'

Sam blinked at him. 'You were the pool man . . . here . . . before?'

'Sure. I'd been coming since they built the place.'

'So . . .' She was not sure how to ask someone if he'd had an affair with the wife of the man you were both working for. 'What made you leave?'

He shrugged. 'They stopped paying. I rang a few times but there was never an answer. The last time, the phone had been disconnected. I thought they must've moved.'

So, no cliché with the pool man after all.

'Are you sure you want me to nuke this?'

Sam nodded. 'Whatever it takes.'

She had become obsessed with getting the house in order before Alan Mitchell returned. Sam had always liked a challenge, to do something that people didn't expect could be done. Like the buffet luncheon she prepared for Ellie's christening, two weeks after she was out of hospital. She glowed as guest after guest commented how wonderful she looked, how amazing she was, how they couldn't put on a party like this, even without having a newborn baby to look after. She also remembered that later in the day Jeff fell asleep in an armchair in the corner of the family room. Anyone would think he was the one getting up to a baby three times a night.

But this time it was not about earning accolades. It was more the sense of control it gave her as the rest of her life was being dismantled, sorted, wrapped in newspaper and packed away in cardboard boxes.

Sam walked back into the house. It had been totally transformed in the past two weeks. The carpet was fresh and clean, every polishable surface was gleaming, everything was in its place. The phone was reconnected, as was Foxtel, and Sam had diverted the mail to a post office box, where she would pick it up directly. Cleaner, gardener and pool man were all booked for weekly appearances.

But for some reason she was curiously dissatisfied. It occurred to Sam that all she had done was patch up the life of a spoilt, overgrown boy who had managed to drive away four wives and who did not even have the most basic of life skills.

She tried not to judge her clients but some of them invited it. Dominic Blair was all style and no substance. Vanessa was genuinely sweet, but the way she just went along with every-thing grated on Sam's nerves. Then there was Guy Hennessey. He had contacted her a few weeks ago, asking her to book the best room in the best hotel in the city and have flowers wait-ing, with a card to 'Suzanne'. Finally, something romantic. Sam had tried to call Fiona to tell her, but she hadn't been able to catch her for a week. She didn't bother to try the following week, however, when Guy asked Sam to do the same thing, but address the card to 'Pamela' this time. And a fortnight later, Tania, and after that, Carly. Or was it the other way around?

Only Ted Dempsey out of the lot of them had a genuine need, yet he was by far her easiest client. Except for Hal, but she could hardly even call him a client. He had done more for Sam than she ever had for him. He'd been away for a few weeks, running training sessions at other offices around Aus-tralia, so she hadn't seen him since their day out. Sam had tried to insist on at least collecting his mail while he was away.

'But I don't get much snail mail these days. You can go and empty out the junk mail if you really want, but I think the super will take care of that.'

'Well, I have to do something!' she insisted. 'Do you want me to arrange to have your carpets cleaned?'

He shook his head. 'They don't need it.'

'What about spring-cleaning your apartment?'

'At this time of the year?'

'It'll be spring by the time you're back. You're in the south-ern hemisphere,' Sam reminded him.

'Still, my place doesn't need spring-cleaning, there's only me. I don't make that much mess.'

She sighed. 'You know, you're a lousy client, Hal.'

'Thanks Sam. And I always speak so highly of you.'

Sam checked her watch now. She was meeting Jeff at the house soon to divide up the furniture. She had only come to

Alan Mitchell's to stock the fridge with a few things – milk,
butter, beer of course, and a chilli con carne she'd made herself.
He was due back any time and she wanted the place to be
perfect. She wanted him to be gobsmacked.

She wanted a bonus.

When Sam arrived home, Jeff's car was parked outside on the
kerb and he was sitting inside it. He got out as she pulled into
the driveway.

'Sorry I'm late,' Sam said as he approached her.

He shrugged. 'No worries.'

She looked at him. 'Have you come from work?'

He nodded. It was interesting to note the deconstruction of
Jeff Holmes, Corporate Executive. It had happened so gradually over the months that it caught Sam by surprise when she
really looked at him now and then. He was wearing casual
clothes to work these days, a concession that had been introduced into the office years ago but one which Jeff had never
taken up. And he was wearing his hair much longer. As it grew
out from the neat, close cut he'd worn for years, it swirled and
kinked into sandy brown waves. Sam had forgotten how wavy
his hair was, she'd forgotten about the curls that clustered at the
nape of his neck. He looked . . . younger, more like the boy she
had married.

Sam opened the front door and Jeff followed her in. He was
moving house too. He had put a deposit on a semi in Rand-
wick. The living areas were tight apparently, but it did have a
small backyard and three bedrooms. Josh wouldn't have to sleep
in the living room any more. Sam wondered how they could
afford it. Jodi's business was obviously doing alright, though she
supposed having two wages made all the difference.

They walked into the kitchen and Sam put her bag on the
bench. 'So, how are we going to do this?' she asked him.

Jeff shrugged. 'However you want.'

'Well,' she began, 'of course you'll take the spare bed from
the study, for Josh.'

'Thanks, that'd be great.'

Sam considered him for a moment. 'You don't have to thank me. I'm not giving it to you, Jeff. You're entitled to your share.'

She didn't want this to be awkward. And definitely not emotional. She'd heard enough stories and seen enough movies about couples fighting over food processors and CD collections. She did not want to go through that.

Besides, Sam had noticed in herself a strange detachment from all the stuff around her. The things that suddenly mattered were a revelation. A tiny worn-out baby's jumpsuit meant a lot more to her than the four-thousand-dollar leather lounge suite, for example.

'Why don't we start upstairs?' she suggested.

Jeff insisted he didn't want anything from the kids' rooms, despite the fact that with Ellie and Jess sharing, some of their furniture was going to have to be culled.

'Well, the girls can work that out. If they want to bring anything to my place, that'll be fine.'

Sam said it was only fair that Jeff take the rest of the furniture from the study. Though she hoped he didn't mind if they kept the computer.

'Of course,' he agreed. 'The kids need it for school.'

She pushed open the door to their room, but she stayed back, leaning against the doorjamb. Jeff didn't venture in either.

'Can you use a king-size bed?' she asked, trying to sound nonchalant.

He shook his head. 'You have it.'

'It would never fit – I'd have to climb directly onto it from the doorway.'

'Oh?' he frowned. 'Your room's that small?'

'I'm taking the second bedroom.'

'Why?'

'To placate Jessica for having to share with Ellie.'

'Did it work?'

'Not really.'

He leaned against the wall, crossing his arms. His expression seemed concerned. 'You shouldn't have had to do that,' he said quietly.

Sam considered him for a moment. 'There are at least five kinds of responses I could make to that,' she returned cryptically, closing the door again and heading towards the stairs. Jeff followed her down to the formal living rooms.

'The leather lounge will never fit in the new house,' said Sam. 'Do you want it?'

He shook his head. 'It won't fit in my place either.'

'What about the dining setting?'

'We don't have a separate dining room and we already have a table and chairs.'

Sam nodded. 'I'll have to sell it then, I guess.' She looked around the room, at the side tables, lamps, cabinets, the prints on the walls. 'Is there anything else you wanted? I really couldn't fit much of this in if I tried.'

'Me either,' Jeff sighed deeply, rubbing the back of his neck. 'Jeez Sam, we had so much stuff it won't even fit into two houses. What were we trying to prove?'

Sam looked down at the carpet, self-conscious. She could feel him watching her.

'That wasn't a dig at you, honestly Sam,' he said. 'I know this place meant a lot to you.'

She shrugged. 'Not any more. It was all I ever dreamed of once, I worked so hard to get it. Now I think I hate it.'

He didn't say anything. She cleared her throat and walked down the hall. 'I was going to ask you if it was okay if I took the furniture out here?'

He followed her into the family room. 'Sure.'

'Mainly I need the sofas, and the table and chairs. If there's anything else you want —'

'No, really Sam. I don't want to take anything you can use.'

She frowned. 'Have a good look, you're sure there's nothing?'

She watched him survey the room indifferently. For some reason it bothered her. Didn't he feel anything? Maybe she didn't want things to be awkward, but by the same token she would have liked to see some evidence that he cared. Even a little.

The doorbell rang into the silence.

'I'll let you answer that,' said Jeff. 'I have to get going anyway.'

They walked back towards the front of the house.

'There's so much more,' Sam told him. 'Kitchen stuff, linen. You're hardly taking anything.'

He stopped at the door. 'Why don't you pack up everything you want and I'll come and take a look at what's left.'

'Are you sure?'

'Absolutely,' he nodded as the doorbell sounded again. Jeff stood back while Sam opened the door to a pair of legs supporting an enormous arrangement of flowers.

'Ms Samantha Holmes?' came a voice from amid the blooms.

'That's me,' she confirmed.

'Then these are for you.'

Sam took the flowers in her arms but now her own view was obscured. 'Thank you,' she called to the man as she heard his footsteps retreating down the path.

Jeff cocked an eyebrow. 'You've got an admirer?'

'Surprised?'

'Not at all.' He watched Sam position the flowers on the hall table. 'Is there a card?'

'There is.'

'Well, aren't you going to open it?'

'Yes, I'll probably do that.'

'Oh, right,' he nodded, realising. 'After I leave?'

'Mm.'

Jeff smiled sheepishly. 'I'll get out of your way then.'

'See you.'

Sam stood at the open door, watching Jeff drive away. Well, that felt good. She turned and looked at the flowers, she had a feeling she knew who'd sent these. She plucked the card from amongst the foliage.

You earned it alright! I've approved your bonus with Sheila.
Now, will you marry me?
AM

Sam smiled. Not if you were the last man on earth, she said out loud, screwing the note up and tossing it in the bin.

Wednesday

From:<h.buchanan@igb.com.au   To:<holmes@webnet.com.au
Subject: *No subject*

Hey Sam, how are you going?

From:<holmes@webnet.com.au   To:<h.buchanan@igb.com.au
Subject: *No subject*

Hello Hal. I'm fine. What can I do for you?

From:<h.buchanan@igb.com.au   To:<holmes@webnet.com.au
Subject: *No subject*

I just wanted to say hello. Am I bothering you?

From:<holmes@webnet.com.au   To:<h.buchanan@igb.com.au
Subject: SORRY!

I didn't mean to sound abrupt. My apologies.

Thursday

From:<h.buchanan@igb.com.au   To:<holmes@webnet.com.au
Subject: Re: SORRY!

You didn't even notice that I asked 'how are you GOING?'

From:<holmes@webnet.com.au   To:<h.buchanan@igb.com.au
Subject: Re: SORRY!

That's very good Hal. Very Australian. We'll make an ocker out of you yet.

From:<h.buchanan@igb.com.au   To:<holmes@webnet.com.au
Subject: Re: SORRY!

I take it that's a good thing?

From:<holmes@webnet.com.au   To:<h.buchanan@igb.com.au
Subject: Re: SORRY!

Never mind.

Friday morning

From:<h.buchanan@igb.com.au   To:<holmes@webnet.com.au
Subject: And Another Thing

You didn't notice my perfect spelling and punctuation either.

| From:<holmes@webnet.com.au | To:<h.buchanan@igb.com.au |
| Subject: Re: And Another Thing | |

But you see Hal, spelling and punctuation are only noticeable when they're not done properly.

| From:<h.buchanan@igb.com.au | To:<holmes@webnet.com.au |
| Subject: Re: And Another Thing | |

Just like housework, huh?

| From:<holmes@webnet.com.au | To:<h.buchanan@igb.com.au |
| Subject: Re: And Another Thing | |

And data security, I hear.

September

Sam heard the doorbell, lit the last candle and blew out the match. That would be Liz and Rosemary. Max had phoned to say she was running late, and Fiona couldn't make it. Tonight was the last chance to have the girls over before the house was sold, at least without the kids around. It was their weekend with Jeff. They were moving in a fortnight and from here on in Sam would be too busy anyway.

'Hi Sam, how are you?' said Rosemary as she opened the door, her voice wavering between sympathy and optimism.

'Fine,' she said with a genuine smile. She was glad they were here, it gave her an excuse not to pack for a night.

'God, the place looks so empty,' Liz remarked as Sam ushered them inside.

Sam had sold off almost everything from the formal living room in one hit, the same day the ad appeared in the paper. It was quality furniture and Sam had kept it at an attractive price. She figured expediency was worth something. When she told Jeff she'd write him a cheque for his share, he flatly refused. He said to use it on the removalist, he should share that cost anyway, it was his children that were moving house as well. She insisted a removalist wouldn't cost anywhere near that much, but he still wouldn't hear of taking any money from her. 'You must have had a lot of expenses moving. The money will help.'

Sam wondered with all the nicey nicey when the kick in the guts was coming. But she didn't have the time to dwell on that at the moment.

'Come on through, the family room is still furnished,' said Sam. 'It's the only room we live in now.' In reality, it was the only room they'd ever really lived in.

As they followed her through the double doorway, both Rosemary and Liz gasped at the same time.

'What have you done!'

Every available surface was covered with candles, mostly white, in all shapes and sizes.

'It looks like a movie set or something!'

'There must be dozens!' sighed Rosemary.

'Sixty-seven,' Sam confirmed.

'You shouldn't have done this just for us, Sam,' Liz chided. 'Must have cost you a fortune.'

'No, you don't understand,' she started to explain. 'I found all these while I was packing. They were everywhere. Some were out for decoration, but I had heaps in cupboards, drawers, every place I looked. All these candles that I had never used. I don't know what I was waiting for.'

'A month-long blackout?' Liz suggested.

'Come to think of it,' mused Rose, 'I've got a lot of candles around the house and I never light them either. And vases. I have so many vases, and yet on the rare times I actually get given flowers, I never seem to have the right size vase.'

'Well, I decided I wasn't going to pack sixty-seven candles

away and get them out at another house, only to put them away in a cupboard and never light them there either.'

'Yoohoo,' called Max from the entrance.

'We're out here,' said Sam.

Max appeared in the doorway. 'Wow, look at this place. It's like a coven meeting. Very atmospheric.' She glanced at each of them. 'Haven't you girls started drinking yet?'

'We were just getting to that, Max,' said Liz, tearing the foil off the bottle she had bought with her. She popped the cork and started filling the glasses Sam had laid out on the coffee table.

'Guess what I heard on the radio today,' said Max. 'Did you know there's a Tupperware party taking place on average every 4.4 minutes?'

'What, around the world?' asked Sam.

'No!' Max shook her head. 'In Australia alone!'

'That's incredible.'

'All that plastic,' Liz pondered.

'That can't be true,' said Rosemary, frowning. 'Every 4.4 minutes? That would mean they were going all through the night.'

'Please tell me she's not that dumb,' muttered Max under her breath, reaching for a glass.

'Let's drink to Sam,' said Liz, holding up her glass.

'No, let's drink to all of us,' Sam insisted.

'But this is a big deal, Sam,' Liz persisted. 'Good luck, all the best . . . um, break a leg. I'm not sure what you're supposed to say at a time like this.'

'May your home resound with laughter, and the sun shine on it from above, so that on each day hereafter, it will always be filled with love,' Rosemary finished, holding her glass towards Sam.

Everyone looked at her, surprised.

'It's on a plaque above our back door,' she explained. 'Mum and Dad gave it to us when we moved in. I've read it every day for the last twenty-two years, so I know it off by heart.'

'Thank you, Rose,' said Sam.

Max plonked herself on the floor. 'Going a bit lowbrow, aren't we, Sherl?' she said, referring to the plastic disposable bowls filled with nuts, chips and olives, set out on the coffee table.

'All my platters are packed away,' said Sam. 'But to tell you the truth, I really couldn't give a toss. Maybe my standards are dropping.'

'That's a relief.'

'Are you going to miss the house?' Rosemary asked tentatively.

Sam looked at her. 'I don't think so. It feels so big these days, especially when the kids aren't here.' She paused. 'You know, they marketed this as the ultimate family home, but it's designed to keep everyone apart – all the separate bedrooms and bathrooms, parents' retreat, family room, formal rooms. You could be in the house all day and not bump into anyone if you didn't want to.'

Max sighed heavily. 'It's like a monument to a broken marriage.'

'Oh, *please*!' Liz remarked drily. 'Who's writing your lines?'

'What was it like when you had to split everything up? All the furniture?' Rosemary asked. 'I've heard that can get nasty.'

'No, Jeff was really decent. He didn't demand anything.'

'There's that guilty conscience again,' said Liz.

Sam shrugged. 'I kind of wished he had, though.'

'What are you talking about?'

'Well,' she tried to explain, 'he didn't care, he didn't seem to have an attachment to anything.'

'Blokes are from Mars or Venus,' Liz shrugged. 'Some other planet anyway.'

'He didn't even mention this,' Sam continued, tapping the coffee table. 'This was the first piece of furniture we bought together.'

'I don't understand,' said Rosemary. 'Did you want him to have it?'

'No! I wouldn't have let him actually take it!' She sighed. 'I just wish he'd wanted to.'

Max frowned. 'You realise you've stopped making sense.'

Sam smiled weakly.

'What's the new house like, Sam?' asked Liz. 'I'm dying to see it.'

'Don't get too excited,' she said. 'You'll only be disappointed.'

'Is it that bad?' Rose winced.

'It's not bad at all,' Max insisted. 'It's . . . cute.'

'Mm,' Sam added dubiously. 'It'll certainly encourage togetherness. The living room's barely big enough to swing a cat in.'

'Why would you need enough room to swing a cat anyway?' Liz mused. 'I never did get that expression. Who goes around swinging cats?'

'There's only one bathroom and one toilet,' Sam continued. 'The kids freaked when they realised that.'

'It'll be good for their bladder control,' said Rosemary.

'That's what I told them,' Sam agreed.

'That is such a mum thing to say,' Max smirked. 'Hey, where's Fiona anyway?'

'She's working back, apparently,' Rosemary explained.

'On a Friday night?'

'She seems to spend a lot of time late at the office these days,' said Liz. 'How's your job going, Sam?'

'It has its moments. I got a marriage proposal the other day.'

'Not from Hal!' exclaimed Max.

'No,' Sam frowned, 'not from Hal. From Alan Mitchell.'

'That name sounds familiar.'

'Think concrete. Anyway, the proposal was only a joke. Though I think he probably would have taken me up on it if I'd said yes. But being his wife on a "for hire" basis is more than enough for me.'

'So, you're still seeing the American?' said Liz.

'I'm not "seeing him",' Sam insisted. 'He's a client.'

They all looked unconvinced.

'So what is it that you actually do for Hal?' asked Max.

'What do you mean?'

'Well, you're always harping on that he's a client, but I've never actually worked out what it is that you do for him.'

'That's true,' Liz agreed.

'Um, well,' Sam faltered. 'This and that. You know.'

'No, we don't.' They were all looking at her expectantly.

'What I do for my clients is confidential, I'm not really supposed to talk about it.'

'Come off it! You're always blabbing about your clients,' Max protested.

Sam felt flustered for some reason. 'The thing is, Hal's away at the moment, so actually I'm not doing anything for him right now.'

'Have you spoken to him?' asked Max.

'No.'

'Emailed?' Liz pressed.

'Oh, occasionally. Just to touch base.'

'You're blushing.'

'I am not.'

'She's blushing,' Liz said to the others. 'There's obviously something going on.'

'Obviously,' Max agreed.

'I'm not listening to this,' said Sam, standing up.

'Sam's got herself a boyfriend,' Rosemary cooed.

'Look, this is me not listening and leaving the room,' said Sam, covering her ears as she walked into the kitchen to get another bottle of wine.

'You know what they say,' Max called after her. 'The more you protest . . .'

A fortnight later

The actual day of moving was probably the least stressful Sam had had in weeks. Because of her disciplined packing regime there was no last minute panic. But she was exhausted and she hadn't been sleeping well. She would go off to sleep alright, usually around one in the morning, when she couldn't stay awake any longer. But then she'd wake after an hour or so and lie there, eyes wide open, telling herself to go to sleep. She would watch the digital clock as the numbers reconfigured with each passing minute and worry about the night slipping away. She'd try harder to fall asleep, which of course was self-defeating as she'd only become more anxious when she remained stubbornly awake. She moved through her days with fog for a brain, her eyelids feeling as though they had to be peeled open every time she blinked.

'Samantha, are you well, dear?' Ted had asked on her last visit.

'I'm fine, just a little tired.'

'When do you move house?'

'Next Friday.'

'That's come around quickly,' he remarked. 'So I won't expect you next week?'

'No, Ted, I can still make it.'

'I won't hear of it, Samantha. You have enough to do, I'm sure.'

'But —'

'Oh, that's right, I forgot to tell you,' he said, tapping his forehead. 'I have an engagement next Thursday. I won't be needing you to come after all.'

Sam raised an eyebrow. 'I don't believe a word of it, Ted.'

'Well, that's your prerogative, Samantha,' he returned. 'Now, are you getting enough help?'

She assured him she was. Rosemary was coming to help her clean the house; Liz and Michael had volunteered for unpacking duty on the weekend, and Max was almost a permanent fixture lately. Sam was going to have to remember to do something special for her after this was all over. Even Bernice had offered to help. Though the day she'd come, all she did was expect endless cups of tea and answers to probing questions about the state of Sam's finances. It had been a relief to drop her home again in the afternoon.

Jeff had collected the kids from school on Thursday after-noon and was keeping them until Sunday afternoon, when he would bring them home to Ermine Street. Although Sam had struggled with the notion that they should be part of the moving process as a sort of closure, she couldn't stand Josh's and Jess's long faces any more. It was better if they weren't around.

It also gave Sam more time to pack what was left in their rooms. Come Friday morning she was up early, had stripped her bed, washed the sheets and hung them out on the line before Rosemary arrived. The removalists showed up at nine and by midday the house was empty and spotless. There was nothing left to do. The truck pulled off down the street as Sam packed the boot of their new second-hand Magna with her own overnight bag, the cleaning gear, the dry sheets off the line and other stray flotsam she'd collected around the house.

'Are you going to be alright?' Rosemary asked.

'Of course!' Sam insisted. 'Thanks for everything, Rose. I really appreciate it.'

'Not at all. I wish I could do more . . .'

'You've done more than enough today, Rose. Liz and Michael are coming tomorrow. And Max is at the new place, waiting to open up for the removalists. Everything's covered.'

Rosemary leaned forward to hug Sam. 'You know, I think you're so brave.'

Sam pulled a face. 'I don't know about brave. I didn't choose this, remember. I'm just doing what I have to do.'

Rosemary looked at her. 'Well, you're an inspiration.'

'Oh, Rose! What could I inspire anyone to do?'

'You'd be surprised.'

Sam waved her off down the street and turned back to look at the house. It puzzled her that she didn't feel anything. Certainly no sadness. None of the children were born while they lived here so it didn't have that emotional tug, thank goodness. She was trying to think of anything significant that had happened here.

Her marriage had ended. That was about it. Max was right, the house had become a monument to a broken marriage. Sam got into the car and drove off down the street. She didn't look back or even glance in the rear-vision mirror before she turned the corner and out of sight.

'Hi Sherl!' Max greeted her from the front door. 'Welcome home.'

Sam had been waiting for the place to grow on her, and she was still waiting. Seventy-three Ermine Street had started life as a simple colonial cottage, but along the way most of the period detailing had been ripped out, updated or otherwise eradicated. Timber windows had disappeared in favour of aluminium; the bullnose verandah had survived, but the posts had been replaced with mock Corinthian columns; brick walls had been rendered with concrete and, for some reason defying both explanation and good taste, painted the sickliest shade of blue Sam had ever seen, certainly on the exterior of a house. Nonetheless, other renovations meant that the house had a workable kitchen and bathroom and an internal laundry. Sam had forsaken style for practicality. *Nothing to do, just move in!* the ad had invited, somewhat optimistically. There was nothing to do if you didn't mind that everything was just a little shabby. She considered it now from the front path. Her house. The first house she had bought on her own. She sighed. That blue had to go.

Sam took a breath and skipped down the couple of steps to the verandah. She smiled at Max. 'Got the kettle on?'

'That's a bit hard when there's no kettle,' said Max as they turned to see the removalist truck pulling into the street. 'But I did bring treats!'

Sam followed her through the empty house into the kitchen. At least it all seemed clean.

'Look!' she said, holding up styrofoam cups. 'Real coffee! And I've got focaccia sandwiches and sticky cakes,' she added, indicating a cluster of white paper bags on the bench.

Sam took a cup from her and removed the lid. 'You're a lifesaver.'

'There are some cool little delis up the road, Sam. You're going to like living here.'

She sipped her coffee thoughtfully. This would be a good time for Max's intuition to be right.

Sam thought she had culled their belongings sufficiently, radically even, but she had obviously overestimated the size of this house. Every room was stacked, almost to the ceiling in some cases, with cardboard boxes. They'd had to clear a path in the living room so the removalists could get through into the bedrooms. Then they had to turn around and rearrange the boxes so the living room furniture would fit. Sam gave up trying to get all the furniture in the right place. It was enough if it was in the right room.

'I think it's time to down tools, Sherl,' said Max around seven. 'We're not going to make much of a dent in all this today.'

'I was hoping to have everything done by the time the kids got back on Sunday,' Sam lamented.

'You didn't really think you'd get it all packed away in two days? I know you're a superwoman, but there are limitations.'

Sam pulled a face. 'Well, maybe not everything. But I wanted the place to look nice. So maybe they wouldn't hate it so much.'

'Sam,' said Max seriously. 'The kids will get over it, and life will go on. You look exhausted. Come on, why don't I duck up the road and buy us a bottle of something? The fridge is cold now.'

She was wavering. For the past hour she had started to feel so tired even the most automatic movement had involved herculean effort. She had to concentrate on putting one foot in front of the other just to walk across the room. But Sam remembered she hadn't even made up her bed yet and she had the feeling that if she stopped now and, worse, started drinking, she'd be sleeping on a bare mattress tonight.

A mobile phone started to ring.

'Is that you or me?' said Max, looking around frantically. 'Uh oh, where the hell did I put my bag?'

'It's me,' said Sam. She walked calmly over to a shelf in the kitchen where she'd placed her phone earlier so that it would be easy to find. 'Samantha Holmes.'

'Hey Samantha Holmes, how're you doing?'

'Hal!' Sam knew an involuntary smile had just found its way to her face, and she knew that Max was watching her and making conclusions about that smile that were, well, if not unfounded, then exaggerated to say the least. She turned her back on her sister. 'You're in Sydney?'

'I am,' he confirmed. 'I flew in this morning, but I had to go straight to the office. I just got home a few minutes ago.'

Sam felt a peculiar kind of thrill that he'd phoned her so promptly. But she was just being foolish. All their girlie talk was getting the better of her. She had to maintain her professionalism.

'So, what can I do for you, Hal? Is there something you need?'

'No,' he assured her. 'I just wanted to find out how you are, where you are. Have you moved yet?'

'As of noon today, I'm a resident of seventy-three Ermine Street, Marrickville.'

'Today?' he remarked. 'So, let me guess, you're surrounded by cardboard boxes, nothing fits where it's supposed to, and you're over the whole moving experience, big time. You were just starting to think about something to drink, maybe a pizza.'

Sam laughed. 'Is that an offer?'

'Absolutely.'

She felt embarrassed. 'I was only joking. Max was just about to go up the road and get us something.'

'So, I'll save her the trip. Who else have you got there?'

'It's just Max and me. The kids are with their father.'

'Okay, what do you like on your pizza?'

Sam faltered. 'You don't have to do this, Hal. You've only just got home yourself.'

'Yeah, from a month of living in hotel rooms,' he said drily. 'Come on, I'm your client, you still owe me. And tonight I'd like some company.'

He took their pizza orders and checked her address again,

saying he'd be there within the hour. When Sam hung up the phone, she tried to avoid making eye contact with Max.

'So, your boyfriend's coming over?'

'Max! He's not my boyfriend, and if you're going to start that again, you can go home right now.'

'Do you want me to leave? Give you two a little time –'

'You're not going anywhere! Do you hear me?'

Max smiled. 'Don't you trust yourself alone with him?'

Sam tried to think of something else to say, something Max couldn't misconstrue. She didn't want to discuss this any more. Discussing it gave it credibility. Discussing it gave Max ideas. Discussing it gave Sam a headache. She wondered if Maxine had any of that Rescue Remedy with her. But Sam wasn't about to ask. It would only add considerable fuel to the fire Max was eagerly stoking in her ridiculously fertile imagination.

'I'm going to get cleaned up.'

When she came back down the hall twenty minutes later, Max wolf whistled.

'Cut it out,' Sam said sternly. 'I put on a clean T-shirt, so what?'

'And I don't believe you were wearing those jeans before,' added Max. 'Or the clip in your hair, or lip gloss and mascara,' she said, coming closer to inspect her.

'I'm just making myself respectable,' Sam insisted. 'I'd do it for any client.'

'Why won't you just admit you like him?' said Max. 'I think it's sweet.'

'I don't like him. I mean, I do like him. But I don't like him the way you're inferring. And whether you think I'm contradicting myself or not as the case may be, I'm not going to get involved with a client because, well, because you don't. It's not the done thing. In an arrangement where someone is, in effect, paying your keep, you should keep a professional distance. Well, to some extent, I mean, I suppose the fact that he's coming round with pizza isn't exactly keeping a distance, but he offered. So it's fine. Because that's what he wanted to do tonight . . .' Sam had forgotten the point she was going to make.

Max raised an eyebrow. 'You always babble when you get nervous.'

'I'm not nervous,' she insisted as a knock sounded at the door and a whole flock of butterflies exploded in her stomach. She tried to calm herself as she squeezed past a column of boxes into the hall. She wasn't nervous, she'd been perfectly fine with Hal before Max started making it into something. She enjoyed his company, he made her laugh. That was all. She took a deep, calming breath and opened the door. Then she saw his face, and something weird happened in her stomach.

'Hey Sam,' he smiled. 'Nice place.'

Oh, don't fall for him, she told herself. You don't need this now.

'Sam,' said Hal, frowning slightly. 'Can I come in?'

She stirred. She'd just been standing there staring at him, like an idiot.

'Sorry, I'm a bit tired. I think I may be walking in my sleep,' she smiled weakly, standing back to let him in.

'Gee, I like what you've done with the place,' he said, glancing around between the cardboard towers. 'Kind of "early department store warehouse".'

'And they say Americans don't have a sense of humour,' Max called from the kitchen.

'And they'd be mistaken,' he returned.

'Okay, comic boy, where's the food?'

'Your sister's quite rude, you know,' Hal said over his shoulder to Sam. 'I could get offended.'

'If you hang around long enough it's guaranteed.'

He settled the pizzas on the bench where Max had made some space.

'And I bought champagne. I think you're supposed to break it on the bow of the house, something like that,' said Hal. 'But I'm for drinking it.'

'I'm with you,' Sam smiled.

'Hey Sherl, do you remember where you packed the glasses?' said Max, who was crouched reading the sides of boxes.

Sam frowned. 'I suppose one of the boxes labelled "kitchen".'

'Oh, which one of the seven thousand do you suppose?'

'Don't exaggerate, Maxine.'

Max opened a box and pulled out a coffee cup. 'Will this do? We could be here all night if we try to find proper glasses.'

'Doesn't bother me,' said Hal, popping the cork. Max felt for more cups as Sam held one out to Hal.

'Hey look,' said Max, unwrapping another. 'Here's that reunion invitation you threw out. You should ask Hal to be your date.'

'You want to ask me out on a date?' he smiled at Sam.

'No, she does.'

'Well, thanks all the same, Max, but I don't know you well enough just yet,' he said, pouring champagne into her cup.

'She doesn't want to go because partners are invited,' Max explained to him. 'She's worried she'll look pathetic all on her own.'

'Max!'

'And I would make a damned attractive partner,' Hal quipped.

'You'd be a lot more attractive if you only got over yourself,' Sam muttered.

'Can't see that happening.'

'Anyway you're not dating, as I recall,' she reminded him.

'I'd make an exception for you.'

Sam took a large gulp of her champagne, ignoring the silly grin on Max's face.

'Hey, wait up,' said Hal. 'We have to make a toast.'

'You know,' said Sam, 'I'm sick of toasts. Can't we just have a drink sometimes without having to make it into a ceremony?'

'But I have a good one.'

'Go ahead.'

'May your home resound with laughter,' Hal began. 'And the sun shine on it from above, so that on each day hereafter, it will always be filled with love.'

Sam and Max glanced at each other, trying not to laugh.

'Don't tell me,' said Sam. 'You used to have that on a plaque on the wall at home when you were growing up.'

'Maybe,' he said cagily. 'Gee, everyone's a critic.'

'Well, thank you for the sentiment. Now drink up.'

'I'm going to the euphemism,' Max said, disappearing through the forest of cardboard. 'Send out a search party if I'm not back in ten minutes.'

Hal picked up the crumpled invitation. 'So, you want to go?'

Sam shook her head. 'It'll only be a lot of posing and one-upmanship.'

'Why do you say that? I've always enjoyed my school reunions.'

'Of course you would, you're successful,' she said. 'You've got plenty to crow about.'

'And you don't?'

'My marriage failed, I used to live in a big house in a good suburb, and now I live . . .' she looked around, '. . . here. And my job is basically to pander to incompetent people.'

'I thought you liked your work?'

Sam shrugged. 'It just doesn't sound like a proper job.'

Hal leaned back against the kitchen cupboards. 'Seems to me you're way too worried about what other people think.'

Sam was trying to think of a pithy response. All she could come up with was, 'This pizza will be getting cold.'

Just then a loud crack sounded, apparently from the ceiling, and the lights flickered, dimmed, then surged again.

'What was that?' said Sam.

'Not sure. At least the lights survived it.'

As soon as the words left Hal's mouth, everything went black. The fridge let out a dying shudder and then fell silent.

'I shouldn't have said that.'

'What do you think it is?' asked Sam.

'Some kind of electrical problem.'

'Well, thanks for that, Captain Obvious.'

'Yoohoo!' Max cried. 'Are you guys still there?'

'Yes, can you find your way?' Sam called.

They heard a thud, and then the sound of a box sliding, hitting something else, then crashing to the floor.

'Shit!'

'Are you okay, Max?' Sam said, suppressing an urge to laugh. The situation should have upset her, she supposed, but she was finding it oddly amusing.

'Far out, it's dark in here. Keep talking, Sherl, so I can follow the sound of your voice.'

'Well, what do you want me to say?'

'That'll do.'

Sam couldn't suppress her laughter any longer.

'What's so funny?' asked Hal.

'I don't know.'

'Here I am,' Max announced, feeling around the kitchen doorway. She thrust both hands forward, jabbing Hal simultaneously in the mouth and the ear.

'Ow.'

'Sorry,' she said, feeling around his jaw. 'That is you, Hal?'

'Well, unless you think your sister has grown a head taller and started to shave . . .' He paused. 'Max, you can let go of my face now.'

'Nice jaw line,' she mumbled. 'What are you giggling about, Sherl?'

'Nothing,' she snorted.

'Are you scoffing all the champagne while we can't see you?'

'Sam, listen to me,' said Hal. 'Have you got a flashlight, some candles?'

'Candles?' Sam burst into hysterical laughter. 'No, I haven't got any candles at all. Not even one,' she breathed, barely able to get out the words. She doubled over laughing, tears streaming from her eyes.

'She's gone completely mad,' said Max. 'I thought this might happen one day. I've got a torch in my bag, if we can just find my bag.'

Sam was still laughing as Max and Hal searched in the darkness, all the while arguing over whether the correct name was torch or flashlight. Max was insisting that flashlight was an American term and should he go into a shop in Australia and ask for a flashlight, he'd be laughed at. Hal, on the other hand, maintained that a torch was something you lit, that natives carried torches through the jungle in Tarzan movies. Sam sank down the wall to sit on the floor, chuckling deliriously.

Eventually they located the bag and the torch. Hal tested it, shining it in Sam's direction. She was still sitting on the floor, and when the light fell on her, she started laughing again.

'What's wrong with you, Sam?' Max frowned.

'Nothing,' she cried happily.

'Well, I'm going out to check the fuse box,' said Hal.

'I'm coming with you,' said Max. 'I'm not staying in here in the dark. Come on Sam.'

'But I'm okay here in the dark,' Sam grinned up at her.

Max walked over and pulled her up off the floor. 'I don't trust you on your own. I think you may be sniffing the floor polish or something.'

They walked around to the side of the house and found the meter box. Hal lifted the lid and inspected the fuses.

'Gosh, this is ancient. I haven't seen these old ceramic switches for a long time.'

Sam started giggling again but Max elbowed her.

'Can you tell what's wrong?' Max asked.

'Probably a blown fuse, but I'm not game to touch anything. I'm going to turn off the main switch so there's no more trouble. But it means you won't have any power tonight.'

'Doesn't matter,' shrugged Sam, grinning.

'Still, you'd better call an electrician. There's probably some kind of emergency service,' he said, closing the cover of the meter box. 'In the meantime, I'll check up in the ceiling in case there were any sparks. We don't want a fire up there.'

'We certainly don't!' agreed Sam, trying to take it seriously, but failing.

Sam found the stepladder for Hal and he took it into the hall where the trapdoor to the roof was located. They watched him climb the ladder and lift the door and then his head disappeared, along with the beam of light from the torch.

'You see, this is why I like men, why I can't write them off altogether,' said Max. 'I would no sooner stick my head up into that narky old roof than fly to the moon. But blokes just do it.'

Hal appeared again. 'Seems to be all clear up there.'

He stepped back down the ladder and propped it against the wall out of the way. 'You'd better call an electrician.'

Sam shrugged. 'I'll do it in the morning.'

'Call somebody now,' said Max. 'Then at least they'll be here first thing.'

'She's right,' Hal agreed. He took his mobile phone out of his pocket and dialled a number. 'Yes, I'm after electrical services, emergency, after hours if possible.' He paused. 'Marrickville.' Another pause. 'Yes please.' He passed the phone to Sam. 'They're connecting.'

Sam stirred, trying to focus. She gave a vague explanation to the person on the other end, who took her details and promised someone would be out first thing in the morning.

'Come on,' said Max. 'We'd better eat the pizza while it's still warm. We won't be able to reheat it.'

They made their way out to the kitchen and stood around the bench eating. Sam didn't feel all that hungry, but in the dark they didn't notice that she was nursing the same piece.

'You'd better come home with me tonight,' said Max.

'No, I have to be here bright and early for the electrician. I wouldn't want to miss him.'

'Then I'll stay here with you.'

'There's no point both of us being uncomfortable,' Sam maintained. 'I'll be fine, I'll just go to bed. I'm dead tired anyway.'

'I could stay,' offered Hal.

'You wish,' Sam scoffed.

Hal turned to Max. 'She has this idea I'm always trying to get her into bed.'

'Methinks she doth protest too much.'

'Okay, you two can leave now,' said Sam, closing the lid of the pizza box. They started to argue with her, but she eventually convinced them she was dead on her feet and just wanted to get some sleep.

But when Sam closed the door behind them, she wished she hadn't been quite so insistent. She felt an ache rise up in her chest. She was just tired. She found her way through to her bedroom with the torch they'd left her, and then she saw the unmade bed. She started to read the labels on the boxes, looking for linen, but her eyes were stinging. Where were the sheets she'd taken off the line? Probably still in the car. Sam suddenly felt overwhelmed. She didn't have the energy to walk out to the car, or even to make the bed for that matter. She found her way back to the kitchen and the torch beam fell on the bottle of champagne. She picked it up and realised there was still a little left. She emptied it into a coffee cup, walked out the back door and sat on the step, looking out into the backyard. No pool, no pergola, just a cracked cement path leading to the Hills hoist, a lemon tree, some nondescript shrubs and a rickety fence with palings missing.

The ache in her chest welled up, constricting the back of her throat. Tears pooled in her eyes before falling over her lashes to trickle down her cheeks. She sniffed, and gulped down half the cup of champagne. She sobbed, just once, involuntarily. Then she drank some more. She wiped the tears with the back of her hand. But they kept coming.

'Sam?'

She sniffed again, looking around. Hal was standing at the side of the house. Light from next door illuminated his silhouette from behind. It made him look ethereal, otherworldly, like he was her guardian angel or something. God, she was so tired she was becoming delusional.

'I tried knocking,' he said. 'There was no answer.'

'Sorry. I didn't hear you.'

'You know you're not very secure here, anyone could just walk straight through that side gate.'

'Oh.' More good news.

'So,' he said, holding up a plastic shopping bag as he walked towards her. 'I saw a Seven Eleven, so I bought you some candles and a bigger flashlight. I didn't like to think of you alone here in the dark. And turns out I wasn't laughed at when I asked for a flashlight. Max can put that in her thesaurus and . . . look it up.'

A noise like something between a hiccup and a sob escaped out of Sam's throat.

'What's the matter?' Hal said as he came closer. She could see his features more clearly now, which meant he could see her tears. 'Hey, I know the thesaurus joke wasn't one of my best, but . . .'

Sam attempted a laugh but it came out strangled. She covered her face as more tears flowed. Hal didn't say anything as he sat down on the step beside her and put his arm around her.

'What the hell have I done? What the hell was I thinking?' she whimpered.

Hal rubbed her shoulder comfortingly. 'Come on, I'll show you,' he said, standing up and putting his hand out to her. She looked up at him, frowning. 'Well, come on,' he urged.

Sam stood and took his hand. He led her to the back corner of the yard and then started walking along the length of the fence.

'This is the boundary of your property,' said Hal. '*Your* property! You own this.'

'Well, the bank's letting me pretend I do.'

He ignored her, continuing on to the opposite corner, where he turned, leading her along the side fence back towards the house. 'All of this is yours,' he said, continuing up the side path past the house. 'An entire building that will give you shelter, keep you warm . . .'

'Not until the power's back on.'

They came out to the front of the house. Hal led her to sit down on the squat brick fence.

'Sam,' he began. '"What the hell you've done" is an extraordinary thing. You've bought a house all on your own. That's a big step, and okay, there are risks. But think about it, Sam, you're one of the lucky ones. Only something like, um, I forget the exact figure, but I'm sure it's less than ten per cent of the world's population owns property, and barely any women. There are people who don't even have a pillow to lay their heads on at night.'

'Did your mother used to tell you to eat your dinner and think of the starving people in Africa?'

Hal looked a little frustrated. 'Are you always so damn negative?'

'Sorry,' she said quietly. 'I know everything you're saying is true. I was just feeling sorry for myself.'

'Well, that's allowed now and then,' he smiled. 'Come on, let's go inside and light some candles and get you comfortable.'

She stood up, returning his smile faintly. She knew she should probably insist that he go home, that she would be alright. But Sam didn't want to be alone. And it was nice to have someone to lean on for a change.

So she let Hal arrange the candles on a tray, and clear a space in the living room. She let him find blankets and a pillow for her. And he let her talk. She told him about Alan Mitchell, and Guy Hennessey, and poor Vanessa, and dear Ted. And sometime either very late at night or very early in the morning, he checked that all the doors were locked, covered her with a blanket, blew out the candles and left her curled up on the sofa where she had drifted off to sleep.

Eight a.m.

Sam blinked. She was lying under the covers on her own bed, on a sheet. When did she make the bed? She looked around the room. Her room in Ermine Street. Everything was unpacked and in place, as far as she could tell. She hadn't realised the walls were so white, they almost glowed from the sun streaming through the windows.

She got up and walked down the hall. The living room was all in order, there were no boxes around, not even empty ones. There were flowers on the table, oddly like the arrangement Alan Mitchell had sent her. What day was it? She knew she didn't get all this done on Friday. There was the blackout, and last thing she remembered was getting sleepy on the sofa, talking to Hal . . .

She heard a car pull up outside and peered through the curtains. It was Jeff. Had she lost an entire day? Was it Sunday already? She watched as the children all bounded out of the car and ran for the house. She walked over to the door and let them in.

'Hi Mum!' they chorused. Their faces were all pink and shiny and smiling. 'Can we see our rooms?'

Why were they all talking like that, in unison? This was very bizarre. They ran off down the hallway and disappeared.

'Hi Sam!' Jeff chirped. 'Wow, the place looks great. Sorry we're early, the kids couldn't wait to get here. Mind if I put the kettle on?'

'There's no power,' she said vaguely.

Jeff laughed. 'Of course there's power!'

He walked out into the kitchen and Sam went to close the door. But as she turned around, Hal appeared on the doorstep, smiling broadly.

'Hey Sam, how're you doing?' he said, walking past her into the house.

'Who's this?' said Jeff warily, coming out of the kitchen.

'This is Hal Buchanan. Hal, this is Jeff.'

'Are you dating my wife?'

Sam was shocked. 'Jeff! That's none of your business.'

'I think I've got a right to know what the mother of my children is getting up to.'

'Stop this, Jeff, you're embarrassing me. Hal is a client.'

'But I think we're friends now. Aren't we friends yet, Sam?'

'Well, I'm her husband.'

'Only on paper, I believe, Jeff,' said Hal.

'I don't think that's any of your business.'

'Jeff!' Sam exclaimed, moving between them. 'There's no need to be so rude.'

'I just want to know what he's doing here.'

'It's top secret, I'm with the CIA.'

'I suppose you think that's funny?'

'No, I don't have a sense of humour, I'm American.'

Sam frowned, looking at Hal. He winked at her.

'Why are you here?' Jeff was almost shouting.

'I'm on a contract –'

'Well get this,' said Jeff. 'Your contract expires now!'

'I don't think that's for you to say, Jeff.'

'Oh yeah?' he leered, taking a step closer.

This was ridiculous. 'Jeff, stop this. You should go.'

'I'm not going anywhere,' he snarled.

Sam stared at him. There were two small lumps protruding from the top of his head, just above his temples. They seemed to be growing as she watched them.

'Look at your head!' Sam screamed as the skin broke and antlers sprouted up and out of Jeff's skull. 'Do something!' she shrieked, turning to Hal. But now he had antlers growing out of his head as well. The two men started to circle each other slowly.

'Stop this,' Sam cried. 'You have to stop it at once!'

She heard loud knocking at the door. 'Is there anyone there?'

'O thank God,' she sighed.

'Hello? It's the electrician.'

Sam jumped up with a fright. The living room was gloomy, there were boxes stacked in front of the window, blocking the morning light.

'Anyone home?' the voice called again from the front door.

'Coming!' Sam replied. She struggled to unravel herself from the blanket and ended up rolling off the sofa and landing with a thump on her knees.

'Just a minute!'

She sat back on her haunches and saw the tray of half-burned candles on the coffee table. She felt a little spaced out. She smoothed her hair and adjusted her T-shirt, before getting up and squeezing past boxes to the front door.

'Hello,' she greeted the man as brightly as she could manage. 'Sorry about that.'

'No worries, love. I better take a look at this meter box then.'

She led him around the corner of the house and down the side path. He lifted the lid of the meter box and frowned, shaking his head. That wasn't good.

'Jeez, it's an antique.'

Sam sighed. She thought she could hear a faint ringing sound coming from inside the house.

'I think that's my phone.'

'Go ahead, love, I'll be right.'

Sam dashed inside and stumbled over boxes and furniture till she reached the kitchen.

'Hello?' she said breathlessly after grabbing the phone off the shelf.

'Hey Sam.'

It was Hal. With huge antlers. God, she was going to have to try to wipe that mental picture from her brain.

'How did you sleep?'

'Oh, um, alright,' she faltered. 'Thanks, you know, thanks for last night.'

'You're welcome.'

Mentally break off the antlers and throw them away. It won't hurt him, they're not even real.

'Is he there yet?' Hal continued.

'Who?'

'The electricity guy.'

'Oh, sure.'

'What did he say?'

'Well, not a lot yet. He just got here.'

'Let me talk to him.'

'No!' Sam declared. 'I can handle it.'

'I'm sure you can. I just want to talk to him.'

'Why?'

'I want to ask him something.'

'Wait a sec,' she sighed begrudgingly, walking out the back door and up the side path to where the electrician was working.

'Excuse me,' Sam began. 'Um, a friend of mine, well, he was here last night when the power blew, and, well, he wants to talk to you.'

'No worries.'

Sam handed him the phone and he held it to his ear. 'Gidday. Yeah . . . Yeah . . . Yeah, it's a shocker alright. Yeah.' He turned and looked straight at Sam, grinning broadly. 'I reckon.'

Sam frowned.

'She is,' he continued. 'Okay, mate. See ya.'

He passed the phone back to Sam and she walked down the path out of earshot.

'What was that about?'

'Nothing. I just needed some electrical advice.'

'You were talking about me.'

'You see, what you have is a condition called paranoia, Sam.'

'What electrical advice could you possibly need?'

'I wasn't sure which way the batteries went in my *electric* shaver.'

'I'm hanging up now.'

'Wait a second. Do you need a hand today?'

'No, it's okay, Max is coming, and a couple of other friends.'

'So? It'll be like a party.'

'Unpacking?' Sam said dubiously.

'Sure! We can drink Coca-Cola and dance and act zany, just like in the commercials.'

'You're a fool, you know that.'

'Ah, come on Sam, can I please come over to your place and help unpack for hours and lift heavy stuff and get a sore back and make your life a little easier?'

He has no antlers. He has no antlers.

'Please?'

'If you insist.'

Fortunately Max was the first to arrive, giving Sam the opportunity to recount the whole dream in detail.

'What do you think it means?'

'Well, what do you think it means?'

'I don't know, that's why I'm asking you!' Sam cried. 'You're the psychologist.'

Max looked surprised. 'I'm barely half a psychologist, Sherl.'

'Which is double what I am. Come on, you must know something about dream interpretation?'

'Strict symbolic interpretation of dreams is passé. You have to work out what the dream means to you.'

'It means I'm going crazy.'

'I'll tell you one thing. Usually the people in your dreams are not actually the people themselves, they represent aspects of yourself. The fact that the two main figures in the dream were men could simply mean that you're struggling with your masculine side. You have to ask yourself, what does Jeff mean to you? What does Hal mean to you? Is one freedom and the other commitment? Is your new life battling it out with your old life?'

Sam listened to her, wide-eyed.

'And the antlers are obviously very significant.'

'What do they mean?'

'Well, they're a powerful male symbol of aggression, domination, even sexuality. You could be wrestling with the need to take your position as the head of the family.'

Sam chewed the edge of her thumb, contemplating.

'Or it could mean . . .' Max said thoughtfully.

'What?'

'That you want to have sex with Hal.'

'Shut up.'

Sunday

Sam lay on her freshly made bed looking around the room, where pretty much everything was in its place. The walls weren't so white, in fact they could probably do with repainting. She wasn't dreaming this time. She hadn't lost a day. Yesterday was very clear in her mind.

Liz and Michael had arrived soon after Max, closely followed by Hal. Of course that created a stir with Liz, who kept cornering Sam when Hal was out of earshot and grilling her about what was going on with the tall, handsome American.

Nothing, Sam had tried to insist.

Yeah right, Liz had smirked, winking at Max.

And Hal only made it worse. He was relentlessly charming, unfailingly polite. He worked like the proverbial trooper, moving heavy furniture around with Michael as though it was fun, climbing ladders, hanging pictures, connecting the TV and video, and reinstalling the computer so it was working better than it did before.

And he was funny. Very funny. He made everyone laugh, often at his own expense. Liz was very impressed. She kept nudging Sam and winking. Sometimes Sam would look up and see that Hal was watching the winks and nudges with a satisfied smile, and next thing those damned antlers would appear on his head.

When Hal brought up the subject of the reunion, of course everyone agreed Sam should go with him. And unless she wanted to make a really huge deal of refusing, she had to concede.

But it was a mistake to get involved with Hal Buchanan. Sam knew it, she just wished everyone else would get it as well. Couldn't they see heartbreak in his broad shoulders and his square jaw and his green eyes and that satisfied smile? Max had been right in the first place. Hal was out of her league. The only reason he could possibly be interested in a seen-better-days thirtysomething mother of three was to fill in time while he was in Australia. And despite the girls' ideas about Sam just having a fling, it was way more . . . complicated than that. She couldn't explain why, it just was.

Sam glanced at the bedside clock. The kids would be here soon, she just needed to lie down for a little while. She couldn't remember ever feeling this exhausted, but at least everything was done. Their rooms were all ready, she'd left only the heavily taped boxes marked DO NOT OPEN!!! for Josh and Jess to unpack themselves. Dinner was in the oven and Sam was crossing her fingers for a pleasant, perhaps even celebratory meal together. She knew it was probably wishful thinking, but if only the kids could be a little happy, a little content this first night together in the house, maybe they could reinvent themselves here as the family they were now. Circumstances might have made them a different family, but Sam didn't want that to be a second-rate family.

She had just dozed off when she heard the knock at the door, and she felt groggy as she hurried out to let them in. Ellie's beaming face was the first thing she saw as her little daughter jumped into her arms and hugged her. Sam held her tightly, looking past her to where Jeff was huddled with Josh and Jess. Their heads were downcast and he had a hand on their shoulders. He was giving them a pep talk, she realised. She felt tears pricking her eyes. She didn't know whether she was grateful to Jeff, or annoyed that he had to.

'Hi Mummy! Is all our things here now?'

'Yes honey.'

'Can I see?'

'Of course.'

Sam set Ellie down and she ran off down the hall. Josh and Jess were approaching, their father between them, still holding each firmly by the shoulder.

'Hi Sam,' said Jeff brightly. 'How did everything go?'

'Alright. We had a slight hiccup with the electricity. I'm going to need a new power board and some of the wiring will have to be replaced. But it's doable.'

'Oh.' He looked concerned. 'That's bad luck.'

Sam didn't know why she had started on a negative. Josh and Jess hadn't even looked at her.

'But kids,' she tried again, brighter this time, 'your rooms are all set up, just how you wanted. Why don't you go and take a look?'

They sauntered off down the hall. Jeff stepped inside.

'It's a nice little place, Sam,' he offered encouragingly.

'Mm,' she nodded.

'I think you'll like being closer to the city. It only took us twenty minutes to get here. I told the kids we might be able to have a night through the week together, now and then.'

Sam didn't say anything, she just gave him a wan smile.

Jeff was watching her closely. 'That's only if it's okay with you.'

She roused. 'Of course it is. Don't mind me, I'm just being vague.'

'You look tired, Sam. I could have kept the kids another night, you know. They are on holidays.'

She shook her head. 'No, it's okay, they had to face it sometime. Life goes on.'

Jeff went to say goodbye to the kids and then he left. Sam could hear arguing from the girls' room. She took a deep breath and walked down the hallway.

'What's going on?' she asked, standing at the door.

'I told Ellie she has to move some of her stuff out of the way,' said Jessica. 'This room is *so* much smaller with furniture in it, Mum.'

'Why does Ellie have to move her things?'

'Because I'm the eldest,' Jess explained airily. 'I should have twice the room she has.'

'That's not fair!' Ellie protested.

'It certainly isn't,' Sam agreed. 'Jess, you're *sharing* the room. Have you got any appreciation of the concept?'

'Why is the computer out in the living room?' Josh asked, appearing in the doorway.

'Because there's nowhere else to put it.'

'Well, why can't it go in my room?'

'Hey!' Jess interrupted. 'That's not fair! As if anyone else would get near it.'

'There's your answer, Josh,' said Sam.

'How am I supposed to do homework and stuff without any privacy?'

'Well –'

'And *stuff*!' Jess taunted. 'Like talking to your friends on ICQ all night?'

'Shut up, retard.'

'Josh –'

'I don't know why you're complaining,' Jess pouted. 'At least you get a room to yourself.'

'Suck eggs,' he smirked.

'It's not fair, Mum!'

'Cut it out!' Sam shouted over the top of them. She was surprised by the volume of her own voice. The kids just stared at her.

'Listen to yourselves!' she continued, lowering her tone. 'I'm sick to death of your whingeing and whining. You're turning into spoilt, rotten kids. Do you know how lucky you are to even have a house? There's like . . .' What had Hal said? '. . . ten per cent of people in the whole world who own houses.' She noticed Jess rolling her eyes.

'Do you think I purposely set out to make life harder for you? Is that what you're thinking? Because let me tell you, I'm doing the best I can to make the most of a bad situation. I've worked so hard to try to make things look nice around here. But I don't know why I bothered. Because no matter what I do, you always find something to complain about. And *that* is what's not fair!'

Her words were echoing around the room. Josh stared at his feet, Jess was gobsmacked, poor Ellie just looked bewildered.

Sam sighed heavily. 'It would just be nice for a change if someone would say "Thanks Mum, for all the trouble you went to".'

She crossed the hall to her room, slammed the door behind her and threw herself on the bed.

Well, that was an all-time-low parenting moment. She'd brought herself right down to the level of a spoilt teenager and ended up sounding as petty and self-absorbed as they did.

She heard low voices for a while, before they moved down the hall and out to the kitchen. A soft knock sounded on the door.

'Yes?'

'It's Ellie, Mummy.'

'Come in.'

Sam turned over on the bed as the door opened and Ellie appeared on the other side, solemn and wide-eyed.

'Come here, sweetheart,' said Sam, patting the mattress.

She walked over to the bed and climbed up next to her mother.

'Are you okay, Mummy?'

'Yes, honey. I just lost my temper because I'm so tired after all the moving. I shouldn't have yelled at you like that.'

'Joshy and Jessie shouldn't yell either,' said Ellie.

'That's true.'

'What does spoilt mean, Mummy?' Ellie asked after a while.

'It means . . . Well, you're not spoilt, Ellie, so you don't have to worry about it.'

'Are Jessie and Josh spoilt?'

'Sometimes they act a little spoilt. They get a lot given to them, and a lot done for them, and they're not always very grateful.'

They were quiet for a moment.

'I like my room, Mummy,' Ellie said eventually.

Sam kissed her on the top of the head. 'You're a good girl, Ellie.'

There was a tap on the door. Jessica peered in tentatively. 'Do you want to have dinner, Mum? I set the table.'

Sam didn't really feel like eating but she had to be the adult now. 'Sure.'

They walked out to the living area. Jess had indeed set the table, she'd even found a decent tablecloth. Josh was lifting the baking dish out of the oven. Sam's immediate impulse was to go and take over, but she looked at the size of him and realised he was perfectly capable. And if he wasn't, he'd soon learn.

So she sat down at the table instead. Josh carried the dish over and set it carefully on a placemat. Jess followed him with the salad.

'Do you want me to try and serve this up?' asked Josh, eyeing the lasagne uncertainly.

'You could give it a go,' Sam suggested.

'I'll get the server,' offered Jess.

Sam knew this change of heart was at best temporary and she'd be lucky if it lasted till tomorrow morning. But it was a start at least.

October 5

Dear Samantha

I had hoped to see you again, but every time I've flown up to Sydney lately I've been in meetings all day, before returning to Melbourne in the evening.

I trust the move to the new house proceeded without misadventure. Enclosed is a cheque to help defray some of your expenses. Use it for whatever you see fit, perhaps even spend a little on yourself.

Please give my regards to the children. I look forward to seeing you all at Christmas.

I want you to know I am very proud of you.

Your sister,

Alex

A week later

Max arrived at six-thirty to babysit, and so she could help Sam with her hair before Hal came to take her to the reunion.

'It's quiet in here,' Max commented, glancing around the empty living room. 'You didn't have to bind and gag the kids on my account.'

Sam smiled. 'Josh and Jess are both in their rooms and Ellie's next door.'

'So how are things going?' Max asked, following Sam into the bathroom.

'Well, it's been pretty much like this all week. Ever since my dummy spit, the kids have been subdued to say the least. I feel a little guilty, but I can't say I'm not enjoying the peace.' She sat down on a stool in the bathroom and handed Max a comb.

'They had it coming, Sam,' said Max, starting on her hair. 'You know I love them to death, but I think they were taking advantage of the situation. They had to get over feeling sorry for themselves sooner or later.'

Sam looked at her sister's reflection in the mirror. 'How did you get so smart without even having kids?'

'Ha! Maybe it's because I haven't had any, did you ever think of it that way?' she said, twisting and pulling at Sam's hair.

'Ow. You sure do hair like a mother.'

Max grinned. 'So, how long before school starts back?'

'They have another week. I'm mentally battening down the hatches. I'm sure the truce will be over then and the next round of assaults will begin.'

'You think it's going to be that bad?'

Sam shrugged. 'They're not saying much, they're probably not game. I'm not worried about Ellie, but I do feel sorry for Josh and Jess – it'll be hard being the new kid at their age. At least they'll be occupied next week – Jess is going to Emma's for a couple of nights and Josh has an end-of-season camping trip with his football team. So it'll be just me and Ellie.'

'And she's made a friend next door?'

Sam nodded. 'Carlos. She says she's going to marry him.'

'So, she'll be a child bride like her mother then?'

'Heaven forbid,' Sam rolled her eyes. 'She's such a sweet-heart, that little girl. She keeps me sane.' She stared into the mirror. 'Jess used to be like her when she was the same age, you know. What happened to her?'

'She's got PMT.'

'No, she hasn't started her periods yet.'

'Exactly. She's got never-ending PMT. She's a bundle of hormones with no place to go. Don't you remember what Alex was like? She grew fangs. And I think Mum was pre-menopausal at the same time. Talk about your Axis of Evil. It's a wonder you and I survived.'

Max finished her hair and Sam stood up off the stool.

'Nice threads, Sherl.'

'Mm,' said Sam, checking herself in the mirror. 'It's another Vanessa outfit.'

It was a simple, fine jersey slipdress with a matching cardi-gan, in a shade of bronze which was quite striking against Sam's colouring. Vanessa had claimed it did nothing for her.

'She's certainly keeping you in style these days,' Max remarked.

'Well, I've given up arguing with her. Every time I see her she's got another two or three outfits that she insists she'll throw in the charity bin if I don't take them.'

'Don't look a gift horse in the mouth, girlie, as Aunty Gwen would say.'

'Do you think it's too slinky though?' said Sam, adjusting the cardigan. 'I don't want to seem like a try-hard. And I'm wearing my stomach flatteners but I think there's still a bulge.'

Max groaned. 'How do you expect to get any sex when you're wearing steel-belted undies?'

Sam glared at her. 'I don't expect to get any sex!'

'Well at least you won't be disappointed.' Max considered her in the mirror. 'You need to push your boobs up a bit.'

'What?'

'You know, give them a hoick, they're looking a bit saggy.'

'That's because they are a bit saggy, Max,' Sam frowned. 'They're like half-deflated balloons. One of the legacies of having children.'

Max ignored her. 'Lean over and let them fall up.'

Sam couldn't be bothered arguing and did as Max ordered. When she stood up, Max tightened the bra straps over her shoulders. 'There, you've got a cleavage now.'

Sam looked in the mirror. 'I don't know,' she muttered, trying to readjust herself.

'Leave them alone.' Max held her firmly by the shoulders from behind, leaning forward so their faces were next to each other. 'You're that gorgeous, Sherl,' she said to Sam's reflection. 'You barely look as though you've left high school.'

Sam screwed up her face, peering closer into the mirror. 'Yeah, until you get a load of all these wrinkles.'

'Ellie would have wrinkles if she screwed her face up like that,' Max declared. 'You've never realised how pretty you are, have you?'

Sam stared at her, she didn't know what to say.

'Remember, I was always dragging along behind you on the way home from school, I saw the heads turn. You could have had any boy, but once Jeff came along, you stuck to him like a shag on a rock.' She paused. 'Apparently you let him take your self-esteem when he left. But I tell you something, Sam, he didn't leave you because you weren't pretty enough.'

Sam's eyes went glassy. 'Thanks,' she said quietly to Max.

'Now, go and have a good time and knock the socks off all those guys who are still probably holding a torch for you.'

They walked back up the hall and Sam tapped lightly on Jess's door before opening it.

'Could you go next door and get your sister, please?'

'What?' said Jess loudly, removing her earphones. She was lying in the middle of the floor with her feet up on the bed. 'Oh, hi Max!' She swung her legs down and jumped onto her knees. 'Hey Max, can we get *Head Over Heels* to watch tonight?'

'What will Josh have to say about that?'

'He won't care if he's allowed to go on the internet.'

Max looked at Sam and she shrugged. 'Whatever gets you through the night, Max. You do realise there'll be no one over thirty in that movie?'

'Well thank God for that!' she winked at Jess.

'Run in next door and get Ellie, please,' Sam asked her again.

'Okay,' she chirped, skipping past them up the hall.

'Gee,' Max remarked. 'Without so much as a protest? Things really have changed around here.'

Sam walked across the living room into the kitchen. 'Oh no, that's because of Carlos's older brother, who, I've been told, bears a striking resemblance to Freddie Prinze Jnr. Do you want a drink?'

'Okay,' said Max. She gazed at the noticeboard while Sam took a bottle of wine out of the fridge. 'So is Jeff going to the reunion?'

Sam swung around. 'What?'

'Is Jeff going?' she repeated.

'Why would Jeff be going?'

'Because it says here,' she read off the invitation, '"To be incorporated with Flinders High Twenty Year Reunion celebration".'

'What?' Sam said in a high-pitched voice. 'Where does it say that?'

Max pointed to the line as Sam scanned the page. 'My God, they put it in fine print. What were they trying to hide? Why would they do this? Why didn't they make it clear? What am I going to do?' Her voice kept getting higher and higher with every sentence.

'Crikey Sam. The dogs in the street are going to start howling in a minute,' said Max, holding her ears.

Sam took a breath. 'I just don't know why they would do this!'

'Have you forgotten that Flinders Boys' and Chisholm Girls' were right next door to each other? Half the students probably ended up together, just like you and Jeff.'

'Oh shit!'

'What are you worried about? Half of them are probably

separated just like you and Jeff as well,' said Max, taking the yet
to be opened bottle of wine from Sam.

'What if Jeff's going?'

'Then you'll get to meet Jodi,' she said absently, looking for
the corkscrew.

Sam's stomach lurched. 'I don't want to meet her!' she
breathed.

Max looked at her, frowning. 'What, never?'

'I don't know. Just not yet. I'm not ready.' Sam bit anxiously
on the edge of her thumb. 'I'll phone Hal and cancel instead.'

'Don't be stupid,' said Max. 'Jeff mightn't even be going.'
She took the phone off the wall. 'Here, ring him and find out.'

'I can't do that! What will I say?'

Max sighed. 'You could try, "Hi Jeff, are you going to the
reunion tonight?"'

'And what then?'

'It depends on his answer!' Max said, exasperated. 'Stop
being such a wally and call him.'

Sam took the phone and dialled Jeff's mobile.

'Jeff Holmes.'

'Hi Jeff, it's Sam.'

'Hi, is everything okay?'

'Sure. Um, I was just ringing to find out . . .' she swallowed,
'um, are you going to the reunion tonight?'

'Yes, I am, as a matter of fact.'

Sam looked wide-eyed at Max, nodding emphatically. She
mouthed, 'What will I say?'

'Sam,' Jeff spoke again. 'Are you going?'

'Well, I'm not really sure,' she said vaguely.

'I'm going alone,' he said plainly. He must have twigged.

'Oh.'

'So, I'll see you there?'

'Um, look I haven't planned anything definite.'

'Okay,' he paused. 'I'll see you if I see you then, I guess.'

'Yeah. Bye.'

She hung up. Max looked at her expectantly.

'He's going alone.'

'Oh, so you're alright then,' said Max, sticking the corkscrew into the bottle.

Sam shook her head. 'No, I can't show up with Hal.'

'Why not?' Max frowned.

'It'd be too embarrassing. Jeff might think there's something going on. I'd have to let him know somehow that there wasn't . . .'

'Why?'

'Because there isn't.'

'Yet.'

'Max! That's not the point.'

'What is the point?'

'Well, I'd have to introduce them, and then there'd be all that polite small talk. I'd rather have root canal therapy.'

'You're being ridiculous.'

'No I'm not,' Sam said firmly, dialling Hal's number. 'Hopefully I'll catch Hal before he's left.'

'You can't call off a date with a guy just before he shows up!'

Sam was waiting for the phone to be diverted to his mobile. 'It's not a date.'

'This is very bad form, Sherl.'

There was a knock at the front door. Max was pouring the wine.

'That'll be the girls,' said Sam. 'I'll get it.'

She walked across the living room still holding the phone as she heard Hal come onto the line.

'Hi, it's Sam.'

'Hey Sam, what's up?'

'There's a bit of a glitch with tonight. Where are you now?' she asked, opening the door.

Hal was standing on the other side, speaking into his mobile. 'I just arrived at your house and this beautiful woman, who incidentally looks way too young to be having her twenty year high school reunion, has just opened the door.'

Sam pulled a face.

'Now she's making a face. It's not very flattering.'

'You're early.'

He looked at his watch. 'Only a little. You know, we can actually carry on this conversation without the aid of a telephone. It's amazing the advances they've made with the human voice these days.'

Sam rolled her eyes, but she was smiling as she turned off her phone. Hal flipped his shut and dropped it into his shirt pocket. 'What's the glitch?'

'Come on in,' said Sam. She was going to have to argue with him as well now because he was sure to take Max's side.

'Hal-*lelujah*!' greeted Max, as he came into the kitchen.

He winced, 'I don't think so.'

'Well, it was "Hal-*itosis*" in the dictionary before that, but I thought it was a bit offensive.'

'And hardly warranted. You'll have to keep trying.'

They'd had this game going since moving day. Max was determined to find Hal a nickname apart from 'handsome', which Hal had tried to insist was fine with him. They acted like some long-lost brother and sister, the pair of them. Max had never got on so well with Jeff, not that there was any reason to make that comparison.

'So what's the glitch, Sam?' Hal asked her again.

'I've decided not to go to the reunion tonight.'

'No you haven't!' Max exclaimed.

'Oh, haven't I?'

'She's in a flap because the ex-husband will be there,' Max explained to Hal.

'Max, if you don't mind,' said Sam in her mother's voice. Or maybe she sounded more like that woman from *The Weakest Link*. 'It's not that.'

'It is too that,' said Max. 'What else could it be?'

There was a knock at the door and Sam went to answer it, giving her a moment to think of something. Jess stood on the doorstep holding a huge bowl covered with silver foil.

'Look what Carlos's Mummy gave us,' exclaimed Ellie, appearing beside her. 'Palaver!'

'No,' Jessie grinned. 'It's *paella*, Ellie.' Then she giggled. 'That's hard to say.'

The flush in Jess's cheeks and the shine in her eyes were a dead giveaway that young Marco Suarez had been home next door.

'She's got six children, she shouldn't be making food for us.' Sam took the bowl from Jessica and carried it over to the kitchen.

'Hi Hal,' Ellie squealed excitedly, running over to him. He picked her up to receive her kiss on his cheek. Well, how great, thought Sam drily, everyone's getting along.

'Guess what?' said Ellie.

'What?'

'I'm five now!'

'I thought you looked older.'

Ellie beamed delightedly. Human nature was just perverse, Sam decided. The young couldn't wait to get older, until that certain point arrived when birthdays became less welcome and more ominous. That certain point was about the age of twenty-two, she reckoned, for a woman at least. For a man it was more like forty-nine.

'So, six kids!' Max was saying, shocked.

'And they're all boys!' Jessica exclaimed.

'It's testosterone central in there,' said Sam. 'I don't know how she does it. Their place is only the size of ours.' She peeled the silver foil off the top of the bowl. 'Well, there's enough here for all of us. Hey Hal, we can stay here and share the paella.'

'No,' said Max firmly, covering the bowl again. 'You're going to your reunion.'

Josh appeared at the end of the hall. 'What's for dinner?'

'Adolescent male. Smell food. Come hunting,' Max chanted, sounding like an Indian chief in a bad western. If Sam had tried that, Josh would have been merciless. But he just smiled at Max, shaking his head.

'Have you said hello to Hal?' Sam prompted him.

'Hi Hal,' said Josh as he passed through the living room to the kitchen. Hal had taken a seat on the sofa and was browsing through a book he had picked up off the coffee table.

'How're you doing, Josh?' he returned absently.

'What's that book?' Ellie asked Hal, climbing up next to him.

'I suspect this is your mommy's yearbook, from when she was at school.' Sam had dragged it out earlier today and had been searching through the photographs, trying to prepare herself. 'But I can't find your mom, there's no one pretty enough.'

Sam glanced quickly at Max and Jess, who both had dopey grins on their faces. Josh mimed sticking his fingers down his throat.

'What's your maiden name?' Hal asked.

'Dris –'

Sam reached out and stuck her hand across Max's mouth. 'Never mind,' she said.

Hal rejoined them in the kitchen. 'So, what's the verdict?'

'You're going to the reunion.'

'No Max, I don't want to.'

'Why not?'

'Oh, you know what I'm like! I talk too much when I get nervous, I talk so much, in fact, that it's like I can't stop and then I start saying stupid things. I'll get everyone's name mixed up and embarrass myself and wonder why I ever agreed to go at all, which is exactly what I'm doing now, so I'd rather wonder here at home than when it's too late and I'm already there, talking nonsense because I'm so nervous.'

Everyone was staring curiously at her.

'That's a demo, I take it?' said Hal, trying not to smile.

Sam just sighed.

'You really don't want to go?' he asked.

'I really don't want to go.'

'Then what would you like to do instead?'

'Good idea!' Max enthused, changing tack immediately. 'Take her out, she never goes out. It'll do you good, Sam.'

Sam hesitated. This was getting much too much like a real date. 'We could stay here and eat paella and watch *Head Over Heels*.'

'I'm not watching that!' Josh protested.

'No, you're getting free rein on the internet,' Max assured

him. She took hold of Sam's shoulders from behind and propelled her out of the kitchen. 'Get the hell out of here and go
and have a grown-up night out, for crying out loud.'

Sam allowed herself to be walked across the room. Jess
found her handbag and hooked it over her mother's shoulder.
Sam glanced at Hal, frowning.

'What have you got there?'

'Your yearbook. We can have a virtual reunion.'

She went to protest, but Max had opened the front door
and was shooing them out. 'And don't be home too early or I
won't let you in.'

Out on the street they looked at each other blankly.

'Any ideas?' Hal asked.

Sam shook her head. 'I should have, I know. But I don't
really get out much.'

'What was that place we went to when you were looking
for a house? There were lots of Italian restaurants.'

'Leichhardt. It's only ten minutes away. We could try there.'

Although it took a while to find a park, it didn't take them long
to find a bright, noisy place with a huge blackboard menu and
room for two diners without a reservation.

After they had ordered, Hal opened the yearbook and began
to flick through the pages. 'You know I'll find it eventually.'

Sam surrendered. 'Driscoll.'

He turned back a couple of pages and his face broke into a
broad smile. 'Look at you.'

'Cut it out.'

'What? You're real cute. You must have had all the boys after
you.'

Sam shrugged. 'Just the one.' Not that she could recall Jeff
pursuing her as such. It was more her latching onto him, like
Max said.

'"Samantha Jean Driscoll,"' Hal read aloud. '"Sam's
favourite subjects were Home Economics and Commerce. She
will start as a Trainee with the State Bank in the new year. Her

hobbies include ice-skating and horse-riding." I wouldn't have thought ice-skating was big in Australia.'

'I went once.'

'Oh?' Hal smiled. 'And horse-riding?'

'Never been,' said Sam, taking a sip of wine.

'So, you lied in your yearbook?'

Sam shrugged. 'Girls always put horse-riding. What are they going to say otherwise? Lie around on my bed all day listening to records and talking on the telephone?'

Hal smiled, shaking his head. He resumed reading. '"Voted most likely to marry and have children." Well, there you go. You did succeed.'

She frowned doubtfully at him.

'Didn't you get married?' he asked.

Sam nodded.

'And you had children?'

'Alright, but –'

'But nothing, Sam,' Hal said firmly. 'Do you think you're the only one whose dreams didn't turn out the way you'd hoped?' He looked back at the yearbook. 'Take Gail Arthur. It says here she wanted to be a model. Well, I'm thinking she had twelve kids to four different fathers, lost her figure, and now she makes her living as a phone sex worker. Julie Hargraves has had time in gaol by the look of her. And Maree Davies had to declare bankruptcy because her husband gambled away everything they owned and left her for the children's nanny.'

Sam was smiling. 'Last I heard, Maree Davies married a missionary and moved to Papua New Guinea. Julie Hargraves was running a successful medical practice. And Gail, well, you might be right about her. I don't think it was twelve kids though. Maybe four or five.'

The waiter brought their meals and refilled their wine glasses. Sam started to prod the pasta gently with her fork. She looked up and Hal was watching her intently.

'You don't really believe you're a failure, do you?' he asked.

'Well, marriage is supposed to last forever. I bombed out on that one.'

'Okay. If you could go back,' Hal persisted, tapping the yearbook, 'would you do it again, knowing what you know now?'

Sam thought about it. 'That's a hard one. I mean, I'd still want to have my kids. I couldn't imagine life without them.'

'So, you would marry the same person despite the fact that it could end the same way?'

'I guess.'

'Then how can you call it a failure if you'd go back and do it again?'

Sam sipped her wine. 'Would you still marry your wife if you had your time over?'

'Well that's a little different.'

She realised he looked uncomfortable. 'Sorry, I shouldn't have –'

'No, it's okay,' Hal dismissed. 'Look, I don't believe my marriage should never have happened. It made me grow up, I think it taught me a few things.'

'Such as?'

He thought for a moment. 'Well, not to get married again, for starters.'

Sam blinked at him.

'At least not for the wrong reasons.' Hal put down his fork and took a mouthful of wine. 'I think people get married because it's the thing to do. You're at a certain age, you've been together for a certain amount of time. It's what comes next. But I don't know whether you really see the big picture, you know, the rest of your life.'

Sam thought about herself at eighteen years of age when she decided she'd marry Jeff Holmes. He had not actually been aware of her plan at the time. But Sam had been quite clear. She wanted to have the family she'd never had. She wanted her kids to live in a big house with a father who came home every night. Now they had neither.

'Imagine if we really could see the rest of our lives all laid out before us,' Sam mused. 'We'd probably run away screaming.'

'No, you said you'd go back and do it all again, remember?'

said Hal. 'And I don't blame you. I would too, if I had what you have.'

'You would?'

'Absolutely. Don't you realise how lucky you are, Sam? You're still a family, despite the fact you and your husband split. You've got those three great kids, I envy you.'

Sam looked across at him, a little surprised. 'Well, it's not too late for you to have a family,' she said tentatively.

'Oh, I think it is.'

'Come off it. Men can have children at any age.'

'Sure, they're biologically equipped, that doesn't mean they're emotionally equipped. My father was too old when I was born. He was like a grandfather, though not so much the kindly type,' he added. 'I always swore I'd never have children late in life.'

'But you're only about forty, aren't you?'

'Sam, even if I met someone tomorrow, it'd be years before I'd be ready to have a child with her.' Hal picked up his fork again and sunk it into his pasta. 'I'd rather not dwell on something that's not going to happen.'

Sam watched him eating. 'That must have made it harder to leave your wife,' she suggested tentatively. Hal glanced up at her. 'You know, if you believed it was your last chance to have a family.'

'I think it was pretty clear that was never going to happen with Lisa.' He paused. 'No, the hardest thing was probably that it spoilt all my illusions about myself. That I would be a better husband than my father. That I could make everything alright.' He was staring at a spot on the tablecloth. 'Your mind can convince you of things that have no basis in reality.'

Sam twirled her fork around in her food. 'I think I dug my heels in and kept on being a wife even when my husband was no longer a husband and the marriage was no longer a marriage.' She heard the words come out of her mouth as though someone else was saying them. Where did they come from?

'How do you keep on being a wife?' Hal asked curiously.

She shrugged, 'Oh, you know, making the house nice, ironing the clothes, doing all the things you do to keep up appearances.'

'That's what being a wife is to you?'

Sam felt self-conscious. 'Partly.'

'But isn't being a wife, by definition, all about the relationship? I mean, you're only a wife if you have a husband, and vice versa.'

'Of course, but there are certain duties and responsibilities that come with the relationship.'

'Sure, to love, honour, in sickness, in health, and all the rest,' said Hal. 'I don't recall "to have the shirts ironed and dinner on the table" in the vows.'

'Maybe that's how you show love.'

'Maybe. But I think a man should love his wife, not for what she does for him, but for who she is.'

Sam picked up her wine glass, considering him. 'Well, that's a lovely sentiment, but I still think most men are looking for the someone who'll iron their shirts and put dinner on the table.'

'Don't lump us all together,' Hal said shortly. 'And don't you think what you're saying is a bit outdated? Women have their own careers, they're independent, they don't get married to look after a man. It's certainly not what I'm looking for.'

Sam frowned. 'I thought you weren't looking right now?'

He looked a little abashed. 'I'm just saying, theoretically.'

'Okay, theoretically, what would you look for in a wife?'

Hal sat back in his chair, thinking. 'Someone I could be myself with, more than anyone else.' He paused. 'Most of the time we're operating undercover, don't you think? We put on so many faces to the world, it would be a relief to have someone you could be completely at ease with. To have that kind of connection, someone who loved you regardless.'

Sam sipped her wine slowly. She couldn't argue with that. Her whole marriage was about putting on a face to the world. Jeff included.

'What were you looking for in a husband?' Hal asked.

She stared into her glass. 'Someone who'd stay,' she said

quietly. She looked up at him and he was gazing at her, almost tenderly.

'That doesn't seem too much to ask for,' he said.

She smiled lamely. 'Apparently it was.'

The waiter came to clear their plates and offer them the dessert menu.

'We'd better have something,' Hal suggested. 'Max will get mad if we go back too soon.' He paused for a moment. 'And that would make her Mad Max. We wouldn't want that.'

Sam looked at him blankly.

'I just made a joke. Didn't you get it?'

'Yes, but it wasn't a very good one. I wouldn't draw attention to it.'

Sam ordered a dessert she knew she wouldn't be able to eat, but she gladly accepted a refill of her glass. When the waiter left them, Hal leaned forward across the table.

'So what are you going to do with the rest of your life, Samantha Jean?'

'That's a big question.'

'You asked me once if I had dreams about what I wanted to be when I grew up. What about you?'

Sam sighed. 'You read it right there,' she said, indicating the yearbook. 'I wanted to be a wife and a mother.'

'Okay, you can check that box,' he persisted. 'What's next?'

'Well, you never stop being a mother.'

'Nor apparently a wife,' he remarked. 'Is that why you went to work for *Wife for Hire*? You had no one to be a wife to any more, so you decided to do it for a living?'

Sam shrugged. 'Maybe.'

'Don't you get sick of running around after other people?'

'That's not exactly what I do.'

'Oh? What do you do then?'

She hesitated. 'Well, even if I do run around after people, so what? What's wrong with that? I like it, most of the time. And I'm good at it.'

'I'll bet you're good at a lot of things,' said Hal. 'And you'll never know if you stay being a wife forever.'

Sam had never thought about it like that before.

'Maybe it's time to move on,' he suggested.

'You know,' she said, picking up her glass, 'I'm beginning to hate that expression.' She took a mouthful of wine. 'Everyone keeps telling me I should "move on", I even keep telling myself! But how do you do that after sixteen years and three children? It's not that easy, you know, Hal, you don't have to have any kind of relationship with your ex-wife if you don't want to. But I'll be attached to Jeff forever because of the kids. How the hell am I supposed to move on?'

Sam realised that her voice was raised, hardly noticeable in the noisy restaurant, but obvious to Hal. He seemed a little taken aback.

'Sorry,' she said, embarrassed.

'Don't worry about it.'

The waiter appeared behind Hal with his coffee and an enormous serve of tiramisu.

'You're going to have to help me eat this,' said Sam.

Hal frowned as the waiter set it down in front of her. 'I'm not much of a dessert man. I'm already sweet enough.'

Sam grinned. 'Oh sure, that's why you're pouring all that sugar into your cup.' She picked up a spoon and scooped up a little tiramisu. 'So, what about you? I don't see you moving on.'

'What do you mean? I've moved ten thousand miles.'

'But you're living exactly the same life here as you were in the US. What's the difference?'

'The climate –'

'What's stopping you from sailing around the world now, for instance?' Sam continued, ignoring him.

Hal laughed. 'About twenty years.'

She frowned. 'Honestly Hal, the way you talk you'd think you were a hundred and three years old. You're just making excuses. Haven't you ever heard the expression "seize the day"? Spread your wings, reach for the stars, take the road less travelled –'

'Oh my God, it's the attack of the killer cliché queen.'

'I'm just saying,' Sam went on undaunted, 'that you could do anything you want, Hal. What's stopping you?'

He sat back in his chair, staring at her intently. 'You're absolutely right. I don't know what's stopping me.'

Sam wasn't sure, but she felt as though she'd unintentionally thrown down some kind of gauntlet to Hal. When they left the restaurant and made their way back to the car, he frequently took her arm, or guided her along with his palm on the small of her back. Sam was afraid he was going to try to hold her hand, so she made it impossible by folding her arms or clutching her bag. She wasn't really *afraid*, she just didn't want him to hold her hand. It was too . . . It would make it really seem like a date. And it wasn't a date. They had just gone out to dinner. Together. Alone. But it wasn't a date. It was . . .

'Sam?'

'What?' she jumped.

'Are you okay? You seem a bit nervous.'

'I'm not nervous, why do you think I'm nervous?'

'It's just the way you're holding your purse,' Hal said. 'Are you worried someone's going to try to snatch it?'

Sam realised she was clutching her handbag to her chest, with her arms crisscrossed over it. She relaxed, slipping the strap over her shoulder.

'The car's this way, remember,' he said, placing his palm midback now, his fingers just curling at her waist. Sam skittered ahead quickly, and felt his hand drop away.

They were quiet during the short drive home. The tension was so thick in the car, you could not only cut it with a knife, you could take a nice big chunk of it, spread it on bread and make a hearty meal of it.

Sam was wondering what would happen when they pulled up in front of the house. She should ask him in for coffee, that was the best bet. But Max had told her once that asking someone in for coffee was code for 'Would you like to have sex?' and even if you were only talking caffeine, the guy would think you were inviting him in for sex.

But surely Hal wouldn't think that, what with Max inside

and a house full of children? And besides, he was her client, this wasn't a date, so the secret coffee code didn't apply.

Hal pulled the car in close to the kerb, cut the engine and turned towards Sam, all far more swiftly than she was prepared for. God, she just realised she hadn't even thought of the 'stay in the car and neck' scenario. Weren't they a bit old for that?

'Do you want to come in for a cup of coffee?' she blurted.

'But you don't drink coffee this late,' said Hal.

Sam looked at him for a moment, confused. Was he using the code? Was this a test?

'No, no, you're absolutely right. I don't drink coffee at night *at all*,' she said emphatically. 'Well, I used to, but not any more, under the circumstances, I really couldn't drink coffee now. With you. I drink chamomile tea, which is an entirely different thing.'

Now Hal looked confused.

'If you came inside, you could drink coffee and I could drink chamomile tea. Maybe Max would have a cup of coffee, but,' she hastened to add, 'she would just be drinking coffee, you know. I don't think she'd want to have a cup of coffee with you, so to speak. Much as she likes you.'

'Sam?'

'Mm?'

'Are you alright?'

'Sure, I'm fine.' I just seem like a nutcase.

'Okay. Well, thanks for the invitation, but some other time. I should go. Sailing tomorrow.'

'Oh,' Sam nodded.

Suddenly, he leaned towards her and Sam flinched. 'Don't kiss me!' she blurted.

Hal stopped. 'What makes you think I was going to kiss you?'

She looked at him, trying to work out his expression. She couldn't tell if he was teasing her. He seemed completely guileless. He reached behind her seat and handed her the yearbook.

'I didn't want you to forget this.'

Oh fuck! She was such an idiot. If only she could just wiggle her nose and disappear like that other Samantha.

'My mistake,' she croaked, not making eye contact. 'Sorry.'

'But,' he said as she went to open the car door. 'Hypothetically speaking . . . what if I was to kiss you?'

Sam jerked around to look at him. Now she could see the glint in his eye. The bugger.

'Mm,' she mused, regaining her composure. 'Hypothetically?'

'That's right. Hypothetically, if I was to kiss you, would you kiss me back?'

'I work for you.'

'You're not answering the question,' he persisted.

'What was it again?'

He went to open his mouth, but Sam thought better of it. 'No, on second thoughts, don't repeat it.'

'So what's your answer?'

'It's the same. I work for you, it's not appropriate to fraternise with a client.'

'Fraternise?' he grinned broadly now. 'That sounds like fun. I wouldn't mind trying a little fraternising.'

'I'm getting out of the car now,' said Sam, opening the door.

'Hey Sam?'

She glanced back at him.

'Thanks, I had a good time.'

Sam felt herself blush. He was staring intently at her, not teasing, just smiling affectionately, tenderly even. It would be so nice to kiss him, if only it wouldn't . . . complicate everything.

'Thanks, me too,' she mumbled, jumping from the car. He didn't drive away until she had opened the front door and closed it again behind her.

'How did it go?'

'Max! You nearly scared the shit out of me!' Sam exclaimed. 'What were you doing standing there in the dark?'

'I was watching out for you. You've been sitting there a while, though not long enough.'

'God, you're nosy.'

'How was your date?'

'It wasn't a date,' said Sam wearily, starting down the hall.

'You're beginning to sound like a broken record.'

'Well, you keep asking the same questions.'

'It's been a year, you know, Sam. You have to move on,' Max called after her.

She groaned. 'The only place I'm moving on to is bed. Are you staying the night?' she asked over her shoulder.

'No, I've got a date.'

Sam stopped, checking her watch. She turned around to look at Max. 'At this time of night?'

'God, you sound like an old fart sometimes,' said Max. She picked up her bag off the sofa and sauntered to the front door. 'Yes, I have a date, at midnight, shock horror! And I might even end up having sex!' she exclaimed, throwing her arms out dramatically.

Sam turned around again and continued down the hall.

'People do that, you know. They have sex!' Max called after her. 'Sometimes they even enjoy it.'

'Lock up on your way out, will you?' Sam returned as she walked into her bedroom.

'If this goes on much longer,' Max persisted, 'I'm going to have to buy you one of those special toys for Christmas, you know, the battery-operated kind.'

'Goodnight Maxine.'

Monday

From:<h.buchanan@igb.com.au   To:<holmes@webnet.com.au
Subject: Saturday night

Hey Sam,
I enjoyed not taking you to the reunion the other night. Care to do it again? I'm guessing the kids are with their father next weekend. Are you free?
Hal

Sam sat staring at the computer screen. This was taking things a step further, no question. She sat, nervously biting the edge of her thumb. She wasn't ready. It was as simple as that. Hal of all people should understand.

From:<holmes@webnet.com.au   To:<h.buchanan@igb.com.au
Subject: Re: Saturday night

Dear Hal
Sorry, the kids will be with me. They start at their new school next Monday, so we're having a quiet weekend.
Sam

No, that sounded too curt. She deleted 'Sam' and added

Maybe some other time.
Sam

But he might take that as an opening to ask again. What about

Thanks for asking.
Sam

Now it sounded too eager.

Thanks for the other night.
Sam

Suggestive?

Thanks anyway.
Sam

Good. Polite, but definitely nonleading. She clicked *Send*, then immediately deleted both his original message and her reply.

Wednesday

The house was very quiet. Josh and Jess were away, Ellie was next door. Sam could hear her own breathing. She started to think about her options. A glass of wine would go down well right now. Perhaps a little music? No, the silence was a novelty, best to indulge in it. What about a bath? She sighed content-edly. That was it. She leaned her head back against the sofa where she was sitting and put her feet up on the coffee table. She closed her eyes. She could feel the chill of the glass in her hand, the warmth of the water lapping around her body, the peace, the quiet.

Then the phone started to ring.

Bugger! For a moment she thought about letting the machine pick it up. But what if it was one of the kids? She sighed, dragging herself up and walking into the kitchen.

'Okay, okay,' she said to no one as she picked up the receiver.

'Sam! You won't believe what's happened!'

Woman's voice, excited, shrill . . . Fiona? God, she hated it when people didn't say who they were on the phone. She had to keep them talking until they gave it away somehow.

'Try me.'

'You really won't believe it. I should make you guess.'

Then Sam got her clue. She heard the drawback on a cigarette. 'Or you could just tell me, Liz.'

'Rose has left Colin.'

'She has not.'

'Oh yes she has.'

Sam didn't know what to say.

'Sam?'

'I don't know what to say.'

'I know, isn't it unbelievable? I mean, she just walked out apparently.'

'Where is she?'

'She's staying at the Ritz Carlton at Double Bay.'

'She is not!'

Liz laughed. 'She is! The world's turned on its ear. Anyway, she called and asked me to pass the message along, and we're all invited for drinks.'

'For drinks? What, she's celebrating?'

'Well, wouldn't you if you left Colin?' Liz remarked snidely. 'Look, I think she might be a little shell-shocked. We'd better get over there. Can you ring Max?'

'Sure,' said Sam. 'I'll see you there.'

She replaced the receiver, but stood staring at it for a minute. What had Rose said to her the day of the move? That she was an inspiration? God, not to do this, surely.

Sam rang Max, who seemed to be only mildly surprised. She said she'd be waiting outside her block in ten minutes.

'What are you going to do with Ellie?' she asked.

'Sorry?'

'Ellie. You know, your daughter. Short, dark hair –'

'Oh God, um, she's next door. I'll have to bring her with me, I suppose. Do you think it'll be alright?'

'Should be an education for her,' Max quipped. 'See you in ten.'

Sam hurried next door and rang the bell. Maria answered it, smiling. She was a small but buxom woman and she always had a smile on her face.

'Hello Samanta!' she greeted. She couldn't quite manage the 'th'. 'You come to have dinner wit us? You can't sit in tere alone, all by yourselves!'

'Oh, thank you, Maria. But I have to go out. I've come to get Ellie.'

Maria's face dropped. 'But where are you going? Does Ellie have to go too?'

'Well . . .'

'Leave her here. She's no trouble.'

'Oh I couldn't –'

'Please Samanta! I love having a little girl around. Can you imagine?'

Sam smiled at her. 'I might be a little late.'

'Pssht,' Maria dismissed. She turned towards the sitting room. Ellie and Carlos were engrossed in the PlayStation. 'Ellie, your mama's going out. You gonna stay here wit us for dinner, *querida?*'

Ellie looked over and nodded happily.

'What do you say to Mrs Suarez, Ellie?' Sam prompted her.

'Thank you, Maria!'

'Don't I get a kiss goodbye?'

Ellie jumped up and skipped over to her mother. 'We just unlocked level four on *Crash Bandicoot!*'

'Well, I'm so happy for you!' Sam bent down and gave her a hug. 'Now, you be polite, and eat all your dinner, and help clean up afterwards.'

'Eh!' Maria grunted. 'She's a baby! Too many rules!'

'Thank you, Maria. I'll owe you for this.'

'Pssht,' Maria waved her off.

She turned at the gate. 'I'll have to mind the boys one night so you and Louis can have a romantic night out.'

Sam could still hear Maria's peals of laughter as she got into her car and started the engine.

When Max and Sam arrived at Rosemary's hotel room, Liz was already there. She opened the door for them. Rose was sitting on the sofa, her feet curled up underneath her. She was wearing a thick white bathrobe, obviously hotel issue. She looked serene.

Sam crossed the room towards her as Rosemary got to her feet.

'Rose, how are you?' Sam said, putting her arms around her. Rosemary hugged her in return. But then she pulled back to look at Sam.

'I'm fine. I'm really okay.' She smiled warmly at her. There was a peace in her eyes that Sam had never seen before. 'Sit, have a drink,' she insisted.

Liz handed them glasses, then went to get the bottle out of the fridge.

'Where's Fiona?' Sam asked. 'Is she coming?'

Sam felt like everyone was looking anywhere but at her.

'She's working back,' Maxine blurted.

'How do you know that?' Sam frowned. 'I was the one who called you about tonight.'

'Well . . .' she faltered. 'She's always working back lately.'

'That's right,' said Liz, coming over to fill Sam's glass. 'Fiona is working back. Now, you've got to hear Rosemary's story, she's bloody amazing.'

'When did it happen?'

'Just today.'

Max and Sam stared at her, waiting. Rosemary seemed so calm, like she was a queen holding court.

'I got into my car this morning and headed along the freeway to work.' She paused. 'Then, at the Lane Cove underpass, I suddenly had an overwhelming feeling. I knew I couldn't drive home along that same road this afternoon. In fact, I knew I couldn't do it, not just this afternoon, but ever again.'

'What?' Sam was stunned.

'Have you told Colin?' asked Max.

'Mm,' Rosemary nodded, sipping her wine. 'I rang him from work and said I wouldn't be coming home. He was a little annoyed, you know Col. He said, "What time will I expect you then?" I said that I guess once I find a place, I'll have to come and get some of my things. I'd let him know. It took him a while to catch on. He kept asking what was going to happen about dinner tonight. I think he was in shock.'

Max started to laugh. 'Rose! I never thought you had it in you,' she whooped, holding her glass up to her.

'But wait,' Sam said. 'You can't just leave and not go back ever!'

'Why can't she?' Liz raised an eyebrow.

'Well, what about your clothes . . . and stuff?' Sam realised that sounded pretty lame in the scheme of things.

'I went out at lunchtime and bought a couple of pairs of undies and a toothbrush. And I've sent the clothes I was wearing to be laundered.' Rosemary smiled impishly. 'That was a bit of an indulgence.'

Sam was shocked. Liz and Max were smiling along with Rosemary. They'd lost all sense of reason. Rose had just left her husband. You didn't laugh and celebrate. This was serious.

'What are you going to do, Rosemary?' said Sam sternly. 'You can't afford to stay here and have your clothes laundered every night.'

'No, I'll shop for another shirt tomorrow. And I'm only staying here for a couple of nights. It was a midweek special thing. I had a voucher out of the newspaper.'

'Serendipity,' Max declared.

Sam stood up and started pacing. 'So you're never going back to Colin? You just get in your car one day and decide you're never going home?'

Rose looked at her squarely. 'There hasn't been one day in the past ten years that I've wanted to go home. It's taken me this long to get the courage to do something about it.'

Sam stood staring at her, breathing heavily. Everyone was quiet.

'I don't understand, Sam. You're the reason I was finally able to do it.'

'Me?'

Rosemary nodded. 'I've watched you in awe. You've handled every hurdle that's been put in front of you. A new job, a new house, and you've got three kids! My boys are grown up, working. I don't have to worry about them. I realised that if you could do it, then surely I could.'

'But don't you see?' said Sam in a small voice. 'I didn't do the leaving. I never would have left Jeff.'

They all stared at her. She sat down again and picked up her glass, gulping down half of it.

'Sam,' Rosemary said after a while. 'You know what Colin was like, probably better than anyone here. Do you think I should have stayed with him?'

Sam slowly raised her eyes to look directly at Rosemary. Sweet, long-suffering Rosemary. How often Sam had wished she'd find the courage to stand up to Colin. He had so thoroughly stripped Rose of any sense of worth, it was a wonder she had the gumption to leave him. She had never been anything more to him than a housekeeper, cook and from what she had hinted, a not always willing sexual partner. He was a Neanderthal brute and Rosemary was well rid of him.

Sam cleared her throat. 'Of course you couldn't stay with him.'

There was a collective sigh in the room.

'Have you made any plans?' Max asked Rosemary.

The conversation took off, but Sam tuned out. She thought about Jeff leaving her. Had he struggled with it? Had it taken him a long time to get up the courage? Did he have a drink and celebrate with Jodi when he finally went through with it?

She didn't want to be this mournful woman but it still hurt. She wondered how long it would keep on hurting like this. How long it would be before she could be as calm as Rosemary. Till she could say she had 'moved on'.

'So, I've already called a couple of agencies,' Rosemary was saying. Sam presumed she was talking about finding a place to rent. 'And I'm going to my first singles party on Saturday!' she finished excitedly.

'What?' Sam frowned. This was too much, surely everyone would agree. But they were all looking at Sam like she was the one from another planet. Or a convent perhaps.

'It's just, well, isn't it a little soon?'

'What do you expect her to do, Sam?' said Liz. 'Dress in black and not go out in public for twelve months?'

'Like someone I know,' Max added pointedly. 'Metaphorically speaking.'

'Sam, I've been in a completely dead relationship for so long,' Rosemary explained. 'I've had no passion, no fun. I want to start living. I don't want to put it off a minute longer. This is the beginning of something for me, not the end.'

It was nearly ten by the time Sam dropped off Max and arrived at the Saurezes' to get Ellie.

'Did you have a nice time, Samanta?' Maria asked, smiling.

Sam forced a smile in return. 'Yes thank you. And thanks so much for having Ellie.'

'Eh!' Maria scoffed. 'She is an angel come down from heaven. Look at her,' she said, nodding towards the living room where Ellie was curled up asleep on the lounge. 'Maybe you will leave her here? Tere is no need to disturb her.'

Sam looked at her little daughter, like an angel from heaven indeed. 'You know, Maria, I think I'd be lonely without her tonight.'

Maria nodded knowingly. 'Of course.'

Sam carried her sleeping daughter inside the house and down the hall. She paused outside the girls' room, feeling Ellie's breath against her neck. Then she turned and walked into her own room instead. She lowered Ellie gently down, pulling the covers out of the way. Then she removed her sandals and drew the sheet and quilt back over her, tucking her in firmly.

Sam walked wearily to the bathroom and stared at herself in the mirror. She should clean off her make-up, but that required more diligence than she could muster at the moment. She undid the clip restraining her hair and tousled it with her fingers. She brushed her teeth, turned out the light and crept back to her room. Climbing into bed, she inched over next to Ellie, putting her arms around her and nestling in close. It was a while since she had slept with one of the kids. It was a while since she had slept with anyone.

Despite having a new house and a new job, a new car even, Sam realised she was not living a new life, not inside her head at least. She was still a wife, a jilted one, but she had not left that role behind. She was like her mother, wearing the label, clinging to what she had once been. But why? What was the advantage in being an ex-wife over a single woman?

Safety. Familiarity. Sam didn't know how to be a single woman. Like Alex said, she was barely more than a child when she met Jeff. She hadn't had any practice.

She closed her eyes and saw Hal, smiling at her the way he had in the car the other night. What would it be like to have a man's arms around her again? She imagined him lying behind her, wrapped around her as she was wrapped around Ellie. She felt his face against hers, his slightly whiskery chin on her neck, his lips on her earlobe. Sam's heart started to race and she felt hot. She unravelled herself from Ellie and turned over onto her back, breathing heavily. She was nothing but a frustrated, fear-ridden, deserted wife, bringing her daughter into her bed so she didn't have to feel so lonely. But it only made it all the more obvious how lonely she was.

Sam threw back the covers and walked out to the kitchen. Opening the fridge, she picked up the bottle of wine she had started a couple of nights ago, took a glass from the cupboard and walked back into the living room. She sat down heavily on the sofa and turned on the television with the remote, lowering the sound so as not to disturb Ellie. She flicked stations. News. News. News. Crappy movie. It must be crappy because Steven Seagal was in it. Sam hated Steven Seagal. But she tossed the remote aside, poured herself a glass of wine, and curled her feet up underneath her, staring at the screen.

Sometime around one, the bottle was finished and Sam couldn't keep her eyes open any more. She turned off the television and walked a little unsteadily to her room, where she climbed into bed, turned away from Ellie and fell asleep.

The following week

'Um, hi, Sam, it's me, Vanessa Blair.'

Of course it was, Sam didn't know any other Vanessas. She wondered why she sounded so nervous.

'Hi Vanessa,' said Sam. 'What can I do for you?'

'Um, well, I was hoping to see you. I need to talk to you about something. Maybe I could come to your new house? I haven't seen it yet.'

She had never seen the old house either, and they weren't exactly friends. Sam wondered what was going on.

'I've bought you something,' Vanessa continued. 'A house-warming gift.'

She really was desperate. Sam could hardly refuse her now.

'Sure, when would you like to come?'

'Are you busy this afternoon?'

'Well, it's the kids' first day at their new school,' she hesitated. Sam was planning to do the grocery shopping and then wait anxiously for them to get home. She wasn't actually planning to be anxious, she just knew she would be. It was probably better to have something to distract her.

'I promise I'll get out of your way as soon as they're home,' Vanessa persisted.

'Sure, let me give you the address.'

When Sam opened the front door, Vanessa stood holding a gardenia covered in gorgeous perfumed blossoms in a pretty terracotta pot.

'Vanessa, it's beautiful! Thank you, you really shouldn't have.'

'No, please, I wanted to,' Vanessa insisted, passing the plant to Sam. 'You've been so good to me . . . to us.'

Sam watched her biting her lip. Her usually sunny smile was eclipsed by an anxious frown.

'Come inside,' Sam offered, holding the door open. She showed Vanessa into the living room. 'Well, this is it.'

'It's charming.'

'Charming' was another one of those words like 'cute' that covered a multitude of contingencies.

'Can I get you a coffee?'

'Mm,' Vanessa wrinkled her nose. 'Maybe a weak tea. I don't suppose you have anything herbal?'

'Sure, how's chamomile?'

'Lovely thanks.'

Sam placed the gardenia on the kitchen bench and made the

tea, while Vanessa made polite observations about the amount of storage in the kitchen, the size of the backyard, the convenient location of the laundry. It was all just patter, making Sam all the more intrigued about what she was doing here. She handed Vanessa a cup and offered her a seat at the dining table.

'You wanted to talk to me about something?' Sam began.

Vanessa looked up abruptly from jiggling her teabag. 'How did you know that?'

'You said so, on the phone.'

'Oh,' she nodded. 'Yes, um . . .' She took a deep breath. 'Well, what it is . . . is that I've found out I'm pregnant.'

Sam had not expected to hear that and she didn't know how to respond. Her immediate feeling was delight for Vanessa – after all, this was what she'd wanted so badly. But Sam could see the demons she was struggling with. Without a doubt Dominic didn't know anything about this.

'What did Dominic say?'

'He doesn't know yet,' Vanessa said quietly.

No surprise. 'How do you feel about it?'

Vanessa stared at her teacup for a moment, before meeting Sam's gaze directly. 'This is all I've ever wanted. There's a part of me that feels so excited, so . . . complete. But . . .'

'What?'

'I'm scared about Dominic's reaction.'

'Scared?'

'Kind of. I want this baby so much, and until I tell him, I can fantasise about how wonderful it will be. I can imagine Dominic crying with happiness. I can see him holding our baby in his arms and falling in love with her, like you said your husband did.' She paused. 'But after I tell him, I don't know whether he'll even let me keep it.'

'What are you talking about? It's not a stray dog.'

'But we didn't plan it. He's going to be shocked, I don't know how he'll react. But I do know he has never let anything get in the way of his plans.'

Sam sighed deeply. 'How did it happen? If his plan is so watertight, surely you were using birth control?'

'Of course,' said Vanessa. 'I was on the pill, and then a few months ago I replaced it with the ovulation method.'

'Dominic agreed to this?' Sam was stunned.

'No . . .' she said vaguely. 'I've heard it can sometimes take months to fall pregnant coming off the pill. I just figured this way, when I finally did talk Dominic into it, I'd be ready, I'd know my cycle and be able to conceive straightaway.'

'But of all people, Vanessa, you should have realised the risk you were taking. You're an actuary.'

She looked guilty. 'It's just, after what you said –'

'After what I said?' Sam exclaimed. 'I didn't have anything to do with this.'

'I know. But you told me once that people usually cope with the inevitable. And that sometimes it was acceptable to blur the truth a little in a marriage.'

Fuck. Sam dropped her head in her hands. 'Vanessa, I was talking about not telling your husband the price of a new outfit! I didn't mean you should lie about contraception.'

'But I was using the ovulation method. I thought it would be alright . . .'

'You work out probability and risk for a living, for godsakes! Don't tell me you didn't know what might happen.'

'This is exactly what Dominic is going to say,' Vanessa said tearfully, her eyes filling. 'He's going to be so angry. I don't think he'll accept the inevitable. I don't think he'll believe it is inevitable.' One tear toppled over her lashes and rolled down her cheek. 'What am I going to do?'

Sam reached over and squeezed her arm. They were startled by the front door bursting open. Josh walked through, dumping his bag as he headed for the kitchen.

'Hello Josh.' Sam felt torn now. She'd planned to give the kids her undivided attention this afternoon, but she couldn't just ignore Vanessa. 'We have a visitor.'

He stopped in his tracks. 'Hi,' he said awkwardly.

'This is Mrs Blair. My eldest, Joshua.'

'Please, it's Vanessa.' She had discreetly wiped her eyes and was smiling brightly. 'Hi Joshua, nice to meet to you.'

He mumbled a response and then proceeded to the kitchen. 'Anything to eat, Mum?' he called.

'I did the shopping today.'

'Sick.'

'Sick's good,' Sam explained to Vanessa. 'Where's your sister, Josh?'

He was standing staring into the open fridge. 'I dunno. Probably licking the footpath outside Marco's place —'

'Shut up, Josh!' Jessica shrilled from the front door. 'We were just talking.'

'Yeah, I know who was doing all the talking.'

'*Shut up, Josh!* Mum, tell him to shut up.'

'Jessica,' Sam said evenly. 'We have a visitor.'

Jess looked around, surprised. 'Oh, sorry. Hello.'

'Hi, I'm Vanessa,' she smiled. 'Nice to meet you.'

Jess smiled in return, before something caught her eye in the kitchen. 'Mum, Josh is drinking juice out of the carton!'

Sam turned around. 'Joshua!'

'Dobber,' he sneered at Jess, wiping his mouth with a tea-towel.

'Josh,' Sam chided. 'I wish you wouldn't use the tea-towels to wipe your face! Put it in the laundry hamper please.'

'I think I should get out of your way,' Vanessa smiled faintly, standing up from the table.

'Sorry,' said Sam. 'I don't think we'll get much peace now.'

'Mum, can I ring Emma?' said Jess, heading for her room.

'Um, could you just wait on a minute, Jess? I'd like to hear how it went today.'

'It was fine,' she shrugged. 'I won't stay on long, Mum.'

Famous last words. Jessica had never had a short telephone conversation in her entire life.

'Bye, nice to meet you,' Vanessa called after her as Jess disappeared down the hall. 'Bye Josh.'

He grunted a goodbye as Sam walked Vanessa to the door and followed her out onto the verandah.

'They're gorgeous, Sam,' Vanessa gushed. 'Josh is so tall and handsome, and Jessica's a doll, with that long blonde hair.'

'They take after their father.'

'They're coping with the move alright?'

'So far, so good.'

Sam had to admit that things had gone incredibly smoothly, helped in no small way by the Suarez family next door. The two of them had happily boarded the bus this morning as though they did it every day. Josh had a newfound status as the older boy. Just as Jessica idolised Marco, Marco idolised Josh. All the Suarez boys thought he was some kind of god on his skateboard, and Joshua was lapping it up. He had even bestowed upon Marco one of his old skateboards, which had been received with reverence and awe by the younger boy.

'You're so lucky, Sam,' said Vanessa wistfully.

Sam looked at her. 'You have to talk to Dominic, you know that, don't you?'

She nodded vaguely.

'As soon as possible,' Sam insisted. 'You're deceiving him, he's within his rights to be upset. And the longer it goes on, the worse it will be.'

Sam noticed her lip trembling. 'Vanessa, you're his wife. In the end you mean more to him than anything, and your happiness will too.'

She wasn't at all sure she believed that, and looking at Vanessa, Sam suspected she didn't either.

'You should try to remember what brought you together in the first place,' she suggested, trying a different tack. 'How did you two fall in love?'

Vanessa was thoughtful for what seemed like a long time. Sam was beginning to think she hadn't heard her, then she cleared her throat.

'I can't remember.'

Sam wandered back into the house after waving Vanessa off. She couldn't do anything for her at this stage. It was up to Vanessa now. Sam walked down the hall and tapped on Jessica's door before opening it.

'Can we talk?'

'Soon as I'm finished, Mum,' she said, covering the mouthpiece. 'Won't be long.

Sam sighed. 'You can ring her back.'

'But –'

'Jessica, just give me five minutes, please. I have to go and pick up Ellie soon. I promise, you can ring Emma back then.'

Jess pulled a face, but she grudgingly told Emma she'd call back in five minutes. Sam half expected her to put on the kitchen timer when they walked out to join Josh, who was busy eating his way through the newly stocked pantry.

'So, tell me how it went today,' said Sam brightly.

Josh shrugged, his mouth full.

'It was fine, Mum, I told you,' said Jess impatiently. 'Now, can I ring Emma back?'

'Jess, five minutes, I said. It's all I'm asking for, you two. Come on, you have to give me something,' she pleaded.

Josh swallowed. 'Mr Pritchard's a dickhead.'

'Josh, language!'

'He is, he gave us homework the first night.'

'I've got him for English,' Jess exclaimed. 'He gave us home-work too!'

Sam listened as they bleated about the same stuff they always did their first day back. The only reference they made to the fact they had started at a new school was to say that they didn't have to do any of that 'dumb crap' and introduce themselves in front of everyone. The school apparently had a buddy system in place for new students, and they were both assigned someone who sat with them in most of their classes. It appeared that rather than being shunned as newcomers, they instead had a bit of kudos, and it sat well with the pair of them.

'Did I hear right? Are they really okay?' Jeff said in disbelief when he phoned later. He'd asked Josh to put his mother on after he had spoken with them.

'I know, I can hardly believe it either,' Sam replied. 'They seem fine. I just worry that it's a little too calm, you know? I'm waiting for the storm to hit.'

She heard Jeff laugh gently. 'You've always been a bit of a pessimist, haven't you, Sam?

Had she? She hoped not. She had never thought of herself as a pessimist.

'I barely slept a wink last night, worrying about them,' Jeff was saying.

'Really?' she said, not able to hide the surprise in her voice.

'You think you have the monopoly on worrying about the kids, Sam?' he asked.

'I didn't mean that —'

'It's okay,' Jeff sighed. 'Fact is, I have always left the worrying to you.' He paused. 'But this felt like it was on my head. They only had to change schools because of . . . what I did. You don't know how guilty I've been feeling.'

That was a huge admission. Which strangely gave Sam no satisfaction whatsoever.

'Guilt never did anybody any good,' she told him, and she actually meant it. 'I think it's time to move on. Seems to be what the kids are doing.'

'Sure,' he said, clearly stunned.

Neither of them spoke for the next few moments. Their lives were moving further apart with every day that passed. Common property had been dispersed or liquidated. They lived at different postcodes. Pretty soon there'd be nothing remaining of the life they once shared. Except the kids. There'd always be the kids.

'I have to go,' said Sam, breaking the reverie.

'Of course, I didn't mean to keep you.'

'Bye.'

November

Sam could not understand why the car had stopped, or why it wouldn't start up again. It just seemed to run out of puff. It had coughed and spluttered a couple of times before gliding to a complete halt.

She looked at the time. There was no way she would make it home for the kids now. She'd been cutting it pretty fine anyway. Sam tried the ignition again. Nothing. She sighed heavily, frowning at the little petrol bowser illuminated on the dash. It couldn't be that she'd run out of petrol, surely? She had never paid that much attention to the little bowser on the four-wheel drive, because of the auxiliary tank. Jeff filled the car every weekend, it was the one thing he did take care of. So Sam made sure she filled this car weekly as well. But she had done a lot of driving this week, an unusual amount in fact.

Sheila had recently passed on another client and Sam had been grateful to pick up some more hours, with Christmas on the way. But now she was not so sure that Mrs Patricia Bowen was worth the trouble. Never had Sam felt more like an indentured servant. Mrs Bowen was obviously under the assumption that Sam had no other clients, no family of her own, no life. Either that or she didn't care either way, which was probably closer to the truth. She was undertaking some minor renovations to her home, apparently for no other reason than it gave her the opportunity to harass people whom she wouldn't normally meet in the course of her daily life, namely building contractors. And Sam. None of the renovations were essential, or even much of an improvement on what was already an overwrought, pseudo-Tuscan mansion of the worst possible pretentious kind. But Mrs Bowen wanted a slightly larger window here, a new set of French doors there, all six toilet suites (Sam had never heard them called that before) replaced, and new door handles throughout. And she expected Sam to search the metropolitan area far and wide for exactly what she wanted, seeming displeased if she found it too easily, and so changing her mind, yet again. Sam wondered how long she could put up with the woman's sheer effrontery.

But now she had her own problems. She sat in the car going nowhere, considering her options. Josh and Jess caught the school bus and they both had a key in case they beat Sam home. She had promised them she would never be far away without letting them know. Then there was Ellie. She didn't like to leave her at pre-school past four o'clock if she didn't have to, it was a long enough day. She might make it, but it depended on how long it was going to take to get the car going.

Sam had a sudden fright. She grabbed her wallet from her bag and started searching frantically through all the pockets for her MRA membership card. She found it eventually and scanned it for details. Damn! She'd forgotten to change the membership over when she bought this car. Surely they would understand? She was trying to remember the policy. There would possibly be a charge involved but that didn't bother her. Sam studied the card again and her heart sank. It was out of date. Her membership had lapsed in September, the month of the move; she must have missed it in all the confusion. She stared disconsolately out the window as the sign on a telegraph pole nearest her came into focus. This was apparently a clear-way zone from three-thirty. Sam checked her watch. It was after three already.

She felt panic rising up inside her, but she had to stay calm and think this through. Someone had to pick up Ellie. If she arranged that, then she could concentrate on the car.

Jeff. He was Ellie's father. It was a reasonable thing to ask, a reasonable thing to expect him to do. She dialled his office number on her mobile and his assistant answered.

'Hello, it's Samantha Holmes, could I speak to Jeff please?'

'Sorry, Ms Holmes. He's in a meeting.'

'Well, this is important. It's an emergency actually.'

'Of course. Then you should probably try him on his mobile.'

'Oh?'

'He's over at the St Leonard's office.'

'Oh,' Sam repeated flatly. He'd never make it in time any-way. 'Never mind then.'

'Is there anything I can do to help?'

'No, thanks, I'll have to make some other arrangement. Don't worry.'

'I'll tell him you called.'

Sam hung up and dialled Max's mobile, praying she'd be

contactable and not in a lecture or something. It was hard to remember her schedule, erratic as it was.

She answered.

'Oh, thank God, where are you?' Sam blurted.

'I'm at uni, Sam, what's up?'

'Are you in the middle of anything important?'

'Well, it depends –'

'I need you to pick up Ellie, if it's no trouble, well, even if it is trouble . . . Max? Max?'

Damn! The line had dropped out. Sam looked at her phone. The battery was low. She had probably one more chance to get through to Max before it went dead altogether. She pressed redial and Max answered immediately.

'What happened?'

'My battery's low, so if it drops out again, try ringing me instead.'

'Sure.'

'I've broken down.'

'Oh no, Sam. Do you know what's wrong?'

'Well, actually, I think I may have run out of petrol.'

'You're joking?'

'Okay, okay,' Sam could hear the snigger in Max's voice. 'You can make fun of me later. In the meantime, I need you to pick up Ellie and go back to the house and wait with the kids. I'll pay you for the taxi when I get there.'

'Don't worry about that. Actually I was just offered a lift home, I'm sure it won't be a problem to detour. But what are you going to do? Have you called the MRA yet?'

Sam sighed. 'My membership has lapsed,' she said in a small voice.

'What!' Max shrieked.

'Look, don't carry on. There's nothing I can do about it now.'

'But what will you do? Are you near any petrol stations?'

Sam looked up the broad sweep of road ahead of her. 'Not that I can see, but I don't want to leave the car to go looking. I'm on a clearway, I think it may even be a tow-away zone.'

'Shit, Sam!' Max exclaimed. 'Tell me where you are, exactly.'

'Well, I'm on Parramatta Road, um, maybe near Annandale, I'm not sure. I'm not at Leichhardt yet, I know that much.'

'So you're heading west?'

'I suppose so, or south maybe. Anyway, I'm on the left-hand side of the road.'

Max laughed. 'God you're a dolt sometimes. You'd always be on the left-hand side of the road, Sherl! Don't move, okay? I'll organise something. And don't worry about –'

But the phone had gone dead. Completely this time. Sam sighed heavily and tossed it into her bag. She supposed she would have to trust Max. She didn't really have a choice.

The next twenty minutes passed more quickly than Sam had anticipated, and more quickly than she would have liked. From the dot of three-thirty, she was steadily assailed by cars whizzing up the outside lane and sounding their horns insistently when they realised she wasn't moving. She had searched everywhere for the hazard lights, but she had never used them before on this car and she couldn't find the switch. A couple of times she thought a car was going to end up in her boot, it came up so fast. None of this was helping to ease her anxiety. There wasn't a thing she could do now. If she had any hope of finding a service station, she should have started looking as soon as she broke down. She had walked back a little way up the road after speaking to Max, but she hadn't seen anything that way either. The area was still unfamiliar to her, she would have ended up on the proverbial wild goose chase if she had gone searching. So she was better off staying put.

Another car roared up behind her, bimping loudly. As the driver swerved past, he stuck his middle finger up at her. God, what did he think, she was doing this just to annoy people? That she got her kicks from parking in clearway zones on a hot day with her engine off and no airconditioning? It occurred to Sam that lifting the bonnet would at least signal to the approaching traffic that she had in fact broken down. She released the lever under the dash and stepped out of the hot car into the even hotter sun.

Her anxiety was hitting an all-time high. She had never broken down before. Actually that was not quite true. Jeff's old Valiant station wagon had broken down once on their way back from the beach. She recalled it was a fanbelt or some such thing. They had walked to a phone booth – it was in the days when phone booths were everywhere – and called Jeff's dad, who'd come to collect them. It was no great drama. Filling in time with your boyfriend when you were seventeen was hardly an ordeal anyway.

Sam lifted the bonnet and propped the arm into position. When she stepped up onto the kerb, she saw that a police car had pulled up behind her. She immediately froze, feeling sick inside. She felt like a criminal, even though she had done nothing wrong, really. Just something stupid. How long did they put you away for that?

'Afternoon, ma'am,' said the policeman as he approached, shadowed by his female partner, who nodded in Sam's direction. 'Having car trouble?'

'Yes,' Sam said, trying to control the waver in her voice.

'Have you called for help?'

'Yes,' she nodded. 'My sister . . .' she was about to say 'will be here soon', but she didn't know what Max was organising.

The policeman was looking at her quizzically. 'Your sister? She knows about cars?'

'No,' Sam smiled weakly. 'She was going to get help. The battery on my mobile went flat.'

'So, she called the MRA for you?'

'Well, no, actually, I'm not a member any more. My membership lapsed, well, it must have come due just as I was moving house, and to be honest, I don't even remember getting the renewal in the mail. Not that I'm blaming the MRA, I'm sure it wasn't their fault. I used to work for them actually. They're very efficient. I must have just missed it because of the move.' Sam took a breath. She realised she was trembling and the police were staring at her, not a little bemused.

'Anyway, I don't really need the MRA. Because I know what's wrong. I'm pretty sure I've just run out of petrol.'

The policeman considered the car, frowning. 'I would have thought this model had an indicator light on the instrument panel. You know, it looks like a petrol bowser.'

Sam sighed. 'It does. It's just that I used to have a four-wheel drive and it had an auxiliary tank, so I didn't really have to think about running out of petrol . . .' She noticed they were both suppressing smiles. 'Look, I'm not usually disorganised. As a matter of fact, I take care of this kind of thing for other people. I'm a lifestyle manager.'

They were now miserably failing the battle to suppress those smiles.

'Whatever you say, ma'am,' said the policeman. 'But I'm afraid this is a tow-away zone and unless you can indicate to me that you'll be on your way shortly, then I'll have to make the call.'

Sam bit the edge of her thumb. She didn't know what else to say. She had the feeling she'd said enough to hang herself already.

'Here's someone,' said the policewoman.

They all looked around as a car pulled up in front of the Magna.

'Anyone you know?'

Sam nodded weakly.

'Looks like your knight in shining armour has arrived.'

The boot flipped open as Hal appeared out of the car, smiling broadly. Sam dashed forward to meet him, out of earshot of the police.

'What are you doing here?' she whispered.

'Max phoned me.'

'Why did she do that?'

'I guess because she thought I might be able to help.'

Sam sighed, exasperated. 'You shouldn't be doing this. It's not . . . appropriate.'

Now Hal sighed.

She didn't know why it bothered her that he'd shown up,

but it did. She was embarrassed about her email brush-off. They hadn't spoken since then and now he was here, rescuing her. 'You're always helping me out. I'm supposed to do this kind of thing for you.'

'Well, next time I run out of gas and I'm stranded on the side of the road, I promise I'll call you.'

'Excuse me, sir,' said the policeman, interrupting them. 'You've brought petrol with you?'

'Absolutely, officer,' said Hal, tapping the can in the boot of his car.

'I think we can leave you and your wife to sort this out between you,' he smiled. 'But if you could get the car moving as soon as possible . . .'

Sam went to say something, but Hal placed his arm around her shoulder. 'Thanks officer. Thank the officer, honey.'

'Thank you,' she said in a small voice.

As the police walked back to their car Sam shrugged Hal's arm off. 'Why did you let him think that?'

Hal picked up the can of petrol. 'What?'

'That I was your wife!'

He grinned. 'Well, it's not entirely untrue, there's a contract somewhere that makes you my wife on a "for hire" basis, I believe. Or so you keep reminding me.'

Sam rolled her eyes. The toot of a car horn sounded behind them, and they both turned and waved as the police pulled away. Hal opened the driver door of Sam's car and felt under the seat for the lever to open the petrol tank.

'You know, you didn't have to do this,' said Sam, watching him. 'I'm not useless, you know.'

'I never said you were useless,' he said, closing the door again. He walked around to the other side of the car and Sam followed him.

'Like I was telling the policeman, it's just that the four-wheel drive had an auxiliary tank, I didn't realise the petrol would run out so quickly.'

Hal undid the petrol cap and handed it to Sam.

'And, okay, I forgot about swapping my roadside service

membership over to the new car. I mean I was in the middle of selling a house and taking care of three kids and working, you know.'

He didn't say anything as he opened the can of petrol and positioned the funnel.

'And the battery went flat on my mobile. So? That could happen to anyone.'

Hal stopped and looked up at the sky. Sam frowned, looking up too.

'What is it?' she said.

'I was just thinking, despite everything, look, the sky hasn't fallen in.' He shook his head. 'What do you know?'

Sam put her hands on her hips, scowling. 'I'm just saying, you didn't have to come, I didn't ask you. Can we just have that on the record, please? I could have taken care of this myself, really.'

'Really, you couldn't. Not this time.' He drained the contents of the can into the tank and held his hand out for the petrol cap. Sam passed it to him.

'Sure, I could have left you stranded here with a dead cellphone and no gas,' said Hal. 'But instead I left work and drove to a gas station and bought a jerry can and filled it and drove out here to help you.' He screwed the cap back on the petrol tank and closed the cover. 'And you know why I did all that?' he asked, picking up the empty can.

'Because you've got some kind of weird saviour complex!' Sam blurted.

He stared at her. 'Excuse me?'

'You're always playing the nice guy. What is it that you want from me? Are you trying to make it so I can't get by without you? Well, I can get by just fine. I don't need you to look after me, I can look after myself.'

Fuck! Where did that come from? Hal was just glaring at her.

He took a calming breath. 'I'm sure you can look after yourself, Sam. I'm sure you can look after everyone and everything and that you don't need anybody. I just came down here today because I care about you, I like you. I like you a lot in fact. God knows why, you're so damned infuriating.' He paused, not taking his eyes off her. 'And you want to know what else? I think maybe you like me too, but for some reason, and I'm not going to presume to analyse you,' he said pointedly, 'you don't want to explore this thing that's between us, this thing that I happen to think could be pretty good.'

With that he turned and walked to his car, put the can in the boot and closed it. He took a handkerchief from his pocket and wiped his hands. Then he came around to the driver side of her car, opened the door and climbed in. She heard him sliding the seat back and then the engine starting up. Sam realised she hadn't taken a breath the whole time.

'So . . .' He stood up out of the car again, looking across the roof at her. 'I'll leave you to it. I'd suggest you stop at the first gas station you come to and fill up. Are you okay for money?'

She nodded meekly.

He paused, gazing up the road for a moment, before turning back to look directly at her. 'I won't bother you any more, Sam. You have my number. You know where I live. If you're ever passing . . . don't hesitate.'

He walked back to his car, opened the door and climbed in. Sam heard the engine rev and then the car took off up the road. She didn't take her eyes off it until it was out of sight.

Sam was livid by the time she made it home. She was angry at Max for sending Hal out to her. And she was angry that Hal had left the way he did. She didn't know why the hell she'd come out with all of that stuff. It must have been the heat, and the anxiety, and the arrival of the police. She'd just been taken by surprise. That was reasonable, wasn't it? Could she explain that in an email to Hal?

But if she did, she'd be making contact again. And what would he take that to mean? He said he liked her. A lot. And he reckoned she liked him too.

Well, what would he know?

She walked in the front door, slamming it behind her. Max looked up from the magazine she was reading. 'Hi, how'd you go?'

'Hal showed up just after the police did.'

'Oh God!' She stood up. 'Is everything okay? Did they let you off?'

Sam nodded. 'Where are the kids?'

'They're all next door. Maria asked me in too, but I thought I'd better stay close to the phone. I've been feeling a bit redundant though.' Max frowned, considering Sam. 'You look pissed off. Want me to make you a cuppa? Or do you need something stronger?'

'What I need is for you to stop butting in and deciding what you think is good for me,' said Sam angrily. Max just stared at her. She obviously wasn't expecting this outburst, but Sam couldn't help herself now that she had started. 'Stop trying to fix me up with Hal! I don't want to complicate my life with a man. I don't need it, okay? Just because it's alright for you to screw around, doesn't mean it's okay for me, do you understand? I can't be irresponsible like you, doing whatever I feel like with no one to answer to. I have a life, and I don't need you interfering in it any more!'

Sam realised she was shouting. She stood there, breathing heavily, while Max picked up her bag and walked quietly past her and out the front door.

Sam sunk into a chair nearby, trembling, tears stinging her eyes. She dropped her head in her hands. Great. She'd lost a friend or a client or whatever the hell Hal was, and now a sister as well, all in the same day. At this rate, losing her mind was not far off.

The next day

Sam usually didn't bother to call in home when she was out so close to Ellie's pick-up time. There was milk in the car that needed refrigerating, but more to the point, she had a thumping headache that needed medicating.

She put the milk away, poured herself a glass of water and swallowed down a couple of Panadols. She walked into the living room and sat heavily on the sofa, leaning her head back. If she could just have five minutes of quiet, it might be enough to ease the pain throbbing away at her temples.

But she doubted it. The headache had started after Max left yesterday. She'd slept fitfully and woken up with it again this morning. And a visit to Patricia Bowen's house of horrors was enough to keep it going strong.

But none of that was the reason she had a headache. Sam was not worried about Max. She would apologise to her and then it would be over. One of Max's most endearing traits was that she didn't hold a grudge.

No, her headache had persisted all night and all day because she couldn't get the whole scene with Hal out of her mind. Her behaviour yesterday was atrocious. It would have been a disaster if he hadn't come along when he did, and yet the way she'd carried on, anyone would have thought the entire thing was his fault.

The truth was, Sam didn't know what to do about Hal. She was only too aware of the attraction between them. What did they call it in the movies? URST — unresolved sexual tension. Well, there was URST in buckets whenever he was around and Sam was finding it harder to deal with. That's why she had put him off when he asked her on another date. That's why she had acted like an idiot yesterday. Her body was willing, but her mind and her heart were staying put, peering at him through a chink in the curtains, suspicious, uncertain, afraid.

Physically, he was all she could think about. At night she found herself lying awake, staring at the ceiling, picturing him coming to her, imagining the way he would touch her, his lips skimming over the surface of her skin . . . and then she would get out of bed and go and splash cold water on her face. She would pace around the house like a caged animal until she felt so tired she was certain she would get into bed and fall asleep. But as she'd drift off he'd be there again, curled up behind her, enfolding her in his arms. And sometimes that was enough, while other times she'd weep quietly, feeling so lonely she almost couldn't stand herself.

Why was human nature so contrary? Always wanting what you didn't have. When sex had been on tap in the marriage, Sam had been disinterested, to say the least. Then it had been all about avoiding sex. But she'd been no different to other married women she knew. The husband always wanted it, the wife always had a headache. It was so common it was a cliché.

So why not just go for it with Hal? He was willing, she was desperate, clearly. They were consenting adults. It all sounded so reasonable, yet the idea made Sam's blood freeze. Fantasies were all well and good. In her fantasies she had firm breasts and a flat stomach, and she was always taller. She was also supremely confident, lying back, letting him revel in her fabulous body.

As if that was going to happen! She hadn't even been able to bear the light on when she'd had sex with Jeff, who'd known her forever and had been there when she'd had babies, for crying out loud. She'd had nothing to hide from him, yet hide it she had, nevertheless.

But her reticence was not just about sex. Hal would be far too easy to fall in love with. He was kind and funny and considerate. And Sam was needy and vulnerable and had been discarded by her husband of sixteen years as though she was a piece of clothing that no longer fitted. If she allowed herself the comfort of Hal's arms, she was quite sure she would fall head over heels and never, ever recover when he went away.

So much for the Panadol, her head was now throbbing so hard it felt as though she'd just walked out of an all-night dance club. Sam wished there was a switch behind her ear so she could turn off all but the most basic brain functions. Then she could operate on a kind of automatic pilot. Think nothing, feel nothing, just get through the day.

She sighed, getting to her feet. She looked at her watch. Josh and Jess should be home by now; in fact, they should have been home when Sam got here. She wasn't worried, they were probably next door. But then she thought she heard voices coming from up the hall. The girls' room was empty, but she could still hear talking. At the end of the hall Josh's door was closed. There were definitely voices coming from inside.

'Josh?' she said, knocking lightly.

'What?'

Sam opened the door slowly. Josh was leaning against his desk, an odd look on his face. There was no one else in the room.

'I didn't realise you were home.'

He gave a slight nod. 'Same here.'

'I thought someone was in here with you.'

He shrugged.

'I heard voices . . .'

Josh sighed heavily. 'I was just practising this stupid speech.'

'Oh?' Sam leaned against the doorjamb. 'What's it for?'

'English. It's so crap, Mum. Why do they make you do speeches?'

'Well, to give you practice. There are a lot of jobs where you have to be able to stand up in front of people and speak confidently.'

'But I don't want a job like that.'

'Okay Josh,' Sam tried not to smile. 'Just say your dream of becoming a professional skateboarder doesn't quite come off, you might find you need to develop some other skills.'

'I don't like speaking in public. I suck at it, Mum.'

'You must have done this a dozen times at your old school.'

'Yeah, but I knew everyone there. No one took it seriously.'

'Oh, I'm so pleased to hear that,' Sam remarked sardonically. 'Look, take the speech with you this weekend, get some help from your dad.'

'No way.'

'Why not? He gives speeches and presentations all the time.'

'Yeah, so he'll think I'm crap.'

'No he won't, Josh –'

'He will, Mum, he's good at like, everything.'

'No he isn't.'

Josh looked embarrassed. 'I meant work and stuff.'

'I know what you meant.' Sam stepped into the room and perched on the end of Josh's bed. 'He's a grown man, Josh, he's had years of experience. But he was "crap" once too.'

Josh looked at her doubtfully.

'You should have heard the speech he gave at our wedding,' Sam insisted, grinning. 'He was so nervous, his head was jerking all over the place, and he kept tripping over his words and stammering. But the worst thing was, he actually forgot my name.'

'He forgot your name?' Josh repeated incredulously.

'He stood there saying, "My wife, um, my wife, ah, ah . . ." until finally the table of his surfing mates all yelled out at once, *"Her name's Samantha!"* '

Josh laughed despite himself. It was good to see a smile on his face. He was such a handsome kid, so much like his father at the same age. Sam had never thought about that before. Josh was almost the age that Jeff was when they had started going out. But he was just a child . . .

The phone started to ring from the kitchen.

Sam jumped up. 'I'd better get that.' She hesitated in the doorway. 'Take the speech with you this weekend, Josh. I'm sure Dad would love to help.'

She ran to the phone and picked it up. 'Hello?'

'I was just about to give up! Where were you?'

Sam took a calming breath. 'I was in the middle of something with Josh, Mum. Sorry.'

'Is he in some kind of trouble?'

God, why did Bernice immediately imagine the worse? No wonder Sam had a pessimistic streak. 'No, Mum. Josh is fine. Thanks for asking.'

'Don't get that tone with me, Samantha. You sound just like your sister.'

Sam ignored that. 'What were you calling about, Mum?' she said as brightly as she could manage.

'Why, am I keeping you from something more important?'

'No, but I will have to pick up Ellie shortly –'

'Would you rather I phoned back at a more convenient time?' her mother said without any attempt to hide her rancour.

'If you'd like to have a nice long chat, Mum, it would be lovely to talk to you later,' Sam said sweetly, hoping some poor angel somewhere was not missing out on getting its wings because she was lying through her teeth to her own mother. She had a feeling she was confusing her myths there, but anyway.

'Actually, I was just calling about next weekend. You haven't forgotten?'

As if Sam had a hope of forgetting the annual Christmas-cake-and-pudding-baking day. Bernice Driscoll phoned her daughters religiously every January to remind them to write it on their new calendars. And she mentioned it each time they spoke from September onwards.

'I'll be there, Mum.'

'And the children?'

Sam steeled herself. 'Ellie's really looking forward to it.'

'Of course she is. And what about Jessica and Joshua?'

'Well, Mum, I don't think Josh will come –'

'Why not?' she demanded.

'Mum,' Sam pleaded. 'He's a fifteen-year-old boy, he's just not interested.'

'I suppose he thinks it's sissy? Doesn't he realise that all the world's best chefs are men?'

'I don't think he could care less about the world's best chefs, to be honest, Mum.'

'Well, there's such a thing as duty, Sam. I taught you that, but it doesn't seem you bothered to pass it on to your children.'

'Mum, maybe you'd understand if you had a boy.'

'Rub it in, why don't you, Samantha? If I had a dollar for every time someone said that to me when I was raising you girls, I'd be a wealthy woman.'

Sam had stopped paying attention. She was contemplating

locking Jessica in a room with her grandmother for a day. Then she'd think that Sam was not so bad after all.

'I hope Jessica's coming? Or do you have no control over your children whatsoever?'

Jess had turned up her nose when Sam brought up the subject a couple of weeks ago, and she was considering letting her off the hook this year. But now she would have to bribe her.

'Of course she's coming, she wouldn't miss it,' Sam said, crossing her fingers. 'Oh, look at the time! I have to run, Mum, I'm going to be late for Ellie. See you next week.'

Saturday

'Yoohoo,' Sam called from the front door of Max's flat. She'd opened it with her own key as usual, expecting to find Max still in bed. But that sounded suspiciously like a vacuum cleaner coming from her room. She walked over to the kitchen and put her bags down on the table. She'd bought bagels and sticky cakes and cappuccino from the deli Max liked. Plus a bunch of bright orange gerberas she was hoping would make her smile.

The vacuum cleaner went silent and Sam turned around as Max appeared in the doorway. There was an awkward moment while they just stared at each other. Sam knew she had to be the first one to speak.

'I brought you breakfast! I didn't think you'd be up and about yet.'

Max just looked at her.

Sam picked up the gerberas. 'And flowers. I brought you flowers.' She breathed out heavily. 'And I also brought an apology.'

'You're taking a while to get around to that.'

She bit her lip. 'I'm sorry for shouting at you, Max. I'm sorry for the rotten things I said – they were completely unfounded, I only said them because I was angry and hot and tired. That's not an excuse, just an explanation.'

Max considered her a moment longer. 'What did you bring me?' Sam could see the smile in her eyes as she picked up one of the paper bags. 'Ooh, canoli. I love canoli.'

'I know.'

'Okay, I forgive you.' Her face relaxed into a smile as she closed the gap between them and wrapped her arms around her sister. Sam felt a great swelling of relief in her chest and tears sprang to her eyes at the same time as a sob unexpectedly escaped from her throat.

Max held her by the shoulders to look at her directly. 'Come on,' she said. 'You didn't really think I'd stay mad, did you?'

'I was just so mean to you . . .'

'Well, like it or not, I'll still be your sister no matter what you do. So you're stuck with me. And I'm stuck with you. And just so we have it straight, I'm not going to stop interfering either.'

Sam smiled, wiping the tears from her cheeks. 'I know.'

Max plonked herself down on a chair and tore open one of the bags.

'I'll put these in water,' said Sam, picking up the flowers and taking them to the sink.

'So what did you do to poor Hal?'

Sam swung around. 'What do you mean? Have you spoken to him?'

'No,' said Max. 'I can only assume by the mood you were in when you got to me, that something must have happened between you two.'

'Oh.' Sam crouched down, looking for a vase in the cupboards underneath the sink. 'It was nothing really. I was just tired and frazzled, like I said.'

When she stood up again with a vase, Max was looking at her, eyebrows raised.

'What?' said Sam.

'That's it?'

She shrugged. 'I was rude to him too.'

'And what did you take him as a peace offering?'

'I haven't seen him,' said Sam, turning away to fill the vase with water.

'Why not?' Max persisted.

'Because,' she sighed, resting the vase on the sink. She started to open the wrapping around the flowers. 'It's complicated.'

'What's so complicated? It happens every day, all around the world. Boy meets girl, boy likes girl, girl likes boy –'

'That's when it gets complicated. Have you got any secateurs so I can cut the ends of these?'

'Yeah right! Like I'd have secateurs,' Max scoffed. 'I'm not letting you avoid the question that easily.'

'What was the question again?' said Sam, scooping up the flowers and plopping them into the vase.

'He likes you. You like him. What's complicated after that?'

'What isn't?' Sam sighed, shaking her head. She turned around and leaned back against the kitchen cupboard. 'I could give you a list. I've got three children, he lives on the other side of the world –'

'He lives ten minutes away.'

'At the moment.'

'So, live for the moment! What's wrong with that, Sam?' Max held out her hands in exasperation.

'I don't know how to do that, don't you understand?' Sam insisted. 'I've been with the same man since I was a teenager. I'm as worldly as a seventeen year old who's broken up with her first boyfriend. And just as fragile.'

Max frowned at her. 'But you always seem like you're handling everything so well.'

Sam shook her head, smiling ruefully. She picked up the flowers and brought them to the table. 'I feel like a china vase that's been broken and glued back together. And okay, the vase looks fine, you don't even notice the cracks until you look up close. But you would never, ever use it again to hold flowers because you're quite sure it would fall apart.'

She set them down in front of Max. 'Yes, I like Hal, and yes

I'm attracted to him. But to follow through on that would be the stupidest thing I could do at the moment. I'm not the kind of woman who can just go out with a guy, see what happens. Maybe that makes me not very modern, I don't know. But that's who I am. I'm not like you, or even Rose, amazingly enough. I don't want the freedom I never had, I wouldn't know what to do with it. The thought of having sex . . .' Sam took a breath. 'It scares me to death. Someone seeing me naked?' She shook her head.

'Is this because of what happened with Sleazy?' Max asked carefully.

'Well, that didn't help,' Sam muttered. 'But I try not to think about that if I can help it.'

'You know,' said Max, 'I'm sure it would be nothing like that with Hal.'

'Of course it wouldn't.' Sam sighed. 'That's the problem.'

'What do you mean?'

'Don't you see, I'm so naïve I'd probably fall hopelessly in love and expect it to last forever. And one day Hal will turn around and go back to the US, and I'm supposed to handle someone leaving me yet again? I've got three kids to look after. I don't have the luxury of another heartbreak. I'm not that strong.'

'Oh Sam . . .' Max said sadly. She got up from the table and put her arms around her sister, hugging her tight. 'You're not ready, that's all. I won't push it any more. I just didn't want you to miss the boat.'

Sam smiled bravely at Max, much more bravely than she felt. 'Anyway,' she said, changing the subject and picking up the newspaper she'd brought with her, 'I'm going to look for another job. No, more than that, a career.'

'You go girl!' Max cried. 'Got any ideas?'

Sam sat down and pulled out the employment section from the paper. 'You'll probably think I'm silly.'

'So? Wouldn't be the first time.'

'Max! I need you to be supportive, please.'

'Go ahead. I promise I won't think you're silly.'

'Well,' Sam went on, taking the lid off one of the styrofoam cups of coffee. 'It's probably a pipedream, and I suspect it would be really difficult to get into. I mean, I have no idea how you'd even go about it. You probably have to know someone, and I don't know anyone. Still, I love the idea of it, and I think it's something I could do. And maybe even my experience with *Wife for Hire* would count. But I'm probably having myself on completely here −'

'Sam!' Max interrupted, exasperated. 'I'd love to hear what it actually is, preferably sometime before the year's out!'

Sam shrugged, sheepish. 'Well, I'm not exactly sure what you call it, but it involves organising parties −'

'What? Catering?'

'No,' Sam shook her head. 'I'm talking about the organising. And not just parties, but conventions, launches, you know, big things.'

'Event management,' Max said plainly, picking up the newspaper.

'Of course, that's what it's called,' said Sam. She looked closely at Max. 'Do you think I'm crazy?'

'Yeah,' Max nodded. 'But that's beside the point. I think you could do event management standing on your head.'

Sam felt flushed. 'Do you really?' she said in a small voice.

'D'oh!' Max cried. 'My God, Sherl, you're the most organised person I know. Mm, not counting the other day, you know, the empty tank, the lapsed membership, the dead battery . . .'

Sam grinned.

Max had been searching through the pages of the newspaper and had apparently found what she was looking for. She opened the paper out and slid it across in front of Sam. 'Here you go, take a look there for a start. Under "Event Co-ordinator".'

Sam began to read the ads. There were only a few. Max stood up and started clearing the table around her.

'What are you doing?' Sam asked.

'Cleaning up.'

Sam frowned. 'That's not like you. What's going on?'

'I do clean, you know. Are you suggesting I live in squalor?' she said airily.

'I'm sorry. It's just, you're not normally so . . . fervent about it.' Sam narrowed her eyes. 'And you were up before I got here, *vacuuming*! Come on, spill. What's going on?'

'Sorry to disappoint you, but it's not very exciting. A friend from uni is coming round to help me with stats. We have an exam next week and I'm dreading it.'

'I thought you loved statistics.'

'Yeah, quoting them, not calculating them.' She shuddered. '*Maths* is involved, Sherl!'

'Well, I'll get out of your way.'

'No, you're fine. There's no rush. Have you found anything there?'

'Mm, only a couple, and I don't have the experience to apply for either of them.'

'That's why you have to make direct approaches.' Max bustled around the room as she spoke, straightening the place up. 'Find the names of companies in the phone book, put together a resume, and send it to them. Then follow up with a call.'

'Oh, I don't know . . .'

'It's how people get jobs, Sam, especially in that kind of industry. I bet they don't even have to advertise entry-level jobs. They'd have people lining up to work for them.'

Sam looked squeamish.

'Look at the way you approached *Wife for Hire*,' Max continued. 'That was pretty upfront. Come to think of it, all those clients of yours, there's bound to be someone who has contacts, Sam. You have to start telling everyone you know –'

'I'm not sure that's ethical.'

'Why not?'

'Using my clients to get myself another job? It doesn't seem right.'

'Oh Sam,' said Max, frustrated. 'You've got to learn to look after number one. *Wife for Hire* will get along without you.'

She shrugged, thinking. 'What about Fiona?'

'What about Fiona?' Max swung around.

'Well, she works for that huge company . . .' Sam hesitated, looking at Max. 'What is it with Fiona? Why does everybody suddenly become all guarded when her name comes up?'

'I don't know what you're talking about,' Max dismissed, turning her back.

Sam stood up and walked over to where Max was sorting through her CDs. She leaned against the wall and folded her arms. 'What's going on?'

Max sighed, putting down a pile of CDs. 'I would be the worst secret agent.' She looked at Sam squarely. 'Fiona asked us not to say anything to you because she didn't want to upset you, and she didn't want you to hate her.'

'What on earth is it?' Sam frowned.

Max took a deep breath. 'She's having an affair.'

Sam's eyes widened. 'Who with? Do we know him? Does Gavin know?'

Max shook her head. 'No, it's all very clandestine. Somebody she works with. He's married too, apparently.'

'Wow,' Sam said quietly. 'But why does she think I'll hate her?'

'Think about it, Sherl,' said Max. She started slotting CDs one at a time into their stand. 'Jeff left you for a woman he met at work.'

'Oh yeah,' she murmured. God, had she become an object of pity now? Poor Sam. Everyone else was 'moving on' and here she was, too scared to even date a guy she'd known the best part of a year. 'Have you seen Rosemary lately?'

Max nodded.

'I've been meaning to call her. She left a message with her new address and phone number. How's she going?'

'She hasn't missed a beat, Sam. She found a place that first weekend, a furnished place, no less. And it's not bad.' She paused. 'You should go and see her.'

Sam nodded vaguely.

'She thinks you're avoiding her.'

'I'm not avoiding her!' Sam insisted. Max raised an eyebrow. 'Okay, maybe I am avoiding her.'

'Why? You should hook up with her some weekend when you don't have the kids.' Max slid the last CD into the rack. 'She's certainly getting around. She's joined all these singles groups and she's out like, every second night.'

Sam winced. 'I could think of nothing worse.'

'Yeah, meeting new people, having fun, what an ordeal that would be.' Max checked her watch. 'Dan should be here by now.'

'Dan?' Sam grinned, arching an eyebrow. 'You didn't say the someone from uni was a *man*.'

Max rolled her eyes. 'A man who's good at *maths*, Sherl! Do you really imagine he'd be my type?'

Sam shook her head. 'Well, I'll leave you to it.' She crossed to the kitchen, tossed her empty cup in the bin and picked up her handbag and the newspaper.

Max followed her. 'You don't have to leave.'

'No, it's okay, I've got grocery shopping to do anyway.'

'Jeez, I think I'd rather be doing statistics.' Max walked her to the door.

'I'm sure you would, with *Dan*,' Sam winked. 'Have fun.'

Max rolled her eyes. 'Fun with statistics. There's an oxymoron.'

'I'll call you,' Sam said as she started down the stairs. 'Don't forget baking day next week.'

'Like I could.'

Late Saturday morning was about the worst time to go grocery shopping, Sam realised on her fifth circuit of the car park. But she had nothing else to do. Weekends without the kids still dragged, despite the odd duty for a client. She had a few calls to make later, she liked to confirm restaurant reservations she had made previously, just so there were no last-minute upsets. And Patricia Bowen had left a list, of course.

A young couple with a shopping trolley stopped just ahead of her and unlocked the boot of their car. Sam pulled over and flicked on her indicator. She might as well wait, there were no other spaces to be had. She watched the couple. They seemed to be enjoying themselves, talking and laughing the whole time they loaded their bags into the car. She couldn't remember enjoying shopping with Jeff that much. Did they ever even go together? Not after the kids, maybe occasionally before that. She imagined they would have been rushing to get through it, having a hundred other things to do. Probably bickering the whole time.

Sam sighed. Did he go shopping with Jodi now? Maybe on their child-free weekends?

The pair were now apparently wrestling over the car keys, he had his arms around her from behind, tickling her, trying to make her give them up. The woman's face was beaming with delight as she finally relinquished the keys. He kissed her lightly, before opening the door for her.

They weren't married, Sam decided. Or if they were, they were newlyweds. Or maybe they were having an affair. He had a family on the other side of Sydney, and he never went shopping with his wife.

Well, you're a bitter old piece of work, Samantha Holmes, she said to herself as the couple pulled out and drove away. She parked the car and strolled aimlessly into the supermarket, collected a trolley and pushed it through the barrier.

Her mind returned to Fiona. Sam wondered who she was having the affair with, how long it had been going on. Did she steal away on the weekends? Surely it would be too difficult to get away from Gavin and the girls? He had them all week. Now that Sam thought about it, what had Jeff done? She knew he'd made the excuse of at least one conference to get away. The rest of the time he'd hung around the house, detached and distant. Sam hadn't known that was because his heart and mind were somewhere else. She wondered why he didn't make more excuses to get out at the time. Jodi wasn't married. Or was she?

Sam hardly knew a thing about the woman who lived with her husband. The woman who cared for her children every second weekend. But that was how she preferred it. These days she only saw Jeff for what he was to them. The father of her children, that's the only role she needed to know about. The only one that mattered to her. And she had to admit that he seemed to be doing okay, better than when they were together. At least the separation had forced him to have a stronger relationship with his children.

Sam wondered if the same would happen to Fiona. She seemed a somewhat distant mother. But that was probably unfair. Men were allowed to go to work and leave their kids without anyone raising an eyebrow. Yet there had been not a few comments over the years about the strangeness of Fiona and Gavin's arrangement, the strangeness of Gavin. In some ways, Sam wasn't that surprised Fiona had been tempted away.

What was she thinking? She was just the same as Gavin, staying home with the kids. Did that give Jeff the right to wander? To find someone more exciting? Why was she more sympathetic to Fiona in the same situation?

Sam sighed – no one really knew what went on between a married couple, behind closed doors. She and Jeff hadn't been close for a long time. Sam had replaced the missing intimacy with striving for a bigger and better house, with stuff to fill it, with a load of activities for the children and a frenetic social calendar for themselves. Anything that would fill the emptiness. And it would have been enough for her. That was the pathetic part. She had settled, if not for a loveless marriage, at least for a passionless one. But it wasn't enough for Jeff. Maybe he had done them both a favour.

Sam blinked, taking in her surroundings. She was in the canned food aisle. She looked in the trolley, it was half full. She did a quick check of the contents and realised it was all stuff she'd intended to buy. It was like when she found herself driving along somewhere, and while she could remember leaving home, there was a whole chunk of the journey about which she had no recollection. It was apparently possible to shop on automatic pilot as well. God, it was such a mindless activity.

The sound of her mobile phone ringing startled her. She felt around inside her bag to answer it.

'Samantha Holmes.'

'Sam? It's me, Jeff.'

Speak of the devil.

'Hi, is anything wrong? Are the kids okay?'

'Yeah, everyone's fine. It's just Jessie. She's okay, but she's not feeling well.'

'What do you mean?' Sam frowned.

'Well, it's not as though she's actually sick, but she isn't feeling the best, you know?'

'Jeff, what are you talking about?'

She heard him sigh. 'She doesn't have an illness as such. But she isn't exactly a hundred per cent . . .'

The penny dropped. 'Oh Christ,' said Sam. 'She's got her period, hasn't she?'

'Yes!' The relief in his voice was palpable.

'Oh, the poor kid. Is she okay?'

'I think so, but she wants to go home, if that's alright?'

Sam wasn't surprised, seeing as her father couldn't even bring himself to say the word 'period'. 'Of course it's alright.'

'She wants her mum.'

Sam unexpectedly felt tears spring to her eyes. She swallowed. 'Well, I'm just at the shops, but I'll finish up right away and meet you at home.'

'I'll give you a head start. See you there.'

Sam turned off the phone and put it away. She felt nervy and teary and sick in the stomach. Her little girl . . . God, it sounded so corny to say she was a woman now. Of course she wasn't. She was still a little girl, but something had shifted.

Sam raced to the personal aisle and grabbed pads with wings, pads without wings, super, light and every size in between, tampons with an applicator, and others in a groovy purse pack. At the front of the store she took one of every magazine on the stands that had a teenage girl on the cover. Sam looked around, frantic. What else?

Of course. Chocolate.

True to Murphy's Law, she ended up on the slowest possible checkout queue. The woman being served ahead of her seemed mildly irritated that her mobile phone conversation had to be interrupted while she entered her EFTPOS details, and she consequently got them wrong twice. But it wouldn't have made much difference. The checkout operator must have been from the remedial intake, she was as slow as a wet week. It never ceased to amaze Sam that all they had to do was run an item across a scanner and still they had trouble with it. She'd had a stint as a 'checkout chick' when she was still at school, but in her day there was no conveyer belt. You had to bend over one trolley, pick up each item and place it in the next trolley, and you had to key in the prices *and* work out the change. All that and they were still twice as fast as most of the girls who served her these days.

She really was starting to sound like her mother.

Sam had just opened the door at home with her first load of shopping when Jeff's car pulled up outside. She carried the bags through to the kitchen and came back to the door to greet them. When Sam saw Jess's face, she knew this was going to be delicate. She was unusually subdued and she didn't make eye contact. She was obviously embarrassed by the whole thing, so as much as Sam felt like gathering her up and rocking her in her arms like when she was a baby, she contained herself.

'Hi, sweetie,' she said lightly.

'Hi,' Jess murmured, walking past her. She continued down the hall to her room.

Jeff had picked up the rest of the bags out of the open boot.

'Thanks,' said Sam. 'Come on through.'

He followed her into the kitchen and set the bags down on the bench. 'I won't keep you,' he said. 'I'd better get back to the other two.'

Sam walked him to the front door. He hesitated, glancing up the hallway, a worried frown creasing his forehead.

'She'll be alright,' said Sam. 'We all have to go through it. One half of the population at least.'

He sighed. 'Yeah, but she's only a kid. How did she grow up so fast?'

'We'll blink, you realise, and it'll be Ellie next.'

'Oh don't say that,' he winced.

Sam watched him. There was more feeling in his eyes than she'd possibly ever seen before. He loved his kids. It made her feel close to him.

'Listen, has Josh mentioned a speech he's doing at school?'

Jeff shook his head. 'What speech?'

'He was practising the other day. I told him you'd be a good one to go to for help.'

Jeff had an odd look on his face, almost bashful.

'But go easy on him. He's a bit in awe of you.'

'He is?'

'Oh, don't worry, I pulled you down a peg or three. I told him the wedding speech story.'

Jeff's face relaxed into a smile. 'Well, thanks for that, I think. I'll see you tomorrow.'

'Give Ellie a kiss for me,' Sam called after him as he turned to walk up the path. He held up his hand in a wave.

She closed the door and strolled thoughtfully back out to the kitchen. She didn't know whether she should leave Jess alone, she might have wanted to come home for that very reason. But Jeff had said on the phone that she wanted her mum. Sam picked up one of the shopping bags and walked up the hall. Jess hadn't closed the door, she was still unpacking. Sam leaned against the doorjamb.

'How are you feeling, kiddo?'

Jess shrugged. 'Alright, I guess.'

Sam took a breath, stepping into the room. She held out the bag. 'I bought you these. I didn't know what you'd prefer, but I suppose you don't know that yet either.'

Jess took the bag and looked inside. To Sam's surprise she grinned, shaking her head.

'What?' Sam frowned.

Jess lifted a plastic bag from her overnight bag and handed it to her mother. Sam looked inside, it was full of much the same.

'Oh, did Jodi get these for you?'

'No,' said Jess. 'Dad went out this morning and bought them.'

'Your father?'

'I thought he must have bought out the whole shop. But it looks like he left some for you!' she giggled.

Sam was relieved to see some animation in Jess's face, and she smiled. 'So, he handled it okay, then?'

'Yeah, he was great. I woke up this morning, and I was a bit of a mess. That was the worst part,' she said, looking embarrassed again. 'I didn't know who to tell. Josh's useless, and Ellie's too little.'

Sam cleared her throat. 'You didn't think you could talk to Jodi?'

Jess shook her head, shrugging. 'She was sick this morning anyway.'

'Oh?'

'Dad said she had a bug. She kept throwing up. Between Jodi and me, he had the washing machine going all morning.'

Sam tried to conjure up a mental picture of Jeff up to his elbows in bloodied sheets and vomit. It was beyond her realm of comprehension.

'He couldn't even say "period" on the phone,' Sam told her.

Jess giggled. 'No, he couldn't *talk* about it, Mum! He got all nervous and flustered. It was pretty funny.'

'What was Josh doing in the middle of all this?'

'Oh, he took off up the skate park.'

Sam was not surprised. She looked at Jess. She had a bit of colour back in her cheeks and her eyes were brighter now.

'Well,' she said, leaving the bag on Jess's bed, 'I guess you'll have enough of these to keep you going till you get married.'

'Like that's ever going to happen,' Jess murmured.

'Oh? Why do you say that?'

She shrugged. 'I don't think people who are married are very happy.'

Sam was a little shocked. It seemed a very jaundiced view of life for such a young girl. At Jess's age all she could think about was getting married. Not that that was a particularly healthy attitude either, come to think of it.

She sat down and patted the bed beside her. Jessica slumped next to her, with only a fleeting roll of her eyes.

'Your father and I had some happy times, Jess, lots of happy times. It's just that we were very young when we got together, and people change. They grow up, and they end up wanting different things. That's why it's better not to marry too young.'

Jess was quiet, listening.

'The thing is, and I'm sure I speak for your dad as well, I don't regret that we got married, or else we wouldn't have had you or Ellie or Josh.'

'Yes you would. We just would have had a different father. Like if you'd married Hal —'

'Jess!' she sighed.

'Just say, you know, pretending.'

'You mean hypothetically?'

'Whatever. If you married Hal, you still would have had us.'

'No, Jessica Lauren Holmes, you are part of your dad and part of me. You wouldn't be who you are if I'd married someone else. And Dad wouldn't be your dad. You wouldn't want that, would you?'

'Mm, I didn't think of that.' Jess traced a pattern on the carpet with her toe. 'Are you going to get married again, Mum?'

'Not in the foreseeable future, Jess.'

'But ever?'

'Ever is a long time. Besides, someone has to ask, you know.'

'What if Hal asked you?'

'Jessica!' Sam sighed, shaking her head. 'Maxine's been filling your head with these ideas. Hal and I are just friends.' She couldn't even say that any more, she realised sadly.

'But what about hypo-thingummy, like you said before?' Jess persisted. 'If Hal asked you to marry him, would you?'

'Hal lives on the other side of the world.'

'So?' said Jess, her eyes shining. 'Maybe we could move to America!'

'And to think I had trouble getting you to move across Sydney!' Sam said dubiously. 'What about your dad? I couldn't take you so far away from him. When would you get to see him?'

Jessica sighed heavily. 'Life's complicated, isn't it?'

'Tell me about it. Now,' Sam said, slapping her knees as she stood up. 'I bought you some emergency supplies that I bet your father didn't think of.'

'What else do I need?'

'Chocolate and magazines,' Sam informed her. 'And later we'll bring out the heavy artillery.'

'What's that?'

'Videos and ice cream.'

Thursday

'There's an attachment to this email, Ted,' said Sam. 'It might be a photograph.'

'I'm afraid I'm not following you, Samantha.'

Sam was enjoying the chance to get to know Ted's son through his emails to his father. It was a wonderful, warm relationship. Hugh Dempsey was an art dealer in London and was, by all accounts, enormously successful. He had an English wife, Susan, and a teenage son, Edward, whom he wrote about with a great deal of affection. He also clearly adored his father and still sought and valued his opinion.

'Hugh has sent an attachment with this email,' Sam explained. 'Has he ever done that before?'

'I couldn't tell you, Samantha. I don't know what it is.'

'In this case it's a photograph, I'm fairly certain. If you want to send something from a different program on the computer, you have to make it an attachment, that's opened separately to the email. Problem is,' Sam murmured, frowning at the screen, 'this one doesn't want to open. You don't have the program on your computer.'

'That's a problem?'

'I'll tell you what I can do. I'll send it to myself and then I'll print out whatever it is and bring it over next week. Unless you'd like it sooner?'

Ted smiled at her. 'I wouldn't have even known it was there, Samantha, so next week is quite soon enough. That's if it isn't any trouble?'

'Not at all!' Sam assured him. She loved being able to do something extra for Ted.

'You're a very clever woman, Samantha,' Ted declared. 'I think you're wasting your talents, you know.'

Sam grinned, shaking her head. He was an easy man to impress. 'I hate to shatter your illusions, Ted, but my son taught me how to open attachments to emails when he was still in primary school, as I recall. It isn't very difficult.'

'It's not just that,' said Ted. 'I often think of you, Samantha. Is this really what you want to be doing all of your life? Running around after other people?'

'First of all, I barely run around after you, Ted. I've told you before, I enjoy coming here on Thursday afternoons, more than anything.' Sam paused. 'As for the rest, well, there's good and bad like in any job.'

'But will this sustain you as a career, especially as your children get older and move on?'

She shrugged. 'I have a few ideas, but I think they're way out of my league.'

'Such as?' Ted urged.

Sam paused. She didn't know whether she should be saying all this to him. But he had become so much more than a client. More like a kind uncle.

'Well, have you heard of event management, Ted?'

'Certainly I have. It's a very exciting industry.'

'Mm, but I think it's really hard to get into. My sister suggested that I tell everyone, even my clients, to get the word around. But I don't feel comfortable doing that.'

'Why not? I've employed many people over the years through personal contacts. It's very reassuring when you're taking on new staff if they come recommended.'

'Maybe you're right,' Sam mused. 'Now, we had better finish this email and add some kind of explanation about the attachment. Goodness knows how many others he's sent you in the past. You're going to have to fess up that you didn't see them.'

'You know I'd prefer not to say anything about my condition, Samantha.'

Sam looked at him directly. 'That's not what I meant. You can easily explain that you'd never noticed the attachments before, and that a friend pointed it out to you.'

'Yes, let's just leave it at that.'

'Though,' she continued carefully, 'I still don't understand why you won't tell Hugh –'

'Samantha –'

'Don't "Samantha" me!' she retorted. 'I read these emails from your son, begging you to come over and spend time with him and his family. He must be heartbroken that you ignore him.'

Ted sighed heavily.

'He loves you, Ted. You're not being honest with him. You're treating him like a child, still trying to protect him.'

Ted didn't say anything for a moment. Sam was worried she had overstepped the mark. But then she noticed he was smiling faintly.

'Of course I want to protect him, Samantha. And I will until the day I die. I'm sure you'll do the same for your own children.'

'I hope as they grow up that they'll want me to be honest with them as well.'

'You think it's that important?'

'Absolutely.'

Baking Day

'Ellie, you mustn't pick the cherries out of the mix, dear.'

'But they're yummy, Nanna.'

'Yes, but it's unhygienic, and besides, you have to leave some for everyone else.'

'I'll get you a whole packet of glacé cherries, honey,' said Sam from across the bench. 'Or better still, fresh cherries. They'll be out soon.'

Ellie clapped her hands.

'That's the way, Samantha, indulge the child's every fancy,' said Bernice. She shook her head. 'Modern parenting.'

'Yeah, in our day there was no such thing as indulging!' said Max drily.

'Don't be smart, Maxine. I didn't teach you to be so smart.'

Max and Sam grinned slyly at each other.

'You think I wouldn't have liked to indulge you?' Bernice went on. 'A deserted wife, struggling away on a pension and a series of menial jobs, just to make ends meet? I'm surprised you can afford to spoil the children the way you do.'

'A packet of glacé cherries is hardly going to break the bank, Mum,' said Sam.

'No, not on its own. But if you say yes to everything they ask for –'

'Mum! Who says I do that?'

'She doesn't Nanna,' muttered Jess from where she was slumped at the end of the bench, her chin resting on her hands. Sam realised she should have added conditions to the bribe it took to get Jessica here. Not just that she had to come, but that she had to look like she was enjoying it. But that was hardly fair. Sam wasn't even enjoying it.

'Mum, I had an idea about Christmas this year,' said Sam, changing the subject.

'Oh, what kind of idea?' said Bernice suspiciously.

'Well, you always go to so much trouble, and you deserve a break, and, well,' Sam hesitated, 'I thought we could have Christmas at my place for a change.'

Jessica sat up straight, suddenly interested.

'Why on earth would we want to do that?' said Bernice.

'I thought it might be getting too much for you.'

'It's not getting too much for me. You'd think I had one foot in the grave the way you're talking.'

'I didn't mean it to sound like that, Mum.'

'Mummy, I have to go to the toilet,' said Ellie.

'Take her, please, Jess.'

'Why do I have to take her?' Jessica whined. 'She's old enough to go by herself.'

'Jess, her hands are all sticky, she'll have to clean up first.'

'She can wash her hands here –'

'Jessica! Will you please just do as I ask without the twenty questions?'

Jess knew when her mother meant business. 'C'mon Ellie,' she grumbled, sliding off the stool.

Sam waited till they were out of the room. 'I didn't want to talk about this in front of them,' she resumed. 'But I don't know where the kids will be Christmas Day. I haven't spoken to Jeff about it yet.'

'What difference will that make?' Bernice frowned.

'I just thought that if they end up with their father this year, at least the house will be full and I might not miss them so much.'

'So, this is all about you, Samantha?' Bernice sniped. 'What about everyone else?'

'I think it's a great idea,' said Max.

'Well, of course *you* would. You'd jump in a fire if Samantha suggested it. Never been any different.' Her expression was scornful. 'But you do have another sister. There's Alexandra to consider. She's coming up from Melbourne this year.'

'I'll call her,' said Sam. 'I don't think she'd mind where we have Christmas, as long as we're together. Isn't that the point?'

'I think she'd want things to be the same as they've always been. Why change now?'

'Why not?' said Max.

Bernice ignored her. 'And then there's Aunty Gwen. Usually you collect her from the nursing home, Samantha. How will we get her all the way to your house?'

'Mum, we used to almost pass the nursing home on our way here from Cherrybrook. Surely you're not expecting me to drive from Marrickville up to Turramurra to pick up Aunty Gwen and then back here to Dee Why before lunch on Christmas Day?'

'Well how else is Aunty Gwen supposed to get here?' asked Bernice, unblinking.

'I hadn't thought about that,' Sam muttered, annoyed that it had become her problem.

'It appears you haven't thought much at all,' Bernice went on. 'Like whether Aunty Gwen would even be comfortable in your house, Samantha.'

'Why shouldn't she be?'

'Well, Sam, I mean, please,' Bernice said as if she was stating the bleeding obvious. 'It's hardly palatial . . .'

'You think this house is a palace?' Max smirked, glancing around.

'It breaks my heart that you lost that house, Samantha,' Bernice continued. 'It was your children's inheritance. I'm surprised you let Jeff get away with it.'

Sam frowned. 'What do you mean, Mum?'

'In my day, your father could up and leave and there was no child support agency to chase any money out of him. By the same token, he couldn't take the house away from me either.'

'Jeff didn't take the house, Mum. I made the decision to sell on the advice of a solicitor. It was too great a debt to carry on my own and I could never have bought Jeff out.'

'Especially with that housekeeping job. If you'd stayed with the MRA –'

'Mother! It's not housekeeping,' Sam insisted. 'Not that there's anything wrong with housekeeping, but –'

'Look, I don't want to go into that right now,' said Bernice dismissively. 'We've always had Christmas here at home, there's no need to change things now. When I'm old and frail like Aunty Gwen, you'll get your chance. Oh, and Sam, while we're on the subject, I'd like those curtains finished for the front room before then.'

Sam sat back on the stool Jess had vacated. 'But you've had the same curtains for years. Why change them now?'

Bernice glanced at her, frowning. 'Why, dear, don't be silly.'

Sam felt anger welling inside her. 'Why is it silly, Mum? Why isn't my place good enough?'

'I didn't say it wasn't good enough –'

'Nothing is ever good enough for you, is it, Mum? I do whatever you ask of me, whenever you want it, no matter how busy I am. But it's never enough. And now I ask this one thing . . .' Sam's voice was breaking. She didn't want to lose it. She cleared her throat. 'Well, some of us don't have the luxury of doing things the way we've always done them. Some of us have had the rug pulled out from underneath us and we've landed on our arses. And we have to find another way of doing things.'

Jess and Ellie appeared in the doorway to the kitchen.

'So I'm going to start now,' said Sam, wiping her hands on her apron, before untying it and lifting it over her head.

'What are you doing, Samantha?' said Bernice, nonplussed.

'I don't want to spend the second weekend of November making Christmas pudding any more. Come on girls, we're going to McDonald's.'

Sam walked over to the doorway where Jess and Ellie were still standing, apparently in shock. She turned them around by the shoulders and marched them out of the house.

Max was draped across the sofa when Sam and the girls arrived home later that afternoon, laden with plastic shopping bags. There was a glass of wine and an opened packet of cheese crackers on the coffee table.

'Make yourself at home,' Sam remarked, dumping the bags.

'Thanks, but I did already.' Max swung her legs off the sofa and sat up. 'I figured you owed me for deserting the good ship Driscoll.'

Sam collapsed wearily into the closest armchair, and Ellie promptly climbed onto her lap. 'Oh, sweetheart, can Mummy just have the chair to herself for a while?' Ellie looked dejected. 'Why don't you go and see if Joshy's next door? Let him know we're home.'

Instantly her face lit up and she jumped off Sam's lap.

'I'll go!' Jessica blurted, dashing for the door.

'No, Mummy said for me to go,' Ellie protested loudly, chasing after her.

'You can both go!' Sam said firmly. 'Jessica, would you please slow down and not stampede into Maria's house like a baby elephant? And close the door behind you,' she added as they flew through the doorway. Jess appeared again, grabbed the door and slammed it shut. Max and Sam winced as it shuddered on its hinges.

'Kids, who'd have 'em?' Sam sighed, easing her head back and closing her eyes.

'So, how do you feel?'

'Buggered.'

'That was a big thing you did today, Sherl.'

Sam looked at her. 'How was Mum after I left?'

'Oh, what do you think? I had to listen to the "deserted wife" lecture all the way through. And back again, I'm pretty sure.' She frowned. 'I don't know, I stopped paying attention after a while.'

Sam smiled weakly. 'I'm sorry I left you there on your own.'

'Don't worry, I'm a big girl. I can choose to stay or leave, just like you did.'

'How did you get away in the end?'

'I told her I had a date tonight.'

'Do you?'

'Not really. I'm going to see a play with Dan.'

'Sounds like a date to me.'

'Sam, I said it's with *Dan*!'

'So? What's wrong with Dan? I like him.' Sam had been pleasantly surprised when Max dropped round one day with Dan. He was a maths teacher training to become a high school counsellor, which made him hands down the most normal guy Max had ever allowed herself to be seen with. He was also quite athletic, another aberration for Max, and he had smiling eyes and an expansive laugh. He came across as someone who was in love with life. And, Sam suspected, her sister as well. They had teased and cajoled each other the entire time and she could almost see the electricity flying between them. All of which Max vehemently denied when Sam put it to her later.

'Let me tell you about Dan, Sherl,' Max was saying. 'Do you know where he is right now?'

'No, where is he?'

'He's playing golf. I could never date a man who plays golf.'

Sam burst into laughter. 'So let me get this straight? You can go out with a man who takes photographs of the carcasses hanging in butcher's cool rooms and tries to pass them off as art, yet you can't date a man who plays golf?'

Max smiled wistfully. 'David Cornish. I haven't thought of him in a long time.'

'I think of him whenever I look at a piece of raw meat. Pass me your glass, I need a drink.'

'Get your own.'

'That would mean I have to move.'

'Okay, I'll get you a drink,' Max relented, walking out to the kitchen. 'Let me explain the whole golf thing to you,' she continued, coming back into the room with another glass and the bottle. 'It's men using long sticks to hit a ball into a hole. The aim is to get through as many holes in as few shots as possible,' she went on, pouring wine into Sam's glass.

'So?' said Sam blankly.

'Come on, Sam! They "play a round", they carry score cards with them! The game simply reeks of sexual conquest.'

Sam regarded her curiously. 'Are you going to donate your brain to medical research when you die? I think they'd be interested in some of your thought processes.'

Max ignored her, returning to her spot on the sofa. 'Anyway, I should never have mentioned anything about Dan to Mum, because when she heard he was a teacher she nearly had an aneurism. Nothing like the thought of a daughter snaring a public servant with superannuation to get the pulses racing!' she added wryly.

Sam chuckled, sipping on her wine.

'She thinks you're going to spoil Christmas now and not show up.'

'I don't know what I'm going to do,' Sam sighed. 'Last year was so hard. I thought everything would be much better by now, but I seem to go two steps forward and one step back all the time.'

'At least you're still going forward,' Max maintained. 'You've got a house, and a job you're good at, and the kids are doing fine.'

'No, according to Mum, I'm spoiling the kids, my job is a joke and my house is a dump.'

'You can't let her get to you, Sherl,' said Max. 'Mum's not going to change at this late stage.'

Sam groaned. 'What if I end up a bitter, twisted, deserted wife like she is? I don't want to live my life blaming an absent husband for all my woes, always thinking if only things had been different.'

'So don't.'

'What if I don't know how to do otherwise? I've only had Mum as a role model.'

'Well, that's determinism of the worst kind,' Max retorted.

'It's just that I can see so much of myself in her, it freaks me out,' said Sam. 'I think she survived by keeping her life so orderly, and I realise that's how I manage too.'

'Is that what you want?'

'I don't want to end up like Mum, but I don't know if I can function any other way.'

'Well, you have to give it a try.'

'How?'

'You made a start today by putting Mum in her place, where you should have put her a long time ago.'

Sam sighed heavily. 'So why do I feel like a naughty kid?'

'Because in the end she's still your mother, and that's a tough hierarchy to break.'

'You did it.'

'But you've always been different, Sherl,' Max said. 'Alex just rode right over her. I ignored her, but you, you always tried so hard to please her. And it's almost impossible to please Mum, unless you're Alex. You're a grown-up, Sam, you shouldn't need her approval any more. God knows she hardly gave it to you anyway.'

'Tell me about it.'

'So let go, break away and give yourself some space.' Max looked at the apprehension on Sam's face. 'What's the worse that can happen?' she persisted.

Sam shrugged. 'She won't speak to me.'

'And what will that mean?'

She was thoughtful. 'She won't call me and ask me to do things for her, she'll stop putting me down for my life choices, and I won't have to run around after her.'

'Sounds like a win/win situation to me.'

December

'Sam? It's Vanessa.'

'Hi, how are you?'

She didn't really have to ask that. Even over the phone Sam could hear the heaviness in her voice.

'I need to see you . . . um, please, if possible.'

Sam sighed. 'I'm run off my feet at the moment, Vanessa. I probably can't fit you in till next week.'

'I'm sorry, I shouldn't be bothering you, but Dominic told me to call.'

'Oh?'

Sam could hear Vanessa breathing heavily. 'He wants you to organise . . .' Her voice faltered. 'He wants you . . . to . . . find a good clinic, where I can get a termination.' She broke into loud sobs.

'Oh, Vanessa, I'm so sorry,' Sam said softly. Bloody pig-headed, goal-orientated, self-absorbed Dominic. 'What are you going to do?'

'I have to go through with it,' she cried. 'I don't have a choice.'

'Of course you have a choice, Vanessa!' Sam insisted. 'It's your baby.'

'What are you saying?'

'Well, you're carrying the baby, you have rights, too. It's not all Dominic's decision.'

'But he said he'll leave me if I keep it.'

Bastard. Sam wanted to tell her that was no great loss. She thought for a moment, listening to Vanessa's sobs. 'How will you live with yourself if you do this? They have counsellors at these clinics, Vanessa. They won't let you go through with it if you're hysterical.'

'Will you go with me?'

Shit. 'Vanessa,' Sam said gently, 'let's not talk about that just yet. You shouldn't do anything while you're so upset.'

'But he said he'll ring you if I don't.'

'Fine, I'll tell him I'm looking into it.' And a few more things besides. 'Give me a couple of days, I'll rejig my schedule and find some time to see you.'

'Oh, thank you, Sam.'

'It's alright. Just try to stay calm in the meantime.'

When Sam hung up she sat down on a kitchen stool, shaken. Dominic was unbelievable. Sam had to wonder if there was more to this, but she knew him well enough by now. He was a royal dickhead. She just hadn't realised the depth of his selfishness, how far he would go to get his own way.

The phone started to ring again. She looked at the clock. Damn, she was late for Patricia Bowen and this was probably her calling to complain now.

'Hello?'

'Could I speak to Samantha Holmes please?' asked an unfamiliar male voice.

'Speaking.'

'Oh, hello Ms Holmes. You don't know me, my name is Andrew Byron. I'm the managing director of Byron Promotional Services.'

Was he a new client? Usually Sheila passed details on for Sam to establish contact.

'How can I help you, Mr Byron?'

'I hope you don't mind me calling you at home. A friend told me all about you, he's been very impressed with some work you've been doing for him. He gave me your number . . .'

'You're really supposed to go through the agency.'

'Agency?'

'Yes, *Wife for Hire.*'

'I'm not sure,' Mr Byron sounded confused. 'You've done some work for Ted Dempsey?'

'That's correct. He gave you my number?'

'Yes, he did. My company organises conventions, conferences, product launches, anything. Ted said you're interested in getting into this kind of work, and he gave you a glowing recommendation.'

'Oh my God!'

'Are you alright, Ms Holmes?'

'Did I say that out loud? I beg your pardon.'

'Don't worry about it,' he said kindly. 'So you are interested?'

'Yes, absolutely. But I don't have any experience,' she blurted.

'Ted told me you're punctual, reliable, dedicated, highly organised, that you juggle a job and a home and three children on your own. He believes you could do anything you set your mind to. That's good enough for me.'

Sam had to say something. Something intelligent preferably. Something impressive would be even better.

'Thank you,' she said in a small voice. Wow. That ought to knock him dead.

'Anyway,' he went on, 'I thought the best way for us to meet you and for you to meet us was to invite you along to watch one of our teams at work. People coming into this industry don't always have a realistic idea of what's involved. They think it's a lot more glamour and a lot less hard work than it actually is.'

'I don't mind hard work,' said Sam breathlessly.

'I don't doubt that, Ms Holmes.'

'Please, call me Samantha. Sam, even.'

'Okay Sam, it's usually the kids straight out of school that have the wrong idea. But I still think it would be good for you to come and have a look at what we do. Are you free on the tenth?'

Sam wasn't going to even bother checking. Anything else could be changed for this. 'Absolutely.'

'Okay. Let me give you the details.'

Thursday

'Samantha, I don't know what to say.' Ted was clearly overwhelmed.

Sam had discovered that the attachment to Hugh's email was a photograph of Ted's grandson. She had decided that her printer wouldn't do it justice, so she'd taken the disc to have it printed digitally and had had it framed as well.

'I had to thank you somehow,' said Sam.

Ted looked confused.

'Andrew Byron contacted me the other day. I didn't expect you to do that for me.'

'But that was nothing, Samantha. A phone call.'

'And a huge recommendation.'

'I was only telling the truth.'

'Mm. Now I've just got to live up to it.'

'That won't be a problem,' Ted assured her. 'So, is this a goodbye gift?'

'You're not getting rid of me that easily,' Sam quipped.

Ted looked back at the photo. 'Well, thank you for this, Samantha,' he said. 'I can't tell you how much I appreciate it.'

Sam watched him, looking at his grandson. 'He's a handsome boy, Ted.'

'Do you think so?'

She nodded enthusiastically. 'I'll say. He's at that age where he's barely still a boy. But give him another year and he'll be almost a man, he'll have lost that boyishness. And he won't ever get it back, it'll be too late,' she added ominously.

Ted raised an eyebrow at her. 'I'd say that was a rather poorly disguised attempt to convince me to make the trip over to see him.'

'Are you thinking of visiting England, Ted?' Sam exclaimed, running with the ball. 'That's wonderful! I can organise all your travel arrangements, you know, I do it for clients all the time.'

Ted looked at her dubiously.

'Just so you know,' she shrugged.

Friday

Sam was trying to get through a few loads of washing before she went to meet Jeff. He'd called a few days ago saying there were some things they needed to talk about. It was true, the holidays were coming up, not to mention Christmas. Sam still didn't know what to do this year. Since the episode with her mother she was trying to push Christmas to the back of her mind. But it never worked for long, with decorations all over the place and every store playing sickly Christmas songs on a loop. Besides, her clients constantly reminded her. Everything had to be done by Christmas. Even if it was something they had left for years, it suddenly had an urgent deadline of December twenty-fifth.

Sam completed the ritual checking of Joshua's pockets before she added his clothes to the washing machine. No matter that she asked him ad nauseam, no matter that she threatened him with worse and worse punishments, he still couldn't get it through his apparently impervious skull that he needed to empty his pockets before discarding his clothes. And so notes from school were destroyed, coins got caught in the hose, and tissues disintegrated, spreading like confetti through the entire load. She reached into the pocket of his school trousers and felt something. As she withdrew it, Sam frowned at the small, sealed plastic packet for half a second before she got such a shock that she dropped it in the laundry tub.

She reached for it gingerly. What was Josh doing with a condom? In his *school shorts*? Maybe it was just one of those things boys did, a badge of honour to flash around. Sam flinched. He was the same age that Jeff had been . . . Oh, this was too hard. Jeff should be involved in this. She'd bring it with her today and discuss what they should do about it.

Sam closed the lid of the washing machine and walked out to the kitchen, tossing the condom in her handbag. She unplugged her mobile from its recharger and took her keys off the hook near the door. Jeff had suggested they meet at a local café, which didn't bother her but it did seem a bit unnecessary. He could have just come here.

Jeff was already seated at a table in the corner when Sam arrived. He looked nervous, she realised as she came closer.

He stood up. 'Hi, Sam. How are you?'

'Fine thanks, Jeff. And you?'

He nodded awkwardly, waiting for Sam to take her seat before he sat down again. A waitress came directly over and they both ordered coffee.

'So what did you want to talk about, Jeff?' Sam asked him, noting his reticence.

'Oh, well, a few things,' he said, avoiding eye contact.

She watched him. He really was nervous. She probably should throw him a line about Christmas. But she didn't know what to say. She would be happy to call it off altogether this year. That was the easiest solution as far as she was concerned.

The waitress reappeared with their coffee and Jeff took a long gulp from his cup. He pushed it to one side and leaned forward, his elbows on the table and his arms crossed in front of him. Defences up, thought Sam, reading the body language.

'I'm trying to do the right thing here, I really hope you'll keep that in mind. This isn't easy, but I thought I should tell you myself, before you heard it . . . some other way.'

Sam wondered if her face had gone white, because it felt as though all the blood had drained down to her ankles. She couldn't imagine what Jeff was going to say, but his demeanour was giving her the shivers.

'Sam,' he said carefully, pausing, watching her face closely.

Oh, for Chrissakes just spit it out!

'Jodi is pregnant.'

Everything went weird all of a sudden, distorted. She could see Jeff, but it was like he was at the end of a tunnel. Her husband was going to be the father of someone else's child. Someone she had never met. The café opened out to the street but Sam felt as though there was no air in here. The light around them had turned blue. Her eyes were stinging . . . Her throat was dry, but she couldn't reach for the glass of water on the table . . . Her hands were trembling too much, she slipped them under her knees. She sat there like a child . . . a tiny child with no voice . . . no power . . .

'Sam?'

She couldn't look at him. If she looked at him she might cry. She was even frightened to blink in case tears formed. He was speaking, but his voice felt like it was coming from far away down that tunnel.

Not planned . . . few months . . . quite ill . . . June next year . . .

Shut up. *SHUT UP!* she wanted to scream. But she couldn't do that here. Ha! Now Sam understood why he wanted to meet in public. Less chance of a scene. And what had happened that other time? They'd ended up in bed. No, he clearly didn't want to risk that again.

Sam felt her breathing steady. She swallowed and her throat was not quite so dry. She reached one hand out towards the water glass, and it obeyed her, not trembling but picking up the glass and bringing it to her lips smoothly and without incident. The ice cubes clinked as she sipped on the cool water. She could do this. She'd just been pushed off a cliff without any warning, but she had managed to hang on and pull herself back to solid ground.

She put the glass down on the table and looked up into Jeff's eyes. He had changed. He was not her husband any more. He didn't even look the same.

'Does . . .' Sam cleared her throat, 'Jodi, have any other children?'

He shook his head. 'No, of course not.'

She didn't know why it was *of course* not. 'Then she must be very happy.'

Jeff shrugged. 'Well, like I said, it wasn't planned. It's still a bit of a shock, to the both us.'

What, was he expecting sympathy now? Her condolences on the imminent demise of their cosy tête-à-tête? They had all the shit ahead of them, literally. Sleepless nights, colic, dirty nappies, and from what the kids had said, Jodi was not the type to handle it on her own as Sam had done. Jeff was in for a rude awakening.

She considered him coolly. 'I hope this isn't going to affect the children.'

'Of course it won't. You know how much I love them, Sam. Nothing's going to change.'

'Well, of course things will change,' she said calmly. 'So you're going to have to think about that and be prepared. You'll lose them if you make them play second fiddle to a screaming baby.'

Ooh, that was bitchy, but Sam couldn't help herself. It seemed to give her strength. She could see Jeff taking it in, feeling the weight of it all. She did almost feel sorry for him. Almost.

He sighed heavily. 'There's something else.'

Sam couldn't imagine that anything could be worse than what he had already told her. She took a sip of her coffee. 'Go on.'

He opened his mouth to speak, then he took another gulp from his cup. He wiped his mouth with the back of his hand and folded his arms in front of him, on the defensive again.

'I think it's time we got a divorce.'

She was falling this time. Off the edge of that cliff, while Jeff stood laughing at her from above.

No! don't lose it, Sam. Think about it. He's not your husband anyway. Not any more. Only on paper. It's time to tear up the paper.

She stared at her coffee cup. 'Does she want to get married?' It was too hard to say the woman's name twice in the same conversation.

Jeff shook his head. 'Not necessarily. She doesn't really believe in all that. But it doesn't seem right for me to be married to someone else when we're going to have a child together.'

It was alright to fuck *someone else* while they were still married and had *three* children together. Now he had a conscience and Sam was the 'someone else'. Fuck him. Fuck them both.

'Fine, we'll get started on it after Christmas, okay?' she said lightly. She wasn't going to show him it bothered her one bit.

'Sure,' he breathed out, visibly relieved. 'You're taking this all so much better than I thought.'

Smug bastard. Did he think she'd crack? Did he hope she would?

'And seeing as you've mentioned Christmas,' Jeff continued carefully, 'I was hoping we might be able to sort that out as well.'

Sam sat back in her chair. She folded her arms and crossed her legs, staring directly at him. 'What do you mean, "sort it out"?'

'Well,' he shrugged. 'You know, I never made any demands last year. I thought that was only fair. So I figure, maybe it's my turn to have the kids this year.'

Sam's mobile phone started to ring. Good. She needed a moment.

'I have to get this, sorry.'

Jeff nodded as she retrieved the phone from her bag and answered it.

'Sam, it's me, Vanessa.'

Damn, she hadn't had a chance to get back to her yet. 'Hi Vanessa, what's up?'

'Something's wrong. I, I think I'm bleeding.'

'Well, are you?'

'Yes,' she sighed.

'Is it heavy?'

'Mm, it's like the start of a period, I've got cramps too.'

Sam sighed inwardly. 'You should call Dominic –'

'I can't,' she blurted. 'He's still angry.'

'Well, is there someone else I can call for you?'

'No one else knows I'm pregnant,' Vanessa explained tearfully. 'Dominic forbade me to tell anyone. There's no one I can call . . .' Her voice broke. 'I'm sorry for bothering you with this –'

'It's alright, Vanessa. Are you at home?'

'Yes.'

'Okay, I'll be there as soon as I can.'

'Thank you,' she breathed.

Sam hung up the phone and got to her feet, picking up her bag. Jeff was looking expectantly at her.

'I have to go, it's a bit of an emergency.'

'Do you want to pick this up again later?' he asked.

'No need,' said Sam briskly. 'You say it's your turn to have the kids for Christmas this year? Well, for all their lives there *was* no Christmas for those kids but for me. I did the planning, the shopping, the wrapping, the decorating, the cooking . . . every-thing. And you did . . . let's see,' she put her finger to her chin, feigning contemplation. '*Nothing*, I believe, would be a *fair* way to describe it. So, on my calculations, that makes it "your turn" in about another fifteen years. Let's pick it up again then.'

Sam turned on her heel and left Jeff sitting there, stunned. She was sick to death of being so reasonable and fair about everything. What was fair about being dumped after sixteen years and three children, replaced with a new partner, a new baby, a new life? Jeff was getting it all. Well, he wasn't going to get Christmas as well.

Vanessa was still in her robe when she opened the door, and it was nearly midday. She had been crying and there were dark circles under her eyes.

'Thanks for coming, Sam. I'm so sorry to do this to you.'

'Don't worry about it, Vanessa,' she dismissed, walking into the apartment. 'You look tired.'

'I haven't been getting much sleep lately.'

Sam looked at her. 'What's happening? Are you still bleeding?'

Vanessa nodded wearily.

'It's more than spotting?'

She nodded again, her head downcast.

Sam sighed, touching her arm. 'You know we're going to have to get you to the hospital?'

Vanessa looked up at her then, there were tears streaming down her cheeks. She sniffed. 'I'd better get dressed.'

'Don't you want to call Dominic? He could meet us there.'

Vanessa's face crumpled and she started to sob. Sam put her arm around her.

'He won't care. He'll be happy it's all over,' she whimpered.

'Oh, Vanessa, of course he'll care. He wouldn't want you to go through this.'

Vanessa wiped her cheeks with the palms of her hands. 'I'll call him later. Once we know for sure.'

At the hospital, the triage nurse was brusque and matter-of-fact. Suspected miscarriage. A doctor would see her soon. They were directed to wait in the meantime. Sam thought about the list of things she had planned for today, but none of that mattered any more. She would have to make some calls but they could wait until the doctor was with Vanessa. She was suddenly tired of being all things to all people, all at the same time. Just being here for Vanessa was enough. It was the best she could do.

After an hour a doctor was available to see Vanessa, and Sam went to make her calls. Patricia Bowen was annoyed but Sam remained firm.

'I was expecting you to talk to the tilers today. I don't like the finish in the powder room. It's going to have to be redone.'

'I'll speak to them before the day is out, Mrs Bowen. I told you, I'm at the hospital and this is an emergency.'

'But it's not as if it's one of your children.'

'No, she is a friend, and she has no one else.'

'Well, you wouldn't be able to just walk out if you were in a regular office job. I don't see why this should be any different.'

'I think in these circumstances I probably would have walked out of a regular office job, Patricia.' She had never used her first name before. 'And I'm asking you to show a little compassion. Your tiles will be fixed. You have my word.'

'I'm having guests at Christmas, this job has to be finished.'

Sam wanted to say, 'Well, if you'd stop changing every little frigging thing, it would have been finished months ago.'

But instead she just said, 'Leave it to me.'

Sam hung up the phone and wandered back to where they had been sitting. A nurse came towards her.

'Mrs Holmes?'

'Yes. How's Vanessa?'

'She's going to need a D and C.'

'So she lost the baby?'

'In a manner of speaking. Vanessa had a blighted ovum. There was never any baby.'

Sam's heart sank. She'd heard of that before. It was a miscarriage by any other name.

'She'll have to go to theatre. They're prepping her now.'

'Can I see her?'

'Of course, I'll take you through.'

Sam followed the nurse through a set of double doors and along a corridor, past a row of small rooms. She stopped outside one.

'She's already had her pre-op meds, so she might be a little groggy. You'll be able to stay just until they come to take her to theatre.'

Sam nodded, stepping into the room. Vanessa looked pale, almost transparent against the white hospital bedding. There was no life in her usually bright eyes, no smile. She was clearly devastated.

'Sam,' she said in a small voice, reaching her hand out.

Sam came closer to the bed and took Vanessa's hand. 'I'm here.'

'They're saying there was never a baby.'

'That's true, but your body was doing everything as though there was one, Vanessa. You don't have to feel embarrassed.'

'But there was a baby.' Her voice was so faint. 'I felt it. I know it was there.'

Sam looked into her sad blue eyes. 'Of course you felt something. Your body was behaving exactly as though you were pregnant.'

'But I felt the baby,' she insisted. 'If it was a girl, I was going to call her Emily, and if it was a boy, Connor.'

Sam felt a pang in her chest. Connor was the name they had picked out for Ellie if she was a boy. She wondered if Jeff would recycle it.

'Do you want me to call Dominic?' Sam said, changing the subject for both their sakes.

She shook her head tearfully. 'He didn't care about the baby, I don't want him here.'

'Listen to me, Vanessa,' Sam said gently but firmly. 'You're going under anaesthetic. He's your husband, he should know.'

'Do they have to get his permission?'

'No, not any more.' At least in this country a wife was no longer the possession of her husband.

'Then I don't care, Sam. Do whatever you think. But I don't want to talk to him.'

Sam stayed with her for a few more minutes until they were ready to send her to theatre. She walked out of the ward, out of the waiting room and out through the exit until she could breathe some fresh air. She slumped against a brick wall. She felt so sad her stomach ached. Surely Dominic would want to be here? He was not so inhuman that he would be impervious to his wife's pain. Vanessa said she could do whatever she wanted. Sam took out her mobile and the small address book she carried with her everywhere. She found his office number and dialled it. She didn't realise it was a direct number so she wasn't prepared when he picked up the phone and announced, 'Dominic Blair'.

'Oh, I didn't expect you to answer the phone.'

'Who is this?' he demanded curtly.

'Sorry Dominic. It's Samantha Holmes.'

'Hello Samantha,' he said expansively, dropping the impatient tone. 'I was going to call you.'

She had to head him off, she knew what he was probably intending to call her about and she wouldn't be able to bear the slightest mention.

'Dominic, I'm with Vanessa. Something's happened, we're at the hospital.'

'My God, what is it, not an accident?'

He sounded distressed. Of course he did. He wasn't totally without feeling.

'No, Vanessa's going to be alright. But she lost the baby.' It was the simplest way to explain it for now.

There was the slightest of pauses. 'Oh, is that all?' She could hear the relief in his voice. 'Well, it's for the best, really, isn't it?'

'I don't think that's how Vanessa sees it at the moment.'

'She'll get over it.'

Sam couldn't speak. She couldn't believe what she was hearing.

'Will I have to come and pick her up? Because,' he paused, checking something, 'I don't think I'll be able to get there till at least five. I have a meeting at three-thirty . . .'

Sam tuned out. He was prattling on about his busy schedule, he didn't ask one question about what Vanessa was going through.

'Dominic,' she interrupted, 'Vanessa's in theatre. She's under general anaesthetic.'

'Really?' His tone was not one of shock or concern, but more of registering an interesting fact. 'Well, she won't be ready to leave for hours yet then.'

'Dominic!' Sam cried, exasperated.

'What? What is it, Samantha?'

'Well, don't you want to be here?'

'What good would I do, she'll be out to it for quite some time.'

'But . . . don't you want to be with her, don't you even care?'

'Of course I care. What are you trying to say?'

'My God, I knew you were selfish, but this is unbelievable.'

'Samantha, I don't think you're being entirely appropriate.'

'Oh, look who's talking! Do you think it's appropriate to leave your wife in hospital while you go to a meeting? Do you think it's appropriate to say that losing a baby is "for the best"? What the fuck is wrong with you?' Sam was almost yelling now.

'Tell me, Samantha, do you reserve the same hostility for someone who deceives her husband and falls pregnant without his knowledge or consent?'

'It wasn't like that.'

'Oh, so you obviously know more about this than I do. Did you advise her, Samantha? Did you tell her how to scheme against her husband?'

'Get stuffed, Dominic.'

'I don't have to listen to this. And I think you can take this officially as the end of our relationship.'

'Nothing would please me more,' Sam declared, hanging up. She stood there, trembling. She felt sick in the stomach. God, she shouldn't have spoken to him like that. She had no right, it was none of her business.

But Vanessa had made it her business. She had asked for her help. If Dominic wasn't such a prick, none of this would have happened and Sam would never have been involved. But Sheila would be hearing about this now and Sam had definitely lost a client, not that she wanted him any more.

She took some deep breaths to calm herself. She didn't have to take that crap from Dominic, she wasn't his wife.

Poor Vanessa was, though. Sam would have to stay around now to explain what had happened, and besides, it was unlikely that Dominic would be here for her. She couldn't leave her all alone.

She wandered back into Casualty and inquired at the desk as to where she should wait for Vanessa. They directed her to the maternity ward.

'Oh, they're not taking her there, surely?' Sam winced. 'She's just lost a baby.'

'She won't be placed in a room with new mothers, but she'll have to go to the ward. There's nowhere else.'

Sam walked despondently to the lifts and made her way to maternity. She knew she was in the right place as soon as she stepped out of the elevator. It was filled with the sound of babies, the smell of babies. It was so evocative. Sam was catapulted back to when her own children were born. The fear, the wonderment, the joy like she had never known before. She walked slowly up the corridor, glancing into the rooms where mothers held their babies at the breast or over their shoulders, patting them gently to soothe them. There were flowers and balloons everywhere, drifts of pink and blue. Sam arrived at the nursery. There were barely any babies kept here any more, they all stayed with their mothers. This was more of a time-out room now. There were just two clear plastic cribs on stands pushed to one side. And inside them, two tiny bundles, wrapped like packets of fish and chips, their dear little heads emerging from the blankets. Sam watched them intently. One was sucking on a huge pink dummy as though her life depended on it, which was fair enough, she supposed. The other, a little boy in a blue beanie, was intermittently smiling, then wincing, then smiling again. Wind. Sam smiled too, faintly. What were they thinking? Was it really just wind, or were they dreaming of things no grown person could ever imagine?

Sam leaned her head against the glass. Jeff was going to have another baby. It would be his, but not hers. It would be a sister or a brother for her own children, but it would have no relationship to her at all. She felt tears creep into her eyes and she sniffed them back.

She walked up the corridor to the nurses' station and asked when Mrs Blair was due back from theatre. After some checking and a phone call, they showed Sam into a private room where she could wait till Vanessa was brought up. She settled herself into an armchair and stared out the window at the other hospital buildings.

She felt so lonely. She didn't want to go home to the empty house tonight. The kids were going to Jeff's. He and Jodi were probably planning to announce the news to them, now that he had 'done the right thing' and told her first. She wondered how they would take it. She really had no idea. The girls would probably be thrilled, it would be like having a doll to play with. She didn't know about Joshua. She remembered when he was born, and now look at the size of him. A newborn baby could probably fit inside one of his shoes. He was almost a man himself.

Sam had a sudden thought. God, she'd forgotten about the condom. Not that she would have brought it up today anyway. She didn't know that she wanted to discuss her son's safe sex habits with his prodigious father. Her head was swimming. She wanted to stop thinking. She leaned her head against the back of the chair and closed her eyes.

Sam blinked, squinting at the lights overhead. Her back was sore and her legs were stiff. She stretched out in the chair.

'Hello,' said Vanessa quietly.

Sam looked across the room. Vanessa was lying on her side on the hospital bed. She looked small, like a child.

'Sorry. I must have nodded off.'

'You've been asleep for quite a while.'

Sam stretched again, arching her neck each way. 'I'm sorry, Vanessa.'

'Don't say that. I should be apologising to you.'

'Nonsense.' Sam stood up and took a step towards the bed. She leaned on the edge. 'How are you feeling?'

Vanessa took a deep breath and turned over onto her back.

'I think I know what people mean when they say they feel like they've been hit by a bus.'

Sam frowned down at her.

'I'll be okay,' Vanessa assured her.

Sam breathed out heavily. 'Vanessa, I have to tell you something.'

'You spoke to Dominic.'

'How did you know?'

'He called the hospital. They put him through.' Vanessa smiled faintly. 'He was very cross with you. He wants to fire you.'

'Don't worry. I quit.'

'Sam, you've been so good to me.'

'But I can't work for you two any more.'

Vanessa looked away. 'There may not be an "us two" any more.'

Sam sighed. She didn't know what to say. They sat quietly. Sam could hear the faint cries of a baby somewhere in the ward.

'You asked me one day how we fell in love,' Vanessa said after a while. 'And I told you I couldn't remember.'

Sam nodded.

'The thing is, I really don't remember. I don't remember falling in love with Dominic. He just walked into my life. We were at uni, and suddenly he had taken over. He's like that, he needs to be in charge. It's not his fault. I just went along. It's what I do.'

'You deserve better, Vanessa.'

'Maybe I don't. Maybe I deserve exactly what I got.'

Vanessa asked to spend the night in the hospital. She was a paying customer, it was okay with them. She would call Dominic in the morning. They had a lot to talk about.

Sam walked out through the corridors, past the rooms of sleeping mothers and their sleeping babies, out into the world again. She had to think for a moment about where she had parked the car. In the dim light of dusk everything looked different. And she was not familiar with this hospital, it was not where her babies had been born. The thought of her children sent a sob surging up through her ribcage and she leaned against a garden wall, catching her breath. Her babies were with their father, their father who was going to be a father again.

Sam wanted to scream. She didn't want to keep having these thoughts. It was like some interminable loop. Like sentimental Christmas songs playing over and over. Enough! Enough already. Give it a rest, she told herself. There had to be other thoughts to have tonight. Other ways to spend her evening. She would go mad if she didn't break this miserable cycle.

It started to rain, just lightly. That fine rain that you can hardly feel as it soaks your clothes, wetting you through to the skin.

Sam saw her car ahead and breathed a sigh of relief. She ran for it, climbing in and locking the doors. She turned on the radio. Some upbeat dance music was playing, the kind Jessica liked. Well, that was fine. It was crap, but it was just what she needed to distract her thoughts.

She started up the engine and drove off but she didn't have a clue where she was going. It started to rain more heavily. Sam drove around slowly, following street signs, stopping at lights, turning corners, but she was aimless. She didn't want to go home by herself. This was not a night to be alone.

Finally she pulled over and cut the engine, but not the radio. She didn't think she could stand the silence. She tried Max's number but the message bank came on. Sam didn't know what to say, so after the beep, she just said, 'It's only me. It's nothing. I'll call you later.'

She sat there for a while longer, watching the windscreen wipers thwack back and forward. The noise started to annoy her so she switched them off. The rain dotted, and then slid down the windscreen. She thought about her options. She could phone Liz, but she didn't want to be with a couple, that would only remind her of how alone she was. She scrolled through the numbers stored in her phone until Rosemary's came up. She pressed *Call* and waited for it to connect.

When Rose picked up, Sam could hear a lot of background noise, music, people laughing.

'Hi Sam! How are you?' Rosemary was shouting.

'Fine, um, okay.'

'What's up?'

'Oh, nothing. I was just seeing what you were doing. Thought I might catch up with you.'

'Sorry? I can't hear you, Sam. It's pretty noisy here. I'm at a club, you'll have to speak up.'

The last place Sam wanted to be tonight was at a noisy club. 'Don't worry,' Sam said loudly, 'I'll call you tomorrow.'

'I can't hear you, Sam! I'll call you tomorrow, okay?'

'Bye.'

Sam breathed out heavily. She started the engine and pulled out from the kerb. After a while she realised she had followed the stream of traffic right into the city. Well that was stupid. She'd have to make her way across town now to get home.

She stopped at lights and looked up. She was at the end of the street where Hal lived. How had she ended up here? She wondered if he was home. Well, she could get that thought out of her head. She wasn't about to go and see him. He'd think she was crazy. She couldn't just show up out of the blue, pouring all her woes onto him. It wasn't appropriate. Although it wouldn't be the first time. And he had said, if she was ever passing . . .

The lights went green, Sam flicked on her blinker and turned into the street.

Twenty minutes later she found a parking spot, which was at least another ten minutes walk back to Hal's building. This was ridiculous, she'd been telling herself repeatedly, and still she had driven around and around looking for a spot. She got out of the car. The rain had eased slightly, but she'd only walked a block when it began bucketing down again. She ducked and weaved between buildings and under awnings, but after a few minutes she was drenched through. Okay. Give it up, Sam. This is now bordering on insanity. Go back to your car, go back to your house, get dry, go to bed. But no matter what she told herself in her head, her legs would not obey. They just kept carrying her onwards to Hal's place. It seemed quite beyond her control.

When she arrived at his building, she stood for a while looking up, wondering if she could count the floors to his apartment and see if there were lights on. But she didn't even know what side of the building he was on. And besides, she could only see raindrops falling. It was funny that, the way you could distinguish the individual raindrops falling out of the sky when light was cast across them.

She was going crazy. She was quite definitely going crazy.

She walked out of the rain to the intercom panel and pressed the button for Hal's apartment. It buzzed then stopped. Sam heard his voice. 'Hello?'

She froze.

'Hello? Is anyone there?'

'Hal? It's Samantha Ho –'

'Sam? Are you okay?'

She felt choked. 'Um, I was just passing. You know . . .'

The door released instantly. Sam pushed it open and walked dripping into the foyer. She tiptoed across to the bank of elevators as one opened. He must have sent it down for her. She hurried over and stepped inside. The doors closed behind her. No going back now.

The lift ascended in the time it took Sam to take one deep breath, trying to collect herself. The doors opened and Hal stood waiting on the other side. Her barely gained composure evaporated. His hair was a little ruffled and there was light stubble on his chin. He was wearing loose trousers and a crumpled T-shirt, obviously not expecting company. But he was still drop-dead gorgeous. She had lied through her teeth pretending to Max all this time that she hadn't noticed how handsome he was. How could she fail to notice those eyes, that jaw.

'Sam, look at you, you're soaked. What happened?'

'I . . .' she swallowed.

He reached for her arm and drew her out of the elevator. 'Are you okay? You're not hurt?'

She thought she was going to cry when she saw the concern in his eyes. She shook her head. 'No, it's nothing like that.'

'What about the kids, are they alright?'

A lump rose in Sam's throat. 'The kids are fine,' she managed to say. 'I'm sorry, I shouldn't have come . . . I'm probably interrupting –'

'The only thing you're interrupting is a bad movie,' he said gently, smiling down at her. 'I'm glad you're here. Come on inside.'

He led her across the hall into an open door, closing it behind them. Sam stood dripping on the carpet.

'I'm sorry,' she said again in a weak voice.

'I'll get you a towel, come on through.'

She followed him down a short hall into what must have been his bedroom. He walked ahead of her into the bathroom and reappeared with a towel, handing it to her. She started to mop her face as he slid the door of the wardrobe open and pulled a shirt off a hanger.

'Here you are. Get dry, you can change into this, or take anything you want.'

Sam nodded, unable to say anything.

'Take your time.' Hal walked back out to the main room, closing the door quietly behind him. Sam let out a sob, burying her face into the towel. What was she doing here? She shouldn't have shown up like this, not after the way she'd treated him.

But he was the only person she could imagine who's company she wanted to share tonight. Sam didn't want to dwell on why that was. She had to pull herself together. She went into the bathroom and peeled off her soaking jeans and her blouse, hanging them carefully over the rail. After towelling herself off, she examined her reflection in the mirror. Damn. Her mascara was smudged and the rain had flattened her hair to her head. She rubbed it dry, but it only looked worse. She crept back into the bedroom and found her hairbrush in her handbag. She picked up Hal's shirt and pulled it on as she walked back into the bathroom.

Sam buttoned up the shirt. It was pale blue, made of soft, well-worn fabric. It almost went to her knees and she had to roll back the sleeves about four times. She brushed her hair smooth, but it didn't really look much better. She frowned at herself in the mirror. She was having one of those moments, imagining what it would have been like if she'd had a glimpse of the future a few years ago, when she was still with Jeff, living in Cherrybrook, still believing they were going to grow old together. She would have been mystified as to what she was doing, dressed in another man's shirt, standing in his bathroom, wondering how she had got here.

Well, she had run ten minutes in the rain and shown up on his doorstep, unannounced and uninvited, that's how she had got here. What was she doing? The last time she had seen Hal he had told her he liked her, a lot, but he'd left it to her to make the next move.

And here she was. Sam bit nervously on the edge of her thumb. What kind of message was she sending him? She considered her reflection sceptically. She decided she was pretty safe. Hal was hardly going to make a pass at her tonight – she looked like a drowned rat.

Whatever, she couldn't stay hiding in his bathroom forever. She walked back out through the bedroom, grasped the handle of the door and opened it determinedly. Hal looked up from where he was sitting at the end of a long sofa, one leg hooked up underneath the other. He stood up. They looked at each other for a moment, not saying anything.

'Hey,' he was the first to speak. 'How're you doing, Sam?'

She thought she was going to melt all over the carpet, but instead she cleared her throat. 'Nice place,' she said, looking around.

It was a simple, open-plan apartment. The kitchen was separated from the rest of the living room by a dark timber bench and large picture windows ran along the length of the outer wall, looking out to the city.

'It all belongs to IGB. I just moved in with my suitcase.'

It was pretty minimalist. There was a distinct absence of

personal effects. It gave the place a sort of temporary look, like a hotel room. Sam wished she hadn't noticed that.

'I suppose you're wondering what I'm doing here?' she said eventually.

'It doesn't matter. I'm just glad you are.'

Sam breathed out. She didn't have a witty reply. Hal picked up a glass of wine from the coffee table. 'I thought you could do with a drink.'

She walked towards him. 'Thanks.' She took the glass out of his hand and he picked up his beer.

'To old friends,' he nodded, clinking her glass with his bottle. 'Take a seat.'

Sam sat down on the sofa, but he hesitated. 'Are you hungry? Can I get you anything?'

She smiled. 'Do you have any chocolate?'

'Fraid not.'

'Never mind then.'

He sat, curling his leg up like before, turning side on to face her. 'This is a surprise, Sam, a good one.'

'I'm sorry for showing up like this.' She took a deep breath. 'After the way I treated you last time —'

'Don't worry about it.'

She shifted to face him. 'No, let me say it. I want to apologise for the way I behaved.'

'Sam, I said don't worry about it.'

'But I do worry about it. You were only trying to help, and . . .' She hesitated. 'I said things I had no right to say.'

She looked at him, he was gazing intently at her. 'You were having a bad day.'

'That's no excuse.'

'Well,' he said softly, 'I forgive you.'

Sam couldn't hold his gaze any longer. She glanced around and noticed a video case on the coffee table. She leaned forward to pick it up.

'This is what you were watching?'

He shrugged. 'Just filling in time.'

She looked at him sideways and read off the back of the

case, affecting a dramatic voiceover. 'This is the story of a crack squad of elite commandoes who were destined to become America's only hope in a power-packed struggle for freedom, set against the backdrop of a world gone mad . . .'

Hal looked at her blankly. 'Were you trying to sound like an American then?'

'Maybe,' she said cagily.

'Ah, you see, where you guys go wrong is that we don't actually *have* an accent.'

'Ha!' Sam scoffed. 'Neither do we.'

'No, Crocodile Dundee, I'm afraid you do. If you want to sound American, you just have to drop your accent. Then you'll sound normal.'

Sam laughed, shaking her head. She looked back at the case. 'What is a "crack" squad, anyway? They're always "crack" squads. What does that mean?'

'I don't know.'

They fell silent. She put the video back on the coffee table. Eventually Hal cleared his throat.

'Do you want to talk about it, Sam?'

She looked at him sideways. 'Well, the more important question is probably, do you want to hear about it?'

'Of course I do.' He looked at her intently. Sam believed him.

She sighed. 'I found out today that not only does my husband want to divorce me, but he's having a baby with his new partner.' Her voice broke a little as she said the words. She took a large gulp of her wine. 'And after that, I had to take a friend who was having a miscarriage to the hospital because her bastard of a husband had a meeting.'

Hal sighed loudly. 'You did have a bad day.' He stood up. 'I'll get you another drink.'

He walked into the kitchen and returned with a bottle of wine, topping up Sam's glass for her. He left the bottle on the coffee table.

'So,' he said, sitting down again, 'you don't want a divorce?'

'Oh, it's not that. I know it's inevitable. It's just such an awful feeling. Like, that's it. All those years, for nothing. A magistrate somewhere can just stamp the papers and it's like it never happened.'

'I don't think it means that,' he said gently.

She shrugged. 'I suppose.'

He was watching her closely. 'And the baby? That bothers you?'

Sam took a tremulous breath. 'I don't know why, but it does. I mean, we weren't going to have any more children, even if we'd stayed together. But he's going to have a whole other family now. Where are my kids going to fit into that? I don't want them to be hurt any more.' Sam blinked back tears, swallowing down some more wine. 'I shouldn't be telling you this –'

'If you say "it's not appropriate", you know I may have to kill you.'

Sam smiled sheepishly. 'I wasn't going to say that. I was going to say that I feel bad always dumping stuff on you. Why do you let me do that?'

He shrugged. 'I'm a good listener. Despite the fact that I'm a man.'

'And you're a good man,' Sam said quietly.

He gazed at her, reaching his arm across the back of the sofa to touch her cheek gently. 'You're not so bad yourself.'

Sam held her breath. This was getting way too intimate.

'Are you sure you don't have any chocolate?' she chirped, jumping to her feet. She threw back the rest of the wine in her glass and felt it go straight to her head. She remembered she'd had hardly eaten a thing all day. She walked around the bench into the kitchen and opened the fridge, peering in. 'Not even for emergencies?'

'Exactly what kind of emergency calls for chocolate?' Hal had followed her and was leaning against the bench, watching her.

'Well, d'oh! Any emergency of course,' Sam exclaimed. 'What's with all the fruit and yoghurt? Are you some kind of a health nut?' She opened the freezer. 'Not even any ice cream?'

'Sorry.'

She turned around to look at him. 'I thought you Americans only ate junk food?'

'Yeah, and what was that about Australians wrestling crocodiles while they're still in diapers?' he returned.

'They're called nappies,' Sam corrected him, closing the fridge and leaning back against the door.

'No, they're called crocodiles,' said Hal guilelessly. 'I'm quite certain about that. And you don't have alligators in this country.'

Sam pulled a face. 'I was referring to your use of the word "diaper". The correct term is nappy.'

'You know, the population of the US is about ten times the size of this country's, and you're telling me which is the correct term?'

'Yeah, well, you know what they say. Size isn't everything,' she retorted.

'But no one really believes that.'

Sam glanced at him. He was waving the red flag of sexual innuendo right in her face. She turned to the pantry cupboard and opened the doors. 'Do you have any cooking chocolate? Chocolate chips?'

Hal shook his head. 'Do you think I bake on the weekends?'

'Don't be sexist, Hal. Most of the world's best chefs are men,' she said tartly. She surveyed the scant contents of the pantry. 'You are a health nut, there's only cereal in here.' She stepped onto one of the lower shelves and tested her weight on it.

'What are you doing, Sam?' Hal asked, watching her climb up the shelves of the pantry.

'Surely you must have *something* with chocolate in it.'

'You're going to fall,' he warned. She felt his hands on her waist, steadying her. 'Come on down from there.'

Sam stepped down carefully, his hands still supporting her. She turned around to face him but he didn't release her, so her arms had nowhere to rest but along his. They were standing close, breathing hard, staring intently at each other. Sam felt light-headed.

'Why are you here?' Hal said in a low voice.

Sam swallowed. 'I can't tell you unless you have CIA clearance.'

She saw the glint in his eye. 'I think it's because you decided you like me a little, after all.'

'You've always had tickets on yourself . . .' She stared at his lips as they drew nearer. 'Don't kiss me,' she breathed.

'What made you think,' he murmured, their faces close, 'that I was going to kiss you . . .' he finished as his lips came down onto hers. Hal was kissing her. She was kissing him back. It was really happening. He gathered her close to him as she brought her arms up around his neck. Her mind started to race. What now? Where would this lead? Did she want it to go there? Was she ready for that? But her thoughts were overcome by sensations, the way his lips felt, softly caressing hers, the way his mouth tasted. Sam wanted to savour this, not analyse it. Hal brought one hand up to cup her face, his thumb stroking her cheek, as she felt him retreating, slowly, drawing back from her mouth while still holding her body close to his, their lips gradually parting, hesitantly, reluctantly. She opened her eyes and he was staring down at her tenderly. He smoothed his thumb across her bottom lip.

'I've wanted to do that for such a long time,' he said softly.

Sam's heart jumped into her throat. 'Well,' she swallowed. 'You'd better not do it again.'

She saw the glimmer in his eyes as he covered her mouth with his own again, their lips moving against each other, their tongues slow dancing to some innate rhythm. Sam felt intoxicated. She couldn't remember kissing ever feeling like this. She didn't know how long they stayed there, crushed up against the pantry cupboard, but the sensations pervaded her entire body until she felt almost delirious. She heard herself moan as she pressed herself hard against his torso, lifting one leg to slide the inside of her thigh against him.

'Oh Sam,' he groaned. They were both breathing heavily as he cradled her head with both hands, covering her face with soft, lingering kisses. Sam had not expected this. She didn't realise how much she wanted him, how much she must have been suppressing it. But she couldn't any more. She started to tremble, imagining him pulsing inside her, their bodies meshed together. She thought her knees were going to give way.

'Hal,' she breathed.

'Mm,' he murmured, his mouth moving to her ear.

'Don't . . . take me . . . to bed.'

He stopped suddenly, drawing back to look at her. 'Sam,' he said gently. 'Are you sure?'

She nodded. 'Yes, um, I mean no. What's the right answer?'

He was searching her eyes. 'Whatever you say it is.'

Sam smiled shyly, taking his hand and leading him out of the kitchen and across the living room. But she hesitated at the door to his bedroom. He brought her hand to his lips and kissed it, then he pushed the door open, taking the lead now, walking her inside. Sam stared at the vast bed. It must have been king size, she hadn't really noticed when she was in here before. Now she was taking in every detail. The bedside lamps were both turned on. She wished they weren't. The light was only dim, but she was going to have to get naked. It couldn't get dim enough. She didn't know if she was going to be able to go through with this. What had happened since they left the kitchen? She would have let him jump her there on the floor if he had tried.

Hal turned her around and tilted her face towards him, bringing his lips down onto hers, melting away her trepidation. Then she felt his hands move down to the first button on the shirt. She automatically reached to stop him.

'What's the matter?' he said gently.

'Oh nothing, sorry.' She took a deep breath. 'I'm just nervous, you know?'

He held both her hands and kissed them one at a time. 'Sam, we don't have to do anything if you don't want to.'

She looked up at him.

'We could just get into bed and hold each other and go to sleep.'

Sam frowned. 'You'd actually be able to do that?'

He smiled at her. 'Probably not, but it sounded noble, don't you think?'

She smiled back. She took a deep breath and started to undo the buttons herself, one at a time, five altogether. Hal bent to kiss her, sliding his hands under the shirt across her shoulders, letting it fall to the floor.

'Um, sorry about the sensible underwear,' she stammered. 'I didn't expect . . . anyone . . . would be seeing it.'

'Well, okay, I'll overlook it just this once.' He smiled indulgently. 'Sam, you're beautiful, whatever you're wearing, or not wearing,' he said, pulling her close against him as he nuzzled into her neck, sending little shots of electricity right through her body. Let go, just let go, she told herself. Then she felt him tugging gently at the clasp of her bra and she froze again, pulling away.

'What is it?'

'Oh, Hal, it's just . . .' She clasped her arms awkwardly in front of herself. 'Well, let's just say I've got to that age where I look better with clothes on.'

'I'm afraid I'd have to argue with you there.' He considered her for a moment. 'Would it help if I took my shirt off?'

She smiled shyly. 'It wouldn't hurt.'

He lifted his T-shirt over his head and tossed it aside. He looked just like she'd imagined. Broad-shouldered, nicely muscled but lean, with a fine spray of hair covering his chest. Sam moved closer to him and laid her cheek against his skin, listening to his heartbeat. He smelled so good. He folded his arms around her, stroking her hair.

'I'm sorry,' she murmured. 'This must be getting annoying.'

'It's okay, sweetheart. There's no hurry.'

He called her sweetheart. She looked up at him. 'You know I've only ever been with Jeff. Except for this one other time with this really horrible man from work, I can barely remember it. It was just after Jeff and I split up, and I was completely drunk.' She took a breath. 'Oh God, you must think I'm terrible.'

'I don't think you're terrible.'

'The thing is, I'm probably not very good at it. I have barely any experience. I was only a schoolgirl . . .'

'Relax,' said Hal. 'I'm an expert. I have sex with lots of women, all the time.'

Sam's eyes widened.

'I'm joking,' he smiled, smoothing her hair back from her face. He took a breath. 'Okay, true confessions. There was an old girlfriend I hooked up with in New York after I left Lisa. I thought it'd help. It didn't. There hasn't been anyone else since.'

Sam stared at him. She hoped she wasn't being naïve, but he was looking down at her with so much tenderness, she found herself believing him. She took a step back and reached behind with both hands, deftly unlatching her bra and letting it drop to the floor. Hal breathed out audibly. She watched his eyes flicker across her body.

'You were wrong, you know,' he said huskily.

'What about?'

'You don't look better with clothes on.' He drew her close to him and wrapped his arms tightly around her. Sam relished the feeling of his skin against hers. She responded to his kisses, matching his urgency, trembling as he lowered her onto the bed. He lay at her side, drawing his thigh across hers, as one hand glided over her skin, lingering at her breast before continuing downwards, tantalisingly, to stroke her belly, his fingers hovering along the edge of her pants. Sam drew her breath in sharply. She watched him, watching her. He was gazing adoringly at her body, but she didn't feel self-conscious. He was making her believe that she was beautiful. She wanted to turn all her thoughts off now and just go with it. He lowered his head and she felt his mouth on her breast as his hand reached her inner thigh, caressing the skin, excruciatingly sensitive to his touch. Sam heard herself moan with pleasure.

Then suddenly he stopped, resting his head against her chest. 'Dammit,' he muttered.

'What is it?'

He lifted his head to look at her. 'Sam, I don't have any, you know, protection.'

She smiled. For some reason that pleased her. Besides, all was not lost.

'Get my handbag,' she said in a low voice. 'It's at the end of the bed.'

He rolled over and picked up the bag, passing it to her. She peered inside, feeling around until she found the condom. 'Here,' she said, handing it to him.

'Well, you're a bundle of surprises.'

She smiled. 'That's it, though, that's all I have.'

'Okay,' he said. 'We'll just have to make it last.'

And he did. He aroused Sam beyond what she had felt for a long time, if ever. He moved his hands and mouth across every part of her body, stroking, caressing, exploring, until she couldn't bear it any longer. All the blood in her entire body felt as though it had rushed to her pelvis, and she ached to feel him inside her. She arched herself against him, parting her thighs and wrapping them around him. He didn't hold back any longer. And as he thrust inside her over and over, Sam lost herself completely. No more thoughts, only feelings. Intense, exquisite, explosive. And then they reached the place, fused together, muscles locked, crying out, before falling back to earth, slowly, breathing hard, collapsing against each other. Sam felt tears welling and she let them flow. She wasn't sad, or maybe she was. Sad, and happy, and exhilarated.

Hal lifted his head to look at her. 'Are you okay?'

She nodded.

He wiped a tear away from her cheek. 'What's this then?'

'I'm just happy.'

'I'm glad you're happy,' he said, staring intently into her eyes. 'I want you to be happy.'

And then he kissed her, a long, slow, lingering, wonderful kiss. Sam was floating. She wanted this to last forever.

'Stay right here,' he said after a while. 'I'll be back in a minute.' He kissed her lightly as he drew away, moving off the bed. He walked into the bathroom and closed the door behind him.

Sam sighed deeply. Now what? No, don't start to think, just

hang onto the feeling. She closed her eyes, but the thoughts took over like gatecrashers at a party. What did this mean? Was this the start of something? Or just two consenting adults doing what consenting adults do? What was she supposed to do now? Stay or go? She was a grown woman, for godsakes, and she didn't know the rules. How was she supposed to know what to do next?

Sam glanced down at her naked body and rolled over, pulling the covers around her. She had felt like the bloody Venus de Milo only moments ago. Hal had made her feel like that. But now she felt self-conscious again. She stared out the window. The venetian blinds were slanted open and she could see the silhouette of the city against the night sky.

She heard the tap running in the bathroom and then stop. The door opened and Hal must have flicked a light switch because the lamps went out. He climbed in behind her and slid across, spooning himself into her back.

'What are you thinking about,' he murmured softly into her ear.

'Oh, I was just wondering if there was someone with a tele-scope trained on us in one of those buildings.'

'Well, I hope they enjoyed the show. Not as much as I did,' he finished, nuzzling into her neck.

'Hal?'

'Hmm?'

'Maybe I should go?'

He lifted his head and she turned to look up at him.

'Do you have to?' he frowned slightly. 'Where are the kids?'

'At Jeff's.'

'Are you having regrets?'

She shook her head. 'Are you?' she asked tentatively.

He stroked a lock of hair away from her forehead. 'Just that there was only one condom.'

Sam smiled faintly and turned back to stare out of the win-dow again as Hal pressed his lips against her shoulder. That wasn't very romantic. He just wished they could have done it again. She supposed she did as well, but was there anything else? Was it more than just sex for him too?

'I'm glad you came here tonight,' he murmured in her ear.

'You are?'

'Mm, the movie was getting boring.'

She nudged him, looking around. 'Can't you ever be serious?'

'I am being serious, the movie was boring. And I am so glad you're here,' he said quietly. 'My only other regret is that it took you so long.'

As he kissed her tenderly, Sam let her doubts melt away, for now. When she turned back on her side, he folded his arms around her from behind, holding her close against him. Sam didn't know where all this was leading. She would worry about that tomorrow. Count on it. But for now she revelled in the feeling of his body wrapped around hers. This was like her fantasy. It was enough for now.

The morning after

Sam blinked. Shafts of sunlight peeked between the city buildings, filtering through the blinds into the bedroom. She could hear Hal breathing in a steady rhythm behind her, feel his hand resting on her hip, his leg nestled against hers. She sighed. She had slept so deeply, she couldn't even remember dreaming.

Morning had arrived with undue haste. Morning meant they were going to have to face each other. Say something. Sam shivered. The last time she had found herself naked in a man's bed, she had fled the scene. But she didn't want to this time. She wanted so much more, and that frightened the life out of her.

She knew this would happen. She knew if she allowed herself to feel anything, it was going to be too much. She started to bite on the edge of her thumb. God, she was so naïve. They had sex, so what? Sex was a physical drive. People did it all the time without making such a big deal about it. Grow up, Samantha, welcome to the real world.

But then she remembered the things Hal said, the way he kissed her. It was so . . . intimate. Not because they were naked, not because of the sex, but because of what was in his eyes when he looked at her.

The phone suddenly rang into the silence. Sam nearly cleared the bed, she jumped with such force.

Hal stirred, snuggling closer. 'Let the machine get it,' he murmured, half asleep.

Sam listened to Hal's brief recorded announcement. *'Can't come to the phone right now. Talk to the machine, I'll get back to you.'*

Then a woman's voice came on the line.

'Janet Murphy calling, Mr Buchanan. Just confirming your travel arrangements. You are booked onto Qantas flight QF 41, departing Monday the eighth of December at eleven a.m., one way, direct to New York. Sydney airport recommends you arrive at the terminal . . .'

Sam wasn't listening any more. She wasn't breathing either. She swung her legs over the side of the bed and sat up. She felt Hal's hand on her back.

'Sam,' he said. 'I was going to tell you.'

She stood up, dragging the sheet with her. 'I really have to get going, I've got a ton of things to do today,' she said, trying to wrap the sheet around herself as she reefed it from the bed. It looked a lot easier when they did this in the movies.

'Sam, wait a second,' Hal said, grabbing at the quilt to cover himself as the sheet slid away. 'Let me explain.'

She walked with some difficulty around the end of the bed, dragging the metres of sheeting, before tripping and falling onto her knees.

'Are you alright?'

She popped up again. 'I'm okay.' She bunched the sheet up around her and headed for the bathroom.

'Sam, wait,' Hal was sitting on the edge of the bed. 'Talk to me.'

'There's nothing to talk about, Hal. You're going home, I've got stuff to do. Life goes on. Let's be grown-ups about this,' she finished, walking into the bathroom and locking the door. She turned around and saw herself in the mirror. She collapsed back against the door, sliding down, her face crumpling as tears rose into her throat. She was such a fool.

She jumped as a knock sounded on the door above her.

'Sam?'

She buried her face into the sheet, stifling her tears.

'Sam?'

She took a couple of breaths. 'I'll be out in a minute,' she called, hoping her voice didn't give her away.

Sam hauled herself up and unravelled the sheet, letting it drop to the floor. She splashed cold water on her face, staring at her reflection in the mirror, the hurt in her brown eyes. She slipped her shirt off the rail. It had dried overnight. Bugger, her underwear was still out there. Bad luck. She wasn't going out again till she was fully clothed. She buttoned up her shirt and pulled on jeans that were still damp, all the more uncomfortable with no underwear, but she'd put up with it until she got home.

Sam bundled up the sheet, took a deep breath and opened the door. Hal was dressed, pacing outside, his hands thrust in his pockets. He stopped when she appeared.

'Sam, I'm not letting you leave until you give me a chance to explain.'

'Sure,' she said briskly, tossing the sheet onto the bed. She spied her bra on the floor and bent to pick it up, stuffing it into her bag. Now, where were her underpants? She got down on her knees.

'What are you doing?'

'Getting my things,' she replied, feeling under the bed.

He knelt down on the floor and took hold of her arm, pulling her upright so she had to face him. 'Will you listen to me, please?' He looked frustrated.

She watched him, waiting.

'Sam, I'm not going home for good. The company called me back to fix a glitch in the system. It's my system. I'm the only one who can do it. I'll be back in a few weeks.'

For a moment Sam felt like throwing her arms around him and holding him tight. But something didn't sound right. She had to stay in control.

'That's fine Hal, you do what you have to do. I'll see you in a few weeks, we'll get together then.'

She stood up and walked out into the living room, rummaging in her bag for her mobile. She found it and tried to turn it on. Damn.

Suddenly Hal grabbed her arm from behind and swung her around. He was past frustrated. He looked upset, even angry.

'Sam, what's this bullshit? Why are you doing this?'

'Doing what?'

'Acting like it was nothing last night, like it was just casual sex. Didn't it mean anything to you?'

She sighed. 'I can't allow it to mean anything, Hal.'

'Why not?'

And then she knew. 'You said you were going home.'

'I told you, it's only for a few weeks.'

'This time. But there'll be a next time. And there'll be a time when you don't come back.'

'How do you know that? I don't even know that.'

'You called it *home*.'

He looked blankly at her. 'It's just an expression, Sam.'

But he'd given it away. He didn't know when the day would come that he would go home, but it would come. And Sam didn't want to be the one left behind again.

'My phone's gone flat,' she said finally. 'I really do have to go.'

His arms dropped from her shoulders and she walked away from him to the front door. He didn't move. He didn't say anything as she left the apartment.

As soon as the lift doors closed, Sam started to tremble. She leaned heavily against the wall of the elevator, but it only took a moment to arrive at the ground floor. She walked out onto the street. At least it wasn't raining today. Sam hesitated. She didn't have a clue where she'd parked the car. All she remembered was that it had taken her probably ten minutes to walk to the apartment building. And most of that had been uphill. She looked down the street uncertainly, before glancing back into the foyer. Hal hadn't followed her. Of course not. He couldn't argue with what she had said. She sniffed back tears and started down the street.

More than an hour later Sam arrived home. It had taken her most of that time to find the car. She'd started to panic, but had calmed herself down again, mentally cordoning off a few blocks at a time and covering them methodically.

She was close to tears when she walked inside the house. She noticed the light on the answering machine flashing, no surprise, but first she had to get out of these clothes. The day had turned steamy and Sam had never felt so uncomfortable, trudging the streets with no underwear, her damp jeans chafing her bare skin. She shed them on her way down the hall into the bathroom. Standing under a cool shower, she let the water wash over her until she felt cold, until any threat of further tears was extinguished. She wasn't going to cry any more. She was going to stop feeling sorry for herself, be an adult and get on with her life.

Sam wrapped her hair in a towel and dressed in the softest T-shirt and old shorts she could find. She was ready to face the answering machine.

She listened to an irate message from Patricia Bowen, followed by another one. Then one from Sheila. Then one from Max. She sounded worried. Then another one from Sheila. One from Rosemary. Another from Patricia Bowen and yet another from Sheila. Sam sighed wearily. Sheila was not happy. She supposed she'd better deal with her first. She picked up the phone and dialled.

'Hello Sheila, it's Samantha Holmes,' she said when Sheila answered.

'Samantha,' she said, sounding like a disapproving school principal. 'I have been calling since yesterday evening. Where have you been?'

It was within her rights to say 'none of your business', but she did owe her some kind of explanation.

'I'm sorry, Sheila, I've been absolutely swamped.'

'Well, I have had Patricia Bowen on the phone to me half a dozen times claiming you've let her down, that you were supposed to deal with something important for her yesterday.'

'Unfortunately an emergency came up.'

'She said something about that. And I know your time is your own to organise, Samantha, but if you have made arrangements with a client –'

'It was for another client,' Sam interrupted. 'I had to make a judgement call.'

'I see. Who was the other client?'

'Vanessa Blair.'

'Oh yes, there was a message from Mr Blair yesterday. I didn't have the chance to get back to him with everything going on.'

'Well, he would have been calling you because he wants to terminate my services.'

'Pardon?'

'There was a crisis with his wife yesterday. He didn't appreciate . . . my involvement.'

'It's not your place to step in between a couple, Samantha. That's not your role.'

'Well sometimes it's hard for me to figure out just what my role is, Sheila.' Sam felt as though a tightly strung cord inside her, which had somehow been holding her together, had just snapped. 'Is it my role to run around after Mrs Bowen listening to her incessant, trivial complaints while she changes her mind every hour, on the hour, and blames everyone around her because they should know what she wants before she does, but she doesn't even know what she wants, so how can anyone else have a hope of knowing?' Sam took a breath, but she was on a roll. 'Or is it to book a termination clinic at Dominic Blair's request because he wants to end his wife's pregnancy, despite the fact that she doesn't? Or is it to take Vanessa Blair to the hospital when she loses the baby in question? Or is it to listen to Dominic telling me he's got a meeting and won't be able to get to the hospital? That it's for the best that Vanessa lost the baby, and not to worry about her, *she'll get over it?*'

Sam's tone had become progressively louder till she was almost shouting.

'Take the weekend off,' Sheila said quietly. 'Don't call Mrs Bowen, I'll handle her. And come into the office on Monday, we need to have a chat.'

Monday morning

Somehow Sam made it through the weekend. She had not heard from Vanessa, but she figured it was best to leave it up to her to make contact. She couldn't imagine what kind of a weekend she must have had.

Max dropped in on Saturday before Sam had the chance to return her call.

'Hey, what's the matter?' she said as Sam opened the door to her. 'You look strange, something's happened.'

Was it really true that people could see it in your face when you'd had sex? Sam wasn't ready to tell Max about Hal, she didn't need the third degree.

'You want to know what's happened?' she said. 'Vanessa Blair had a miscarriage, I abused her husband, I've probably lost another client as well and my job is on the line. Oh, and Jeff wants a divorce because he and Jodi are having a baby.'

Max just looked at her wide-eyed. 'Fuck!'

She couldn't stay long, she was meeting Dan for another non-date. And she had also not been on a date with him the night before when Sam had left the message on her machine. If she kept not dating him like this, things were going to get serious. Or not.

Sam had spent the rest of Saturday cleaning. With a vengeance. She'd always found it enormously therapeutic to throw herself into housework, it helped clear her mind. Not that it worked quite so well this time. Although she fell exhausted into bed that night, she still couldn't get Hal out of her mind when she closed her eyes. And now she had reality to shape her fantasies. She knew what his body felt like lying against her, the warmth of his arms around her, the way his lips tasted . . . But there had been no messages from Hal, and he hadn't called all weekend.

The kids made no mention of the baby when they arrived home Sunday afternoon. Sam didn't want to bring it up if they knew nothing yet. She wasn't able to check with Jeff, he didn't come inside when he dropped them home, sending his apologies via Jess – 'Dad said to say hello, but he was running late for something or other'. He was avoiding her. Sam supposed she could hardly blame him.

Josh and Jessica had left on the bus nearly half an hour ago, and Sam was just about ready to leave to take Ellie to pre-school. She would go and see Sheila after that. She had spent most of Sunday bringing all her records up to date, gearing herself up for the showdown. Sam had mixed feelings about the whole thing. Except for Ted, she could happily give up all her clients, she'd had enough. But what was the alternative at the moment? She was due to meet Andrew Byron at the Darling Harbour Exhibition Centre tomorrow, and she was understandably hopeful about her chances. But that was all she had. And there was a mortgage to pay, mouths to feed, and only half her Christmas shopping done.

She picked up the briefcase she'd packed for her meeting with Sheila, and her handbag, and Ellie's backpack and sunhat and Zoey the zebra, which she had insisted on bringing today. Sam carried it all to the front door, juggling as she undid the deadlock. The door fell open as Sam turned around to call out for Ellie.

'Eloise Holmes, where are you? We're going to be late!'

She appeared at the end of the hall. 'Sorry Mummy. I had to go.'

'You just went a minute ago!'

Ellie shrugged. 'But I had to go some more.'

Sam smiled. 'Well, I guess when you gotta go . . . Come on, we'll be late.' She watched Ellie skip across the living room, suddenly stopping dead in her tracks as she looked past her mother.

'Hal!' she squealed delightedly.

Sam swung around as Ellie ran past her out the front door and into Hal's arms. He scooped her up, looking warily at Sam over her shoulder.

'Hey,' he said tentatively.

Sam couldn't say anything. She seemed to have lost the faculty of speech.

'Is this a bad time?'

She shook her head vaguely.

'Where have you been, Hal?' Ellie blurted. 'Why don't you come to visit us any more?'

'Sorry Ellie, I, uh, haven't had the chance.'

'Did you know Santa's coming soon? And I'm going to be an angel in the play at kindy. And we're going to have a party . . .'

Sam watched Hal listening patiently as Ellie prattled on. What was he doing here? Didn't he have a plane to catch? Was that his taxi parked across the street?

'. . . maybe you can come and see me in my play,' Ellie was saying.

'No, Ellie, Hal's going away,' Sam said, finding her voice. She looked directly at him. 'He won't be able to come and see your play.'

Hal didn't flinch from her glare. 'I will miss your play, Ellie. But I'll see you after Christmas.'

'Promise?'

'Promise.'

'Ellie, hop in the car, sweetheart, and wait for Mummy.'

Hal put her down and she skipped over to the car. He looked at Sam. 'I won't hold you up. I just wanted to see you before I left.' He took a breath. 'There's something I have to say to you.'

'Okay,' she said quietly. She watched him shift from one foot to the other, glancing around as if he was collecting his thoughts from the atmosphere. Finally, he put his hands on his hips and looked directly into her eyes.

'Do you have any idea what a frustrating woman you are, Sam?'

She hadn't seen that coming.

'You react before you know all the facts, you do it all the time. And Jesus, do you react,' Hal declared, raising his arms. 'You can be very pig-headed when you want to be, Sam. Sometimes you should talk less and hear people out before you go making up your mind.'

Sam swallowed. 'Are you through insulting me yet?'

'See? You're doing it again. Jumping to conclusions, not hearing me out.'

She just looked at him.

Hal took a breath. 'Okay, first off, I think it's a bit rich for you to be pissed at me because I didn't tell you I was going away. I haven't heard from you in weeks, not since the last time you freaked out.' He paused for effect. 'I had no idea you were going to show up the other night, I certainly wasn't expecting what happened.' He sighed, rubbing his forehead with one hand. 'But Sam, I don't know how you can "not allow" it to mean anything. I couldn't get on that plane today after what happened, not without sorting this out. I couldn't, even if I wanted to. There's some kind of hold you've got on me . . .'

Hal stared down at the ground. Sam watched him, barely breathing.

He looked up again and met her eyes. 'I don't know what it is, Sam. I just have the feeling that if we don't give this a chance, we'll both end up regretting it.'

What did he just say?

'You tell me you don't feel the same way,' Hal continued quietly, 'and that'll be the end of it.' He paused, watching her. 'But think before you speak for once, would you?'

No fear of that. Sam couldn't speak right now even if she wanted to. Her heart was pounding against her ribcage and she felt as though she could quite possibly throw up.

'Well?' Hal said after a while.

Sam swallowed. 'I can't say that,' she croaked.

He looked confused. 'I'm sorry?'

She took a deep breath. 'I can't say that I don't feel the same way.'

He regarded her curiously. 'That double negative cancels itself out, doesn't it?'

She shrugged.

'So you *can* say you feel the same way I do?'

She nodded shyly.

His shoulders visibly relaxed and he breathed out heavily. 'Okay then,' he said, the relief apparent in his voice. 'So, I'll be back sometime around the middle of January,' he continued calmly. 'Sometimes people go away, Sam, and they come back.'

She looked up at him and he held her gaze, steady and unblinking.

'I have something for you.' He reached into the pocket of his jacket and pulled out a small, flat gift box, about the size of a pack of cards. He went to hand it to her but her arms were full.

'Here,' he said. 'Give me some of that.'

Hal took Zoey and the sunhat and Ellie's bag. Sam put her briefcase down beside her and opened the lid of the box. She frowned as she drew out a set of keys. They had a large label attached to them. '"Fourteen Marine Drive, Palm Beach,"' she read. 'I don't understand?'

'It's yours. Well, for January anyway.'

Sam was mystified.

'Call it a Christmas present. For you and the kids.' He paused. 'You said you'd like to lie on a beach for a month sometime.'

She looked up at him, her eyes wide. 'You did this for me?'

'Not exactly,' he shrugged. 'I booked it, well, some time ago, not realising of course that I would be away. For a while. A *short* while,' he emphasised. 'But it would be a waste to have it sitting there empty till then.'

Sam fingered the keys, still stunned. 'I don't know what to say.'

'Say that you'll think fondly of me while I'm away and be glad to see me when I get back.' Hal was looking intently at her. 'And then maybe we can work out what happens after that,' he added quietly.

Sam felt her face go hot. 'Okay,' she swallowed.

She noticed a smile in his eyes as he nodded faintly. 'Good. That's settled then.'

'When are you leaving?' she asked.

He indicated the taxi. 'I'm on my way to the airport now.'

'Let me take you —'

'No, it's okay. I didn't mean to hold you up, you were on your way out.'

'I only have to take Ellie to pre-school, then I have a meeting later.'

He seemed uncertain.

'Come on,' she cajoled. 'This is one of those things I really should be doing for you.' She didn't want to say goodbye like this, in a rush, her stomach all twisted in knots. 'Please?'

He grinned down at her. 'Well, you don't have to beg.'

He paid off the taxi driver and transferred his bags into the boot of Sam's car. Ellie started up her chatter as soon as he climbed in the front seat. Where was he going? Why? For how long? Children were lucky. It was alright for them to be blunt and, well, just plain nosy. They didn't have to disguise their curiosity in veiled, roundabout questions.

'What would you like me to bring you back?' Hal was asking her.

'You don't have to do that, Hal,' Sam said, but they both ignored her.

'I'd like, um . . . a present!' she exclaimed.

'Okay,' he laughed. 'A present it is.'

When they arrived at Ellie's pre-school, Sam glanced at Hal. 'This'll only take a minute. Say goodbye to Hal, Ellie.'

Ellie appeared in the gap between the front seats, clutching her zebra. 'Can you take Zoey with you?'

'Ellie, Hal can't take a stuffed zebra all the way to America with him!' Sam chided.

'But Zoey's never been to 'merica.'

'Won't you miss Zoey if I take her, Ellie?' Hal asked her.

She looked at him seriously. 'Yes, but I know you'll look after her. And as soon as you get home, you'll bring her straight around to our place, won't you, Hal?'

How did she get so cunning? She was only five, for godsakes.

'I'll take her,' said Hal as Sam went to protest. 'She'll be good company.'

Ellie beamed as she reached around to hug him. 'Be good Zoey!' she said, thrusting the zebra into his arms. 'Bye bye, Hal!'

Sam took Ellie inside and returned to the car a few minutes later. 'What time is your flight?' she asked Hal.

'Eleven o'clock.'

She checked her watch. It was going to be tight. She pulled out from the kerb, mentally working out the best route at this time of the day. And what on earth she was going to say to him as they drove along. How were they supposed to make light conversation after what had just passed between them? Sam wished Ellie was still in the car. She'd been a good buffer. Maybe light conversation was exactly what was needed. It was probably all Sam was capable of at the moment anyway.

'Will you spend Christmas with your family?' she asked.

He shrugged. 'Portia's not really a Christmas kind of person. She calls it the Festival of the God of Consumerism. She usually boycotts it.'

'That's not a bad idea,' Sam muttered.

'Besides, she's on the other side of the country, I don't know that I'll get the chance to see her. Maybe I'll stop over on my way back.' He glanced at Sam. 'You'll have a busy Christmas, I guess, with the kids and all.'

'Mm.' Now Sam wanted to talk about something else. Anything else. 'I have a job interview the day after tomorrow,' she chirped.

'No kidding? What kind of job?'

'Well, the company does event management, conferences, that kind of thing,' she explained.

Hal smiled broadly. 'Way to go, Sam. Sounds perfect for you.'

She shrugged. 'But it's only an interview. Well, it's not really a proper interview, I don't even know if there's an actual job. And I don't have any experience. And I'm a bit old, they probably want someone much younger. With training.'

'Don't worry, that positive attitude you've got going will make up for all that,' Hal said drily.

She glanced across at him. He was watching her, he seemed thoughtful.

'Don't sell yourself short, Samantha Jean,' he said in a quiet voice. 'You have absolutely no reason to.'

Hal believed in her. Ted Dempsey obviously believed in her. Maxine and Alex believed in her. Maybe it was about time she started believing in herself.

'Okay,' she said softly.

As they approached the airport, Sam offered to park the car and come into the terminal. But Hal insisted she just drop him off outside.

'I can check myself in,' he assured her.

She followed the signs to the two-minute drop-off zone. What could she say in only two minutes? Bugger all. Sam's thoughts raced as she tried to think of a dazzling parting remark, something Hal would remember. Something that would make him think fondly of her as well.

She stopped the car and turned off the engine.

'No need –' Hal started to say as Sam jumped out. He climbed out of his seat and looked at her across the roof of the car. '– for you to get out,' he finished.

Sam shrugged and walked back to open the boot. Hal joined her, still holding Zoey.

'Oh, here, let me take that,' said Sam. 'I'll hide it until you come back.'

'No,' he resisted. 'A promise is a promise.'

Sam frowned at him. 'You're actually going to take a stuffed zebra halfway across the world on a business trip?'

Hal was unzipping his suitcase. He flipped it open and began rearranging the contents of his bag to accommodate Zoey.

'Hal, you can't –'

'I told Ellie I would take Zoey with me,' he said over the top of her protests. He pushed the lid of his suitcase down firmly and zipped it closed again, looking directly at Sam. 'And I'm a man of my word.'

He picked up the bag and his briefcase and Sam closed the lid of the boot.

'Hal!' she blurted. He looked at her expectantly but she still hadn't thought of anything to say.

'I'll be seeing you then,' he said.

Now or never. Sam took a step closer and reached her arms up to his shoulders, but she didn't want to have to yank his head down to her. Instead she turned him around and stepped up onto the kerb, bringing her face level with his. She looped both arms around his neck and pulled him close, kissing him purposefully, deliberately, trying to convey . . . well, she hoped he got the drift. He was obviously taken aback at first, but he relaxed into it, moving the arm holding the briefcase around her.

Sam pulled away slowly, a little self-conscious.

'What was that for?' Hal said quietly.

'I don't know,' she shrugged.

She stepped off the kerb and skirted backwards around the car. 'Have a good trip,' she called, before disappearing inside the car. As she pulled away she could see Hal in the rear-vision mirror, standing in the same spot. He hadn't moved. He watched her until the road curved around and she was out of sight.

Sheila tapped the pen on her desk. 'You're too emotionally involved, Samantha. You can't work effectively like this.'

'I don't know how you can avoid it when you're dealing with people on such a personal level,' said Sam. 'They all want to be friends, confide in me.'

'That's because you're so good at this, Samantha,' Sheila said matter-of-factly. 'You have the rare ability to combine warmth and efficiency. You're one of the best lifestyle managers I've ever employed.'

Sam didn't know what to say. Sheila didn't mean it as a compliment. She wasn't one to flatter. She just called it as she saw it.

'So, you've proven yourself now.'

'Sorry?'

'Do you think you're the first jilted wife who's ever joined us to make some kind of point to her husband?'

Sam was gobsmacked.

'In my experience, men don't leave because of a messy or disorganised house. Sometimes it's quite the opposite. Funny, we make it so important,' Sheila said, almost wistful. 'So,' she snapped out of it, 'I knew we wouldn't have you for much longer. You were bound to burn out soon. It always happens to the best ones.'

Sam looked at her sheepishly. She may as well be honest. 'I am looking at my options actually.'

'Well,' Sheila said, unperturbed. 'We should discuss how you can begin culling your clients, starting with Mrs Bowen, I presume?'

Sam nodded vaguely. 'If that's okay.'

'Of course it is,' Sheila dismissed. 'It's the only way we'll keep her as a client at all. She's very dirty with you. I've told her I'll take care of her personally from now on.'

'You're brave,' Sam muttered. 'I didn't realise you still took on clients.'

'I reserve myself for the particularly challenging ones. They only come along from time to time.' She looked up at Sam. 'That's how I avoid burnout,' she winked. 'So, is there anyone else that you'd like to offload, or who you think could be easily passed along to someone else?'

'Well,' said Sam, picking up her briefcase, 'I have all my records with me.'

'Excellent. Let's take a look.'

'You know I can't afford to do this right away. I still have a mortgage.'

'Of course. We'll start the process now, but it will take months, and you can keep on as many clients as you wish. It's up to you.'

Sam smiled gratefully. 'You're being very good about this.'

'What's the point of making it unpleasant, who wins out of that? It's not good for either of us, it's certainly not good for the clients.' Sheila paused. 'You're going to make a new start for yourself, Samantha, regardless of what obstacles I put in your path. I'd rather you left us with a sense of accomplishment, and perhaps even a nice word to say about us.'

When Jeff called that night to talk to the kids, Sam made sure she answered the phone. She walked into her room and closed the door.

'Hi,' he said warily. 'Are any of the kids around?'

'Sure, I just want to talk to you about Christmas first.'

She heard him sigh. 'Look, I understand where you're coming from, Sam. It's fair, I suppose.'

'Well, it's good of you to be so understanding, but I was coming from somewhere completely selfish. It shouldn't be about what's fair for me, or you, for that matter. It should only be about what's fair for the kids.'

He didn't say anything.

'So they should have Christmas with you this year.' Sam paused, giving him a chance to take it in.

'Thank you, Sam.' She could tell he was stunned.

'But I was going to ask a small favour.'

'Of course.'

'Well, I hope it's a small favour. Maybe you won't see it that way.' She took a breath. 'But would you mind if they have the morning here? I just thought that way it probably doesn't complicate the whole Santa issue for Ellie, you know. And . . . oh, damn.'

'What is it?'

'I'm trying to sound like I have noble intentions. But I just don't think I could cope without them on Christmas morning,' Sam swallowed, pressing her eyelids to stem tears that were perilously close.

'Then they should spend Christmas Eve with you,' Jeff said plainly. 'I'll pick them up later the next morning.'

Sam sighed, relieved. 'Thank you.'

'Thank you.'

They were silent for a moment. Sam composed herself. 'I'll get one of the kids now.' She walked towards the door. 'Oh, by the way, have you said anything to them . . . about . . . your news?'

'Ah, no, not yet,' Jeff stammered. 'We thought it was better, maybe, to wait a little longer.'

Mm. Because you never know when the ex-wife's gonna blow.

'Well, whatever . . . they won't hear anything negative from me,' Sam finished.

'Thanks Sam, that means a lot to me.'

'Okay,' she said, leaving the room. 'I'll get Jess.'

Sydney Exhibition Centre, Darling Harbour

Sam arrived at the main entrance at twenty past nine, ten minutes before she was due to meet Andrew Byron. She had spent a ridiculous amount of time last night deciding what to wear. This was a trendy industry, but she didn't want to look like mutton done up as lamb. Nor did she want to come across as too conservative. She didn't feel that a regular interview-type outfit was appropriate. Besides, Mr Byron had not spoken as though this was a formal interview. Sam finally settled on simple black trousers, flat shoes and a short-sleeved turtleneck jumper. She was neat and tidy and comfortable for work, but quite acceptable if it turned out to be more formal.

Someone burst through a door behind her and charged off down the street in a hurry. Sam wandered over to stand by the open door, watching the hubbub inside the vast pavilion. There were rows and rows of canopied stalls, some brightly striped, others bearing brand names. She tried to remember whether Mr Byron had mentioned what this was all about. Some kind of gardening show perhaps? There were no plants in evidence as yet, but there were workers everywhere. They were up on ladders, stringing up banners, assembling yet more stalls, dashing around like chooks with their heads cut off. It did, however, seem like organised chaos. People weren't frantic, just busy. Sam sensed the adrenaline in the atmosphere and found it irresistible.

She was so absorbed, in fact, that she hadn't noticed someone approaching.

'Samantha Holmes?'

She jumped a little, her eyes coming to focus on a pleasant-looking man who was probably around her own age. He was wearing a suit and tie, and a broad smile.

'Andrew Byron,' he announced, thrusting his hand out towards her.

Sam took a moment to respond. 'Sorry,' she said, clasping his hand. 'I was expecting someone older. You said you were a friend of Ted's,' she added vaguely.

'I am a very old friend of Ted's,' he confirmed. 'I went to school with his son.'

'Hugh?'

'You know Hugh?'

Sam shrugged. 'Only through cyberspace. I handle Ted's correspondence. Hugh's an avid emailer.'

'Yes, I know, that's how we keep in touch.'

She frowned. 'Oh, perhaps you shouldn't mention anything about me to Hugh —'

'I know,' he assured her. 'Ted's secret is safe with me. Though I think the old bloke's mad, and I've told him as much, in politer terms. Of course he should tell Hugh about his condition.'

Sam nodded. 'That's what I keep telling him as well.' She

suddenly wondered if she was sounding gossipy. 'Not that it's really my place, or my business.'

He smiled. 'Ted thinks the world of you, Samantha. I'm sure he would respect anything you had to say.'

She felt herself blushing.

'And I have enormous respect for anything Ted has to say,' he added. 'Which is why I was happy to set up this meeting.'

'Well, I can't tell you how much I appreciate it, Mr Byron.'

'Please, it's Andrew.'

Sam nodded shyly.

'Now, unfortunately I'm not going to be able to hang around for long,' he explained. 'I have a client meeting, that's why I'm wearing this straightjacket,' he said, indicating his suit. 'We're not usually so formal on the job.

'So, let me find Denise, she'll take care of you, show you the ropes.' He touched Sam's elbow lightly to guide her along past a row of stalls. He stopped where a young man was intent on attaching a banner across the front of one of the stalls.

'Brad,' Andrew said, 'have you seen Denise?'

'Sure,' he grinned. 'Big woman, dark hair . . .'

'Very funny, Brad. Brad's the team clown,' Andrew explained to Sam. 'Brad Moss, this is Samantha Holmes. She's considering coming to work for us.'

She was considering?

'Hi,' Brad smiled, shaking her hand. 'It helps if you're a little crazy.'

'If that's the case, I should fit right in.'

'So you don't know where Denise is?' Andrew persisted.

'She'll be around somewhere, boss. Follow the voice.'

They smiled knowingly at each other. As they walked along further, Andrew explained that Denise was his most senior manager and arguably the best event co-ordinator in the business. He introduced Sam to more members of the team as they came to them. Not all the people working here today were his staff, he told her. Many were contractors, the tent hire people, for example. They'd come in, do their job and leave. The team were responsible for co-ordinating all the various contractors, and then the exhibitors, as well as liaising with the venue management, sponsors and any number of other interested parties.

'It's a juggling act,' said Andrew. 'You have to keep a lot of different people happy and try to meet often conflicting needs. You've got to be a master of negotiation and diplomacy. And you have to do it all to a deadline.'

Sam noticed that all the team members were wearing a dark green T-shirt with 'Outdoor Living Expo' plastered across the front and 'Green Team' on the back. They also sported a small set of headphones each, not unlike the type Sam had worn when she worked in the call centre.

She and Andrew had come to the end of the aisle. From here the space opened out and it appeared they were setting up some kind of stage. There were tracks of lights being lifted into position, backdrops being hung, while another group was building what looked like timber framework at the far end. A row of trestle tables along one side served as the administrative centre apparently. There were three members of the 'Green Team' manning computers and phones, surrounded by cardboard cartons and stacks of papers.

And in the middle of it all there was one voice going non-stop, over the sound of hammers and saws and power drills and phones ringing. A largish woman, wearing a vibrant overshirt that was as loud as her voice, paced back and forwards across the stage area, barking orders into her headset at a breathtaking rate.

'Trev, Trev, Trev, no I don't think so. Tell them if they leave ten dozen orchids here now, they'll all die . . . No, Justine, that's no good . . . Well, Trevor, remind them that they were not expected until Friday, so it's not on our heads and as we don't have the watering system connected yet THEY WILL DIE! Can I make myself any clearer? Am I going to have to come out there, Trevor? I hope not, Trevor. That's the boy . . . Justine, if they unload there how the hell do they expect to shift five tonnes of bush rock from the other side of the venue? . . . Yes, Stephanie, that'll work, but have them come down tomorrow, yeah? We can't handle it today . . . You know, Justine, you can tell them that if they had actually bothered to follow the delivery instructions which we went to great trouble to fax ahead, we wouldn't be having this discussion . . . of course, that's assuming they can actually *read* . . .'

'I'm guessing we've found Denise?' said Sam.

Andrew smiled down at her. 'Come on, I'll introduce you.'

They walked across the stage area, stepping carefully over leads and around ladders.

'Denise,' Andrew said loudly.

She swung around, holding her hand up, obviously in the middle of another conversation. 'Well done, Trev . . . Yeah, Friday. We'll have the system on by then. Andrew, what can I do for you?' she finished without missing a beat.

'I want you to meet Samantha Holmes. I mentioned she'd be dropping by.'

'So you did.' She grasped Sam's hand firmly. Denise was an attractive woman with sparkling hazel eyes and a cap of shiny dark hair. She exuded energy. 'So do you get Sam? Shall we call you Sam?'

'Yes, absolutely.'

'Well, it's just not good enough!' she boomed suddenly, dropping Sam's hand. 'I said today, by four! You can tell them we'll be looking for another supplier.'

Andrew noticed Sam's startled expression. 'You get used to her after a while,' he assured her. 'Denise, do you want to turn that off for a minute, it's a bit distracting.'

'Too bloody right,' she agreed. 'Same with that fucking hammering. It's driving me crazy. Hey, Bob the Builder, TAKE FIVE!' she bellowed towards the back of the stage area.

A chorus of '*Denise!*' came back at her from around the pavilion. All the green T-shirted workers were holding their ears and wincing.

'Whoops,' Denise whispered. 'Sorry guys, I'm signing off now.' She unhooked the headset from her ear and looped it over her shoulder. 'Who's for a cup of coffee?'

'I have to get going,' said Andrew, checking his watch. 'Meeting.'

'On your bike then, I'll take care of Sam.'

'Good to meet you, Sam,' said Andrew, shaking her hand. 'We'll talk again soon.'

'Thanks for everything,' said Sam.

He shook his head. 'You can thank Ted.'

Denise led her over to a trestle table set up with an urn, cups and catering size tins of coffee and biscuits. 'What will you have?'

'Coffee thanks.'

'Good,' said Denise, making them both a cup. 'You've gotta like caffeine to survive in this business. Caffeine before and during. Alcohol after,' she winked. She handed Sam a cup. 'So, you're interested in working for us?'

'Very,' Sam nodded, sitting in the chair Denise indicated.

'What kind of experience have you had, Sam?'

She sighed. 'Well, in this actual industry, not a lot. In fact, nothing to speak of. But I've been working as a lifestyle manager the past year.'

Denise raised her eyebrows. 'Pardon my ignorance, but what the hell's a lifestyle manager?'

'I work for an organisation called *Wife for Hire*. We provide a service for busy executives –'

'You're having me on!' Denise exclaimed.

'No,' Sam said in a weak voice.

'You're not like, really a *wife*, in the full sense of the word?'

'No, no!' Sam assured her. 'It's not that kind of agency.'

'Thank Christ for that, I was starting to wonder,' said Denise, slurping her coffee.

'No, we do all kinds of things, from paying bills to organising renovations to planning dinner parties.'

Denise nodded. 'Fair enough, a lot of that experience will help you here. It's just on a greater scale.'

Sam glanced around the vast auditorium. 'That's an understatement.'

'Take what's going on up there,' she said, indicating the stage area. 'There are live demonstrations every day during the expo, headlining with the *Backyard Blitz* team. So what do you think would be involved in setting up for them?' she said, folding her arms and leaning back in her chair.

Sam looked momentarily bewildered. 'Well, a backyard for starters.'

'Right, that's what they're building up there. A kind of simulated backyard for them to "blitz". So take it from there.'

'Well, there'd be so many things they'd need. Plants and equipment, though I suppose they'd supply a lot of that themselves . . .' Her voice trailed off as she became lost in thought. 'Okay, so you would have to establish who your contact is, and liaise with them to find out what they are bringing with them, and what we would have to provide. I mean, to begin with, what kind of space do they need, power, water –'

'You'll do fine,' said Denise with a satisfied smile.

Sam looked at her. 'There's a lot more to it than that.'

'You don't have to tell me.' Denise considered her for a moment. 'Do you have children, Sam?'

She nodded. 'Three.'

'Phew.' She leaned forward. 'Let me tell you something. We get these kids showing up fresh from a six-month stint at college and they want to tell us how to do it!' Denise shook her head. 'Had this little slip of a thing start the other week, and she had a fabulous idea for decorating the pavilion.' She was making no attempt to hide the sarcasm in her voice. 'Paper flowers, she said. Paper fucking flowers! They showed her how to make them at college. Honestly, I thought Brad was going to strangulate a hernia, he was trying so hard to stop himself from laughing.'

Sam grinned. 'Funny, I don't see any paper flowers around.'

'Yes, well, I told her that she could practise her origami techniques on the twenty thousand brochures that needed folding. She thought I was joking.'

'What happened to her?'

'She decided that perhaps we were not the company for her. Brad was quite devastated,' Denise chuckled. 'Frankly Sam, give me a woman who's done an eight year old's birthday party and I'll show you an event organiser.'

Sam smiled. 'Well, I've done a few of those.'

Denise drained her cup and got to her feet. 'I've got to get back to work. Can you hang around?'

'I was planning to.'

'How are you at folding brochures?'

'I just can't believe how fabulous it is!' Sam enthused.

Max had been listening patiently to Sam rave about her day for the last half-hour, virtually without a break.

'I'm getting the idea.'

'Oh, okay, I'm going on a bit.'

Max grinned. 'It's alright. It's good to see you so charged about something, Sherl. You haven't been a very happy camper lately.'

Sam looked at her. 'Sorry.'

'You don't have to be sorry.' Max walked round the kitchen bench and opened the fridge, peering inside. 'I'm glad things are looking up. Got anything to drink?'

'Sure, sure, sorry, I should have offered,' Sam moved her out of the way and reached for a bottle on the lower shelf. 'I wish I had some bubbly. I feel like celebrating.'

'You can do that just as well with still wine,' Maxine assured her.

Sam started to open the bottle while Max found glasses.

'You know the best thing,' Sam said, picking up the thread again, 'is working with other people. It made me realise that I've worked on my own most of my life. I mean raising children is a very solitary occupation. And then there was the call centre.' She drew the cork out of the bottle. 'Sure they called you a team, but all day you're stuck in that cubicle on your own with only a voice down the phone line to relate to. Then with *Wife for Hire* I was working on my own again. But today I was part of a team, there was always someone to talk to, someone beside you to help, work with you, throw around ideas. It was . . . fantastic!'

Sam had been waving the bottle around as she spoke, and finally Max grabbed it out of her hand and poured them both a glass.

'I'm raving again, aren't I?'

Max smiled, handing her a glass. 'It sounds like you've found your niche.'

'I have, I really have. I think things are really going to come together for me now, Max. I can feel it.'

'So when do you start for real?'

'I called Andrew Byron this afternoon and he said I'm welcome to observe as often as I like, but I'll start officially at the end of January, when I get back.'

'Get back from where?'

Sam had forgotten to tell Max. 'I have the use of a house in Palm Beach for the holidays.'

Max's eyes widened. 'Wow, who did you have to sleep with to score that?'

Sam turned to open the fridge again. 'Just Hal.'

'What did you say?'

'I don't know what to give the kids for dinner,' she mused, staring inside the refrigerator. 'It's too hot to cook tonight.'

'Sam!' Max exclaimed, grabbing her by the arm. 'Did you just say you slept with Hal?'

'Not in so many words,' Sam said calmly. 'I think you asked who I had to sleep with, and I said, "Just Hal".'

'Sam!' she squealed. '*Sam!*' she squealed again, hugging her. 'Why didn't you tell me?'

'Because I knew you'd carry on like this.'

Max drew back to look her in the face. 'Aren't you happy about it?'

'Yeah, I think so. Now anyway.'

'When did it happen?'

'Last week. Friday, actually.'

Max gasped. 'Why didn't you tell me?'

'I haven't had the chance.'

'But I saw you on Saturday.'

'I was still confused on Saturday.'

Max looked at her. 'Come on,' she grabbed her hand and started for the back door. 'Out here, away from the kids. You're going to tell me everything.'

'But I have to start dinner.'

'I'll shout takeaway,' Max dismissed. 'Oh, and grab that bottle.'

They sat on the back step while Max made Sam recount everything, though she reneged on some of the more intimate details. Talking about it made it seem more real, reinforcing that it actually had happened, it was not just one of her fantasies.

'So, how was it?' Max asked, nudging her. 'I mean really, *how was it?*'

Sam sipped her wine. 'It was pretty bloody wonderful,' she said slowly.

'You're in love!' Max swooned.

Sam felt her heart drop into her stomach. 'Slow down! I've only slept with him once.'

'Yes, but I know you, sister. You married the last guy you slept with,' Max reminded her. 'Not counting Sleazy, of course. So it's a fair comment.'

'Look, I'm not going to allow myself to even think about whether I'm in love with him.'

Max was thoughtful. 'You're becoming an avoidant.'

'What are you talking about?'

'Psychological theory on attachment types. It's very well documented. You used to be an *anxious ambivalent*, but now you're turning into a *fearful avoidant.*'

'Which is better?' Sam frowned.

Max grinned. 'Oh, don't worry, they're both dysfunctional. The anxious ambivalent is the clingy, dependent type. If they're rejected they may become ambivalent about showing emotion and so they use avoidant coping strategies. Which is what you've been doing with Hal.'

'You think I was dependent and clingy with Jeff?'

'Well, maybe not on Jeff the man. But you were dependent on the relationship, don't you reckon? The whole wife-and-mother gig. It was what gave you a sense of identity. So now you're avoiding attachment because that didn't work out.'

Sam was thoughtful. 'What about you?'

Max laughed. 'Oh, I am the absolute *Queen* of avoidance, haven't you noticed?' She took a sip from her glass. 'But I'm coming around.'

Sam looked slyly at her. 'Dan?'

Maxine nodded.

'I like him,' Sam said simply.

'I know you do.'

They both sat lost in their own thoughts.

'So what's normal?' Sam asked eventually.

'We prefer not to use the word "normal",' Max warned. '*Secure* attachment is the ideal. You know, you see it in the toddler who is happy to wander away from Mum, while keeping her in sight. The child who can separate without trauma.'

'And the adult who will risk starting a relationship without knowing how it will turn out?'

Max smiled. 'You said that, I didn't.' She took a sip from her glass. 'Speaking of mothers and separating from them, have you decided what you're going to do about Christmas?'

Sam drew her knees up, hugging them. 'I can't tell you how much the thought of it fills me with dread,' she said quietly. 'I've told Jeff he can have the kids. He's going to pick them up about eleven.'

'That was very generous of you.'

Sam shook her head. 'No, it was the right thing to do.'

Max leaned over against Sam. 'Maybe you should come to Mum's. You don't want to be here on your own.'

'The thing is, I think I'd rather forget it was Christmas at all once the kids are gone. It might be easier that way.'

Max looked at her doubtfully.

'What do you think I should do?' Sam asked earnestly.

She paused. 'I think you should do whatever feels right for you. Stop worrying about everyone else. You've got to start looking after yourself.'

Christmas Day

Sam had prepared everything ahead so that she would be able to give the children her full attention for the morning. She was up at six with Ellie, though they had to wait another hour for Jess and Josh to emerge. In the meantime they shook presents, played at guessing, giggled a lot, and Sam generally revelled in the anticipation of her little daughter who still believed in Santa and magic and happily ever after.

When the others woke, Sam sat back and watched them open their presents. She knew she had spoilt them this year. She wasn't trying to compete with Jeff, it wasn't like that. He had contributed to their Santa presents anyway and he seemed just as eager to overdo it as she was. Clearly they were both over-compensating for everything the kids had been through. It was probably not realistic, nor the wisest thing to do. But Sam couldn't help herself.

After the presents were opened, she made ham and eggs for breakfast and tried to get the kids to linger at the table. But with new toys to play with, and clothes to try on, and make-up to test, they were soon off again. The knock on the front door at eleven came too soon. Ellie ran at her father before Sam had barely opened the door.

'Daddy, Santa came last night! Come and see!' she blurted.

Sam smiled. 'Come in, Jeff. Merry Christmas.'

'Merry Christmas, Sam,' he returned as Ellie dragged him inside.

She stood back as the kids showed off their booty to their father and he made all the right noises. Sam looked at her three beautiful children and her heart filled. The older two were all kitted out in their new clothes. Joshua was dressed head to toe in heavily labelled skate gear, large enough to fit someone twice his size, but with his height and his shock of blond hair, he could carry it off.

Jessica unfortunately looked like a prostitute. Sam knew as soon as that thought entered her head that she was channelling

Bernice; however, she did worry that there was too much make-up and too much skin showing. But Jess was young and gorgeous and enviably firm, and Sam thought what the heck, why shouldn't she flaunt it? It wouldn't be long before she'd be so obsessed with what was wrong with her that she'd never be so carefree again.

And Ellie looked like a little angel. Sam had paid way too much for a totally impractical but stunning white dress with gold stars dotted around the yoke. She knew Ellie would barely get any wear of it outside of this Christmas, but she couldn't resist. Oh well. Maybe Jeff would have a girl and they could pass it on to her.

Whoa! That thought certainly snuck up on her.

'We should get going,' Jeff said tentatively, glancing in Sam's direction.

'Of course. Go get your things, kids,' Sam prompted them. She went to the hall cupboard where she had stored the bags of carefully selected, beautifully wrapped presents she had bought for everyone in Jeff's family. She probably should have left it to him, but she had always done it, and she still wanted to have some kind of presence as the children's mother. She wanted them to know that she was coping, that her children were doing fine and that she could still manage everything as before. It was probably pathetic or ridiculous. It was probably both of those things.

But she had drawn the line at buying something for Jodi. Sam had made an offhand but well-placed remark to Jessica that perhaps they should shop with their father for Jodi's gift, he would know what she wanted. That was the best she could do.

'Mummy, can I bring the postcards from Zoey to show everybody?' Ellie was asking.

'Of course you can, sweetheart. They're on the fridge.' A different postcard had arrived on the three consecutive days leading up to Christmas. Zoey at the Empire State Building, at the Statue of Liberty and at Central Park. She certainly got around. Ellie was thrilled, and Sam was not a little chuffed herself.

She walked her family out the front door and stood on the

verandah to say goodbye. Ellie gave her mother a huge hug, but the others went to walk past.

'Excuse me,' Sam admonished good-naturedly. 'Hugs are compulsory on Christmas Day, it's the law.'

Jess pulled a face that combined eye-rolling with a resigned grin, and leaned forward to kiss her mother, squeezing her briefly. 'See ya Mum.'

Sam looked up at Josh who was considering her with a twinkle in his eye. Before she knew what he was doing, he wrapped his arms around her and lifted her off her feet. Sam shrieked.

'Merry Christmas, Mum,' he said, settling her back down again. She smiled, watching him leap up the steps to the footpath to catch up with his sisters.

'Thanks for this, Sam,' Jeff said seriously. 'Mum and Dad said to say thank you as well.'

Wonders never cease. Sam shrugged. Jeff seemed hesitant. She'd better give him permission to go.

'I'll see you in a couple of days,' she said lightly.

'Right, okay.' And then, unexpectedly, he leaned forward and kissed her on the cheek. 'Merry Christmas, Sam.'

She mumbled the same back and he turned to join the kids. They were just climbing in the car when Sam heard Ellie cry out, 'Hi Jodi! Merry Christmas!'

Sam froze. Shit! Jodi had been sitting in the car this whole time. Of course she would be, Jeff had said he'd need to leave at eleven to make it to his parents' in time for lunch. He wouldn't want to have to cross the city again to go back for her. Sam supposed that was why he had not parked directly in front of the house. She could make out a figure in the front seat, but she was relieved she couldn't see her clearly. Sam knew she was going to have to face meeting her one day. But not today. Not Christmas Day.

Sam went inside and closed the door behind her. It wasn't Christmas Day, it was Tuesday, and the bathroom needed cleaning.

By five that afternoon Sam had cleaned the entire house. Her hands were withered and waterlogged, and the house smelled of disinfectant and furniture polish. She was exhausted, but she didn't want to stop. She had to keep occupied. If she turned on the television it would be wall-to-wall, *Very-Brady-Christmas*-type schmaltz which, although nauseating, would probably have her in tears before long.

Sam remembered she hadn't checked her emails this week. That was a very un-Christmas type of activity. She made a cup of coffee and carried it to the computer, opened the program and clicked on *Check Mail*. After a moment the box appeared announcing she had new mail. Sam liked that little box. But her heart missed a beat when she saw 'Hal Buchanan' next to the subject 'Merry Christmas'. Sam felt her hand trembling as she clicked on his name. Just three words appeared.

I miss you.

Sam drew her breath in sharply and tried to suppress the lump in her throat. But it was no use. Her face crumpled and the tears flowed. She was crying because it was Christmas Day and her children weren't with her, because her estranged husband had kissed her on the cheek while his pregnant partner sat in the car, because she'd never had Christmas away from her mother and her sisters, and because this lovely man, who was all the way across the other side of the world, had thought of her today.

A knock on the door made her jump. She grabbed some tissues, wiped her eyes and blew her nose. When she opened the door, Max was standing there smiling, a bottle in one hand and a Tupperware container in the other.

'So, has he jumped off the bridge yet?' she asked.

'What?'

'Jimmy Stewart. Aren't you watching *It's a Wonderful Life*?'

'I didn't know it was on.'

'Sherl, you're the only person I know who has their own copy of that movie,' she said, walking past her into the house. 'Come on, let's put it on. It's Christmas.'

'The idea was to try to forget it's Christmas, remember?' Sam answered as Max thrust the bottle and the container into her hands.

'As if!' she exclaimed, searching through the row of video tapes. 'You can take the girl out of Christmas, but you can't take Christmas out of the girl.'

Sam smiled weakly.

Max looked around at her. 'Have you been crying?'

She swallowed. 'A little.'

'Why?'

'I got an email from Hal –' To Sam's own surprise, her voice broke and she started to sob.

'Sherl,' Max exclaimed, putting her arms around her. 'What did he say?'

'He said he missed me,' she wailed.

Max held her by the shoulders. 'But that's good, isn't it?'

Sam nodded. 'I don't know what's wrong with me.'

'You've been sitting here alone on Christmas Day getting miserable, that's what's wrong with you. What have you been doing with yourself?'

'Housework.'

'Well, that's just sick,' said Maxine, turning up her nose. 'No wonder you're depressed. But it's not too late to salvage the day.' She took the bottle back from Sam. 'Look, it's the customary bottle of Baileys from Aunty Gwen, and there's plum pudding in that container.'

Sam eyed her. 'Did Mum send this?'

'No, I had to mount a covert operation to smuggle it out.'

Sam followed Max into the kitchen. 'She hates me, doesn't she?' she asked.

Max shrugged, taking glasses down from the cupboard. 'She'll get over it.'

Sam opened the container. 'Yum, you even remembered the custard.'

They were halfway through the movie and further through the bottle when there was another knock at the door.

'Who do you reckon that'll be?' said Max, not moving.

Sam hauled herself up off the sofa. 'Only one way to find out,' she said, walking towards the door.

'Merry Christmas Sam.'

'Alex! What are you doing here?'

'You know what they say. If Mohammed won't come to the mountain . . .'

Sam beamed, throwing her arms around her sister, before she remembered that close physical contact was not really Alex's thing. She blamed her lack of inhibition on the Baileys, though it occurred to her that Alex didn't recoil.

'Come in,' Sam said, showing her into the room. 'You're on your own?'

Alex nodded. 'I left Gordon and Isabella to clean up with Mum. He's a lot more patient than I am. Here, I brought my bottle of Baileys from Aunty Gwen.'

'Yay!' said Max. 'We were getting low. I'll get you a glass.'

Alex's lip curled slightly. 'I don't think so.'

'Oh, come on, it won't kill you, Alex,' Max said, walking out to the kitchen.

'The house is charming, Sam,' Alex declared, glancing around.

Sam looked at her dubiously. 'You reckon?'

'I wouldn't say it if I didn't think so,' she said archly. 'It's much more you than that other big showplace you were living in.'

'What do you mean, much more "me"?'

'Warm, friendly, homely. That kind of thing.'

'I'm homely?'

'In a good way,' she dismissed. 'Now, I told Mum to get off your back and to think about giving you a hand once in a while.'

'You did?'

'I explained to her that you're on your own and you need her support. She harped on as usual about how she had no such help, and I reminded her who cared for us every school holiday.

They may barely have been speaking to her, but Nan and Pop still did the right thing by us.'

'What did she say to that?'

'Nothing of course. What could she say?'

'Well, I'm going to see her tomorrow, I never intended to make it a cold war.'

'Just don't give up any of the ground you've gained, Sam.'

'Okay,' she murmured.

Max returned with a glass for Alex. 'I was trying to think of the last time we were all together like this. Just the three of us,' she said.

They fell silent, dredging through their memories. Sam had the feeling they'd never been alone, just the three of them.

'I think we should make a toast,' she said, picking up her glass.

'I thought you were sick of toasts?' said Max.

'This one is special,' Sam insisted. 'To my sisters. For always being there for me, each in your own way. I'm so glad you're in my life. I don't know what I'd do without you,' she finished, sniffing.

'It's the alcohol,' Max nodded at Alex. 'Makes her a bit cheesy.'

They clinked glasses. Alex took a tentative sip of her drink. 'I suppose it's not too bad with ice.'

'Take a seat,' Sam said.

'Oh, you're watching this,' said Alex, noticing the television. There was an uncharacteristic softness in her voice. 'I love this movie.'

'Do you?' Sam wouldn't have thought that such an unashamedly sentimental movie would be quite to her sister's taste. But then, how much did she really know about Alex anyway? 'We could rewind it to the beginning if you like,' Sam offered.

'No, this is my favourite part.' She settled back into her chair. 'Imagine, seeing what the world would be like if you'd never been born.' She stared at the screen, taking a long sip from her glass.

'Our dear departed father might have stayed around, I guess,' Max suggested.

'You didn't fall for that line, did you?' Alex raised an eyebrow. Sam and Max looked at her.

'I don't believe Dad left because of us. Nothing's ever that simple, is it, Sam?' she said pointedly. 'It was just a convenient excuse.'

'Why did he need to bother with an excuse? He never came back,' said Max.

'No, I meant it was an excuse for Mum.'

'What are you talking about?'

'I think that in order to cope, to save face, she had to find a reason that had nothing to do with her, that wasn't her fault and that would put all the blame squarely on Dad's shoulders.' Alex paused. 'She was devastated when he left, you girls were probably too young to remember. So she's spent a lifetime loudly protesting that she was wronged by a no-good man, to make herself feel better. The irony is, it didn't work.' Alex paused to drain her glass. 'And look at the effect it's had on us. How were we ever supposed to feel okay about ourselves? Little wonder I married a father figure.'

'I knew it!' Max exclaimed.

'Don't get me wrong. I love Gordon very deeply. He's a good man, and devoted.' Alex reached for the bottle and topped up her glass. 'Samantha, you married when you were barely out of school, rushed into playing happy families and treated your own male child like he was some kind of trophy.'

'Did I?

'You did,' they said in unison.

'Sorry about that.'

'What about me?' said Max.

'Isn't it obvious? You choose men that you could never take seriously because you don't want to get serious. You use them like playthings, no commitment, no attachment, because you wouldn't dare risk someone abandoning you.'

Max frowned at her. 'Did you ever do psychology?'

Alex smiled. 'I didn't need to. You can read us like a children's book. A line drawing and a handful of words on a page.'

Max and Sam sat suitably chastened. They both reached for the bottle at the same time.

'What if we had been born boys?' Sam mused while Max refilled their glasses. 'I wonder what our lives would have been like then?'

'I think I would have been gay,' Max decided.

'Why?'

'Because I can't imagine being attracted to women in that way.'

Sam grinned, shaking her head. 'I wonder if I would have been more independent? Waited a bit before getting married. I don't think boys have the same dreams about growing up to become a husband, do they?' she sighed. 'What about you, Alex? How do you think life would have turned out for you if you had been born a man instead of a woman?'

She considered the question. 'Well, I'm in senior management with a global organisation. As we speak, my spouse is back at my mother's house with our child, washing dishes. And I'm here having a drink with you two, who would have been my brothers.' She arched an eyebrow. 'I think my life would probably be exactly the same if I were a man.'

Max and Sam hesitated for a moment. They weren't certain, but it sounded like Alex was making a joke. They both looked at her and saw the smile in her eyes, before all three of them burst into laughter.

When Sam waved her sisters off it was after eleven. She was agreeably tired and she felt sure she would sleep well tonight. She went around the house locking doors and turning off lights. But as Sam passed the computer she paused. She hit a key to bring up the screen again. After a delay of a moment or two, Hal's email reappeared. Sam clicked on *Reply*, and typed in 'I miss you too'. She hesitated only briefly before clicking *Send*. Then she quit the program and took herself off to bed.

Boxing Day

Sam sat in the car on the street outside her mother's house. She had been sitting there for a full ten minutes now, and no over-whelming urge had possessed her and magically transported her into the house. She was going to have to get there the normal way, through sheer force of will. She sighed heavily, picked up the bag of gifts she had brought with her and stepped out of the car. As she approached the front door, Sam could feel the appre-hension in her bones. It shouldn't be such a nerve-racking, unpleasant experience to visit her own mother. How had it come to this?

She knocked on the door and waited an unreasonable length of time before she heard footsteps coming up the hall. Bernice must have known it was her and she was clearly taking the opportunity to make her squirm.

'Hi Mum!' Sam said brightly as the door opened. 'Merry Christmas.'

Bernice stood there, holding the door knob, unmoved. 'It's not Christmas any more, Samantha. It's Boxing Day.'

'It's still the Christmas season, and you know what they say, 'tis the season . . .' Her voice trailed away as she watched her mother standing stock still, her face set hard. Sam took a deep breath. 'Aren't you going to ask me in?'

'So today you want to come in?'

Sam wasn't going to be drawn. 'Yes, thanks Mum,' she chirped, walking past her and through into the living room. 'Aunty Gwen has left already?'

'Alex and Gordon are taking her home right now, as a mat-ter of fact. I'm sure Alex would have told you that last night.'

If she had, Sam probably would have waited until she was sure Alex would be here. She could use the moral support.

'Well, these are from me and the kids,' said Sam, holding out the bag. 'Perhaps I should keep Aunty Gwen's present to give her myself?'

Bernice clasped her hands together. She didn't take the bag.

'Yes, Samantha, perhaps that's exactly what you should do. You ruined Christmas for her by not coming, and then dragging your sisters away like that –'

'I didn't drag them away.'

'They went to see you.'

Bernice was determined to make this unpleasant. What had Alex said yesterday? Don't lose the ground she'd gained. Sam had the chance, for the first time in her life, to be honest with her mother. She couldn't change Bernice, but she could change the way she related to her, or more correctly, reacted to her.

Sam put the bag down on the nearest armchair. 'Okay, Mum, I'm not going to do this. I refuse to any more. If my being here upsets you so much, then I should go. And if you're going to persist with the tone and the putdowns, I'd rather leave and save us both the grief. It's up to you.'

Bernice stood there, her face pinched. Sam had her over a barrel. She would have to state plainly that she wanted Sam to leave and that wasn't how Bernice did things. She preferred to pick away at the scab than rip it off and expose the wound to the light.

'I was just making tea. Would you like a cup?' said Bernice, changing tack and saving face in one fell swoop.

'Thank you.' Sam followed her mother into the kitchen. Bernice flicked the switch of the kettle and opened a cupboard door for cups.

'So, how was yesterday? Did you have a good Christmas?'

Bernice shrugged. 'It was quiet. Isabella had no one to play with.'

'I'm afraid that couldn't be helped. My kids wouldn't have been here regardless.'

'So now Jeff is dictating when he has the children?'

'No,' Sam said firmly. 'It was his turn this year. In fact he was kind enough to wait till Christmas morning to pick them up.'

'Hm, happy families!' Bernice smirked.

'I hope so, Mum. I hope we can all still manage to be happy despite what's happened.'

'Well, good luck with that,' muttered Bernice, pouring water into the teapot.

Sam leaned forward on the bench, considering her. 'You've never been very happy, have you, Mum?'

Bernice was clearly taken aback. 'I beg your pardon, Samantha?'

'I'm just saying, life doesn't appear to have made you very happy.'

'Well, what do you expect? It wasn't so easy being left on your own with three children, thirty odd years ago.'

'You think it's easy for me, Mum?' Sam raised an eyebrow. 'This is the hardest thing I've ever been through.'

'Well, imagine what it was like for me,' she said squarely.

'I'd like to. Why don't you tell me?'

Bernice breathed out. 'I feel like I'm on *Oprah*,' she muttered.

Sam folded her arms, waiting.

'When your father left, Maxine was only tiny, I cried all day, every day, I couldn't stop.' Her voice was brittle, guarded. 'It seemed to be beyond my control. I was certainly not normally predisposed to tears.'

'It sounds like postnatal depression.'

'Oh, for the love of . . . why does everything have to have a fancy label these days?' Bernice shook her head. 'I was upset. Of course I was, your father had walked out and left me with three small children.'

'You should have got help, nowadays you can get counselling –'

'I saw a counsellor. The sister at the hospital clinic arranged it after I cried all the way through my postnatal check-up.'

'That's great. That you saw a counsellor, I mean.'

'Oh, please!' she frowned. 'It was a complete waste of time. I had to do all the talking to keep the conversation going. He just sat there, nodding, repeating things I said straight back at me. The man was a fool. He gave me a prescription for some pills, but I tore it up when I got home.'

Sam wondered whether their childhood would have been

better or worse if Bernice had ended up addicted to Valium, which was probably all they were offering back then.

'Why did Dad leave, do you think?'

Bernice looked up abruptly. 'Maxine was another girl. Three strikes and he was out the door.'

'Do you really think that's all it was?' Sam asked carefully.

'What are you suggesting?'

'I'm not suggesting anything. I was just asking a question.'

'Well, then, what are you implying, Sam? That it was some-how my fault?'

'I didn't say that, I wouldn't say that,' she said levelly. 'He left you with three kids, there's no excusing that.'

'Exactly,' Bernice agreed. She handed Sam a cup of tea. 'I did everything for that man. I washed and cooked and cleaned and cared for his children. He couldn't have asked for more in a wife.'

Sam felt a chill right through to her heart. She was her mother's daughter.

Bernice reached for a tin on top of the refrigerator. 'I know you don't make Christmas cake any more, but do you still eat it?'

Sam didn't take the bait. 'Yes, thanks Mum, I'd love some.' She watched her mother cut the cake and arrange the pieces on a plate. 'So, if Max was a boy, he would have stayed and we would have been a happy family,' Sam suggested.

Bernice bristled. She didn't look at Sam. 'Yes, I suppose so,' she said, dismissively. 'Let's sit down, shall we?'

Sam followed her out to the living room and they sat opposite each other, across the coffee table. She wasn't going to get anywhere talking about their father. Bernice had a black and white view of her marriage, which the passing of so many years had set in stone. It was impossible, and perhaps even unreasonable, to expect her to have a different perspec-tive now. But there was something else Sam had always wanted to ask.

'What happened with Nan and Pop?'

'You have a lot of questions today, Samantha.'

She shrugged. 'I just always wondered why you didn't speak to them.'

'We spoke.'

'Come on, Mum. I was young, I wasn't stupid.'

Bernice sighed. 'They never liked your father. They tried to talk me out of marrying him.'

'Well, they had a point,' said Sam.

'Would you be sitting here right now if they'd succeeded?' Bernice returned sharply.

Sam blinked. 'No, of course not. You're absolutely right,' she said quietly. 'What happened?'

Bernice shrugged. 'I got on with my life and they moved up to Taloumbi after your pop retired. When your father left, they wanted to help, give me money, take care of us. But I wasn't about to give them the satisfaction,' she said smugly, sipping her tea.

'But you let them take us in the holidays?'

'When I started working I had no choice. But that's the only thing I ever let them do for me.' She replaced her cup in its saucer. 'I showed them.'

Sam felt a pang in her heart. Just exactly what had she shown them? Whatever it was, it wasn't worth the estrangement that persisted between them all those years. Nothing was worth that.

What an awful place to inhabit all that time. Lonely and self-righteous, proving her mettle to who knew any more? Who cared? She looked at Bernice, and suddenly she was no longer the formidable mother of her childhood.

There's the sad woman whose husband left her, and she never, ever got over it.

Sam made a silent vow that her life was going to add up to more than just surviving. Maybe she was her mother's daughter, but she wasn't going to repeat her mistakes. She didn't need to prove anything to anyone, she just wanted to be happy. She got to her feet and picked up the bag of gifts from where she'd left it earlier. She moved around the coffee table and sat on the couch next to her mother.

'Why don't you look at your presents, Mum?' said Sam. 'Ellie made something for you at pre-school.'

Palm Beach

'Maybe it's that one!' Jessica exclaimed, pointing towards a huge white mansion on the hilltop.

'I doubt it.'

They had arrived at Palm Beach and were winding their way slowly up to the crest of the hill, the kids getting more excited and unrealistic by the minute.

'It's number fourteen, isn't that right, Josh?' Sam asked.

He was navigator for the trip. Sam was annoyed that the stereotype about women and maps had proven true, at least for her family. But she wasn't giving up on Ellie yet. She just had to learn to read first.

'That must be the place over there,' said Josh, pointing ahead.

'I can't see any house,' Jessica declared.

On the eastern side the houses dropped down away from the road, so there was often only a garage or carport visible at street level. Sam spotted the number fourteen on a rickety mailbox next to a small weatherboard garage with a faded olive-green door. She steered the car onto a driveway paved with flagstones, stopping in front of the garage door.

'Are we here, Mummy?' said Ellie excitedly.

'I think we are.'

'Where's the house?'

'Let's go and find it.'

They got out of the car and made their way down an over-grown path, past a twisted wisteria vine, banana and pawpaw trees and, to Sam's delight, a frangipani in full bloom. The back wall of the house came into view across a small patch of lawn.

'Is this it?' said Jess, turning up her nose.

It was a simple, single-storey cottage, clad in the same dirty green weatherboards as the garage.

Sam smiled. 'It's perfect.' She found the key in her handbag. 'Just wait till you see inside, I bet the view is spectacular.'

They followed her into a darkened hall. The atmosphere was slightly musty, as if the house had been closed up for a while. Sam couldn't wait to throw open all the windows and doors to catch the breeze coming up from the ocean. The end of the hallway opened into a large room with a kitchen at one end. The opposite wall was apparently almost entirely windows, but they were concealed by a run of drab beige curtains. Sam found the cord to open them and as they swept aside, a view across the whole of Palm Beach was revealed. As she had predicted, it was spectacular.

She unlocked the doors and slid them back as a fresh gust of sea air flooded into the room. They stepped out onto a wide deck that appeared to be suspended above the tree line of Norfolk Island pines. From here they could see the full curved sweep of the beach below them, from the rocky outcrop at the southern end, all the way to where it mushroomed out to form the Barrenjoey Headland to the north.

'Wow,' murmured Jess.

'Awesome,' Josh added.

'Look Mummy,' cried Ellie. 'There's a lighthouse!'

Sam picked her up, perching her on one hip. 'So there is.'

'Can we go and see it one day, Mummy?'

'I don't know. We'll have to find out if it's open to tourists.'

'What's a toowist, Mummy?'

'Well, that's what we are,' Sam laughed. 'We're "toowists"!'

'I bags first dibs on a bedroom,' Josh blurted suddenly, dashing back inside.

'That's not fair!' Jess whined, following him.

Sam set Ellie down with a sigh and walked back into the living room.

'I bagsed, Jess!'

'But you've got a room to yourself at home, and at Dad's. I should get first choice here.'

'Says who?'

'Listen to me, you two,' Sam said loudly enough to get their attention. 'This is my holiday too, and I don't want to spend it refereeing your arguments. Now, can you please try to be reasonable for a change?'

'But Mum, I should get to choose. How come he gets everything?'

'Why don't you check out the rooms before you start arguing over them?'

As it turned out, there were six bedrooms in total and the issue was resolved. The house was deceiving from the outside. It was one of those places that had been tacked onto over time, rooms added according to need, resulting in a rabbit-warren floorplan that the kids proclaimed 'heaps cool'. There had been few other changes, though Sam was pretty sure a wall had been knocked out in the large room facing the deck. The bathroom was the original 1950s pink and grey, but clean and well kept. The floors had been stripped back to timber throughout, the furniture was dated, the kitchen basic but adequate. Sam loved it. There was something right about a holiday cottage that was slightly daggy. You wouldn't want to live in it, but it was a nice place to visit.

'How many sleeps will we be here for, Mummy?' Ellie was perched on the kitchen bench, munching on an apple while Sam packed the food away.

'You're staying for two whole weeks! That's fourteen sleeps, which takes up all your fingers and thumbs on both hands, and more.'

'How many more?'

'You have to count four toes as well,' said Sam, tickling Ellie's feet.

She giggled. 'When are we going to the beach, Mummy?'

'As soon as I pack away all this.'

Ellie climbed down off the bench and wandered out to the balcony. Sam watched her staring out to sea, her chin resting on the handrail. She turned around to look at her mother.

'It's so pretty, Mummy,' she called. 'Are we going soon?'

Sam looked at her watch and then at the boxes of groceries. Bugger it. They would still be here later, and it was already after two.

'Go tell your brother and sister to get ready.'

Two weeks later

'I wonder what the poor people are doing today?' pondered Maxine, peering out from under an enormous straw hat, her eyes shielded with dark glasses.

Sam laughed lazily from her deckchair. 'At least two of them are sitting on a balcony overlooking Palm Beach, sipping margaritas.'

'To handsome Hal,' said Max, raising her glass. 'For providing the location.'

'And to Dan, Dan, the Margarita Man,' added Sam.

'Dan makes a mean margarita, I'll give him that.'

'*Dan* is perfect,' Sam insisted. 'Especially since he volunteered to take the kids down to the beach for a game of cricket.'

'The thing is, he'd *rather* be down there playing cricket. He's a bigger kid than the lot of them. I think he might be hyperactive, he always has to be doing something. He wears me out.'

Sam glanced across at her with a wicked grin.

'Shut up you.'

'I didn't say anything.'

'Yes, but you were having impure thoughts.' Max sat up, looking at Sam. 'Speaking of which, when are you expecting Hal?'

'I'm not sure. I haven't heard from him since Christmas.'

'Well let's hope he's not too far off, so you two can make the most of the time alone.'

Sam had invited Max and Dan up for a few days, and in return they'd offered to take the kids to Jeff's, saving her the trip back and forth.

Max considered the frown on Sam's face. 'What's up?'

She shrugged. 'I'm still a little squeamish at the idea of being here all alone with him, for an extended period of time.'

Max laughed. 'It's a hell of a job, but someone's got to do it, right Sherl?' She sat up and faced her directly. 'Would you *please* get over yourself for a while? I'm not going to give you a lecture, I'm on holiday. But drop the defences, Sam, you're on holiday too. When Hal shows up, just relax and enjoy yourself. Go with the flow.'

'But what if it's like on TV, that as soon as the unresolved sexual tension is, well, resolved, the show always flops?'

'What?' Maxine screwed up her face.

'And remember, we're in rebound territory,' Sam continued breathlessly. 'We're both just out of painful break-ups, which is probably what drew us to each other in the first place, but is that enough to sustain a relationship? I have to wonder. And anyway, sustaining a relationship is a whole other problem, given that second time around it's even more likely to fail. I mean, you'd know the statistics, Max – isn't the divorce rate higher for second marriages, not that I'm talking about marriage, I mean, that's not even on the cards, talk about jumping the gun. But what if –'

'*Sam!*' Max cried. 'What if the friggin' sky falls in!'

Sam looked at her, startled.

'Would you stop being so full of doom and gloom? Quit worrying about what might or might not happen in the future. Life's not that certain. God, anyone would think you had some kind of terrible ordeal ahead of you, instead of a couple of weeks at Palm Beach with a bloody gorgeous man. What is your problem?'

Sam took a deep breath. 'You're right. Of course, you're absolutely right.'

Max swung her legs onto the deckchair, leaned her head

back and pulled her hat down over her face. 'You would have saved me a lot of trouble if you'd realised that a long time ago.'

Wednesday

The kids had been gone for three days and Sam had finished the only book she'd brought with her. She might have to drive out tomorrow to find a bookshop or at least a newsagent, or she'd go stir crazy.

It wasn't that she was bored all the time. During the day she went for long walks, swam in the ocean, took unbelievably self-indulgent naps and read. But at night she would start to feel edgy. There was a TV, but no video player, and there was never anything decent to watch over summer. Sam would turn on mindless programs and next thing her thoughts would wander. What day was it? How long had she been here? How long did she have left? How long had Hal said he'd be away? He hadn't been specific, but she thought he'd mentioned mid-January. Wouldn't that mean he'd be back by now? Maybe he had to go straight back to work here? Maybe he'd call on the weekend? Maybe she would go crazy if she kept on this train of thought? *Train*? Trains ran to schedules along a single track. Her thoughts were more like dodgem cars, careering all over the place out of control.

Sam was startled by a loud knock at the door.

'Yoohoo! Mr Buchanan, is anyone there? It's the agent for the house.'

Sam hurried up the hall to the flyscreen door. A smiling, middle-aged woman stood on the other side, wearing a neat navy blue suit and carrying a handbag and a clipboard.

'Oh, hello! Mrs Buchanan, I presume?' she chirped.

'Um . . .' Sam didn't really want to have to go into complicated explanations. 'How do you do?' she said as she opened the door and offered the woman her hand. 'Do you want to come in?'

'No, no, I don't want to bother you. We just like to check in with our tenants after a couple of weeks, make sure everything's okay, they aren't having any problems.'

'Oh no, everything's fine,' Sam nodded. The woman just looked at her, smiling. 'Mr Buchanan's not around, unfortunately,' Sam added. 'He was called overseas for work. But he should be back any day now.'

'Oh, what a shame,' the woman frowned with her eyes, but her lips were still smiling. 'And after he went to so much trouble to get the place.'

'He did?'

'Yes, we tried to direct him to the central coast,' she hesitated, 'It's a little more affordable, or accessible, shall we say? But he said he didn't have the time, and he was desperate, and well, frankly, he's very charming, isn't he?' she laughed, touching her hand to her cheek self-consciously. 'So anyway, the owners of this house are abroad at present, and they're putting it up for sale when they return. They didn't intend to use it this summer. We made a few calls, and eventually they agreed. I think they felt sorry for him, seeing as it was so close to Christmas.'

'It was close to Christmas?'

Her eyes widened. 'Oh dear, have I dobbed him in?'

'Um . . .' Sam didn't know what to say.

'I bet I know what's happened here,' she nodded her head knowingly. 'He was supposed to organise your holiday this year, wasn't he? And he forgot. Typical male,' she finished, rolling her eyes.

'Something like that,' Sam said with a faint smile.

'Please don't tell him I blabbed. He seemed like such a nice man.' She paused. 'Did you two meet over there?'

'Pardon?'

'In the States. He is American, isn't he? Or is he from Canada?'

'No, he's American. We met here.'

'Oh, that's nice.' The woman smiled again. She was a very

smiley woman. 'Well, I don't want to take up any more of your time. Please don't hesitate to contact the office if you need anything.' She opened her clipboard and slipped out a business card. 'I'll give you my card. I bet he forgot to leave one with you.'

'Thank you.'

Sam closed the screen door and pulled the main door shut as well, now that evening was coming on. She wandered back up the hall and into the kitchen, tucking the card under a magnet on the refrigerator. She poured herself a glass of wine and walked out onto the deck, leaning against the railing.

So Hal had only rented this place just before Christmas? Why did he tell her he'd had it for 'some time'? She wondered which weekend he had come up here. Was it before she went to his place that night? Why would he rush about frantically to rent a six-bedroom holiday house for himself when he knew he was going to be in the States? He must have rented it after they'd spent the night together. Why did he go to so much trouble? A smile crept onto her face, all of its own accord.

Her mobile phone started to ring. The kids had already phoned her today but maybe Ellie wanted to talk again. She did that sometimes when she was at her father's. Sam hurried inside and grabbed the phone off the bench. 'Hello?' she said, answering it.

'Hey Sam, how're you doing?'

Her mouth went dry and she felt goosebumps creeping up her legs and her arms. It was not a little distracting.

'Sam? It's me, Hal.'

'I know,' she said, finding her voice. 'Sorry, hi, when did you get back? Are you back?' she blurted.

'I flew in this afternoon.'

Her heart sank. He wouldn't be coming up tonight if he'd only just got home. 'How was your flight?'

'Long. How's everything there?'

'Wonderful. The house is terrific, Hal, the kids had the best time.'

'Had?'

'Mm, they're with their father. Max came up to collect them.'

'So you're having a holiday now?'

'I guess . . .' Sam murmured. Ask him. Just say the words. Sam could feel herself trembling inside. Relax and enjoy yourself, Max had said. She took a deep breath. 'Um, are you . . . well, were you thinking . . . well, would you like to come up?'

Hal breathed out heavily. 'I thought you were never going to ask.'

Sam heard a knock at the front door. 'Oh, could you hold on? There's someone at the door.'

She hurried up the hall. It must be the real estate woman again. She unlocked the door and swung it back. Hal stood on the other side of the screen door, his phone in one hand, a couple of bags and Zoey the zebra in the other.

'Hi honey, I'm home,' he said, looking straight into her eyes.

Sam couldn't move. 'Hi,' she said, her voice barely making it out of her throat. There was something else she ought to say, she knew there was, but she couldn't think what.

'Can I come in?' Hal asked eventually.

Oh, that was it. 'Yes, yes, of course, come in,' she said, stirring. He opened the screen door and stepped inside. They stood there looking at each other, still holding their phones.

'I'm going to hang up now,' said Hal into his, a smile playing at the corner of his lips. Sam nodded, and they both turned off their phones. Hal slipped his into his pocket.

'You brought Zoey,' she remarked, for the sake of saying something.

'And I brought you something too,' he said, passing her a brightly coloured gift bag. He set his overnight bag down on the floor and lay Zoey across it.

Sam peered inside the bag and smiled. It was filled with chocolates. Just about every kind of chocolate bar she'd ever seen, and some she hadn't.

'Emergency rations,' he explained. 'And there's some quality American stuff in there too.'

'Thank you.' Sam felt overcome. Hal was here, they were

alone. He had an overnight bag with him. 'Um, do you want
. . . um,' she stammered. 'Would you like me to show you
around?'

'I have seen the place.'

'I know.' She turned down the hall. 'Just before Christmas,
wasn't it?'

He followed her into the living room.

'Wasn't it?' she repeated, folding her arms, waiting for an
answer.

'I can't remember exactly.'

'The agent popped in earlier.'

Now Hal looked sheepish.

'Why did you say you rented the place a while ago?'

He sighed heavily. 'Because, if I'd told you I got it just for
you, you would have used the "A" word.'

Sam frowned.

'You would have said it's not "appropriate", and then you
would have given me the whole client spiel again, yada, yada,'
he sighed dramatically. 'It was easier to stretch the truth.'

She smiled shyly. He took a step closer, gazing at her
intently. Sam turned to the windows. 'Have you seen the view?'
she said lightly. 'It's fabulous.'

'Yes, it's a fabulous view,' he replied in a low voice, but she
knew he wasn't looking at the view at all. He reached for her
hand and laced his fingers through hers. Her heart started beating faster. She couldn't look at him, her eyes remained fixed out
the window, not that she could have described what she was
looking at.

'Are you hungry?' she asked.

'No.'

'Would you like a drink?'

'No thank you.' He stepped closer, till their bodies were just
touching. 'I missed you.'

'I know, I got your email.'

'And I got yours.'

She felt his lips brushing against her hair. It made her
tremble.

'I haven't shaved my legs,' Sam blurted suddenly.

Hal smiled down at her, a little taken aback. 'Well, that's a relief, neither have I,' he said. He reached up to remove her hair-clip, raking his fingers through to free her hair. It sent shivers down her spine. 'You have the most beautiful hair, and you always keep it tied back,' he murmured, cupping her face.

'Oh, and I don't have any, um, you know, thingummys,' she breathed.

'Look in the bag,' he said with a glint in his eye.

Sam realised she was still clutching the bag of chocolates. She foraged through them and drew out a long strip of small sealed plastic packets. She smiled. 'You're an optimist.'

'Funny, people always tell me I'm a realist,' he grinned. He took the bag from her and tossed it on a nearby chair. Then he pulled her close to him.

Sam felt a rush of emotion. The way he was looking at her, holding her. She wanted him. Go with the flow, Max had said.

'You weren't going to kiss me . . .'

'No . . . what made you think that?' he murmured as his lips sank into hers.

The next morning

Sam lay awake, watching Hal sleep. She'd thought the sun streaming through the sheer curtains might wake him, but he hadn't stirred. He was dead to the world. Jet-lagged probably. And maybe a little worn out as well, she smiled.

They had made love for hours, indulging in the fact they had condoms to spare this time. Sam felt like a teenager. Though not quite. As a teenager, sex had certainly been ener-getic, but it was also clumsy, often rushed, and ultimately unsatisfying a lot of the time, for her at least. And to some extent that pattern had endured into their marriage. Sam had read the magazine articles about bringing the spark back into the bedroom, but it felt forced, even embarrassing. It was better just to go on as they always had. Jeff usually made some kind of effort to tend to her needs first. If it wasn't working she just faked it to move him along. Their sex life had been like painting by numbers. No invention, no spontaneity. No passion. And then it had died out all together.

With Hal it was all passion, unbounded and seemingly inexhaustible. Sam felt completely uninhibited. He had a way of making her feel she was the most beautiful woman in the world. And he was no clumsy teenager. She didn't want to dwell on how Hal knew the things he did, she was just grateful for it.

She looked at him now, so peaceful and boyish as he slept. A wave of emotion washed over her, so intense it frightened her. It was scary to feel like this, to be thinking this way. To fall in love again was a huge risk and Sam didn't know if she was brave enough or strong enough to chance it.

Hal took a deep breath in and out. He blinked his eyes a couple of times and then looked straight at her. 'Hi.'

'Hi.'

'What are you looking at?' he said, his voice husky.

'You.'

He edged closer to her. 'What were you thinking about?'

'You,' she smiled.

'What's the matter?'

'Nothing.'

He touched his thumb to her forehead. 'You get this little crinkle here, between your eyes, when something's worrying you.' He leaned forward and kissed it. 'I love that little crinkle.'

Then he looked back into her eyes. 'And I love you.'

Sam swallowed. 'You shouldn't say things like that, you know,' she said quietly.

'Why not?'

'Because a girl is inclined to believe that kind of thing.'

'Oh? That's bad?'

'Well, she might think you really meant it. And she'd rather you were honest.'

'Okay, let me try again.'

Sam's heart lurched.

'I love the little crease on your forehead,' he murmured, kissing it again. He looked back at her. 'And I love you, Samantha Jean.'

She stared at him, tears springing into her eyes.

'So you can stop worrying.' He closed his arms around her, turning over onto his back so that her head came to rest on his chest.

Sam lay there listening to his heart beating as his breathing settled into a rhythm. She raised her head to look up at him.

'Hal,' she said softly.

He didn't stir. He'd drifted off to sleep again.

She watched him for a moment. 'I love you too,' she whispered.

The day was blue and bright and sunny, like every other day had been since Sam had arrived at Palm Beach. Hal had dozed for another half hour before hauling himself out of bed and insisting they do something active and outdoors before he slept the whole day away.

'And if I do that, I'll never get over this jet-lag,' he explained. 'I'll be up all night.'

'You won't hear me complaining,' Sam had muttered salaciously. Which had landed them back in bed.

Another hour later they emerged into the sunshine and onto the beach. When Hal headed for the rock pool, Sam dragged him into the surf, insisting it would do more to wake him up and clear his head.

Afterwards they sat on the beach, her back against his chest, letting the sun dry them off. Hal pointed out the sailing boats rounding Barrenjoey Head.

'I'll take you sailing this week.'

'I don't think so.'

'Come on, you made me go in the surf.'

'Oh please,' Sam dismissed. 'You can hardly call this surf.'

'There are waves,' he protested.

'They're wussy waves.'

'What does that mean?'

'What?' Sam peered around at him.

'Wussy.'

'Oh. Weak, cowardly, you know, that kind of thing. You're a "wuss" if you think that's real surf out there.'

'Then you're a wuss if you won't come sailing with me.'

'No I'm not. I'm just not interested.'

'What are you so afraid of?'

She shrugged, turning to look out to sea. 'I'm not afraid.'

He wrapped his arms around her from behind. 'Tell me,' he urged gently.

Sam rested her head back against his shoulder. 'Well, I still don't understand how you can have any control. What if the wind's blowing against you?'

'You can sail against the wind.' He spoke softly, close to her ear. 'In fact, you have to learn how, because you won't always have the wind behind you. But you can't just sail right into it, you have to tack or reach. And sometimes you can go as fast reaching, in fact faster, as when you're running with the wind.'

'What if the wind gets too strong though, and you can't sail against it? What if it's too hard?'

'Well, if there's a storm, sometimes you have to ride it out as best you can. You shorten sail, and you don't make much headway, but at least you stay afloat until it passes.'

'Or the boat capsizes,' she sighed, 'and you end up being washed up onto the rocks, battered and bleeding. Or else you drown.'

'Sam!' Hal chided. He turned her around to face him. 'I know you've been through a lot, but you can't really think life's that grim, can you?'

She smiled. 'I thought we were talking about sailing?'

He smiled back at her, pulling her close to him. How had she turned into this bleak, pessimistic person, so sure that life would disappoint her? There must have been a time when she was happy and at least a little hopeful. At Nan and Pop's she remembered feeling happy, hiding in the dunes, following Pop's footsteps. She'd felt happy when her children were born. A crystal clear, pure type of happiness that depended on nothing more than their mere existence in the world. And she must have been happy with Jeff, at least early on. They were always striving *to be* happy, but had they ever made it? Had she stopped long enough to know if she was happy?

Sam realised she felt happy right now, just sitting on a beach, leaning against Hal. Maybe happiness only came in moments, and you had to grab those moments whenever you could, as often as they came your way, and wring every joyful drop out of them.

She jumped to her feet. 'I'll race you back to the house,' she said, her eyes full of mischief, flicking Hal with her towel.

'Hey, wait up,' he called after her, but she was already halfway up the beach. She was headed for a track the kids had found which was a shortcut back up the hill. Sam could hear Hal gaining on her and it sent shivers right through her.

She hit the track. It was steep and narrow, overgrown with bamboo and fishbone ferns. Hal was not far behind but she was more sure-footed, having trekked through here at least twice a day for the last couple of weeks. She knew where the ground was uneven, where to duck the branches. Hal didn't. Sam could hear him cursing behind her as she came out from the cover of the trees and onto the road. She was short of breath, but somehow she found the energy to sprint down the street. She was just opening the door of the house as Hal made it to the other side of the lawn.

'Samantha!' he called with mock menace, and she shrieked, running up the hall. In a few strides he'd caught her and Sam swung around, throwing her arms around him, fastening her mouth onto his. They were both panting as they kissed each other hungrily.

'Sam,' Hal gasped eventually, 'you're gonna give me a heart attack.'

'Old man,' she murmured against his lips.

'Right,' he said, lifting her off the floor and striding into the bedroom. He tossed her back onto the bed and she lay there, laughing, as he climbed on top of her, looking down at her with a glint in his eye. 'Did you say old man?'

Sam thought she heard something out in the main room. It was the silly ring tone Jess had programmed into her mobile.

'That's my phone,' she breathed. 'I should get it.'

'Oh, I don't think so,' he murmured huskily. He unravelled the sarong she had wrapped around her and then slowly, deliberately, he began to peel her swimming costume down, covering every square inch of her body with soft, feathery kisses.

The curtains lifted as the salty breeze fluttered across them. Sam lay back, closing her eyes, her breath coming in short, uneven gasps. She felt his tongue warm on her skin, his fingertips, his limbs sliding against hers. She tasted the warmth of his mouth as it found hers again. She felt his hands clasping hers tight, where they lay above her head. Then she felt him moving inside her, sending spasms like a ripple effect out from deep inside her belly. She could feel his blood pulsing, his heart beating against her chest, his breath warm on her neck when he eventually collapsed against her. She felt utterly, blissfully spent. She felt happy.

'I love you,' he murmured.

Sam held her breath. She knew she should say it back, so that he could hear her this time. She didn't know why she was hesitating, what was stopping her.

Hal lifted his head and gazed down at her. 'What's wrong?'

'Nothing,' she insisted.

Sam heard the phone ring again. She groaned.

'Don't worry about it,' Hal said. 'You can check your calls later.' He shifted off her, lying at her side. 'Tell me what's on your mind.'

'I'm fine, Hal.'

'No, you're not,' he said gently, touching her forehead. 'You've got that little crinkle again. You're not okay with this yet, are you?'

Sam turned onto her side, facing him. 'I don't know,' she said quietly.

'What is it?'

She thought about it. 'It still feels a little unreal.'

'Feels pretty real to me,' he said, nuzzling into her neck. Then he drew back to look at her again. 'Tell me what you mean.'

'Well,' Sam thought about the best way to explain herself, 'you know Lyle Lovett and Julia Roberts?'

He frowned at her. 'Are you heading somewhere particular with this?'

'Trust me,' said Sam. 'Did you know Lyle Lovett and Julia Roberts were married once?'

'Vaguely.'

'Mm, well, that's because it only lasted about five minutes,' said Sam. 'Everyone knew it would never work, because they weren't in the same league. Like you and me. Get it?'

Hal looked confused. 'So, you're saying I'm like Lyle Lovett?'

'No, *I'm* like Lyle Lovett.'

'Then I'm like Julia Roberts?' he frowned.

'Work with me here, Hal.' She sighed. 'The thing is, you could get anyone –'

'Sam! Cut it out.'

'It's okay, Hal –'

'No it's not, I'm not going to listen to you talk like that. You're a beautiful woman –'

'Well, of course you're going to say that.'

'That's right! Of course I'm going to say that.'

'Hal, I'm lying naked beside you, it would be impolite to say otherwise.'

'No, it would be untrue to say otherwise.'

She was about to go on when Hal put a finger to her lips. 'Sam, this is one of those times you really should stop talking.' She just looked at him as he stroked her cheek. 'I wish you could see yourself the way I see you. You really have no idea how beautiful you are, do you?'

There was nothing she could say to that.

'Who comes up with these ideas, Sam?' He leaned forward

and kissed her softly. 'And what league are you in if you're someone who's easy to talk to, laugh with . . .'

'Who has three kids?' Sam murmured against his lips.

Hal smiled. 'They earn you bonus points.' He pulled her close, kissing her persuasively until her mobile phone started to ring again.

'Bugger,' she breathed. 'That's the third time,' she said, sitting up.

'Leave it,' he urged.

'I can't, remember the three kids?'

She tried to gather her sarong around her, but Hal was lying across half of it. 'Can you move, please?'

'I'd rather watch you run off naked.'

'You and the rest of Palm Beach,' she said. 'The curtains are all open out there.' He shifted off the sarong and Sam grabbed it, wrapping it around herself as she hurried out of the room.

The phone had stopped by the time she got to it, but the number appearing on the screen was Jeff's mobile, so she returned the call.

'Oh, hi Sam,' he said when he answered it. 'I've been trying to contact you for the last hour or so.' He sounded serious.

'What's wrong?'

'Um, look, everyone's okay, really. It's not that bad.'

Her stomach turned to lead. The words were supposed to reassure her but they had the opposite effect. 'What's happened?'

'There's been a bit of an accident –'

'What? Who?'

'Just calm down and let me explain –'

'Don't tell me to calm down, Jeff!'

She heard him sigh. 'It's Josh. His arm. We don't know for sure yet, he hasn't been to X-ray –'

'Oh God! Where are you?'

'Casualty.'

'Which fucking hospital?' she cried.

'Prince of Wales.'

She hung up the phone and stood there trembling. She didn't even know what had happened, but she couldn't listen to Jeff's patronising voice another second. She had to get to her son.

Hal appeared in the doorway, half dressed. 'What's wrong?'

'Josh is in the hospital,' she said briskly, striding past him.

'Christ, what happened?'

'I don't know.' She opened the wardrobe door and yanked a dress off its hanger. 'It's his arm, apparently. They're waiting for X-rays.'

'What did he do to it?'

Sam grabbed underwear from a drawer in the dresser. 'I don't know, okay? Stop hassling me!'

'I didn't mean to hassle you, Sam.'

'Look, I didn't ask any questions, I just want to get to the hospital, okay?'

'Sure,' said Hal. 'I'll drive you.'

'I can drive myself,' she snapped.

'Sam,' he said firmly, taking her by the shoulders, 'you're upset, you shouldn't be driving a car in the state you're in.'

'Don't patronise me!' She was almost shouting.

Hal looked squarely at her. 'I'm not patronising you, Sam. But just think about it for a second. Do you want another accident in the family today?'

Her face crumpled as a sob escaped from her throat. Hal went to pull her closer to him, but she backed away. 'We have to hurry,' she said, wiping her eyes.

She dressed quickly. Hal pulled on a T-shirt and went around the house closing the windows and locking them. Sam didn't know what to bring with her. She wouldn't be back tonight, she didn't know when she'd be back. It was too hard to think about it, so in the end she just grabbed her handbag and her phone.

They didn't speak as they headed out of Palm Beach. They were sure to hit peak-hour traffic when they got closer to the city, but for now the roads were relatively quiet. Sam wished she was already there, at the hospital, so she could see for herself that Josh was alright. But they were more than an hour away and there was nothing she could do about it. She could call Jeff for more information, but she was so close to the edge she knew she'd just freak out again. Hal pulled up at traffic lights and reached across to squeeze her hand. She didn't look at him, didn't respond in any way. She couldn't deal with him now. When the lights turned green, he released her hand and drove on. Sam stared vacantly out the window. She tried to focus on the steady beat of the car tyres as they crossed the seams in the concrete road. Anything to stop the thoughts tormenting her mind. She was having sex while her son was having an accident. She'd ignored her phone ringing. She *always* answered the phone when the kids weren't with her. She was angry with Hal for telling her to leave it, she was angry with Jeff for placing her son in danger. But more than anything, Sam was angry with herself.

When they arrived at the emergency entrance to the hospital, Sam barked at Hal to let her out. He pulled over immediately.

'I'll find you inside as soon as I've parked the car,' he said as she jumped out.

Sam hurried breathlessly through the doors and directly over to the reception desk.

'My son is here somewhere,' she blurted. 'How can I find him?'

'Name please,' said the woman automatically.

'Samantha Holmes. Um, his name is Josh. Joshua Holmes.' Sam spelt out their surname.

The woman keyed it into her computer and squinted at the screen. 'Okay, he was sent up to X-ray, let me just check if he's back,' she said, picking up the telephone.

Sam clutched her arms around her anxiously and turned to face the waiting room. She heard a squeal, 'Mummy!' and then Ellie appeared from between the rows of seats, running towards her. Sam stooped to give her a hug. 'Hello darling, are you alright?'

'Yes, but Joshy braked his arm!' she exclaimed.

God, Sam still didn't know anything. Which arm? How badly was it broken? Jessica was coming over now. Where the fuck was Jeff? She supposed he was with Josh, but had he just left the girls out here on their own? Then Sam noticed somebody shadowing Jess, walking behind her. She froze. It had to be Jodi. Why did she have to deal with everything at once?

'Hi Mum,' said Jess.

'Do you know where your father is?' Sam said impatiently, ignoring the woman standing behind her.

'He's with Josh.'

'Excuse me, Mrs Holmes?' said the woman at the desk. Sam turned around. 'Your son is back from X-ray. I'll take you through to him if you like.'

'Thanks.' Sam didn't know what to do with the girls. She couldn't even look at Jodi, much less engage her in conversation.

'Hal!' Ellie cried, running across to him as he appeared through the doors. He lifted her into his arms and carried her over to where they were all standing.

'I have to go to Josh,' Sam told him. She wasn't going to bother with introductions or any other pleasantries. They could sort themselves out. 'Can you stay with the girls?'

Hal nodded. 'Sure, go on.'

Sam followed the woman through swing doors into the large, open ward. She spotted Josh at the far end. Jeff was sitting in a chair beside his bed.

'I can see them,' Sam said to the woman. 'Thank you.'

Jeff stood when he caught sight of her. 'Sam, I was just about to come out to see if you'd made it yet.'

She ignored him and walked to the other side of the bed. 'How are you, honey?' she said gently, stroking Josh's hair. His arm was loosely bandaged and strapped to a back slab. She leaned down to kiss his forehead.

'Mum,' he whined, pulling a face.

'He's a bit groggy,' Jeff explained. 'They had to give him something for the pain.'

Sam looked up at him then, for the first time. 'What did the X-rays show?'

Jeff swallowed. 'His wrist is fractured and he has another break further up, near his elbow. It's displaced, they're going to have to do an open reduction.'

'What does that mean?'

'They have to use pins and a plate to set the bone. It has to be done in theatre under a general anaesthetic.'

'Shit,' Sam breathed. She paused, looking at him grimly. 'What happened?'

Jeff looked guilty, as well he should. 'He fell off a bike.'

'A bike?' Sam frowned. She had assumed this had happened skating. Josh hadn't ridden his bike in ages. And he'd never taken it to his father's place. 'What bike?'

'It was a trail bike. There's a place just outside Sydney –'

'Do you mean a *motorbike*?' Sam raised her voice just slightly, conscious of her surroundings.

Jeff nodded. His face had turned white.

'Wasso cool, Mum,' Josh slurred, his eyes barely open.

'You took a fifteen-year-old boy motorbike riding?' Sam exclaimed in a shrill whisper. 'What the hell were you thinking?'

'It's perfectly safe –'

'Obviously it isn't!'

That stopped him in his tracks, momentarily. 'Look, we can't talk about this now, here.'

'Fine!' Sam glared at him. She turned to Josh. 'Honey, we're just going out to check on the girls. Are you alright?' she said gently.

'Mm,' he grunted. His eyes were closed now.

Sam marched out of the ward and through to the waiting room, Jeff trailing behind her. She spotted Hal on a bench against the far wall, with Ellie on his lap. Jessica was next to him and beside her, Jodi, Sam presumed. She still had not really looked at the woman. From this distance she took in that she was wearing a dark top and she had long, mousy-coloured hair. Hal got to his feet as they approached.

'How's Josh?' he asked, concerned.

'His arm's smashed to pieces by the sounds of it,' said Sam. 'He's going to need surgery and a metal plate and God knows what else.' Everyone was standing in a circle, looking awkward. She was going to have to say something. 'This is Hal Buchanan, a friend of mine. Hal, this is Jeff.'

The two men shook hands. 'How're you doing,' said Hal.

Jeff cleared his throat. 'This is Jodi,' he said, looking at Hal.

'We've introduced ourselves,' Hal explained.

Jeff glanced at Sam. 'Sam, Jodi.'

This was excruciating. Sam barely looked at her, she just nodded in her direction. 'Jeff, what were you doing taking Josh motorbike riding?'

'I went too, Mummy!' Ellie chirped.

Sam glared incredulously at Jeff.

'The girls were only on minibikes,' he explained.

'I can't believe this,' Sam said, clenching her teeth.

'Look, it's a big family amusement park. They provide safety gear, they take all the appropriate measures, it's not dangerous –'

'So help me Jeff, if you say one more word about it being not fucking dangerous, I'll slap you!' Sam blurted.

Hal and Jodi moved discreetly away, ushering the girls over to the other side of the waiting room.

'Your son has been injured, for crying out loud!' Sam continued. 'When are you going to get it through your thick skull that it was dangerous? And stupid. And reckless!'

'He could have done it skating –'

'But he didn't, did he!' she cried, raising her arms. People were starting to look, but Sam was oblivious to them. 'I can't trust you with the kids if you're going to do things like this!'

'What are you saying, Sam?' Jeff said grimly.

'Clearly I've been way too lenient. I'm going to have to rethink the whole access arrangement.'

Jeff clenched his jaw. 'I don't think you get to decide things like that.'

'Alright,' she sneered, 'we'll take it to court and let a magistrate decide then.'

'Sam,' he sighed, 'I realise you're upset –'

'Don't fucking patronise me, Jeff!' she said, raising her voice. People were definitely looking now.

'But you're being ridiculous,' he said firmly. 'You think you can stop me from seeing my children just because one of them had an accident while he was with me?'

'You let a fifteen year old ride a motorbike, Jeff!' she cried. 'It wasn't an innocent, unavoidable accident. It was dangerous and foolish. And you didn't get my permission.'

'I don't need your permission to take my son to a registered fun park,' he sniped. 'Go right ahead, Sam, take it to court, see how far you get.'

She folded her arms defiantly. 'You think this is the only thing I have against you?'

'Sam, stop this.'

'What about the time Josh ran off from your place?'

He stared at her. 'I can't believe you're bringing that up now.'

'I'll bring up whatever I like, Jeff. You're not going to get your own way this time. You created this whole mess, you can live with the fallout.' Sam stood glaring at him defiantly. 'You can go now. There's no need for you to be here any longer. I'll stay with Josh.'

'Then I'll take the girls.'

'No way, you're not having the girls.'

'Well, what are you going to do with them? Whatever's going on in your head, Sam, I've got rights, and if you want to make this difficult, then I will too. I don't even know your boyfriend. I don't want the girls going home with him.'

'But it's alright for them to stay with you and *your* girl-friend? I never got a say in that!' she shrilled. 'And anyway, he's not my boyfriend.'

'I don't care. They're not going with him,' Jeff said, resolved.

Sam was furious. 'Right. You stay with Josh. Sleep in a chair all night, I don't give a fuck. What time are they taking him to theatre in the morning?'

'They haven't said yet.'

'Fine, I'll be here first thing. I'll get Max to stay with the girls.'

Jeff sighed heavily. 'It doesn't have to be like this, Sam,' he said, his tone softening.

She just looked at him. 'Apparently it does.'

Sam sat in the car, trembling with rage. She had gone back into the ward to say goodbye to Josh, but he was completely knocked out by the painkillers. She left without another word to Jeff, standing impatiently aside while the girls said goodbye. She watched Jodi out of the corner of her eye. She was almost the biggest surprise today. She was nothing like Sam had expected. She was a lot older, for one thing – she couldn't have been much younger than Sam. And she was, to put it bluntly, pretty ordinary. You could pass her in the street without taking a second glance. Sam had always imagined that Jeff had left her for someone young and stunning. She didn't know if it bothered her more or less that Jodi was neither of those things.

Hal drove them home to Marrickville. They had travelled down from Palm Beach in his car and Sam was not sure what she was going to do about getting her own car back, at least for the next couple of days. She'd have to work it out later. The tension was palpable all the way home. The girls said nothing, obviously subdued by their mother's outburst. She hoped they hadn't heard most of it. She'd never wanted her children to have to witness that kind of thing. But she couldn't protect them forever, that fact was becoming patently clear to her after today's events.

Hal pulled up in front of the house and cut the engine.

'Thank you,' she said curtly. 'Come on, girls, out you get.'

'What are you going to do about a car?' Hal asked as she opened the door. 'Do you want me to pick up some things for you? You won't have any milk, or bread –'

'I'll be fine, I'll sort something out,' she dismissed, getting out of the car. Jessica helped Ellie out of the back seat and Sam closed the door. She handed Jess her keys. 'Go on inside.'

'Sam,' Hal called from inside the car. She bent over to look at him. 'You're sure you don't want me to hang around?'

'I need to get the girls settled and call Max,' she said briskly. 'Thanks for the lift home.'

'Sam, don't shut me out,' he said in a quiet voice. 'Not after . . . everything.'

'This isn't about you,' she returned. 'I just want to be with my kids.'

She straightened up and closed the car door. She walked determinedly down the path to the house and went inside without so much as a wave in Hal's direction. She picked up the phone and dialled Max's number. Thankfully it was her and not her machine that answered.

'Hi Max,' Sam breathed. 'How early can you get here in the morning?'

'Why? What's going on?'

But Sam couldn't speak any more. She just burst into tears.

Friday

Max had come to the house soon after Sam called and had stayed the night. Sam only gave her sketchy details – she couldn't go into the whole drama with her at the moment. It was enough that Josh had broken his arm and was in the hospital. Max didn't suspect there was anything more.

Sam left the house while they were all still sleeping. At the hospital, Josh had been moved from Casualty to a ward overnight. When she found her way there, he was awake but groggy.

'How are you feeling, Josh?' Sam said gently, after kissing him on the forehead. He didn't protest this time. He looked frightened and much younger, like a little boy.

'He's had a bad night,' said Jeff from his seat beside the bed. He looked dreadful, he must have hardly slept. There was a harshness in his eyes when they met Sam's. 'He couldn't get comfortable with his arm strapped like that, and he was in a fair bit of pain.'

She stroked Josh's forehead as Jeff spoke.

'They're coming to take him shortly. They've already given him something to relax him.'

'Pre-ops,' Sam nodded. 'You'll be alright,' she said to Josh. 'The worst of it will be over soon. Once your arm is set in plaster, you're going to feel a lot better.'

He looked up at her bravely, but Sam could see the fear in his eyes. A nurse and an orderly arrived soon after, and Jeff and Sam followed as they wheeled his bed down to theatre. Sam stood holding Josh's hand while the paperwork was completed. He held on tight. When they were ready to take him in, she kissed him on the forehead, and so did Jeff. She smiled bravely, trying to show Josh that she wasn't worried, when in fact her insides were like jelly. The doors closed as they pushed his bed through, and after that they couldn't see him any more.

'You should go, Jeff, get some sleep,' said Sam. 'You look terrible. I'm staying anyway.'

He shook his head. 'No, I want to be here when he wakes up.'

'Fair enough.' She paused. 'Well, take a break then, get some coffee. Do you have any calls you have to make?' she said, strategically avoiding Jodi's name.

'We have to talk, Sam.'

She sighed. 'We will, but not now. I'm not up to it. And I don't think you are either.'

'I'll be the judge of that,' he said firmly.

Sam looked at him. She could see hurt and anger in his eyes, but also a kind of resolve.

'I know you were in shock yesterday,' Jeff began. 'I understand that, honestly I do, I'm not being patronising,' he added. 'But you said some things that I believe were unreasonable, and if you take the time to think about them, once Josh is home and he's okay, well, I think you might have a change of heart. That's if you want the best for the kids, which I know you do, I know that's all you've ever wanted. And it's all I want too.'

Jeff didn't usually talk so fast. Sam knew he was quite upset. She had to put him out of his misery.

'Of course I was being unreasonable,' she said plainly, watching the expression on his face shift. 'Thank you for putting it down to shock. I hope that's what it was. Or else I've turned into some kind of crazy, psycho bitch from hell.'

Jeff looked dumbfounded.

Sam sighed heavily. 'I know we have a lot to talk about, Jeff. But I'm really not up to it right now. I wouldn't be able to think straight and I'm likely to say something else I'll regret. Can we just get through today, wait till we know Josh is alright?'

All signs of anger faded from his features. 'Of course.'

They took a seat and waited together in silence. Sam was glad Jeff was there beside her. He was the only other person in the world who cared about Josh as much as she did. It was right that they were sharing this. It was right that they were both here for him.

Jeff went home soon after they were shown into Recovery to see Josh. Sam stayed with him for the rest of the day. The hospital's policy was to keep patients in for four hours after general anaesthetic, in case of complications. Josh bounced back quickly, being so young, and he was clearly experiencing relief with his arm secure. It wasn't long before he complained he was hungry, and he woofed down the tray of food that was brought to him. Sam phoned Max around midday to let her know when they were likely to be home.

'Hal's called a couple of times,' Max told her.

'Oh?'

'He didn't want to bother you at the hospital, he just wanted to know when to come and pick you up. He said you should give him a ring.'

'I'll get a taxi.'

'Why? Hal said it's no trouble. He's waiting to hear from you.'

'Well, he can wait,' said Sam impatiently. 'I've got enough on my plate without worrying about him as well.'

'What's going on?' said Max. 'Have you two had another fight?'

'No,' Sam insisted. 'He's . . . it's all too much to deal with at the moment, okay?'

'He just wants to give you a lift, Sherl, what's so hard to deal with about that? It'll make things easier for you.'

'Look, I'll talk to him later. For now, I just want to bring Josh home as soon as they say so. I don't want to be waiting around for a lift.'

'Oh, so you'll wait around for a taxi instead?'

'Maxine!' Sam snapped. Then she took a deep breath. She had to start controlling her temper. 'Please, just trust me that I'm handling things the best way I know how. I'll talk to Hal later. And I'll see you in a couple of hours.'

When Sam and Josh arrived home the girls were absorbed in a video, but they stopped it long enough to fuss over his cast.

'Very impressive, Josh,' Max remarked. 'You'll pull the chicks with that.'

'Can I write my name on it, Joshy?' Ellie pleaded.

'Maybe tomorrow,' Sam interrupted. 'He's still a little sore.'

'Can I go on the internet, Mum?' asked Josh.

He must have been having withdrawals by now. 'I suppose so, for a little while.'

'It's not going to hurt my arm, Mum,' he pointed out.

'No, just your brain,' she quipped.

The girls went back to their video and Sam walked out to the kitchen. Max handed her a glass of wine. 'Here you go,' she said. 'I figured you could use this. You had nothing in the fridge so I called Dan and he picked up some things. Just the basics — you know, milk, bread, chocolate. And dinner's in the oven.'

Sam hooked her arm around Maxine's neck and hugged

her. 'You are a wonderful woman. And Dan is a wonderful man, make sure you thank him for me.'

'Speaking of wonderful men,' Max said carefully, 'Hal rang again.'

Sam sighed, taking a mouthful of wine.

'What's going on, Sam?'

She looked at Max. 'More than I can handle.'

Max frowned at her.

'When I got to the hospital yesterday, I freaked out at Jeff, I made a huge scene in the middle of Casualty. I said I wasn't going to let him have the kids any more, that I'd go to a magistrate if I had to.'

Max whistled. 'Still, you were in shock.'

'Well, that's my excuse and I'm sticking to it.'

'But what's that got to do with Hal? Are you worried he thinks you're a nutter?'

'Oh, it's a bit late for me to start worrying about that.' She sighed. 'It's not that. I just don't think this is the right time for me to be starting a relationship.'

'Oh, not this again.'

Sam shrugged. 'I haven't worked myself out yet, how can I be any good to anyone else?'

'You think that people in relationships are all worked out, Sam?'

'No, that's why so many of them are stuffed. I've already had one disaster, I don't want another one right on top of it.'

'Sam, you're doing the avoiding thing —'

'Sure I am,' she agreed. 'I'm avoiding stress and pain and heartbreak. Look what's ahead of me. I have to sort things out with Jeff. Josh is going to need extra attention for the next month or two, physio, God knows what else. Ellie's starting school in a couple of weeks. And I'm about to start a new job. I can't cope with a relationship on top of all that.'

'So take it slowly.'

'Max, this would have to be the slowest courtship in history,' Sam cried. 'We've been skirting around the edges for almost a year. If it was going to work, it would have by now.'

She felt a cramping pain in her chest as she said the words. She looked squarely at Max. 'I have a terrible feeling that Hal is the absolutely right person at the absolutely wrong time.'

By nine o'clock the children were all in bed, Max had left and the house was quiet. Josh had insisted he wasn't tired and that he would read in his room for a while, but when Sam went to check on him, he was out like a light, a surfing magazine opened across his chest. She was worried about him, he was sure to have another unsettled night's sleep. She left his door open so she would be able to hear him from her room. She needed to get to bed herself, but she was not so sure she'd be able to get to sleep.

Sam heard a knock at the front door. She had an uneasy feeling she knew exactly who it was going to be.

And she was right. As she opened the door, Hal was standing on the verandah, a faint, sad smile on his face, his eyes filled with concern.

'Hey Sam, how're you doing?' he said quietly.

Oh, she was not ready for this.

'Okay,' she croaked. She stepped out onto the verandah, closing the door behind her.

'You don't want me to come in,' he said in a resigned tone.

'The kids are all in bed. I was just headed there myself.'

'How's Josh?'

'He'll be alright.'

'What about you?' he said gently.

She shrugged. 'I'm just tired.' She couldn't look at him.

Hal reached up to stroke her cheek with the back of his fingers. Sam caught her breath. 'Don't . . .'

He let his hand drop. 'Don't do this, Sam. Not again.'

She lifted her eyes to meet his. 'What do you mean?'

'Don't use this as another excuse to back away from me,' he said squarely.

'I'm not,' Sam faltered. 'It's not an excuse.'

He folded his arms, watching her. 'Then what's this about?'

Sam could feel tears welling in her chest. She had to keep calm if she was going to get through this. She took a breath. 'I just can't cope with all of this right now. At the beach, alone with you, it was wonderful, Hal. But it wasn't real life. I was kidding myself. I have three kids, a job, an ex-husband. That's my life, I can't pretend it doesn't exist.'

'I never asked you to do that.'

'You asked me to ignore the phone,' she returned, biting her lip.

He frowned. 'What?'

Sam cleared her throat. 'I should have answered my phone.'

'It wouldn't have made any difference,' said Hal. 'Josh's arm was already broken.'

'I realise that. But at least I should have picked up the damned phone!' she said, raising her voice.

'What difference would it have made?' Hal cried.

'It would have made a difference to me!' Sam was shouting now. Her words echoed in the space between them.

Hal glared at her. 'You'll find any damn excuse, won't you, Sam? Any opportunity to see the worst. What's wrong with you? What the fuck does it take to make you happy?'

'I don't know,' Sam swallowed, staring up at him earnestly. 'I honestly don't know. I'm beginning to think it's a family curse.' She took a breath, trying to collect herself. 'I feel like I don't even know who I am. I was somebody else in my marriage. I play-acted a role for sixteen years, and now this is real life without the safety net and I'm not sure if I can do it.'

'Then let's do it together,' he urged.

She met his eyes directly. 'Don't you see, Hal, I have to do this for myself. You can't fix it this time. You can't make it right.'

'But I love you, Sam. And I think you love me,' he went on. 'You've never said the words, but I've seen it in your eyes –'

'Of course I love you,' Sam blurted.

He stared at her, breathing hard. 'Then we can make it work,' he insisted, grasping her hands. But she shrugged them off.

'Just loving each other isn't enough, Hal! Jeff and I loved each other once. So did you and Lisa. My father must have loved my mother enough to marry her. Love is overrated!' she declared, raising her arms. 'You might have a few good years, as long as you're not being jealous or possessive or pissed off with each other for some reason. But you do have passion and that keeps you going, you put up with all the rest. Then after a while the passion fades, you can't be bothered being jealous or possessive, you're just pissed off. You've got bills and a mortgage and all the rest of the shit, and you stop having sex and you don't even like each other any more,' she cried, her voice breaking. 'And then it's just awful. I don't want to go through that again.'

'It doesn't have to be like that, Sam,' said Hal.

'But it seems to be how things turn out, more often than not,' she said sadly. 'You turn into some kind of crazy person, standing in a crowded hospital waiting room, screaming at the father of your children, the man you vowed to love for the rest of your life.'

'He was the one who left you.'

Sam stared at Hal. 'That's right. He did.'

He held her gaze for a moment before turning away, sighing heavily. He rubbed his forehead with his hand, and then turned back to look at her again. 'So what are you saying?' he said, frustrated. 'You're going to cocoon yourself so you can't possibly get hurt again? What kind of a life is that?'

'A less complicated one.'

'But life is complicated, Sam!' Hal insisted. 'It's messy, shit happens, that's how you know you're alive. You can't keep everything neat and tidy and organised.'

'I'm going to have to try. For the sake of my children.'

'And what about your needs?'

'It's not about what I need.' She breathed out heavily. 'Please understand, Hal, this isn't your fault. It's nothing you've done. I just don't want to be this crazy, out-of-control person any more, flying off the handle at people I care about. People who deserve to be treated better.'

Sam saw the pain in his eyes. He looked away, staring down at the ground. They were silent for a while. Eventually he thrust his hands in his pockets and lifted his gaze to meet hers again.

He sighed. 'I never got to take you sailing.'

Sam had contained herself till now, but she couldn't stop the sob that escaped from her throat. She dropped her head as tears brimmed over her lashes. Then she felt Hal's hand on her chin, lifting it, wiping her tears away with his thumb. His face was close to hers.

'Don't kiss me,' she said in a small voice.

He stared at her for a long time. Then his hand dropped away from her face. He turned and walked up the steps and out the gate. Sam went inside, closing the door behind her. But she had to hold her stomach as sobs wrenched from deep inside her. She slid down the wall to the floor, hugging herself, as though she might be able to stop her heart from breaking. But she couldn't. And she realised then that she had never felt this before.

Saturday

Jeff pulled up outside the house at eleven o'clock. When he'd called to check on Josh, Sam had invited him over. She was emotionally exhausted, what little sleep she'd had only seemed to make her feel more tired. But she knew Jeff wanted to see his son, and they still needed to talk.

The kids were all out front, Josh basking in the attention of the neighbourhood and the exalted status he was enjoying since becoming the survivor of a motorbike accident. There would be no room left on the cast by the time it had been signed by all his fans.

Sam wandered out after a while, having allowed Jeff time to talk to the kids and meet their friends.

'Hi,' he said when he saw her.

She smiled faintly. 'Hi.'

He took a couple of steps away from the pack. 'They seem like a nice bunch of kids.'

'They are.' She hesitated. 'Would you like to come inside for a drink? We can talk while they're occupied.'

'Okay.'

'Jess, keep an eye on your sister,' Sam called. 'We're just going inside.'

'Why do I always have to look after her?' Jessica whined. 'Why can't Josh do it?'

'Because at the moment he's only got one good arm,' Sam replied. 'You don't have to do anything, just keep an eye out.'

'And you be good for your sister, Ellie, and stay away from the road,' Jeff warned.

'I will, Daddy!'

'Jeff,' Sam began, after she'd made coffee and they'd taken a seat on the sofa. 'I'm sorry about the scene at the hospital. I was angry –'

'I know. You apologised already.'

'Not properly.'

'Sam, I understand. It's over, okay?'

'Okay. Thanks.' She paused. 'But we still have to talk about what happened.'

He looked at her, waiting.

'We need to discuss things like this. When we were together we would have talked about something like taking them motor-bike riding.'

'And you would have said no.'

'That's unfair, Jeff. I haven't always liked all of your ideas, but I've accepted them when you've insisted. Jessica's mobile phone, for example.'

He looked sheepish.

'I don't expect you to seek my permission or approval for what you do with the kids, that was just my anger speaking.'

Sam paused. 'I do trust you, Jeff. In fact, I think you're a better father now than you were when we were together.'

'Thanks. I happen to agree with you.'

'I just feel I still have a right to take part in deciding,' she continued, 'or at least knowing about what they're doing when they're with you, especially if it's something new or out of the ordinary. And the same goes for you,' she added. 'There's so much we should be discussing. What they're allowed to watch on TV, curfews –'

'I thought you said you trusted me?'

'I do,' she insisted. 'That's the point. I want your input.'

'You didn't seem to want it while we were together.'

'You didn't offer it.'

'Touché,' he smiled.

'The thing is, we're still their parents, we have to have a relationship. I think we should be more honest, or less wary with one another.'

'I'd like that.' He took a deep breath. 'I've missed you, Sam.'

'What?' She looked incredulous.

'I have,' he insisted. 'I mean, I don't want to get back together or anything. But I miss having you as a friend.'

Sam considered him thoughtfully. 'Were we ever friends, Jeff?'

'I think we were.' He paused. 'A long time ago.' He set his cup down on the coffee table. 'You know, I've always loved this table. Remember when we got it?'

'Do you?' she frowned.

'Sure,' he nodded. 'It was when we first got married. Mum and Dad gave us their old lounge suite, but we couldn't afford a dining table. So we bought this with money Aunty Sal gave us for our wedding, or engagement . . .'

'It was for our wedding, and it was your Aunty Kath on your dad's side,' Sam corrected him.

'Whatever, it was the first piece of furniture we ever bought together.'

'You do remember.'

'Of course I do. We ate here every night for the first year or so. You used to set it like a table, with a cloth and everything, and you wouldn't let me turn on the TV while we ate.' He paused, smiling faintly. 'I liked that we kept it all these years.'

Sam sighed. 'Well, why didn't you ask for it when we were dividing up the furniture?'

'I thought you'd want it.'

'I did,' she hesitated. 'You could have asked though.'

He gave a rueful half-laugh. 'If I wanted to fight, I would have just stayed with you.'

She thumped him lightly on the arm.

'Sorry.'

Sam was thoughtful. She had not spoken this honestly with Jeff in a long time. She might as well open the floodgates the rest of the way. 'Can I ask you something?' she said tentatively.

'Sure.'

She took a breath. 'What was it like for you? Was it hard . . . to leave?'

She saw the surprise register in his eyes, but he hesitated only for a second.

'It was the hardest thing I've ever done in my life,' he said solemnly. 'I struggled with it for months. I didn't want to end the marriage, put the kids through that. Hurt you. I didn't want to be the bastard going off with another woman and destroying my family.'

Sam stared at him, her chest tightening.

'But that night, the night I told you, it was the right thing, or the only thing I could do. It was like, one day I didn't know and the next day I knew for sure.' He looked at her squarely. 'I couldn't lie any more and I couldn't stay.'

She swallowed down the lump that had lodged in her throat.

'I know this has been hard on you, Sam. But if it's any con-solation, it's been the worst year of my life as well.'

Once upon a time, Sam would have said, 'Well, you made your bed . . .' But she didn't feel like scoring points over him.

'I suppose you had your family's support at least. Mum blamed it all on me.'

'You think my parents didn't blame me?' Jeff said. 'They were furious with me. My father told me in no uncertain terms to zip up my trousers and go back to my wife and family where I belonged.'

Sam was shocked. 'So when you wanted me to invite them over to see the kids –'

'I was just passing the buck. They had a lot more sympathy for you than me. They gave me hell.' He shook his head, remembering. 'You know, there must have been a dozen times I thought about coming back, if you would have had me.'

'Really?'

He nodded. 'One time, Jodi kicked me out when she found out I'd nearly slept with you –'

'How did she find that out?'

'I told her, of course,' he shrugged. 'Anyway, I was staying in a hotel. You weren't answering my calls and Jodi wasn't speaking to me. I wondered what the hell I'd done to my life, and everyone else's.'

They were quiet for a while. Sam was trying to process all this new information.

'You know you scared the life out of Jodi the other day,' said Jeff. 'At the hospital.'

'I scared the life out of everyone in that room,' Sam returned.

'Yeah, but she's been terrified of meeting you all along.' Jeff picked up his cup, but hesitated before drinking from it. 'She didn't want to meet the woman I found so hard to leave behind.'

Sam was gobsmacked. 'Do you think I wanted to meet the woman my husband replaced me with?'

'I didn't replace you, Sam,' he said seriously. 'You were a good wife, a good mother. You did all the right things. But I didn't feel part of it. I found myself living a life that didn't feel like it was mine, I didn't even recognise myself any more.'

The tears were stinging behind her eyes. She sniffed.

'When I said I thought the marriage had been over for a long time,' he continued, 'I really believed it.'

'I know,' Sam said in a small voice. 'You were right. But I would have stayed anyway.'

'I think you deserve much more than that,' he said quietly.

The front door burst open and Ellie ran inside. 'Mummy! Fatema's dog had puppies, can we have one?'

'Who's Fatema?'

Jess came in behind her. 'You know, she lives two doors up from the Suarezes. You should see how cute the puppies are. Can we have one, Mum?'

Ellie climbed onto Jeff's lap. 'Can we, Daddy?'

He glanced across at Sam. 'That is entirely your mother's call. Don't bring me into it.'

'She'll just say no,' said Jess, stepping across Jeff's legs, past the coffee table.

'Mind the cups, Jess,' Sam warned. 'And why do you think I'll say no?'

'You mean you won't?' she exclaimed, her eyes shining, as she plonked herself on the sofa between her parents.

Josh appeared in the doorway.

'Hey, Josh,' Jess called. 'Mum said we can have one of the pups!'

'Sick!'

'I didn't say that!' Sam protested.

'You gotta come and see 'em, Mum,' he said, planting himself on the coffee table facing the rest of them.

'Careful of the cups, Josh,' said Jeff.

The kids started talking excitedly about which pup they would choose. The girls wanted a female but Josh was adamant. He was already outnumbered by females in this house. The dog had to be male. Sam looked around at her family. They hadn't been together like this since Jeff left, and maybe for some time before that. She realised that perhaps they had reinvented themselves finally, as the family they were now. And it wasn't second-rate at all.

Sunday

'Hi Hal? It's Max here. Maxine Driscoll.'

'Hey Max. Is anything wrong?' He sounded concerned. 'Is Sam okay, the kids?'

'Everyone's fine,' she assured him. 'I just have a favour to ask you.'

'Sure.' Hal paused. 'What can I do for you, Max?'

'Sam's car is still up at Palmy. She asked if I could go pick it up, and I thought if you were headed back up there, I'd hitch a ride.'

Max heard him sigh. 'She really doesn't want to see me, does she?'

'It's not that.'

'Oh, I think it is.'

'Hal, she just doesn't want to leave Josh right now,' Max insisted. 'You know what she's like.'

He didn't say anything.

'Don't go getting all broody on me, Handsome. I wasn't the one who dumped you.'

He laughed then, a sort of feeble half-laugh. 'Aren't psychologists supposed to have empathy for other people?'

'Fine, I'll give you empathy if you give me a lift up to Palm Beach.'

Hal picked up Max on the street outside her apartment an hour later. He had no plans for the day and he knew he had to go back to the house sometime. It was better not to have to go there alone.

They made small talk as they travelled through the city to the north side. Eventually Hal cleared his throat.

'How is she?' he asked, looking at the road ahead.

'Crazy.' Max paused. 'Like a fox,' she added, with a lift of her eyebrows. Hal frowned at her.

'Mad as a meat axe,' she continued. 'Nutty as a fruitcake.

Around the bend, off with the fairies. As thick as two short planks. A few sandwiches short of a picnic.'

Max considered Hal's blank expression. 'You wanted empathy,' she shrugged.

'I'm not sure you have a real clear grasp of what the word means.'

'Do too,' she declared. 'But in order to feel empathy you have to put yourself in the other person's shoes, see how it is for them. And as I've never been dumped, it's a bit difficult for me.'

'You've never been dumped?'

'That's right. Not since my father,' she added wryly. She glanced across at Hal. 'Maybe this will help. She told me you were the right person at the wrong time.'

He shook his head doubtfully. 'If you're the right person, you're the right person, wouldn't you say, Max? There isn't a wrong time.'

'Like I said, there's a kangaroo loose in the top paddock, if you get my drift.' She saw the bemusement on Hal's face. 'Obviously not. I mean she's crazy,' Max explained. 'Actually if you want to know the truth, she's scared. Scared she'll start counting on you. Scared you'll go back home. Scared you'll leave her like all the men in her life have done so far.'

'I wasn't going to leave her,' Hal said seriously. 'I tied up some loose ends while I was back in the States, signed divorce papers, that kind of thing. And I've made a business commitment that's going to keep me here for a while. I wanted to tell her all that, but I didn't get the chance. She never gave me the chance.'

Max considered him. 'You love her, don't you?'

He nodded.

'I mean, you really love her,' she persisted.

He glanced at her. 'Yes, I do.'

'Can you tell me why?'

'I'm sorry?'

'I've never understood exactly what you saw in her.'

Hal gave her a look of sheer disbelief.

'Oh,' said Max. 'That came out wrong, didn't it? Of course I adore Sam. I know how wonderful she is. It's just, well, you're a very eligible bachelor, Hal, and the reality is –'

'We're not in the same league?' he finished for her.

She smiled, relieved. 'You understand what I'm getting at.'

'So you're the one that's been filling her head with that nonsense.'

Max looked blankly at him.

'How come you can see how wonderful she is, and you don't think I can?' he asked her. 'We're not all the shallow bastards you take us for, you know, Max.'

'I'm sorry, Hal,' she winced. 'I didn't mean it like that. How can I make it up to you?'

He sighed. 'Talk some sense into your sister.'

'Hmm,' she mused. 'Easier said. But, okay, if I'm going in to bat for you, you're going to have to give me something to work with, some consumptive poet stuff.'

'Excuse me?'

'You know, deeper than the ocean, higher than the highest mountain . . . that kind of thing.'

He smiled, shaking his head as he pulled up at a red light.

'Hal?'

'I was just thinking about when we first met . . .'

'Who, you and me?'

'No, me and Sam.'

'Oh, good, go on.'

'I told her I wouldn't dream of sleeping with her. Something like that.'

Max frowned. 'This is your best material, Hal?'

'The thing is, the next time I saw her, that was pretty much all I could think about.' He sighed. 'I wasn't looking for anyone, Max. I thought the *Wife for Hire* thing was ideal. I could have someone show me around, no expectations, no strings attached. And then before I knew it . . .'

He was gazing off into the distance. A car tooted behind.

'The light's turned green,' Max prompted him.

He took off again. 'You know, my ex-wife and I were what

you'd call the perfect couple. We had everything going for us, and it ended in disaster.'

'I reckon,' Max nodded.

Hal frowned at her. 'You know about that?'

Max cringed. 'I swear we had to hold her down and beat it out of her. It was ugly.'

He shook his head. 'Nothing's sacred, is it?'

'Not between women, especially sisters.'

He breathed out heavily. 'Anyway Max, you would have said that Lisa and I were in the same league. But I never felt this way about Lisa.'

Max was watching him. He had that faraway look again, staring fixedly at the road ahead.

'I feel a connection with Sam I've never felt before.' He paused. 'I'm more myself with her than with anyone I've ever known.'

They were quiet for a while, until eventually Max cleared her throat. 'Nicely put.'

He glanced at her. 'Much good it does me.'

Max considered him. 'Have you ever heard the saying "When you love someone, set them free"?'

'Sure I have. I've seen it on those cheesy posters, with a sunset and a bird in silhouette in the background.'

'Okay, you're having a go at me.'

'No, I'm not,' he cajoled. 'Well, maybe a little. But go on, what were you saying?'

'Look, I realise it's a cliché,' said Max. 'But it is true. If you really believe you two belong together, then you're going to have to trust that she'll come back to you. You just have to give her a chance to miss you.'

'What if she doesn't?'

'Then like it says on the cheesy poster, she was never yours to begin with.'

A week later

Sam peered through the curtains as Liz's car pulled up outside. The girls had not had a night together for months. In fact it was longer than that for Fiona. But apparently she'd made a commitment to Liz that she would come tonight, and had even accepted her offer of a lift. The kids were with Jeff for the weekend and Sam was due to start her new job next week, so it would probably be their last chance to get together for a while. She went to the front door to greet them.

'Hi Sam!' exclaimed Rosemary, rushing ahead of the others. Rose was a different woman these days. She had joined a gym and become something of an exercise junkie. In the process, she'd dropped weight, her skin glowed and her eyes sparkled. She'd also bought a new wardrobe and had her hair cut shorter and streaked. But Sam knew it wasn't just the exercise and new clothes. Rosemary was doing something for herself for possibly the first time in her life. She exuded confidence. But she had lost none of her sweetness.

'Thanks for inviting us over, it's so good to see you, you look fantastic, how is Josh?' she bubbled, without taking a breath.

'Josh is doing fine,' said Sam. 'He's just frustrated he can't ride his skateboard.'

Rosemary frowned. 'Oh? I thought it was his arm that was broken? Why can't he skate?'

'It is his arm, but Rose, I'm not about to let him on a skateboard with a broken arm.'

'Oh yes, of course, silly me,' she babbled happily. Still as sweet, just as dumb. 'Here you go,' she said, handing Sam a bottle of champagne. 'To celebrate us all being together again.'

'Hi darl,' drawled Liz, stooping to kiss her on the cheek. 'I need to use the loo. I've driven all over Sydney rounding up this lot.'

She dashed up the hall and into the bathroom.

'Hi Sherl,' said Max, with Fiona coming up behind. 'I'll

get the drinks going, eh?' She grabbed the bottle from Sam and went to join Rose in the kitchen, leaving her to face Fiona.

'Hi Sam,' Fiona said in a small, nervous voice.

Sam tried to reassure her with a smile. 'How are you, Fiona?' She felt no animosity, she never had. It was everyone else who had thought she would have a problem.

'Um, fine, okay, you know,' Fiona shrugged uncertainly.

Sam leaned forward to give her a hug. Fiona hesitated before responding, obviously a little taken aback.

'You haven't seen the place, have you?'

Fiona shook her head.

'Come on, I'll show you around. It'll only take half a minute,' she joked.

Fiona stopped Sam at the doorway to her bedroom. 'You do realise how much respect I have for you, for the way you've handled yourself and made a new life for you and the kids.'

Sam leaned against the doorjamb. 'Thanks, Fiona.'

'I just . . .' She hesitated. 'I'd like to explain my situation –'

'Fiona, you don't owe me an explanation.'

'But you're one of my closest friends,' she insisted. 'I want you to understand.'

Sam shrugged. 'I do understand.'

Fiona frowned at her. 'But you don't know anything.'

'I know that you're a good person and that you'd always try to do the best for your children. And that you wouldn't mean to hurt anyone.'

Fiona nodded slowly, her eyes glassy. 'I just feel so guilty. Gavin has stayed home with the kids all these years, he's made all the sacrifices . . . It wouldn't be fair to him . . .'

'Do you love this other man?'

Fiona shrugged. 'I think so. We can't take it any further at the moment, regardless. He's married, his children are quite small, much younger than mine. But we can talk, we have so much in common. And it's passionate.'

'That doesn't last,' said Sam, hating herself for being such a cynic.

'I know. And I'm not sure that I'm prepared to give up my family life.'

'But on the other hand, if the marriage is dead . . .'

'What are you saying, Sam?'

Liz came out of the bathroom, propping herself against the wall near to them.

'I don't think you should stay if you're unhappy.'

Fiona and Liz both looked at her, startled.

'You've come a long way, baby,' Liz remarked.

Max appeared at the end of the hall. 'What's everyone doing standing around here?' she said. 'The wine's poured, but I couldn't find a platter in the fridge, Sam.'

'I haven't made one up yet,' she sighed. 'I've got all the stuff though.'

They regrouped in the kitchen. Sam opened the fridge and passed out containers of olives and packets of cheese. There were boxes of crackers and chips already on the bench. They started picking from the containers, slicing off hunks of cheese with a steak knife, eating crackers straight out of the packet.

'This is not very elegant,' Sam remarked.

'Still tastes the same,' said Max. She picked up her glass. 'Cheers everyone.'

They all murmured 'Cheers' and sipped from their glasses.

'Sam,' said Fiona after a while, 'you were saying that I shouldn't stay if I'm unhappy . . .'

'Whoa,' said Max. 'What have we missed?'

'I was just telling Fiona that she's got to work out whether her marriage is worth saving. I don't know that mine was.'

They all stared at her.

'If Jeff hadn't had the affair, we probably would have lived out our lives together, grown old as two bitter, resentful people, barely able to speak a civil word to each other.'

'So you think it was a good thing that Jeff had an affair?' Rosemary asked, perplexed.

'Not exactly. The right thing would have been to come to me and tell me he was unhappy, long before he ever had the affair. But then again, if we could have talked like that, he might not have been so unhappy.'

'Am I hearing you right, you're not blaming yourself?' said Max.

'No!' she insisted. 'Jeff had the affair. But we were both to blame about the state of the marriage. We'd stopped talking, stopped sharing what was important to us. We were walking along paths that were slowly moving apart and we didn't even realise until we couldn't reach each other any more.' She sighed. 'It's sad, especially for the kids. No matter how well we try to get along separated, they'd still rather we were all together.'

'That's what's stopping me,' said Fiona. 'I want to give the girls a normal life.'

'What's normal?' said Rosemary. 'I stayed because I thought it was the right thing to do. Now the boys are getting a dose of living with their father without me around as a buffer. You know what Brendan said to me the other day?'

Everyone shook their heads, waiting.

'"How did you put up with him for so long, Mum?"'

'Still,' Fiona sighed, 'they're a lot older than my girls.'

'I know,' Rosemary nodded. 'No one can tell you what's right for you. You're the one who has to live with whatever decision you make.'

'Have you ever regretted leaving, Rose?' Liz asked.

'Not for one minute of one day,' she said plainly. 'That doesn't mean I'm deliriously happy all the time. I'm often lonely, and I'd like to meet someone, but I'm trying to be patient about it. There's plenty of sex out there, but not a lot of commitment.'

'So what are you going to do?'

She grinned wickedly. 'I'll just enjoy the sex for now.'

Everyone burst into laughter, dispersing the grey cloud that had settled on the group.

'When do you start your new job, Sam?' asked Liz, changing the subject.

'You've got a new job?' said Fiona. 'It feels like you only just started the other one.'

'I've been with *Wife for Hire* more than a year now. But I'm not giving it up entirely. I'm keeping a few clients, like Ted Dempsey. I still see him every week.'

'What about that handsome American?' asked Liz. 'What was his name? Hal?'

'He hasn't been a client for quite a while.' Sam glanced at Max, expecting some smart comment, but she didn't make one. She probably knew by now that Sam wouldn't tolerate mention of Hal. She had tried to talk to her about him after their drive up the coast together, but Sam had cut her off. Max probably thought she was being hard, but she didn't realise how painful it was.

'And what happened to the nice woman who was married to that dickhead?' Max asked, thankfully moving the conversation along. 'She used to give you all those great clothes.'

'Oh, Vanessa and Dominic? They separated actually. She's home in Armidale at the moment, her parents have a property there. I think Dominic's still hoping they can sort it out. I don't like his chances though.'

'So what's the new job?' asked Fiona.

'Well, I don't know what to call myself exactly. I'm going to work, part-time at first, for an event management firm.'

'Wow! That's fantastic, Sam. And by the way, you can call yourself an events co-ordinator,' Fiona added.

Sam looked at her dubiously. 'Oh, I think entry-level, general dogsbody is the best I can hope for, for now.'

'Don't be so hard on yourself,' Fiona insisted. 'If you don't believe in yourself, no one else will. And you certainly have the skills.'

Sam looked at the mess on the bench. 'Hmm. I think they're going to need some honing.'

'Now's about the time that I usually grab her head and hit it against a wall,' said Max drily.

'There'd be a lot of weekend and night work, wouldn't there?' asked Rosemary. 'How are you going to manage with the kids?'

Sam nodded. 'I've talked it over with Jeff. He's actually

hoping to cut down his hours at work, perhaps even change jobs so he'll have more time with the baby.'

'What baby?' everyone but Max shrieked at once.

'Oh, that's right, you wouldn't know of course. Jeff and his partner are having a baby.'

'Good grief. How did that happen?' asked Rosemary, wide-eyed.

'The usual way, I suppose,' Sam dismissed. 'Anyway, he's happy to be more involved, do some of the ferrying around after school, that kind of thing.'

'You're very lucky things are so amicable between you,' said Fiona.

'You wouldn't have said that a week ago,' said Max, raising an eyebrow.

Sam pulled a face at her. 'So, tell the girls all about your boyfriend, Max.'

'You've got a boyfriend?' said Liz. 'What, one that's lasted longer than a fortnight?'

'Mm. I can't seem to shake him off.'

'You mustn't be trying hard enough this time,' Sam quipped.

Max looked at her, folding her arms. 'I'm thinking of cookware, pots and kettles namely. And the colour black.'

'I'm not following this at all,' Rose frowned. 'Is he a chef?'

'No, he's a teacher,' said Sam. 'She met him at uni, he's studying to be a school counsellor.'

'Yes,' Max sighed. 'It's true. Despite all my efforts to the contrary, I've ended up with the straightest guy on the planet.'

'So it's serious?' said Liz.

'Yeah, way too much a lot of the time, I keep telling him he needs to lighten up.'

'He's absolutely lovely,' Sam told them. 'He treats her like a queen, makes an absolutely perfect margarita, and he's great with the kids.'

'You marry him then,' Max rolled her eyes.

'Are you talking about marriage?' Sam said breathlessly.

'No, he is. Incessantly. But I told him I can't possibly marry him.'

'Why not?'

'His name is Dan *Watson*.'

'So, he has a bland name. That's not really a good enough reason, Max.'

'Think about it, Sherlock. You and I would be Holmes and Watson. It's too corny for words, it has to be an omen. A bad one.'

The girls were all laughing.

'And,' she continued, 'you have such a crook sense of humour, Sherl, it's only a matter of time before you say something really lame like, "Elementary, my dear Watson". I'm not prepared to take that chance.'

'Well, I think we should drink to Mr Watson,' said Fiona, picking up the bottle. 'And wish him luck – he's going to need it.'

'Should I be offended?' Max asked suspiciously.

'Not at all,' Fiona assured her, refilling her glass. Liz covered hers with her hand.

'I'm fine.'

'You've hardly touched your glass,' said Sam. 'Are you on medication or something?'

'No,' she shrugged. 'I'm driving.'

'And you haven't been outside for a cigarette,' said Rosemary. 'What's going on, Liz?'

She gazed around at the group, a slight serene smile on her lips. She looked like the Mona Lisa.

'I'm pregnant,' she said simply.

Everyone's jaw dropped at the same time as though they'd rehearsed it.

'At first I didn't know what to think.' Her voice was quiet and steady. 'I was scared. I'm too old, Will's going to be sixteen this year, what about my job? But dear Michael,' she paused, looking dreamy. 'He acted like he'd just won Lotto. So, I had all the tests, because of my age, and it turns out we're having a perfect baby girl, and we're naming her Charlotte.'

They were all stunned, staring at her.

'So there you have it,' Liz murmured softly.

Sam sniffed. 'It's wonderful. Congratulations,' she said, crossing the room and throwing her arms around Liz. The others all milled around, taking turns to hug her, blotting tears from their eyes, laughing at their own mawkishness.

'Let's drink to all of us,' Max announced, picking up her glass. 'To babies, weddings, divorces, the whole catastrophe. At least none of us can say life hasn't been interesting.'

Ferncourt Primary School

'You have to be very brave and try not to cry. I know it seems scary, but it's not really.'

Ellie looked seriously at her mother.

'I'll try to remember that,' said Sam, who was crouched down at eye-level with her daughter. She looked at her, all dressed in her brand new, green-checked uniform, her dark hair pulled back into two pigtails as requested, and tied with green ribbons. The uniform was a good fit, but for some reason uniforms always looked too big on the first day at school.

'Daddy, I hope you brought a hankie for her, because you know what she's like.'

Sam smiled, despite the ache in the back of her throat. Jeff crouched down next to her, taking hold of Ellie's hand.

'You have a wonderful day, sweetheart,' he said.

'I will, Daddy.' Just then the bell rang. Her eyes lit up. 'That's the bell!' she exclaimed. 'We can go in now!'

She threw her arms around Jeff's neck and hugged him tight. Then she turned to Sam.

'Mummy,' she admonished, touching Sam's forehead. 'You've got a sadline. You have to be happy.'

Sam put on a smile that she hoped looked happy, while she struggled to keep the tears at bay. But as she hugged her baby daughter, who was not a baby at all but a big schoolgirl, she finally lost the struggle. Tears filled her eyes and she was frightened to blink in case they streamed down her cheeks.

Ellie stepped back to look at her mother's face and shook her head. 'I knew it,' she said, her hands on her hips.

Sam sniffed, carefully blotting under her eyes with the corner of a tissue. She couldn't speak though, she didn't trust herself. She stood up next to Jeff.

'I have to go now. Take care of her, Daddy.'

'I will.'

Sam steeled herself as Ellie lined up with all the other schoolchildren. From behind they looked like rows of backpacks with legs and little heads poking out at the top, wearing oversized hats. The teachers were welcoming them to big school, but Sam tuned out. She had to concentrate on holding herself together. She took a deep breath in and out, and then she felt Jeff's hand interlocking with hers and holding tight. She glanced at him and he smiled reassuringly.

Finally they got the lines moving. Ellie turned around once as she came to the door of her classroom. Her face was beaming as she waved excitedly at them. They waved back. And then she was gone.

'Let's get out of here,' Sam gulped. They turned and walked smartly across the playground and through the gate. When they were out of sight, she let out a sob. She felt Jeff's arms close around her and she didn't resist, leaning against him. Sam realised that she didn't feel anything, only comforted, like she would if it was Max. Which was something of a relief.

'Are you alright?' he said after a while.

She pulled back from him. 'Yeah, sorry about that,' she sniffed.

'It's okay.' He watched her dab at her cheeks with a tissue. 'I don't remember you being so upset when the other two started.'

'Well, Josh was all macho and brave. A bit like Ellie, come to think of it,' she smiled. 'I was relieved as much as anything. But by the time Jess started, I knew just how much you lose them when they start school. It's never the same again. They're out in the world, there are other people who influence them, other people they admire. They have relationships that have nothing to do with you.' Sam paused, wistful. 'I was a mess on Jessica's first day.'

'I don't remember,' Jeff said vaguely.

'Well, you weren't around.'

'I wasn't?'

Sam shook her head. 'Jess woke up early and got dressed so that you could see her in her uniform before you went to work. But you didn't come to the school.'

'The things I missed,' he muttered ruefully.

'Well, you're going to get to do it all over again,' Sam reminded him.

He sighed. 'It frightens the hell out of me. I've been spouting all this stuff about wanting the chance to do it differently, now I'm going to get found out for the big fat fraud that I am.' He paused. 'It was all you, Sam, you held us together. How am I going to do it?'

'You'll be fine,' she said, linking her arm through his as they walked back to where the cars were parked. There was something she wanted to say to him. 'Jeff, the other day you said I was a good mother and a good wife, that I did all the right things.'

He nodded.

'Well, I just want you to know that while I was so busy playing that role, I forgot that I was supposed to be having a relationship.'

Jeff stopped abruptly and stared down at her.

'I lost myself too,' Sam continued. 'And I didn't even realise it. And maybe I never would have if you hadn't jolted me out of it.'

He was clearly overcome. 'Thanks for telling me that, Sam,' he said softly.

'My pleasure,' she smiled. She walked on towards his car.

'We did alright, didn't we?' Jeff said, following her. 'They're good kids.'

'It's not over yet,' said Sam.

'I guess not.' He took his keys out of his pocket. 'Have you got something to keep you busy today? You're not going to go home and pine for Ellie, are you?'

She shook her head. 'I have to take a client to the airport, and then I have my first meeting with the events company.'

'So, the new career takes off?' he remarked. 'Go knock 'em dead, Sam.'

She smiled. 'I'll do my best.' She considered him briefly before reaching up to kiss him on the cheek. 'Bye.'

Jeff stood watching till she got to her car. She opened the door and looked back at him, waving as she climbed in. When she pulled off up the street she saw him in the rear-view mirror, still watching as she drove away.

The International Terminal was not particularly busy, so they didn't have to line up for long to check in.

'You don't have to wait, Samantha,' said Ted. 'I'm sure you have other places you could be right now.'

'Always trying to get rid of me,' she replied, shaking her head.

She had finally talked Ted into going to London to visit Hugh and his family. The moment he'd shown signs of relenting, Sam had immediately booked a flight and informed Hugh so that he couldn't change his mind.

'I thought Andrew told me you were starting today?' Ted asked her.

Sam nodded. 'There's a meeting at one. I have plenty of time. Why don't we get a cup of tea?'

They sat at a table with a view of the tarmac. 'I think airports are so exciting,' said Sam.

'Have you ever done much travelling, Samantha?'

She shook her head. 'I had babies instead.'

'You're not missing much, let me assure you. The places are wonderful, it's the actual travelling I'm talking about. Airports and customs and endless queues. And the flights. From Australia, everywhere is a long haul. It takes its toll after a while.'

'Oh, that reminds me,' said Sam, digging in her bag. 'I got you something for the "long haul". Talking books,' she explained, passing him a package. 'Apparently you can ask for a tape player on the plane.'

He smiled. 'Thank you so much, Samantha. You're too kind.' He paused, seeming to search for words. 'You have made such a difference to my life over the past year. I hope you know how much I appreciate it.'

'I do know,' she said, looking down at her teacup. She knew it was going to be hard to say goodbye – she couldn't help wondering if he'd ever come back.

'You have to promise me you'll have the most wonderful time possible. They're all so excited that you're coming. I don't think they'll ever let you go.'

Ted reached across the table and squeezed her hand. 'Do you think you're going to get rid of me that easily?'

Sam arrived at the offices of Byron Promotional Services at ten to one. The company occupied the ground floor of what was a fairly nondescript brick building in Surry Hills. She walked into the reception area and gave her name to the very young woman at the desk.

'Oh, sure, right, Andrew said you'd be coming today,' she said, checking her watch. 'You're early.'

'Sorry.'

'Not a problem,' she dismissed. 'Come through and we'll see who's here.'

Sam followed her around the partition wall into a vast, open office area that appeared to be virtually deserted. Amongst the haphazard groupings of desks and cabinets, Sam could only see one woman working at a computer.

'Where is everybody?'

'Out,' she answered simply. 'As you can imagine, most of our work is on site.'

'Of course,' Sam nodded.

'I'm April, by the way.'

'Please, call me Sam.'

'Okay, Sam,' April smiled. 'Andrew isn't in, I think he told you that? But anyway, that's his office over there,' she said, pointing to one end of the floor. 'And this is the conference room here,' she said, walking to the opposite end. It was a large glassed-in room with windows to the outside, facing a small green courtyard. From the office area, the room looked like a light-filled prism, bright and inviting.

A young man appeared from around the corner, carrying a cup of coffee. It was the same young man she had met at Darling Harbour that day, Sam was certain.

'Hello!' he said brightly. 'Sam, isn't it?'

She was surprised that he remembered her name. 'Brad?'

'Got it in one.'

'You two know each other?' asked April.

'Sam came to check us out at the Outdoor Living Expo, if I remember right.'

She nodded.

'Then I'll leave you to it,' said April. 'I'd best get back to the desk.'

'Thanks,' Sam said.

'Would you like a cup of coffee?' Brad asked her.

'Oh no, that's okay.'

'Don't be shy,' he said. 'Come on, Denise is still ten minutes away, I might as well show you where everything is.'

He took her back around the corner to a small kitchen area where two young women were making coffee. It seemed everyone was young.

'Rachel, Kate, this is Sam, or do you prefer Samantha?' Brad asked her.

'No, honestly, I always get Sam.'

'You're Andrew's friend, aren't you?' asked Rachel.

'Well, friend of a friend.'

They made coffee and carried it back around to the conference room. Sam felt self-conscious that she had been given a free pass in. She hoped it wasn't going to cause resentment amongst the rest of the staff. She would have to work hard to earn their respect, to make them believe she was capable of the job. She just needed to convince herself first.

'This is a lovely room,' said Sam as they settled around the vast conference table.

'Best spot in the building,' Brad agreed. 'North light, trees to look at. It's a regular utopia.'

'Bloody men!' shrieked yet another young woman, charging through the door. Sam recognised her from the Outdoor Expo.

'Stephanie,' Brad said. 'This is Sam. She's just starting today.'

'Oh, hi Sam, I think we met?'

Sam nodded. 'At the exhibition centre.'

'What happened?' Kate asked Stephanie.

'Bloody Ben,' she said, shaking her head. 'I told him to get back with the car, I had a meeting at one. So what does he do? Calls me from somewhere out near Parramatta. *At twelve-thirty!* "Oh, sorry babe",' she said, affecting a dopey voice, '"I just looked at the time." He's such a moron.'

'Guys just don't have the same sense of responsibility. They think in a different way than we do.'

'No, the problem is, they *don't* think at all.'

'Um, you guys,' Brad said, clearing his throat. 'You do actually remember I am a male, when you're having these "all men are stupid" conversations?'

'You don't count, Brad,' said Rachel dismissively.

Sam thought Brad was cute. He had the scruffy thing down pat – scruffy sandy hair, scruffy goatee, ditto shirt, jeans. Jess would think he was 'hot'.

'You know what I reckon would be excellent?' Stephanie asked the group. 'An all-female events company.'

'Yeah!'

'We should start one!'

'Ah guys, what about me?'

'Imagine, only women in the office –'

'BORING!!' Denise boomed, coming through the doorway. 'With a capital B and all the other letters as well.'

'Hi Denise,' the group chorused.

'God, I could think of nothing worse than a women-only workplace,' she declared, walking briskly to the other end of the conference table. 'Where's the fun if you don't have any men around? Hi Braddles. How are you, darling?' she winked at him.

'But women are better at this business,' said Stephanie. 'Men are not natural organisers –'

'Of course they are,' Denise scoffed, dropping a load of folders onto the table with a thud. 'God, how do you think they run corporations and countries –'

'And wars,' Kate added.

'Badly most of the time,' muttered Stephanie.

'And why can't they remember to put the garbage out?' said Rachel.

'Because,' said Denise, 'they all have wives who run around doing everything for them to prove how indispensable they are. Until they get jack of it and then wonder why their blokes can't close a drawer without being nagged.'

'So it's all our fault, Denise?' said Stephanie drily.

'I'm just saying there are men who are lazy and there are women who are lazy, men who are disorganised and women the same. And there are men who are perfectly capable, and women who are control freaks. Sam, hi, how are you?' she said, without drawing a breath.

Sam was startled Denise had noticed her. 'I'm fine, good thanks, Denise.'

'Have you met everyone?'

She nodded.

'Let's get on with it then, shall we? First item on the agenda. The O-Mega launch.'

'The computer company?' asked Rachel.

Denise nodded, slapping an overhead sheet on the projector and switching it on. An image of a bright orange, round-edged computer monitor appeared on the screen.

'They're bringing out a range of decorator hardware, colours to match your décor, brighten your office and make your day,' she said in a monotone, reading off a piece of paper.

'Didn't Macintosh do this, like years ago?' Stephanie frowned.

'That's right,' Denise said, passing brochures around the table. 'Now everyone wants to get on the bandwagon. I'm just waiting for the first retro computer to come out. You know, like those bulky toasters and 1950s-style blenders? Next they'll bring out big chunky beige monitors with tiny little screens, which take up twice as much desk space.' She laughed at her own joke. 'Okay, where do we start, good people? Who can tell Sam what's the first, most important decision?'

'Location, location,' the group murmured automatically.

'A bit of enthusiasm, please!' Denise exclaimed loudly. 'And why is it important to decide on location before anything else?'

'The location will dictate the style, size, atmosphere –'

'Thank you Bradley, you will get a gold star in your workbook.'

'Teacher's pet,' muttered Kate, grinning at him across the table.

'Now everyone, look at the bumf I've handed around. Concentrate. See the launch in your mind.'

Silence descended upon the group. Sam flicked through the advertising material. She hoped Denise didn't expect anything from her. Surely she was just an observer at this stage.

'Well, there are the regular exhibition spaces, at Darling Harbour or Homebush,' Rachel suggested.

'Blurgh!' Denise pulled a face. 'Where's your imagination, sunshine? And this is a *launch*, don't forget, not an expo. It will be invitation-only, we don't need a great big cavernous warehouse. It has to be more intimate than that, it has to be sexy.'

Sam stared at the pages. Brilliant, contemporary, works of art, cutting edge, sculptural, state of the art . . .

'What about,' she mused. Everyone lifted their heads at once to look at her. Shit. She swallowed. 'Oh look, I'm probably way off beam here.'

'Go ahead, Sam,' Denise urged. 'Sometimes the best ideas are the ones that sound crazy at first.'

She took a breath. 'Well, it's only because they're making

such a big deal about them being arty and contemporary and everything . . .'

They were all waiting.

'What about the Museum of Contemporary Art?'

Denise smiled broadly. 'Well, that doesn't sound crazy at all!'

'They have function rooms, don't they?' said Kate. 'A friend of my sister's had her wedding reception there.'

'Yeah, but it might be better to mount it like an exhibition,' Stephanie suggested.

'That's what I was thinking,' said Sam.

'Fabulous,' declared Denise. 'Okay, I'll leave it with you, Sam. The launch is in two months, we'd better have it confirmed by next week.'

'Sorry? What do you want me to do?' Sam was gobsmacked.

'Well, you'll get in touch with the MCA, check out our options, run it by me . . .' Denise was waiting for it to register with Sam.

'Okay, sure,' she said determinedly. 'I'll get right on to it.'

'And well done you,' Denise added. 'It's a truly stupendous idea.'

Sam felt herself blushing. She picked up her cup and took a gulp of coffee.

'Invitations, anyone?' Denise continued.

'This will be for IT people?' asked Brad.

Denise consulted one of the folders in front of her, scanning through a couple of pages. She handed them to Brad. 'Looks like it. But there are retailers there, media of course, a bit of everything really.'

'You want me and Kate to mock up some invitations?' said Rachel.

'Sure, show me something no later than next week, okay?'

'If these are all techno types,' Sam started, surprised to hear her own voice again. 'Um, well, wouldn't they communicate by email?'

'Yeah,' said Brad. 'But so much email goes around, they're likely to take it as junk and just trash it.'

'I was trying to get someone's attention once,' Sam continued. 'And I finally sent a series of probably half a dozen emails,
so that the subject lines all read as one sentence when they
appeared in the inbox.'

'Do you understand what she's talking about, Brad?' Denise
asked.

'Yeah, sounds cool,' he said. 'Is it foolproof?'

Sam nodded. 'If you know the trick.'

'Alright, you two work on that together,' Denise resumed.
'Rachel and Kate do the hard copy invitations. Next . . .'

'Did it work?' Brad muttered under his breath.

'Sorry?'

'Did you get the someone's attention?'

'Oh, yes, I did.' Sam felt the pang in her chest that always
accompanied thoughts of Hal. She worked very hard at suppressing such thoughts. She pushed them so far down that
instead they surfaced in her dreams. Vivid, sometimes erotic,
but always heart-wrenching dreams, so real she'd wake up in a
sweat. Like the one she had all the time, where she asked him
to kiss her and he walked away.

'That's it, ladies and gentleman,' Denise said finally, about an
hour later. 'Now run along, there's a lot of work to be done.'

Sam stood up as the others filed out of the room. She hesitated, watching Denise pack up her folders. She cleared her
throat. 'Um, Denise?'

'Yeah?' she said, not looking up.

'Well, um, I'm just a bit concerned that I've bitten off more
than I can chew. I'm untried in this industry, maybe I'll stuff
up . . .'

'Maybe the sky will fall in, too.'

'What did you say?'

Denise stopped to look at her. 'You haven't heard that
expression before?'

'No, it's not that. Just a lot of people have been saying that
to me lately.'

'And rightly so, by the sounds of it,' Denise remarked. 'God
help us and save us, Sam, if you never try, how will you know

whether you can do it? Imagine if Thomas Edison had thought he couldn't do it? Or . . .' She clicked her fingers in the air. 'Oh, I dunno, I can never think of examples when I want them. And then tonight in the bath it'll suddenly come to me.' She stared at Sam. 'What were we saying? Oh yes! Worrying never got anyone anywhere.' She picked up the stack of folders. 'Besides, you do have some experience, I recall. Where were you working before . . . *Girls for Rent*?'

Sam suppressed a grin. 'No, *Wife for Hire*.'

'That's it. You have to go for it, Sam. Let's see what you're made of. Don't forget, you have us, you're not on your own. If you slip up, we'll be there to make sure the whole thing doesn't fall into a crashing heap.'

'Like a safety net?' Sam suggested.

'A safety net,' Denise nodded. 'Good analogy. Now, come along, we'd best find you a desk.'

Two months later

The door opened just as Sam pushed the key into the lock.

'Sam!' Max exclaimed. 'Do you realise what time it is?'

'Oh, I'm so sorry, Max, I didn't mean to keep you this long.'

'It's not me I'm worried about,' said Max, following Sam into the living room. 'It's almost ten o'clock. You can't keep working these hours.'

Sam threw herself onto the sofa. 'I won't have to after tomorrow. The launch will be over. Besides, all the hard work is done. Denise said a well-organised function runs itself.'

'And what about the next one? You can't keep up at this pace!'

Sam was lying flat on her back, a cushion over her eyes. 'We've switched places,' she remarked.

'What are you talking about?'

'You're doing the impersonations of Mum now.'

'Oh, she called by the way.'

'What did she want?'

'Nothing. Only to wish you all the best tomorrow.'

'What do you know,' Sam murmured.

'Have you eaten?'

'Mm? Somebody handed me a muffin at some stage. I think I ate it.'

'Do you want me to fix you something?'

'No, I'm too exhausted to eat.' She sighed heavily. 'And that bloody dog has been keeping me up at night with his crying. They all begged me to get him, but do you think they hear him at night?'

'Of course not. They're kids. Their antennae aren't tuned to night crying,' said Max. 'Why don't you just bring him inside?'

'I do! I put his basket right near my bed. But he's only happy if I actually hold him.'

'You should have got Jeff to take him while he's a puppy. Give him some practice.'

Sam grunted from under the cushion.

'Was that a snore?'

'Almost.'

'Well, I have to get going,' Max declared. 'I've got an early start tomorrow. Dan wants to go for a run on the beach in the morning.'

Sam lifted the cushion to stare at her sister. 'You go running?'

'Get real!' Max exclaimed, horrified. 'I lie on the beach and doze, and then we go and have brekkie at a café together.'

Sam looked at her wistfully, tucking the cushion under her head. 'That sounds nice.'

Max considered her for a moment. 'Do you miss him?'

Sam was about to say 'who', but there was no point playing that game. She just nodded instead.

'So what are you going to do about it?'

She sighed loudly. 'To be honest, Max, I have to check my

diary before I scratch myself these days. We would probably have broken up if we were still together, with the hours I work.'

'Mm,' Max pondered. 'You realise you didn't actually answer the question just then?'

'What was it again?'

'What are you going to do about the fact that you miss Hal?'

Sam hesitated. 'I don't even know if he's still in the country.'

'He told me he was involved in business that was going to keep him here for quite a while.'

'Oh? You've never mentioned that before.'

'You haven't wanted to talk about Hal before,' Max declared. 'You haven't let me so much as utter his name. There's a lot I've wanted to say to you, but you haven't given me the chance.'

Sam looked at her. 'Go ahead. I'm listening.'

'Sherl, he loves you so much. He told me he felt a connection to you he'd never felt before, and that he could be more himself with you than anyone else, something like that.'

Sam swallowed. 'He said that?'

'Yes, he did. I didn't even have to twist his arm.'

She sighed. 'Well, I think he got over it. He's not exactly breaking the door down. I haven't heard a word from him all this time.'

'Give the guy a break, Sherl!' Max exclaimed. 'How many times is he supposed to come back only to have you turn him away again? It's about time you put yourself on the line.'

Sam was thoughtful. 'I don't know if I'm ready to do that.'

Max crossed her arms. 'Are you happy right now, Sam?'

She shrugged. 'Why wouldn't I be happy? My kids are doing great, I'm getting along with my ex-husband, I have family who love me, friends, a wonderful job . . .'

'But?'

'There's no but.'

'There is so a but,' Max insisted.

'Come on, Max!' Sam stood up and started to pace around the room. 'You're the last person I'd expect to fall for that clap-trap. That I need a man to make me happy.'

'I'm not saying that,' she said calmly. 'Look at me. I didn't need a man, I didn't even particularly want a man. But then I fell in love with Dan. And you know what? I can live without him, I just don't want to. Why do you think I finally said yes?'

Sam stopped pacing and looked at her.

'Of course you don't need a man to make you happy,' said Max. 'But I'm not talking about some theoretical man. I'm talking about Hal. He's a real person, and he loves you and you love him and that's why, despite all that you have in your life, you still feel empty.'

Sam stared at her, tears stinging behind her eyes.

'You know what I was thinking about the other day?' Max asked her.

She shook her head.

'The reason you never got a dog before. You always said it would make too much mess and ruin the garden and just be one big hassle. But you never thought about how much joy a dog would bring, did you? And now that you have him, would you ever give him up?'

Sam smiled faintly. 'You realise you're comparing Hal to a dog?'

'Try to overlook that, it was the best I could do at short notice,' Max dismissed. 'Sam, I just want you to be happy, to be filled up. Not to be living this perfect, orderly, empty existence. Don't you realise that's how it was with Jeff all those years?'

She just stared at Max, biting her lip.

'And think about it, it's the way Mum's been all her life.'

Oh God, Max was right.

'You don't think I've moved on?' said Sam in a small voice.

'Oh, of course you have, Sherl,' Max exclaimed. 'You're amazing, I'm so proud of you. But I think there's one more step you have to take.'

Sam smiled feebly as a tear escaped and trickled down her cheek. Maxine walked over to her sister and put her arms around her, hugging her tight.

'Call him, Sherl. He's worth it.' She pulled back to look at her. 'So are you.'

Sam sniffed. 'I'm afraid.'

Max smiled. 'We're all afraid, Sam.' She took hold of both her hands. 'Go get some sleep. Have a fabulous launch tomorrow – knock 'em dead. We'll talk about this later. Count on it.'

Sam saw her to the door and waited until she drove away in Dan's car. She closed the door and leaned against it, thinking about Hal. There was barely a night that she didn't think about him, didn't yearn for him, didn't lie in bed imagining his arms around her. She tried so hard not to, but it was like being told not to think of pink elephants.

But what was she so damned afraid of? She loved Hal so much it had paralysed her. She couldn't bear to lose him, so she had decided to live without him. What kind of weird, self-defeating logic was that?

The kind that was taught at the Bernice Driscoll School for Martyrs.

Well, enough already.

Sam walked over to the computer and pressed a key to bring up the screen. She sat down and opened the email program and then her work mailbox. The dog started to whine.

'Okay, okay, keep your shirt on,' she muttered. 'You're just going to have to wait your turn, pooch.'

Museum of Contemporary Art

Sam stood tapping her feet to the music being piped through the sound system. Brad had given her quite a rundown on the psychology of music and how to choose appropriately for the function, for the response you were hoping from the people who attended. She had understood less than half of what he'd told her, but that was the same as everything else so far. Sam had been on her steepest learning curve ever, but she loved it. It was exciting and exhilarating and frantic and fun. She loved the energy of all the younger staff, but none of them were a match for the indomitable Denise. She had energy to burn, she was loud and smart and incurably upbeat. Sam easily understood why she had the undying devotion of every staff member.

Her voice drifted into Sam's ears through her headset. She was humming along with the song that was playing.

'And baby, baby you ring my bell,' she started to sing, 'And the next line rhymes with that as well . . .'

Sam switched her speaker on. 'Denise!' she hissed into her mouthpiece.

'What, love?'

'Don't give up your day job.'

'Is that a crack about my singing?'

'No, I would never criticise my boss.'

'Ha, you'd be the only one then. Hey, check out the talent in this room. I thought all computer geeks were ugly, like that guy, whatsisname? Billy Bob Gates?'

'Are the caterers set up yet?' asked Sam.

'Everything's going fine,' said Denise. 'Ooh, ooh, major spunk sighting, ten o'clock.'

Sam spun around. 'Where?'

'Wrong way! If you're at six, where's ten?'

Sam turned in the opposite direction.

'Wrong again!' Denise groaned. 'For a bright girl, you have a shocking sense of direction! Look towards the main door, then to the left.'

'Well why didn't you just say that?' Sam turned around and then she saw him. 'Oh my God!' she breathed.

'Told you,' Denise continued. 'He's a bit of alright, isn't he?'

But Sam wasn't listening any more. Her heart was beating so fast it pounded in her ears as her legs propelled her in his direction. He turned slightly, gazing around the room until his eyes fell on her. His face broke into a warm smile as Sam's knees went weak and her stomach turned to jelly. He started to make his way towards her.

'What are you doing, cheeky?' Denise asked. 'You're not just going to walk right up to him?'

Sam ignored her. She circled around a clump of people, losing sight of him momentarily, and then suddenly he was standing in front of her, large as life.

'Hey Sam, how're you doing?'

'Hal,' she said, her voice barely making it out of her throat. Without thinking, she threw her arms around his neck and held him tight, relieved to feel his arms close around her without a moment's hesitation. Everything came back, the feel of him, the smell of him, the taste of him, all of it. This was nothing like hugging Jeff or Max or anyone else.

'Sam! Don't accost the clientele!' Denise trilled in her ear.

'Shut up,' said Sam.

'Excuse me?' Hal said, drawing back to look at her.

'Sorry, I wasn't talking to you,' she explained, indicating her headset. 'I'm turning you off.'

'On the contrary,' he smiled.

Sam smiled back at him, switching the two-way off and removing her headset. 'So, fancy meeting you here?'

'Well, you know, it was an odd thing,' said Hal, guileless. 'I got this strange series of emails that I think were meant to be an invitation . . . but they were all out of sequence,' he added.

She knew that'd get his attention.

'Oh, I've heard that's the fault of the server,' Sam nodded. 'Apparently you can't control the order they send your emails.'

Hal smiled. 'Well, whatever, I couldn't resist,' he paused, looking at her intently, 'to come check it out.'

Sam felt her heart racing. 'So you're still there?' she said, her voice coming out weird. 'At IGB I mean.'

'Not so much these days.'

She wondered what he meant by that. There was such a lot she wanted to ask him, to say to him.

'And look at you,' he said admiringly. 'This is all very impressive, Sam,' he added, looking around the room.

'Oh, I don't know,' she shrugged. 'It's the first event I've actually helped co-ordinate.'

'Looks like it's a success. Congratulations.'

'Thanks.'

She realised then that he had hold of both her hands, or she had hold of his, she wasn't sure how it had happened.

'How are the kids?' he asked.

'They're good, great.'

'Josh's arm is healed?'

'Mm,' she nodded. 'He got the cast off a few weeks ago. And Ellie started school.'

She noticed his features soften. 'Oh really? How'd she go?'

'Like a duck to water.'

They stood, holding each other's gaze, holding each other's hands. All around them was colour and movement and noise, but Sam felt disconnected from it all. There was only Hal, standing there in front of her, with his beautiful eyes, and his gorgeous jaw, and a smile that warmed right through to her heart, making her realise just how much she had missed him.

'Hal!' she blurted, at precisely the same moment that he said her name. 'Oh, you go ahead.'

'No, you first.'

She took a breath. 'Well, I um, I've been thinking about you a lot, Hal.'

'You have?'

Sam nodded. 'Thing is,' she swallowed. 'Well, the thing is, or should I say "here's the thing", like you would say. That's if you had anything to say. And I don't know if you do. And I don't blame you, because you weren't the one who said those things that night. That was me. And, um, maybe I was wrong, or maybe I was right at the time, but I have moved on . . .' her voice trailed away. Hal was just watching her, a faint, bemused smile on his lips.

'Sam?' said Brad, coming up behind her.

She turned abruptly, dropping Hal's hands. 'Oh, Brad, this is a friend of mine, Hal Buchanan. This is Brad Moss.'

They shook hands. 'Nice to meet you,' said Brad. 'Sorry to interrupt, but I have a message from Denise.' He looked at Sam. 'She said to say that you know how she told you that a well-organised function runs itself? Well, she lied.'

'I'll let you get back to work,' said Hal.

'See ya,' Brad said, disappearing again.

'Um, do you have to run off?' Sam asked, anxious not to leave things unsaid. She had the feeling she hadn't been making much sense when they were interrupted. Though Hal should be used to that by now.

Hal smiled. 'No, I'll wander round now I'm here.'

'Good,' she said, repositioning her headset. 'We'll talk later, okay?'

He nodded and Sam turned away, dashing through the crowd, switching on her two-way. 'Hi Denise?'

'Oh, you're back on line?' came her voice through the earphones.

'Sorry about that,' Sam blurted.

'Don't apologise, honey, I'd have stopped work for him too. But we've hit a few snags.'

'Where are you?'

For the next two hours Sam was flat out, the entire team was. There were no major disasters, just a whole series of minor ones. From too few waitstaff, to technical hitches, to running out of alcohol because more people had turned up than expected. Sam's email trick had been a little too successful at getting attention. It had obviously been forwarded willy-nilly, and a whole lot more people had received what was supposed to be a limited invitation. But the executives from O-Mega were beaming, so Denise was unconcerned, and unflappable as usual. Sam passed Hal a few times as she dashed this way and that through the crowd. She'd catch his eye and smile, and he would smile back. But as the evening wore on, it occurred to her that she hadn't seen him for a while. And much later, when the crowd was thinning, Sam realised he was no longer there.

She had a feeling of panic. She suddenly felt lost without him. Empty, alone. She couldn't just let him walk out of her life again. But maybe he had already. He wasn't here and he hadn't even said goodbye. She felt as though she'd been on a fast and had walked into a sumptuous banquet, but hadn't quite made it to the table before they cleared it all away.

'Congratulations, Sam,' Denise announced, striding across the almost empty room, waving a bottle of champagne. 'Come on, let's celebrate.'

'Should we?'

'Yes, it's okay, all the guests are gone.'

'No, I mean, should we be celebrating?' Sam said meekly. 'There were so many stuff-ups.'

'No more than usual,' Denise insisted. 'You expected that nothing would go wrong? Dear oh dear, Sam. Where's the fun if it all goes smoothly to plan?' She considered Sam, her eyes narrowing. 'You're one of those anally-retentive control freaks, aren't you? The ones with the immaculate houses and no pile of ironing under the stairs? I bet you even label your videos.' She didn't wait for an admission. 'We'll soon knock that out of you. Hey, Brad, Sam here doesn't think we should celebrate.'

'This is Denise's tradition,' he explained, coming over to them. 'She puts on drinks after every function. Don't mess with the system, Sam. It's the best thing about working with her.'

'The *best* thing about working with me, did I hear you say?' Denise eyed him. 'I've got your number, boyo.'

Brad found some glasses in one of the caterers' boxes and Denise opened the bottle and poured the champagne. 'Well done, good and faithful servants,' she said, raising her glass. 'Drink up before the others find us and scoff the rest!'

They pulled chairs around into a small circle as the other members of the team drifted over.

'Hey Sam,' said Denise. 'What happened to Mr Tall, Dark and Heavenly you were talking to?'

Her heart sank. She didn't want to have to start answering questions about Hal.

'Oh, the American guy?' said Brad.

Sam thought Hal had said barely more than a few words to Brad. 'How did you know he was American?'

'We had a yarn later,' Brad explained, reaching into his shirt pocket. 'He was sorry he had to leave, but he asked me to give you this.'

He handed Sam a business card. It was printed with raised blue lettering. Just a phone number and a few simple words.

Sail Away
Day and overnight charters
Hal Buchanan

Saturday

'Where are you going?' Sam asked Jessica when she walked into the kitchen dressed in her best clothes, full make-up and her hair contorted into a kind of bird's nest Sam recognised as high teenage fashion. 'Max will be here soon.'

'I'm going up to the Metro with Fatema. We're meeting some of the girls from school there.'

'But I have to go out,' said Sam. 'Max is coming over to babysit.'

'Mum,' said Jess, rolling her eyes, 'I hardly think I need babysitting any more. I'm like, nearly fourteen!'

'Let's call it supervision then.'

'I told you I was going out, Mum. You've been on like, the lost planet of Atlantis or something lately.'

Sam couldn't be bothered explaining that Atlantis was not a planet. And besides, Jess had a point in there somewhere. She had been feeling pretty spaced out.

'Well, I suppose it's alright. But you have to keep in touch with Max and let her know your movements. Take your mobile phone with you.'

'I don't have a mobile phone,' Jess replied offhand.

'Yes you do.'

'I *used* to, like, yonks ago. But Dad took it off me.'

'Oh? Why?'

'Supposedly the bills were too high,' she remarked airily. 'He said he'll think about it again in a couple of years. I thought he would have told you.'

'No,' Sam murmured. That little gem must have slipped his mind.

There was a knock at the back door. Jess dashed for it. 'That'll be Fatema.'

Sam was surprised to see Fatema wearing a . . . she wasn't sure what it was called. Unfortunately, tea-towel was all that came to mind.

'Hi, Fatema,' Sam said. 'I didn't realise you wore a . . .'

'It's called hijab, Mum,' Jessica informed her.

'Yeah,' said Fatema. 'Dad makes me wear it in public. He thinks it keeps the boys away.' She pulled a face. 'Unfortunately, he's right.'

'All the more for me then!' Jess quipped.

'That's only if they're blind,' said Josh from the living room.

'Shut up!' said Jess. 'Did you know Josh is going to see his girlfriend, Mum?'

'Have you got a girlfriend, Josh?'

'No,' he insisted. 'Shut your trap, Jess!'

'We're going,' said Jess lightly. 'See ya, Mum.'

'Okay, call Max from a pay phone,' Sam sang out as they disappeared through the back door.

'Righto!'

Sam wandered into the hall. Josh was standing in front of the mirror, painstakingly trying to make his hair look like he never combed it at all. She remembered she hadn't said anything to him about the condom in all this time. It had completely slipped her mind.

'Josh,' she began tentatively. 'Do you have a girlfriend?'

'Mu-umm,' he frowned.

She sighed. 'It's just that, well, there was something I was meaning to talk to you about.'

He glanced at her warily. 'You're not going to have one of those talks with me?'

'Well, kind of . . .'

'Mu-umm,' he cringed. 'I don't have a girlfriend. She's just a . . . a girl.'

'Hear me out, Josh.' She took a breath. 'A few months ago, before Christmas actually . . .' She'd better just spit it out. 'The thing is, I found a condom in your pocket.'

His cheeks stained hot pink. 'So?'

'Well, it did make me wonder –'

'Mum!' Josh exclaimed, clearly embarrassed. 'What did you think, I was gonna use it or something?'

'What were you doing with it?'

He groaned. 'We had a class on safe sex in Personal Development and we had to put a condom on a banana.'

'Why did you still have yours?'

'They ran out of bananas.'

Sam suppressed an urge to laugh. 'Oh, okay. So that's all it was?'

'Yeah. Jeez Mum, don't be gross.'

'Sorry, I won't bring it up again.' She went to walk back out to the kitchen.

'Hey,' he called after her. 'What did you do with it anyway?'

'What?' Sam swung around, she could feel her own face burning red now.

'What happened to it?'

'Um, well, um,' she stammered. 'I must have thrown it out, obviously. I mean, it's not like anyone here needed it,' she blurted.

'Okay, Mum, don't have a cow.' He picked up his skateboard. 'I'm goin'.'

'Where exactly are you going?'

'Just hangin'.'

'Where exactly are you hanging?'

Josh sighed. 'Laura Tierney's place, okay? She lives round on Gattica Street.'

'Okay,' Sam said lightly. 'Call Max and tell her what time you'll be home, please?'

'Yeah,' he grunted, walking out the front door.

Sam unplugged her mobile from the recharger and slipped it into her bag. Then she took out a compact mirror to check her face, for the fourth time in the last hour. She took a deep breath to calm herself as Ellie burst through the back door.

'Mum, can me and Max take Mambo for a walk when she comes?'

Sam heard a knock on the front door. 'Well, that's probably Max now, you can ask her yourself.'

Ellie ran to the front door and opened it.

'Hey Jelly Belly! What's happening?' said Max, hugging her.

'Can we take Mambo for a walk?' Ellie pleaded.

'Ooh, I dunno. That sounds suspiciously like physical exercise, Jelly.'

'He's only a pup, Max,' Sam reminded her. 'If you walk to the end of the street and back, he'll be exhausted.'

'Okay then! Go fetch his bridle and saddle him up.'

'Yay,' Ellie cheered, running out to the laundry.

'Where is everyone?' said Max.

'They've all deserted you. Jess has gone to the mall, and Josh –'

'– has a hot date,' finished Max. 'I saw him out the front.'

'Did he tell you he had a date?'

Max nodded.

'He denied it to me.'

'That's because you are the mum and I am the "way cool" aunt.'

'Well, "way cool aunt", thanks for doing this. I was going to ask Jeff but he had some family thing with Jodi's people.'

'No worries,' said Max. 'It gets me out of wedding invitation shopping with the future "MIL".' She sighed. 'She is a lovely woman, but her attention to detail borders on obsessive/compulsive. And I thought Dan was conservative. He's like the Andy Warhol of the family. Wait till she finds out I'm wearing a purple wedding dress.'

Sam had been ignoring Max's constant references to

coloured wedding dresses. Last week it was hot pink. And before that, lime green.

'Where are you going again?'

'I told you, I have an appointment.'

'Mm,' Max shrugged. 'You look nice.'

'You think so?'

She nodded. 'Very nautical. With the blue stripes and all.'

'Is it too obvious?' Sam frowned.

'Too obvious for what?'

'Never mind.' She picked up her bag. She could feel the anticipation rising in her chest and she felt almost giddy. 'I really do appreciate this, Max.' Suddenly she lunged forward and hugged her sister tightly.

'What's going on, Sherl? You're not dying or something, are you?'

'No, no, nothing like that,' she beamed. 'Do I tell you enough that you're a big, crazy nut and I love you? And you're going to be so happy with Dan. And I'm going to be happy too. We're all going to be happy!'

Max was frowning at her. 'I think you need to get the doctor to adjust your Prozac dose, Sherl. You're going way off the Richter scale here.'

Sam looked at her watch. 'Whoops! Better dash. Don't want to miss the boat.'

The traffic was heavy down to the marina and Sam was finding it increasingly difficult to keep her cool. She was dead on time when she finally found a space in the car park, and that only made her more nervous. She had planned to be ten minutes early. Oh well, the sky was not about to fall in.

She did one last check of her hair and face before getting out of the car and locking it. She pulled a note out of her bag and read the directions for where she had to go. After a couple of wrong turns, she eventually made it to the right place and started along the timber pier. She spotted Hal before he saw her. He was bent over, uncoiling rope from around a kind of hook on the deck of a sailing boat. He looked up as she approached and stopped what he was doing, dropping the rope. He straightened, watching her as she stepped down onto the floating pier alongside.

'Hi!' she said brightly, her heart in her mouth.

'Hey Sam.' He was clearly surprised.

She looked along the length of the boat. 'This is fantastic, Hal. Is it really yours?'

He nodded, still bemused. 'And the bank's.'

Sam smiled. 'Well, you did it.'

'I did.'

Hal gazed down at her. He seemed awkward. Sam watched him, unfazed.

'Sam, I'm glad you came, I really am.' He hesitated. 'Thing is, I've got a booking,' he checked his watch, 'right about now.'

'Name of Smith?' she asked.

'That's right.'

'That'd be me.'

His face was blank for a second, until Sam almost heard the clink as the penny dropped. He shook his head, smiling. 'Smith, eh? That's original.'

She shrugged. 'You fell for it.'

Hal considered her. 'Well, Ms Smith, you look just like a woman I used to know.'

'Oh really? What was she like?'

'Beautiful,' he sighed. 'But complicated.'

'What's wrong with complicated?'

'Nothing, nothing at all. I like complicated. She didn't so much.'

Sam took a step closer to the edge of the pier. 'So what happened?'

He gazed at her steadily. 'She didn't want me around after a while.'

'Mm, maybe it wasn't that. Maybe she just needed some time to work out what she wanted.'

She noticed he took a deep breath. 'So what does she want now?'

Sam went to climb aboard. Hal reached out his hand to help her, and she held it firmly as she stepped across onto the boat.

'She wants you to take her sailing.'

One Year Later

'No, Carlos, I told you already, I'm not going to be your wife
any more.'

'Why not, Ellie?'

They were sitting on the back step, alternately tossing a ball
to the dog, who would fetch it and return it, waiting eagerly
for the next throw. At this point it was unclear who would get
tired of the game first.

'Because Mummy said when I grow up I don't have to be a
wife, I can be anything I want, even a vents manager like her.
She said she's not going to be anybody's wife ever again. That's
what she told Hal.'

'Did he cry?'

'No, silly. He's a growed-up man!'

'My dad cries sometimes.'

'Does he?'

Carlos nodded seriously. 'He cried when Brazil won the
World Cup.'

'Well, Hal doesn't have anything to cry about. He says he's
the happiest man in the whole wide world. Mummy says she
loves him to bits and everything, and she's always kissing him.
And he's still going to live with us. He says he's never, ever
going to leave.'

Carlos rested his elbows on his knees, cupping his chin in
his hands. 'I don't get it. If your mum loves kissing Hal so
much, why doesn't she want to be his wife?'

Ellie screwed her nose up, thinking. 'Probably 'cause she did
it as a job and she got sick of it.'

Carlos shrugged, taking the ball from Mambo and tossing it
towards the back fence.

'I'm still gonna have a wedding but,' Ellie said firmly. 'I'm
gonna wear a white dress like Max did at her wedding, and my
bridesmaids will have purple dresses, like Mummy and Aunty
Alex and me and Jess did. But I won't have Mummy and Aunty
Alex, because they'll probably be a hundred years old by then.

I s'pose I'll have Jess. Marco can be her partner. That should make her happy.'

'Can I come too?'

'Yes!' Ellie said, exasperated. 'You have to be *my* partner. You can wear a black suit like Dan, and have a flower on the collar bit, just there,' she finished, pointing to his chest.

Carlos looked confused. 'So we're gonna have a wedding, but you're not gonna be my wife?'

'Uh huh,' she nodded.

'Will we have babies?'

Ellie thought about it. 'I'm not sure. Not two at a time, like Jodi. Her tummy was so big I thought it was going to explode. And Daddy says that one baby has a turn of sleeping, and the other one has a turn of crying, all day long!' Ellie grimaced. 'Maybe I'll wait and see what Max's baby's like when it comes out. She's only having one this time.'

Mambo returned with the ball, dropping it at their feet and looking expectantly from one to the other.

'Will we have a dog?' Carlos asked.

'Oh definitely,' Ellie nodded. 'Maybe even two.'

Dianne Blacklock
Call Waiting

Ally Tasker is trapped in a dead end teaching job and a relationship that's going nowhere. Her dreams of a fulfilling life after art college didn't include cleaning up after bored school children and being a doormat for her yuppie boyfriend. What she really wants is to be more like her friend Meg – at least she has turned her art training into a lucrative job in computer design, not to mention having a doting husband and a gorgeous baby son to complete the package.

But when Ally's grandfather and sole relative dies, she returns to the Southern Highland home of her childhood where she must confront painful issues from her past that her safe life in the city has allowed her to ignore. Meanwhile Meg is not as happy as Ally imagines. Dissatisfied with the pretty picture her world projects, a restless Meg longs to inject more passion and spontaneity into her life – but at what cost to her family's happiness?

Sometimes you have to risk all you have to realise what is worth saving.

'*Call Waiting* is full of genuine warmth and gentle humour . . . the perfect example of utterly relaxing escapism'
CATHY KELLY

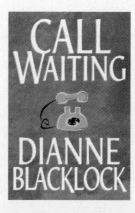

Ilsa Evans
Spin Cycle

Ever had one of those weeks when you've been soaked, put through the ringer and hung out to dry?

On Monday morning, this twice-divorced mother of three was bemoaning her boring life that left her feeling deflated and unhappy. By the end of the week she wishes that was all she had to worry about.

In the space of seven days her life is picked up and spun around when she discovers her mother's getting married again (for the fourth time), her older sister is pregnant again (for the fifth time), her younger sister lands the perfect boyfriend (who is very fanciable), her sister-in-law is running a brothel, her new next-door neighbour is going to be her ex-ex husband. Oh, and she's been arrested, her best friend's gone missing and the pets keep dying. All in the same week she sacks her therapist because she thinks she can work it all out for herself. But can she? And how can she work it all out if she doesn't even know what it is she wants to work out?

Kris Webb and Kathy Wilson
Sacking the Stork

Sophie presumed 'making sacrifices for your children' meant giving up
Bloody Marys and champagne for nine months. When she thought
about it that is . . .

But then two blue lines appear on her pregnancy test.

How does a baby fit in with a hectic job, a chaotic social life and the
absence of Max, the y chromosome in the equation, who has moved
to San Francisco?

Support and dubious advice are provided by an unlikely group who
gather for a weekly coffee session at the King Street Cafe. It is with
Debbie the glamorous man-eater, Andrew the fitness junkie, Anna the
disaster prone doctor and Karen the statistically improbable happily
married mother of three, that Sophie discovers the ups and downs of
motherhood.

And when an unexpected business venture and a new man appear
on the scene, it appears that just maybe there is life after a baby.

Written by two sisters who live on opposite sides of the world,
SACKING THE STORK is a novel which tackles the balancing act of
motherhood, romance and a career, while managing to be seriously
funny.

Jessica Adams
I'm A Believer

Mark Buckle is one of life's natural sceptics. He's a science teacher who'd rather read Stephen Hawking than his stars and he's highly suspicious of Uri Geller. And don't even mention feng shui or crystals. Most importantly though, Mark Buckle absolutely, positively, doesn't believe in life after death.

But then his girlfriend, Catherine, dies in a car crash. And everything changes.

Within days of her death, Mark sees Catherine sitting by his bedside wearing the dressing gown that he packed away in the bag bound for Oxfam. Next, he discovers that he can hear her and she him. Mark has some questions he wants answered . . .

By the end of the year, Mark Buckle, super-sceptic, will be a believer. But not before his dead girlfriend finally sorts out his love life for him.

Praise for I'M A BELIEVER:

'Even complete cynics will fall for the many charms of I'M A BELIEVER'
NICK EARLS

'Adams puts a refreshing spin on the boy meets girl scenario, guiding her flawed but likeable hero to the heights of love from the depths of despair'
VOGUE

'Funny, sad, quirky – and very real. Adams has done it again'
MAGGIE ALDERSON